RanGe

I Am ~~Just~~ Not Junco

BOOK FOUR

By J. A. Huss

RanGe

I Am ~~Just~~ Not Junco
BOOK FOUR

By J. A. Huss
Find me at
Jahuss.com

Edited by RJ Locksley
Cover design by J. A. Huss

ISBN-13: 978-1-944475-76-5

Dedication

To all the nerdy, geeky people who love this SF shit, birds, and dark books with a touch a realism, and hot winged dudes as much as I do. Because I love the fuck out of SF, birds, dark, gritty books and hot winged dudes.

Prologue

Peak City basks in the glow of dawn, all the natural color washed out of the high-rise buildings that wind their way up the side of the mountain, replaced with a hazy orange that reminds me of sherbet. The Goat lurches a few times as I pick up speed to enter the tunnel that will shuttle me through the mountain and into the valley where I have an appointment with death.

I've never been sanctioned to work outside my father's explicit instructions but life has changed considerably in the past few months. Mrs. Strauss showing up at the house to take me back to school a week early, my father not being home all summer, no birthday week, Gideon went missing, and HOUSE's cryptic message that led to this opportunity. All weird shit that's been screaming at me to prepare.

And that's exactly what I'm gonna do.

Prepare. For the fucking shit to hit the fucking fan because I can feel it. It's definitely coming.

The road twists after I leave the tunnel and I guide my aging vehicle onto an almost hidden dirt track. I'll leave tire marks but it's pretty windy today. I'm confident that the dust will swirl and scatter long before anyone enters this forest with forensic equipment, so I don't give a shit.

Let them figure out who killed the Peaks mayor. Like I care. I could kill him from point-blank range at high noon during the Patriots' Day parade and probably get away with it.

All I want is the biometrics so I can get the connection as payment because I need what they have.

I turn off the main track at the 13.28 mile mark and I lurch up and down as the pine needles reach out and slap the side of the Goat.

My smile brightens as I pull out into the clearing and spy the swirling eddy, then swing around and mow down several saplings to partially conceal my vehicle. They'll see that too, the way I flattened the aspens. But fuck it.

I brought just enough supplies to get me through this job and a possible firefight on the way out and that's it. Ten rounds for the rifle, a TZi with four pre-loaded ten-shot mags, and a bottle of water. I check my timeclip and hoof it downstream another quarter of a mile, then find the tree I scoped out last weekend and climb.

The pine resin sticks to my hands as I make my way to the proper bough, another possible giveaway that I am the shooter if I am caught, but again—who fucking cares?

My timeclip buzzes against my skin and I check upriver.

There.

He's busy navigating the rapids and the kayak is being jostled this way and that, just like every other time I've seen him out here. He's not really great at this kayaking stuff. I mean, he's been practicing this stretch of river for two months if I believe what they told me.

And I do believe them. They have a look about them that says 'we know shit'.

So, yeah. He's not that great at kayaking because even I could navigate this baby-ass, wannabe whitewater and I've only been kayaking a few times.

I take out my rifle, don't bother with the bipod, just brace Big Boy against the tree limb, and scope my ticket to freedom as he weaves his way towards death.

He's so fucking close I barely need to aim. His head splatters fractions before the muffled shot rings out in the early morning dawn and I pack it up, swing my way down the tree, then haul ass back to the Goat.

His kayak is waiting for me, swirling in the strong eddy upside down.

I leave Big Boy and my pack on shore and then wade in to the river, swim over to the dead man, and find his left hand. My knife slices open his palm and I cut the biometrics away from the tendons, rinse it out in the water, stuff it in my vest pocket, and then jam him up against some rocks to hold him down just long enough for me to get back into the RR.

He's got no one downstream today, he never does on Wednesdays, so I'm not really worried about the whole getaway thing.

I leave him there, not even looking back as I thrust the Goat in reverse and the aspens spring back up, bent but not broken. I shove it in first and then spin my wheels a little as I leave the way I came.

Sometimes I think it's unfair that I'm such an efficient killer. I mean, they really have no chance once I'm set on taking them out. No chance at all.

The ride back to the RR is uneventful. Even as I pull up to the Council 3 border crossing and hand over my passport, I am calm.

The border guard is older, not anyone I recognize. He smiles at me. Flirting maybe, which is disgusting because I'm barely sixteen years old for fuck's sake. His eyes take me in, notice my wet civilian clothes, and then he finally glances down to read my credentials. His whole attitude changes and I watch his eyes with slight amusement. He tries to avoid my gaze as he makes to address me properly.

"Senior Cadet Captain Coot. Welcome back to the Rural Republic, sir."

"Thank you, it's always a pleasure to come home." I've only been gone two hours but you gotta say something when they tell you that shit. Just protocol.

The guard salutes me as I pull away and I light a cigar and let the wind whip my hair around my face as I haul ass down the road.

The only thing that could fuck this up now is if my dad suddenly appeared.

But he's not around. Hasn't been for months.

The rendezvous occurs in an old house with a crazy slanted roof that sits on top of a cliff out by Ramah. It used to be an artist's retreat, way back before the RR was even a nation, back when it was the State of Colorado in the United States.

But now it's just an old slanted house that can barely withstand its own weight.

I pull up and get out, not taking care to be quiet or to check the familiar old Jeep I'm parked next to. If there's one person from Stag Camp who never underestimated me it was James. I walk through a doorway that lost its door decades ago.

He smiles as I enter and I grab the biometrics from my vest and toss it to him. "Now hand it over, James."

He laughs at me. "Hi, Junco. Nice to see you too. I'm fine, thanks."

I shake my head and smile a little. James has been a big guy my whole life and even though I've grown up, he never seemed to get smaller to me. His gut got a little wider over the years, his light brown hair has always been a little too long, his shirts a little too loud, and his face a little too soft for what he's known for, but he never lost his hardcore-ness. He taught me everything I know about shooting and then some. "Fuck that, James, just give me what I need. I have to get back to school before Strauss comes to get me for piano this afternoon."

"Why do you let her run your life like that, Junco? Shit, enough with the piano already. You're fine. You don't need it anymore."

"I do need it, James. I'm just really good at hiding it. Now give me the info."

"I got it right here." He tosses me a thick yellow envelope tied up with several rubber bands.

I snap off the bands and thumb through the documents. "So, what do I do? Just go up there with this stuff and then what?" I look up to him, my eyes asking for help.

"That's it. You show up and give them the envelope."

I take a deep breath and let it out.

"Here, give me your arm, Junco. I'll scramble the tracking for twenty-four hours. That's all I can give you, OK? You get these little interruptions all the time, so it won't look strange."

"I do?"

He swipes a small device over my tracker and laughs. "We're not perfect, shit happens. So, shit's happening today. Twenty-four hours though, and don't cut it close because it's not that reliable."

"And this will absolutely work? Are you sure?"

He's busy buttoning the small biometrics panel into his front shirt pocket but then looks back at me. "I just told ya, I set it up, Junco."

I shrug. "Nothing is what it used to be, James. Everyone's gone crazy. My dad—"

"You stay away from him now. Hear me? I'm serious. Just stay away."

I don't want to listen to this so nodding is the quickest way to get past it. "And they won't report me?" If they report me I'm fucked.

He walks over to me and gives me a squeeze. "They won't, Junco. I've already made the deal. These guys are friends, OK?"

I pull away.

"But you need to get up there tonight, you understand?"

I swallow. "Everyone's coming back to school today, so it will be crazy. I'll be able to get out no problem."

"Yeah, well, don't let anyone know anything. If they see you, stop and wait a few hours and try again. In fact, when you go back, park out there by the barn, where Michael parks. Then go out later and leave from there."

"It'll be chaos in the barn today, horses being delivered, remember?"

"Not during new cadet orientation, Junco."

"That's true. And you're sure my dad's not coming for the welcome ceremony? He's never missed one before." I want him to come. I miss him and he's been strange for the past few months. I need him to come be nice to me for a while.

"He's not, Junco. And if he does show up? You stay the fuck away. This is an order."

"But why?"

His face becomes serious as he looks down at me. "Junco, trust me. You don't want to know. Just drop it. Drop him. I'm sorry, I know you two were close, but this is the only way. I wouldn't lie to you, Snowbird. But I'm not gonna tell you everything, either. So just do what I say."

"And Gideon? Have you seen him?"

He huffs out some air and this time his words come out as a growl. "Goddamn it, Junco, I said drop it."

"So I'm alone. I have no one. Is that what you're telling me?"

"That's exactly what I'm telling you."

I swallow and turn away, hoping he'll stop me and… I don't know. Hug me or tell me he's still here for me. Or that Gid will be around soon and it'll all be OK. Or maybe, if I'm really lucky? He'll say happy birthday, sorry everyone missed it this year.

But he stays silent and lets me walk out.

I get in the Goat and drive back to school and when I get there my eyes are puffy and swollen from the tears and the wind.

Chapter One

I wake screaming, but only on the inside.

Isten.

It's the only word I know, the only one that exists in my vocabulary. When the screams cease I say it over and over.

And over.

And over.

It never stops, his name is always on my tongue and even in the nightmares, when I am consumed with the vision of my hair swaying in the red gel as it passes before my open eyes, as I relive the pain when my body writhes up and out of the tank, Isten's name is still there.

"Isten," I murmur into the silence.

"No, Junco. Isten is gone."

I know this. *I know this.*

"I know, Junco."

Lucan plucks the words right out of my head with little effort. And I cannot even explain how much I appreciate that right now. That he and Gideon can hear my thoughts. Because I have no desire to talk.

Even the soft whisper of Isten's name is too much. I need the silence and the darkness.

"Open your eyes, Junco. I need to leave soon, but before I can do that, I must talk to you. I must know that you will hear me."

I do not open my eyes.

"Junco."

No.

"Please."

His request is somber, not a demand, a favor, maybe? I open my eyes but the darkness is still there. That darkness is not going anywhere.

"Thank you, now look at me." He waits a few heartbeats to see if I comply on my own before once again adding, "Please."

He releases his tight grip on my body as I turn, then repositions one hand on my shoulder while the other gently pries my chin upward, forcing me to meet his gaze.

A smile from him. "I have to go, Junco. I've overstayed my welcome." He thumbs back to the wings jutting out from his shoulders.

It's weird seeing Lucan with wings. Especially demon wings. They have no feathers, just a bat-like membranous skin that stretches taut, spanning the phalanges that mimic the bones of a hand, albeit greatly elongated.

My eyelids shut tightly at the thought of being in this room alone, forbidding the tears from escaping. I made a deal with myself yesterday. I'd give up crying if I could just count something besides heartbeats. Heartbeats aren't enough anymore. I need the counting far more than I need the tears. I can control it, it's just a temporary defense. I'll only do it when I have to.

I can control it.

So I force the tears back and open my eyes again.

Lucan is still there, waiting, watching.

"I have to leave Earth today, but I'll be back tomorrow, OK?"

I don't answer.

"We have to talk, Junco. There is a lot you need to know, but not today."

No, it's never today, is it? Today is never a very good day for anything, is it?

"Today, just try and leave the bedroom. Can you do that?"

I breathe hard for a few seconds, forbidding the tears. I forbid them because I really need to count.

And then they're gone and I nod. *I'll try.*

I look up at him and know he doesn't believe me. I can't read his thoughts like he can read mine, but I can read his face.

"Gideon is here."

Isten overtakes me again and I just want to crawl under the covers and die. His memories are always there, memories I should not be privy to without him.

"Junco, I said Gideon is here."

"I know, Lucan."

My reacquaintance with speech lights up his face. "You will be OK until tomorrow? I'll be right back."

"I'm…" I cannot even bring myself to say the lie. "I'm not OK, Lucan."

He sighs. "I know, Junco. But you will be, I promise."

I shake my head as I fight back the memories.

"Gideon is here."

"I know," I whisper, irritated. "I appreciate that. I love him and I'm glad he's here to help me—"

Lucan's laugh cuts me off. "He's rather pissed off at your self-pity, actually. He'll be in here shortly to throw you out of this bedroom, so please, Junco. Just get up and get ready. He won't tolerate your moping."

Moping? Is that what he thinks this is?

"Quitting, maybe that's a better word. Quitting. You're not a quitter, Junco. You must gather yourself."

"Right. Gather myself. Just go away. I'll be fine." If there's one thing I know how to do well, it's gather myself. Push that shit down and forget about it. "It's funny though, all that gathering I've done has gotten me exactly squat,

Lucan. Nothing but pain. What's the difference? Between unraveling and gathering? The problem still remains the same, right?"

His smile falters at the recollection of the chat we had, long ago, before I was violated in a tank of goo for two years. *No matter how you choose to look at things, with emotion or logic, the problem doesn't change. Only your reaction changes.* Well, big fucking deal. You still end up in the same place—either dying of cold or dying of the poison fumes from burning the wheat beetle-infested wood.

Which do you choose, Junco? That's what he asked me. *To die or die?*

I think today I'll choose… to die, yeah that's it. Today is a good day to die.

But maybe tomorrow I'll choose to die instead.

It's so stupid. Nothing makes any sense at all.

"Faith, Junco. Sometimes you just have to muster up a little faith that things will get better."

But they won't get better. I know this. I feel it inside me, in every molecule, every atom, every subatomic particle that makes up my body. I feel the wrongness of everything. "Faith is a waste of time."

"Mostly," he replies. "Yes, mostly it is. Faith always takes second chair to action. But sometimes, Junco, you're the only one playing the song and you've got no one else there to rely on. In those times, faith really does help. So you have to have a little faith."

"That's funny, coming from you." I peer up into his eyes. They are a lovely blue-green now. Not the blue like when he's in his Archer form. The need to know suddenly overtakes my prior urge for a fight about faith. "Were your eyes green as a man?"

He lets out a small laugh. "Yes, very green. Are they green now?"

I study them. No, not really green at all. More like aquamarine. I've never seen such eyes in all my life. I gather myself and continue. "You seemed pretty happy when I said my faith was gone. Now all of a sudden you want me to find it again?"

He releases me abruptly and sits up in the bed. "Will you get up, or shall I make you?"

I take a moment to think about it but he doesn't wait. He shoves me off the bed and I plunk to the hard tile floor, a sharp pain radiating up my spine as my hip takes the brunt of the force. He's in front of me now, pulling on me, and then I'm standing there, Gideon's boxers almost falling down my legs.

I tug them up self-consciously.

Lucan laughs. "You smell, you look ridiculous, and you need to sit in the sun for about a week, Junco. I expect you to be well on your way back to normal by tomorrow night when I call. We have to talk and I won't tolerate your—" He stops for a moment to reconsider his word. "Quitting."

I stare at him. His body armor is made up of tiny black scales, a very smooth metal I know from touching them over the past day or so. They clink and chink with his movements. He looks like something straight out of the angel apocalypse. All he needs is horns. "Do you ever have horns?" I hear my mouth ask.

He shakes his head and disappears.

Shit, I really wanted to know the answer to that one.

Chapter Two

Selia and Gideon are sharing the apartment I woke up in, but thankfully after I take a shower and clean up, stopping several times in there to force the tears back when my fingertips find the scars along the back of my shoulders, they're nowhere to be found when I venture out of the bedroom and into the hall.

But there is a strange man standing out on the terrace talking on a comm. I begin to turn to bolt when he catches me. I stop and wait as he dismisses the call and walks back into the apartment in a rush.

I step back a little at his decisive movements.

He stops. "Sorry, Junco. I didn't mean to scare you. Gideon and Selia will be back shortly."

I nod and retreat, hungry, but not able to subject myself to a stranger no matter how badly my stomach is rumbling.

There is no screen in my room, there are no books, no devices to fiddle with, or comms. So I just sit on the edge of the bed and listen with my head cocked slightly for movement beyond my door. There's a small terrace but it's nighttime, and it's way too early to allow myself to look at the stars. I need to work up to that one or I'll be totally gone.

So I just sit in the darkness and wait.

But even after Gideon arrives—I can hear him talking as he moves through the rooms—he does not come to me. Selia says my name once or twice in a hushed whisper, but nothing ever comes of it.

And after hours of waiting I force myself to accept the truth of what is happening. I get up and walk across the room, gulp down the dread, open the door, and walk through.

They are playing cards on the terrace. Gideon, Selia, that guy from earlier, and several other men dressed in uniform. The Asian guy, the one who scared me back into the bedroom, nods at me and everyone turns.

I want to shrivel up and die at the attention.

My chest heaves as it draws in breath after breath and I'm just about to turn when Gid calls for me. "Snowbird," he says calmly. "Come join us."

I finish my turn and shake my head, then make my way into the kitchen to find food. There's a very nice autocook—the kind we had at our house back in Council 3. We always had maids and cooks and housekeepers, so my dad never cooked and I only did on special occasions— Christmas and stuff—or when camping, but I'm a pro at autocooking. My finger traces down Gideon's menu on the side of the machine and I choose seafood. The salty smell of the ocean outside has piqued a craving.

I stand still, dreading footsteps.

But none come.

The machine beeps and I set my meal on the countertop, then walk around and set myself on the tall stool. I eat it all and still, no one comes to bother me.

And when I'm done I just sit there and stare. I can hear Selia asking to come check on me, but Gideon says no. A very forceful no.

Selia does not argue.

So I sit by myself.

And come to the conclusion, after many loud and boisterous bursts of laughter from the poker-playing group later, that these people do not care one way or another if I join them on the terrace.

So I slink back to my dark room, crawl under the familiar covers, and count the seconds until I fall asleep.

When I wake his name is on my tongue once again.

Isten.

The tears spill out before I can stop them, but I get it in check. I need the count, I tell myself. *I need it, I need it, I need it.*

"You don't need it, Junco."

I do. I need it.

Gideon slips into the bed beside me. "You can't go on like this. You have to snap out of it, Juncs."

Silence from me.

"Just let the tears out. You need to cry more than the counting."

I shake my head. "I do not want to cry."

He breathes out with my words. "Please don't do this."

I sniff away the unwanted runny nose. "Do what." It's not a question. It's a half-hearted attempt to stall what needs to be said.

"It's a sickness, Junco. You know this. How many conversations have we had about it?"

"Too many."

"Is that why you wouldn't come outside?"

"No," I lie.

He sighs and turns me around. "You can cry, ya know. No one will stop you."

I know this. I've cried lots of times since leaving the camp behind. I've cried in front of my whole team, Tier, Ashur, Lucan. They've all seen me cry.

But this is different. I *want* to count. Those little counts, the heartbeats, those were nothing compared to what I need to count now. But two weaknesses is one too many.

So I will not cry. And I will not count what I need to count until I get rid of all the crying urges. Because once I start, I won't stop.

"You can talk about it if you want."

I don't want. I cannot even imagine what will come out with the words. Something bad, of that I'm sure. "Where's Tier?"

"On Amelia." It's the same answer I get from Lucan when I ask him.

"Why? Why is he hundreds of millions of miles away when I'm right here?"

"I'm not sure, Junco," he lies. I know Gideon well. And that was a lie.

"Go away."

He does go and as soon as the door closes behind him I am up and moving towards the window. I stop myself before the sky comes into view. I stop.

I am stopped.

But I look, and lean forward a little, stretching to catch a glimpse.

And when I do I smile.

Because they're not there.

And then I laugh. They're not there! It's cloudy!

Gideon's boots move away on the other side of the door and I don't even care that he just caught me. I don't care. I feel the dark place inside me. It's back. That motherfucking bitch has opened up my dark place and I will get her for this. I will not rest until I have wreaked evil and destruction on everyone who had a part in it.

That bitch violated me.

Violated me. For two years.

I know who I am. I know *exactly* who I am. And soon, everyone else will too.

.

Chapter Three

I stay in my room until it's almost time for Lucan to return the next day. The urge to cry is almost one hundred percent in check now. I've overcome it, like an immune system might overtake a foreign invader of the body. This makes me laugh as I stand out on the terrace. What the hell happened to my antigens, for fuck's sake? That bitch—

Stop, Junco. Just let it go for now.

I breathe out and the anger spews into the air like a disease.

There are no poker games tonight. Gideon gave in and made the luxury palatial apartment off-limits to the guards. That's who all those guys were. Just guards. It seems so silly to have been afraid of them. I mean, I could probably take them all at the same time if I really wanted to apply myself.

Stupid, Junco, they're here to protect you, not fight you.

Right, I know that, too.

I'm better now. Better than I was last night, that's for sure. I don't even have the urge to look up at the stars, it's not time yet. Soon, but not yet.

"Oh, I'm so pleased, Junco!" Lucan is standing next to me with a smile on his face.

"Pleased about what?"

He locks his arm in mine. "You're outside, dressed, fed?"

I nod.

"Excellent. That's excellent."

"What am I, a toddler? Some small child who gets a gold star for not wetting herself?"

He laughs. "Oh, you *are* back." He stops to laugh again. "I was so worried about you, but see? Gideon was right, you cannot be coddled too much. It's counterproductive—counter-intuitive was what he said, actually—to be coddled."

"That's the dumbest thing I've ever heard. Everyone wants to be coddled once in a while."

He nods. "Yes, that's true. Do you require more coddling?"

I smile. "No, I've had enough, thanks."

He remains silent as he gazes out at the ocean. It's lovely here, really it is. I mean, who wouldn't want to recover from tragedy in a place like this? Paradise. This is paradise. The beaches are white, the water is a stunning blue-green, and the temperature—mixed with the gentle wind that the Sargasso Sea is famous for—is perfect.

Gideon's penthouse apartment has a view that almost makes you want to cry when the sun sets and there aren't that many people here on our atoll, most of them live on the other neighboring islands, so it's nice and private.

It's funny when I think about it. Ironic maybe. Because one of my last memories of my old life on Earth included a silent wish to spend some time on this very same massive artificial floating island.

I wanted to vacation here. And now that this is where I ended up—it's not enough.

It's never enough with me. It will never be enough with me.

Something is wrong with me.

Lucan clears his throat to pull me back to him, but he seems reluctant to start the conversation so I start instead. "So, *do* you have horns?"

He puffs out a laugh. "I can if you want me to."

"But would you ever, I mean, if no one ever asked you to have them?"

He nods. "Yes, I have horns at times."

"How about hooves?"

He looks down at me, his eyes bright with laughter. "Hooves, too. Is that scary?"

"Hardly," I snort. "But it is sorta cool…" We stand in silence again so I ask another one. "Is it that bad? That you can't bring yourself to say the words?"

His smile fades and he nods. "Let's do it another time. Is that OK?"

"Hey, it's your party, right? As long as it won't kill me to not know, I'm good with denial."

He laughs again. "It will not kill you."

"Good, then let's talk about Tier. Where is he?"

"In the Band. On Amelia. He's been running the worlds since I left. I've been back a few times, mostly to fight with Gib and Rache. We are like brothers in that respect. We often fight, but nothing too serious. They've forgiven me for leaving."

Oh. That was an unexpected revelation.

"But," he continues, "they have never cared for Tier, so they are still angry about that."

I snort at this. "Yeah, I guess. I mean the whole Deliverance thing, right?"

"Right. Yes. But it turned out better than expected?"

The question mark at the end surprises me. "You have to ask?"

"You came out behind on that one, Junco."

He's right. I'm the only one who lost that fight, besides the people I killed to get the privilege of killing myself, that is. "Well, I'm glad you and your brothers are on better terms and all, but when can I see Tier?"

"He will come soon. Let's not talk about Tier, let's talk about the future."

"I thought that was for another time?"

"No, that was a conversation about you, Junco, and what you are now. That can wait, I think. But the future is upon us. We must get ready for it. Very soon the High Order will be here to judge me and if we're not ready for them, it will not turn out well."

"Not turn out well, as in… they might be angry? Or not turn out well as in the end of the world?"

"The latter."

"Oh." Well, that's just wonderful.

"But we have a plan and we will require your help. Will you help us?"

I shrug. "Sure, I guess. Is it difficult, what you need?"

He shakes his head. "No, not difficult, it just requires accurate timing."

"OK." I mean, really. What am I gonna say? Hey, thanks for rescuing me from my evil mother who violated my body for two years, no, sorry I can't help you evade aliens when they return to Earth to punish you, whatever that means?

No, obviously I'm not going to say that. "What happens if we don't have the timing down?"

"Many people will die, Junco."

"How many?"

"It depends. Tens of millions if we are lucky and all goes well. Tens of billions if we are unlucky and are unable to get things working in time. Everyone, if we fail to initiate."

"Oh."

He looks down at me and brushes a fingertip along my cheek. The chills run up my spine and burst out onto my arms. He notices and the heat rises in my face. "I need you, Junco. I require your help. Will you help me?"

His words are so soft I almost don't recognize them as Lucan. "How could I ever say no? I mean, I will help, want to help, but you don't really think I'd refuse, do you?"

"I don't know you very well, I have to admit. You are capable of quite a bit more than I imagined. Gideon has revealed some things and…"

I lose track of his words for a moment. "What things?" I ask, interrupting. "What did Gideon tell you?"

"You had a difficult childhood, that's all."

I frown. "Please don't ask about that. It's my past, do you understand? If I wanted to share it, I would. It feels… wrong for you to know things that I've kept close."

"I do understand, Junco. I've kept things close myself. I didn't ask, he simply… offered. As a way of explanation."

Explanation of what?

I know he hears that question inside my head but he chooses to ignore it.

"I have to go now. I cannot stay, but Ashur is around, just ask Gideon or Selia to call him if you need anything."

I nod. "OK."

"Try and relax for a few weeks, Junco. Think of this as a vacation. Rest. Will you rest?"

Oh, the irony is back. I almost laugh but I'm afraid that might cause Lucan to worry about my sanity. So I simply shrug. "Sure, whatever."

He leaves me there, a look of hope across his face.

I almost feel guilty for the lies of omission.

Almost.

Chapter Four

The sunset leftovers still cling with blurry determination to the edge of the fading horizon, mixing perfectly with the deep azure blue of the Sargasso Sea beyond the breakwall.

I've been sitting out here all evening feeling a little sorry for myself but no one seems to have noticed. Not Selia, who's been busy all day with her pilot lessons. Not Gideon, who barely knows I'm alive these days. I might as well stayed in the tank for all the attention he gives me. Not Lucan. He's been missing since that talk we had out on the terrace a few weeks ago.

And no one else has even bothered to visit. No one.

Unless you count Isten's memories.

So I sit around here on Sargassum, this massive artificial island resort that for some reason Gideon decided to make his home base years ago. And when I think about it too long it really pisses me off. That he'd come here. To paradise. While I was back in the RR falling to pieces and going insane with the lies and the guilt and the violence.

The water laps gently against the flat black rock I sit on. The security of the seawall prevents the sound most beach-loving people crave. Breaking waves. There are no breaking waves on the interior atolls of the resort. And this small, privately funded and guarded island is far inside the protective circle.

A flyer passes over and my eyes track it as it lands on the tall building behind me.

Who could that be? My heart beats a little quicker. Maybe they didn't forget? Maybe it's my dad!

Junco?

Yeah?

Come home. Now.

My face brightens. The flyer *is* for me. I gather up my towel and jump across the rocks until I make the sand. My feet dig in as I jog back towards the massive high-rise and then I force myself to stop and walk calmly as I pass the guards and wait for my elevator.

My guard today is Sho—some warrior Gid has kept close over the years for whatever reason. He's the one I was afraid of that day I came out of my room. I'm still afraid of him to be honest. I'm pretty much afraid to talk to anyone these days so I don't look at or speak to him as he follows me into the elevator, I just tap my foot impatiently as we ascend and when the doors open my heart is buzzing with excitement.

I catch a flurry of black wings ascending the terrace stairs, going up to the flyer pad on the roof, and look over to Gid for an explanation.

Gid looks away.

My legs kick into high gear and I take the steps two at a time and burst up to the pad just as he's about to climb in his waiting flyer.

"Tier?"

He stops mid stride but doesn't turn.

"Are you leaving? Without even saying hello to me?" My eyes burn and my throat clenches up as the words leave my mouth.

His head drops and his chest heaves a little. And then he turns and I step back.

He's glowing green with anger.

"I didn't come to see you, Junco. I had a message for Gideon."

"Oh." I feel the tears but control them. "Well, you can stay now that you're here."

He shakes his head. "I'm not staying."

"Why? I mean, are you mad at me?"

He laughs. "Is that a real question?" He storms over to me, pushes his body up against me and stares me down, emphasizing the height difference between us. I have to tip my head up severely to meet his gaze.

A challenge. He's challenging me.

I squint up at him, annoyed. "What the hell are you doing?"

His hair is cropped short, much shorter than when I saw him last and he's wearing a black uniform but it's not Aves like we used to wear. It's got a lot of little things dangling off it. Like a service uniform. Or an officer's uniform. An officer of excessive rank. He is definitely running something, and it's not just some elite warrior team, that's for sure. From the ribbons and medals I'd say it was an army.

"I'm doing my best not to smack ya down to the ground, Junco. That's what I'm doing." His growl comes out with such venom I step back and look away. "I came here to deliver a message and believe me, if there was anyone else to deliver it, I wouldn't have come."

I keep my head turned. "Why? Why are you acting like this? Why haven't you come to visit?" I look back and wait to see if he will answer. "I've only been here a few weeks, Tier. I have no way to leave. I'm stuck in the middle of the Atlantic Ocean. How could I have found a way to see you on my own?"

"Fuck, yer so stupid."

The shock leaves my body as a gasp. "What?"

"Ya think I want ta see ya after what ya did? Really, Junco? Ya think I'd just forgive something like that?"

"Something like what? Like what, Tier?"

His face dips down to mine and he bares his teeth at me. They are not the same teeth I remember. Fangs, almost. "You had a choice back there in the Runout valley, Junco. Us or them." His head motions behind me and I turn to find Gideon and Selia standing at the top of the stairs.

I swallow. "That's not fair."

"Not fair, eh?" He pushes me this time and I stumble backward. "Not fair? What's not fair is the baby ya killed when you let that bitch take ya."

Now it's my turn to growl. "Fuck you. *Fuck you!* I didn't let her do anything!"

He storms towards me again and Gideon covers the distance between us at a run. "Don't touch her again, Tier. Or I fucking swear—"

Tier's bright green eyes look up and find Gideon. "Ya swear what? What? You'll do what, exactly, Gideon? Because I'd like nothing better than fight ya to the death right now." He clenches his fists and turns away from me, still talking. "You had a choice, Junco. I told ya." He turns his rage back to me. "I told ya I wanted ta quit. So we could have a normal life. And what did you do? You chose chaos and death, just like ya always do. This incessant fascination you have with death, it makes me *sick*."

I'm silent.

"That was my child too."

The tears slip out.

"And ya killed it." He breaks our stare and looks over to Gideon. "For him."

My chest starts to heave as breathing becomes difficult.

"Gideon told me what ya said."

I look over to Gid and he turns away.

"That you killed yerself because you just wanted to die. You never cared about saving me."

I shake my head, but he continues.

"Ya never trusted me."

I'm breathing funny now, the air coming and going in gasps.

"You only care about yerself, Junco. And I can't live like that. You don't need me because ya don't need anyone. You only want what you can't have and ya know why? Because then you can blame yer failure to get these impossible things on yer horrible fucking life. On all the things those people did ta ya. Ya never look at yerself and ask how you contribute to yer own unhappiness."

Lucan appears behind him in his ancient armor and black wings, looking like Satan straight out of Dante's Inferno.

"Tier, that's enough now." His voice is soft and gentle, like when he talks to me.

Tier looks to the side but doesn't turn. He takes a deep breath.

"Come with me, we'll go home."

I'm shocked at both of them now. "He cannot go home, Lucan. He doesn't get to say that shit and just leave! I didn't choose Gideon over him, I just didn't want to leave him there! What was I supposed to do? He's my partner!"

Tier flies at me in a rage before anyone can stop him. He slams me down on the ground and the air bursts out of my lungs like a wind storm. He sits on my chest, restricting my breathing, and then leans down just like Isten did back on the rifle range.

My words come out in a sputter. "I didn't choose Gideon, Tier. I didn't!"

His eyes abruptly stop glowing and become calm as he whispers down at me. "Ya absolutely did, Junco. I wanted what you had ta give. So bad. And you chose death over me. Ya gave that bitch her chance to ruin us and unlike you, Junco? When she gets a chance to win she takes it. She doesn't throw it away. Ashur already had Gideon. I would never have left him there. Never. I know he's yer partner and I was gonna take care of him for you."

I swallow and stare into the hurt he's got penned up behind those eyes.

"I always trusted you and you never trusted me. You gave it away to Ashur, to Isten, to Lucan, to Moju, to that piece of shit clone of Aren and even that fucking nobody Kush. Ya slept with him the minute ya left my cell that night. And I never told ya nothing about that or the way ya broke down on stage after ya killed him. You killed yerself over Kush, Junco. Not me."

I turn my head again but Tier reaches down and grabs my chin, forcing me to look at him as he hurts me in ways I never imagined possible. With a simple look of disappointment.

"So here we are."

I nod up at him. "Here we are." My lips fall into a deep frown as I forget everything I promised myself about giving up crying. The tears stream down my cheeks and I start to sniffle wildly to stop the snot from running down on my lips. "I love you, Tier."

He's not swayed. His face grows more and more hateful as the seconds pass and I can't get myself under control. "No, Junco. You don't. You love Lucan now." He gets up and reaches down to pull me up as well, spinning me around by my shoulders so we are both facing Lucan. "And I'd just like to tell ya congratulations. He's a hell of a guy."

And then he pushes me out of his way and covers the distance to the flyer in a determined walk. Lucan meets him halfway and the two of them get in the vehicle together.

Lucan reaches out and grabs the door and swings it closed and they take off.

My face stares up at the night sky as the shrinking flyer disappears. Leaving only stars that are practically begging for me to pay attention to them.

I walk back down the stairs and Gideon and Selia follow me in silence as we enter the apartment. There's a cake and some balloons on the dining room table that I missed rushing past to catch up with Tier.

They didn't forget.

And ten minutes ago my life would've been complete with this simple expression of friendship.

But now I am lost. Utterly lost.

I stop at the table and read the card.

"Happy birthday, Juncs."

I break down in sobs and Gid turns me around and hugs me close. "He's just angry, Junco. He'll come back around. He was so hurt after Inanna took you, I can't even explain it. And we fought over how it ended back there. A lot. I'm partly to blame because after I came out of the medical tank I turned it all around and made it his fault that you were taken. And he was stupid enough to believe it, so I rubbed it in, used it. It's my fault he's angry and now that he knows you're OK and safe, all that shit that scared him is coming out, that's all. He still loves you. He'll come back around."

I wipe my nose on my arm as I pull myself back together and take a deep breath. "I need my dad, Gideon. Does he have a comm? Can I call him? I need to—"

"Sure, Junco." He pulls his comm out of his pocket and makes the connection, then hands the little tech over to me. I walk out on the terrace and listen as it buzzes over and over again.

A woman finally answers. "How can I help you, Gideon?"

"It's Junco. May I speak to my dad, please?"

She draws in a breath. "He's not here, Junco. But I can take a—"

I end the connection and hand the comm back to Gideon. "He's not there."

Selia is suddenly in my space, her head dipping under my hair to look me in the eye. "Junco, let's go out tonight. You want to come with me over to the main atoll?"

I keep silent.

"It's better than sitting here crying, Junco. It's your birthday, so let's just go check out the island. You've been cooped up on this little private beach long enough. You need to get out."

I hear the crack of a suborbital entering the Sargassum air space and nod my head as I shed the hurt like skin. "Yeah, OK. You're right. I need to get the fuck out of here."

Chapter Five

The door to my dorm room is ajar when I finally make it back to school after picking up the weapons. James was right, there were no issues. They did the code test in front of me for both the SEAR knives. I had a hair sample from Gideon to check his knife. I was worried for nothing. They were nice guys and even gave me the name of a professional who needed some extra help down in Low Dallas.

I walk in silence towards my door and take out my gun.

Listen.

Snoring?

I kick the door open and Aren jumps up from my bed, looking around wildly as he tries to wake himself up.

"What're you doing here?"

He smiles as reality comes back. "Waiting for you, beautiful."

I cock my head at him. "Beautiful? You drunk or something? Does my dad know you're here?"

He walks towards me and flashes me one of those winning smiles that make his eyes brighten, even in this dim light of pre-dawn, but keeps silent.

"What?" I ask.

"He knows I'm here, Junco. I told him I wanted to come back and teach tactical strategy for a year."

"Why?"

He takes my hand. "To spend this last year with you, Junco. Shit, you're so dumb sometimes. Ya know that?"

I pull my hand back, confused. "What're you talking about? Since when?"

He shrugs. "Since now. That's not good enough for you?"

I throw my pack down on the bed. "You want to date me?"

He laughs and pulls me close to him. I think about resisting, but I don't. I like Aren. I've thought about kissing him more than once and I'm coming up short on people who care about me these days, so I let him keep hold.

"Just go with it, Junco. Don't fight for once." His face loses the smile and I tip my head up to look at his expression. It's serious. "I wanna love you, OK? We have a whole year together, your dad even said so."

This draws me out of my trance for a second. "Did you talk to him today?"

He nods. "He's real busy, said to tell you hi."

I pull away and turn around to let my smile out. The relief washes over me so completely I have a moment of dizziness, but I hide it by rubbing my eyes and sitting on the bed.

"I've been waiting for you all night, where the hell were you?"

I huff out some air and my hair blows up over my face. "Doing a whole lot of illegal bad shit, Aren. That's where I was." I let out a deep breath. "God, I'm so glad you're here. I was even thinking about you on the drive home, ya know?" He sits down next to me. "I was thinking how it fucking sucks to have no one this year, right? I swear, you're like a gift from God." I look up at him and smile and his face is so serious it takes me back for a moment. "What?"

He blows out a breath. "What did you do, Junco?"

I crack a smile. "You promise not to get mad at me?"

He nods, but he looks worried. "Yeah, OK. I promise."

"And you promise not to tell my dad? I mean, he probably wouldn't care as long as I never get caught, but still. Don't tell him, OK?"

Another nod.

"I killed the Peaks mayor."

He stands up and pulls his fingers through his hair and turns away. "Why?"

I shrug. "I needed his biometrics to get an extra SEAR knife for Gid and me. They take them away to control us, and we're sick of it."

He just stares at me like I'm some kind of monster.

"What? It's not fair, my dad even said so. Matthew should not be allowed to take away a part of my body. It's a violation. And I know Gid feels it too. It hurts us to be without them, Aren."

"Did Gideon put you up to this, Junco?" His face is so serious I almost panic at telling him.

"No. He doesn't even know. I haven't seen him in more than six months, he went missing over the summer and no one knows where he went, not even my dad."

"Who else knows?"

"Just James. Why?"

"Junco," he takes my face in his hands, "you don't say another word about this, you understand? Ever. You hear me?"

I swallow and nod. "Yeah, sure. I wasn't gonna tell anyone but you're here, so..."

"Not even Gideon."

I crinkle my face at him. "Why?"

"Please, just listen to me, OK?"

I shrug. "Whatever. I can keep a secret, you don't have to worry about that."

He breathes out his relief and I watch him visibly shake off his apprehension. "OK, well. Besides killing the Mayor of Peak City, stealing some United Republics biometrics, and then purchasing two globally illegal weapons, what the fuck else you been up to lately?"

I laugh and push him back on the bed. "Ya know, Aren, if you'd have told me you wanted to date me I'd have been all over you years ago."

He laughs. All the way up to his eyes. "Is that right?"

I lean down and kiss him. His hands are suddenly all over my body, my shirt is off and my pants are unbuttoned before I even draw back to see how serious he is.

His half-mast gaze is all the proof I need. I lift his shirt off too and then he tackles me and makes the last twenty-four hours of stress and unhappiness melt away.

Chapter Six

It takes me three minutes to twist my excessively long hair up into a pony and throw on a pair of soft and faded denim jeans, a pair of brown leather field boots, and a white tank top. Then I sit on the bed in Selia's room and mope while she does her hair and make-up in the bathroom. The house audio is blaring some upbeat music with a female singer when Sel pops her curler-cluttered head out of the doorway. "This is that Cora chick I was telling you about, Junco. She's playing tonight in the arena on the main atoll. Wanna go see her?"

"What for?"

Selia stares at me like I'm a zit mucking up her perfect facial skin or something.

"Uh, I mean, do *you* want to go see her?"

She fiddles with a wayward curler as she talks. "Have you ever been to a concert, Junco? Ashur told me—"

"I've been to plenty of concerts, Selia. Jasus, you people think I'm an infant the way ya'll act like I've never been anywhere. I've traveled all over the world, I've seen Asgarth—"

"Junco, I mean like a *rock* concert?"

"What's the difference? It's music, right?"

She shakes her head and disappears back into the bathroom, but she doesn't stop talking to me. "Ashur said you never really had a teen phase, so ya know. I was just wondering if you wanted to go out. Act a little more like a young person and not quite so much like a grandma who happens to like cutting off heads. Have some fun and all that."

It bothers me that she knows so much about Ashur these days. Apparently she was in the Band for an extended period of time while my body was being mutilated by Inanna. He even paid for someone to fix that nasty head scar and her war-ravaged ear. I barely recognize her with the long blonde hair and her revealing tropical paradise wardrobe.

My hair is not the same either, but it's not exactly blonde. Yet, anyway. Blond hair is something all Archers get eventually but it takes a while. Gideon's is more brown than blond but I've been told I was morphed up a lot more than just one level while it was my turn to be held prisoner in Inanna's torture tank for Stag kids, so I guess that's why my hair is much lighter than his. It looks sun-streaked with parts that are very dark still. It's a total fucking mess and it hangs way down my back when not up in a pony. It catches on stuff and waves in my face and I find my fucking hair stuck to everything. I should just shave it off so I'd have a good six months before I ever had to think about it again.

All Archers have blue eyes as well. Gideon's eyes were always blue, but mine were hazel, so they aren't quite blue yet. They have freaky blue splotches running through them now, though. Color that looks like it's desperately trying to push away the green and brown that used to dominate in there. I have no idea how people can stand to look at me to be honest. Everything about me is a clusterfuck of hazel.

"Ashur knows nothing about my teen years, Selia. Not even Gideon knows what I was doing, so you guys can keep your pity talks to yourselves, I'm not a child, I might not have had screens and rock concerts, but I had work. And I defy you to tell me how that's not applicable to real life."

Selia comes out of the bathroom, her eyes darked up, her lips glowing and pink, and her naturally golden hair flowing down her back in large bouncy ringlets.

She's beautiful.

And I'm jealous of how easily she fits into her own skin, at how she can make small talk with strangers—even the guards in the elevator and downstairs in the lobby. And most of all, at how she always seems to be smiling.

Selia is more than beautiful, she's glowing. She's ravishing. And she's Ashur's girlfriend. Long-term girlfriend. Committed girlfriend, like if they were not involved in all this end-of-the-world shit they'd be picking out china patterns and writing each other love promises.

I haven't see Ashur since I've been back, but I've heard how Selia talks to him on the comm. Makes me want to puke.

And makes me a little jealous, too.

Not that she's with Ashur, he and I have never quite recovered from the whole Deliverance/Kush thing back on Amelia. I'm jealous because I know Ashur tells Selia how he feels about her. I know because she's always ending her calls with that stupid love promise.

Tier never did that with me when we had our little post-Deliverance holiday. He was affectionate and tender, but he never said sweet things to me.

But I'm no Selia, so I guess I understand.

And it should come as no surprise that Ashur fell in love with her while I was away being morphed. Selia looks happy.

I have a permanent frown, I'm afraid to talk to anyone except Gid and Sel, and I feel like my brain has been forced inside a body I've never met before. Even when I came out of the tank with wings back on Amelia I never felt this detached from myself. My replaced fingers and missing scars just make it worse. When a nightdog eats two of your fingers and a psycho slices a SEAR knife down your jawline, you're supposed to have to live with the consequences of those things forever.

And when you cut yourself in half to save the man you love, there should be evidence of that.

But my scars have all been erased. Every bite from the mutants in the Stag, every prairie lion claw mark, every battle wound I've ever had inflicted on me is gone. Even the one I inflicted on myself.

Just gone.

On the outside anyway.

The inside is another thing entirely. Memories of a brother I will never see again haunt me every fraction of a second—waking or asleep. I say his name in my head almost continuously. Every heartbeat says *Isten*. When I breathe in I say *Isten*. When I breathe out I say *Isten*. When I stop I say *Isten*. There is no rest from the pain, only a shallow reprieve that allows me to function for fractions at a time.

But reprieves are only temporary. A postponement of the inevitable, and nothing else. My mind is tempered by the reprieve, but this strength will not last forever.

Selia is suddenly in my face. "You're not wearing that tank top, Junco. I mean," she looks me up and down and her eyes stop on my chest, "you really gotta play up your assets." Her face brightens back up as she beams at me. "I'll find you another top. The jeans are OK, not great, but with the boots you almost look like a sexy cowgirl."

Cowgirl? What the fuck kind of drugs is she on? These are surplus *military* boots for Christo's sake. "I'm not really going for sexy, Selia. Just comfort."

She snorts in the closet but doesn't answer me.

Her room is nothing like any room I've ever had. It's not girly like my princess room, or minimal and modern like my secret room or my rooms on Amelia.

It's homey. Comfortable. Just a mess of this and that—nothing that matches or has any sort of style to it. In fact, most of her furniture is downright ugly—that rattan shit that makes me think of old people communities in the Texas peninsula.

But somehow it fits her. She makes it beautiful. Selia makes everything more beautiful.

Gideon kicked me out of his room, with the big luxurious bed covered in an Egyptian cotton duvet and piles of downy pillows, the first chance he got. So my current room is Gideon's guest room which has a sort of not-lived-in tropical-tourist thing going on. Not rattan, thank God, but more like regular summer camp for twelve-year-olds—two sets of bunk beds of all things. Two! Like he rents this place out as a holiday home when he's off killing people and needs stacked beds to accommodate large family reunions.

I snort at that thought. As if. As if we ever had one of *those*.

Nothing in that room is mine. Not one thing. Even the clothes were purchased with Gideon's credits in the gift shops downstairs and I had to have these boots overnighted to me because all they had in stock were flip-flops and strappy sandals.

I don't mind flip-flops for the beach, but I don't do strappy anything.

So to recap, Selia is beautiful, easy to talk to, and well-adjusted.

Right. Got it.

I'm a mish-mash of rural Farm girl and avian killing machine, afraid to talk to strangers, and well on my way to a severe psychological disorder that cannot be controlled.

This night is starting to sound like fun already.

Selia appears in front of me holding a brown leather bustier.

"No. I'm not wearing that."

She pouts. "Why not? You'll look great."

I'm about to answer with several cognizant reasons when she whips the tank over my head and spins me around, flattens the bustier to my chest, places my hand over it, and proceeds to try and zip it up.

The zipper sticks in the small of my back.

"Shit, Junco. You put on some pounds. Suck it in for a second, will ya?"

I do and she tugs on the sides of the leather and the zipper at the same time until it gets past the force of tension and slides up my spine.

She spins me around again and smiles. "Sorry about the pounds remark. The weight looks really good on you actually. You were always nothing but muscle and bone, but now—" she looks me over a little and clicks her tongue. "You're all curvy and shit."

I sigh as I wiggle and give the girls a little adjustment inside the bustier. I've noticed the extra bulk myself and I'm sure this will really fuck up all my defense moves, so it sorta pisses me off that Inanna made me downright pudgy compared to how I used to look. Soldiers don't need curves, just muscles.

It's funny though, I don't weigh any more than I did before this morph. I guess the wings were replaced with fat and that accounts for the whole conservation of mass going on. It's like my body is a chemistry equation that must be balanced—an honest-to-God stoichiometry puzzle. The problem is, I'm never sure if the products are better or worse than the reactants.

Selia pushes me to sit down on the bed, pulls the elastic tie out of my hair and starts to brush it with long even strokes. I hate brushing it. Strands come off and fly all over the place. They stick to my arms and clothes and drive me crazy.

I just sit there and let her do her thing. She comes at me with some kind of flat-iron and drags it down my hair to make it even and straight. It hangs lower now but it's not as unruly, so that's good.

I balk at the make-up but Selia slaps my hand away and orders me to sit still.

I do.

It's so much easier to let people do what they want than it is to fight them.

When she's done I don't even bother looking in the mirror. Who cares?

Not me.

We walk out to the living area where the elevator doors are open and waiting for us but there's no one inside. Gideon's voice carries back into the house from the terrace and I spy him and Sho out there. Gid has no shirt on and his upper body is golden brown from the sun. He's got some mirrored sunglasses on even though the sun has set and a cigar dangles from his lips. They seem to be a permanent fixture in his mouth these days. The few times he's gotten close to me the smoke on him is all I can smell. It makes me think of us at home. I frown at that thought. Thinking of camp as home is wrong.

Isn't it?

Gid's Archer scars are pale marks that partition off his back, the large triangle coming to a point somewhere below the waistline of his cargo shorts.

If he was Tier, I'd call that sexy. I might even have to see where that line eventually stops.

But this is just Gideon. He's not sexy. He's just Gideon. In fact, he's sort of an asshole these days and I'm not really sure if that's left over from the tough-love act of the first few days where I refused to come out of the bedroom, or if he's really holding something against me.

I've never even bothered to look at my own Archer scars, but both they and the wing bumps are mostly hidden by my hair. Selia says it's not so unusual to have such marks. Apparently people do all sorts of weird things to their bodies, up to and including scarring themselves on purpose.

I sigh.

Life.

It's hard for me these days.

Nothing much makes sense. Especially since everyone I thought was close to me is now distant. They all have lives beyond me, life went on without me. And as stupid as it sounds, this shocks me.

Sometimes I wish I'd never come back.

I push down my thoughts of Tier and think of Lucan instead. How could he leave me standing there like that out on the terrace? After all that shit Tier said? After that bullshit promise to love me for millennia. It was the ultimate betrayal in the middle of an unimaginable shunning by the most important person in my life.

I swallow down my pain and watch Selia go out on the terrace to tell Gid we're leaving.

Sho comes back inside and stops when he sees me. "Shit, Junco. You clean up nice. Want me to follow you guys around tonight to keep the weirdos away?"

I frown and turn away as Selia comes back inside with Gid and answers for me. "No, that's OK, Sho. We'll be fine."

Sho laughs so I turn back to look at him a little closer and he winks. He's good-looking with his mixture of Asian and Western features. I probably insulted him with my reaction.

"Hold on, I'll come with you guys." Gideon grabs his shirt and slips it on and we all walk towards the elevator together.

I half expect Selia to tell him no but I've noticed that she takes orders from Gideon without question these days. Always. I've been wondering where that directive comes from but haven't had the desire to actually ask for a chain of command flow chart yet.

The ride down is uneventful. It's a private elevator and only goes to our apartment, so that's how it's supposed to be. But the lobby is another thing altogether. When I came up it was empty but now it's bustling with people waiting near the canal for transport over to the other atolls.

"Shit," Selia sighs, "I guess everyone's got the same idea tonight."

I guess they do.

"Oh!" she exclaims, jerking on my arm as we walk out into the marble-floored atrium. "Look, that's her! Cora! She's staying here. I bet that was her suborbital we heard earlier."

Our atoll is pretty exclusive and from what I'm told, my dad and Gideon own the entire thing. It's well guarded, mostly for my sake these days, but also for famous people who want privacy. Gideon tugs on Selia and me, dragging us over towards the transport line.

"I don't want to go to the concert, Selia. You and Gideon can go, I'll just stay—"

"No. You're not going back upstairs. We don't have to go see her, but you're staying with us tonight, Junco. I've had enough of your moping bullshit." She stares down at me, her blue eyes flashing.

"Fine." I watch the rock star talk on a comm across the atrium and dial up the scope sight I inherited from Isten so I can try and read her lips. I'm not real good at that but I've accessed the sphere on my vision screen several times using the machine parts of me, so I reach into some of the weird circuitry winding its way through my body and try for a connection to her comm.

I almost smile at my success.

"I just got here, goddammit! I have an entire year of tour dates ahead of me and he goes and pulls this bullshit—"

Uh-oh. The rock star's not having a good night.

"I *will* come back, after my show, and then you tell him my lawyer will ream him in the ass for this fucking shit—"

Someone must cut her off because she stops mid-sentence, then continues. "I'll have the pilot ready the sub and be back in Texas later. And so help me God, if that bastard doesn't give him back tonight. Tonight!" She screams that last part and even Selia and Gideon turn to see what's going on. She catches her outburst and dials it back down. "I'll call you when I land."

The comm disappears into a large bag hanging off her shoulder and she adjusts her hair and walks over towards our transport line. She stops right next to me and I have to elbow Selia to stop her staring.

The boat comes and Gideon directs Sel and I to get in, but the rock star stops him with a hand on his shoulder.

"Do you mind if I ride with you guys? I'm just going over to the main atoll."

Gideon pushes up his sunglasses and looks her up and down like he's buying a horse or something, then waves her into the boat with a smoldering cigar.

She sits across from Selia while Gid sits down on the other side of me. Selia starts flattering the strange woman and I just watch and soak her all up. Her hair is short and spiky, colored several shades of pink, and she's wearing dark sunglasses even though the sun's been gone for hours. Her outfit is not much different than mine really. Jeans and boots, although hers are the sexy kind with tall heels and not the practical kind made for marching. And a tank top. If Selia hadn't changed my shirt we'd almost look like we planned to wear the same thing. She's also got a lot of jewelry that clinks when she moves and her lips are bright red.

Gid puts his arm around me and pulls me into him, trying to hide my face from her I think, but I can't stop watching Cora. She's one of those people who suck up all the energy in a room, or a boat, and then project it all out in front of them.

She watches me watch her and then offers a hand. Something she did not do for Selia. "I'm Cora, and you are?"

I just stare at her and she pulls her hand back.

"She's mute," Selia barks, "can't talk." I turn my eyes away and bury my head into Gideon's chest so Cora can't see me smile. Selia is so strange. She makes up the weirdest shit when we go out in public. I don't look much like the old Junco these days. The hair, the curves, the lack of scars and the extra fingers.

But some people look at me like they know. They know exactly who I am. It freaks Gid and Selia out so Selia comes up with these stupid lies. If the lie was always the same it would be one thing, but she pulls out different shit, like being mute, all the time.

Cora doesn't let it go and I feel Gideon tense when she starts talking again. "Really? A mute, huh? I had no idea they still have mutes. I mean, didn't they invent the synthetic voice box like forty years ago?" I turn back to watch her and can't stop the smile. Cora slips her sunglasses down her nose to reveal large bloodshot gray eyes. "Does she at least have a name?"

Gideon takes over. "Her name is Astrid. But she doesn't talk and that's the end of it."

Cora ignores Gideon and stretches out her hand again. "Nice to meet you, *Astrid*."

I reach out and shake her hand and she winks at me.

Gideon tells the driver to stop at the next atoll and we leave the rock star sitting there in the boat, her mouth dangling a cigarette in a knowing smirk as we make our getaway.

Chapter Seven

We exit the canalwalk and enter the nearest hotel, walk straight through to the other side, and catch the next boat over to the main atoll. None of us speak but it is clear that both Gideon and Selia are troubled that the rock star recognized me so easily.

We're floating down the main canal, getting ready to line up to debark, when I break the silence. "We should just go home if you're worried."

Selia shakes her head and Gideon actually sneers at me. "We're already out, Junco. It's just weird how she picked up on you right away."

"Maybe she recognized Selia? She's been on screens more than I have."

Selia winces in my peripheral vision and I know they're lying to me about something. It doesn't matter though, I've suspected it since the second day back when they took out the screen in my room. They thought I was delusional that first time I woke up. But I wasn't. There was a screen on the wall and then it was gone. I figure the whole world's talking about me, but I'm not interested enough to find out what it is they're saying.

Gideon puts his arm around me and pulls me in for a hug. "It's nothing, I'm sure. We're not gonna let it ruin your birthday, Junco. We're gonna have a nice time tonight, OK?" He leans down and kisses me on the head. "When's the last time I got to see you for your birthday? It's been too long. I'm gonna make up for it tonight."

God, I love him.

I know Tier thinks I chose Gideon, but it wasn't the same kind of choice. Neither was Lucan. I don't want them or need them in the same way I need Tier.

Gideon is just a very special friend and Lucan… Shit, I have no idea what Lucan is to me. I'm clearly not all that important to him if he finds it so easy to walk away from me. And I get it, Tier is like a son to him. Fine. He's allowed to choose Tier. But don't tell me you love me, will love me for thousands of years, and then walk away when I need you.

I can get that from pretty much everyone else in my life. I don't need any more fucking part-time friends.

This is what makes Gideon such an attractive choice as my eternal partner. He never wants more. And he never *makes* me choose. He's just there.

And he loves me unconditionally. He's seen me do things that will condemn me to Hell, and still, he loves me. Would do anything for me. Would die for me.

And I would definitely do the same for him and I do not regret my actions back in the Runout valley. How was I supposed to know Tier would save him? Tier wanted to kill him in the tunnels. I'm no mind-reader.

Our boat finally reaches the dock and we get off and slip into the crowd. Gid holds my hand like he's my boyfriend and Selia sticks to my shoulder like a bodyguard.

The crowd in the casino is not that thick but I can hear the cheering coming from the arena farther down the island and figure most people are probably going to the show.

Gid lets go of my hand and walks off to the bar to get us some drinks. I'm twenty-two now. Totally legal. It feels weird because it seems like it was just a few days ago when I was getting ready to turn twenty. The morph stole the time in between and there is no way to get it back.

Selia drags me outside to a table near the dance floor and we sit. The club is not crowded and the cheering from the arena tells me the rock star has arrived. I check my vision screen. An opera is about two and a half hours long. I raise my voice over the throbbing beat. "How long do you think that Cora show will last?"

Gid shows up and hands us drinks. Selia has some girly thing but Gid hands me a beer. Selia takes a long slurp of her concoction and then comes up for air and looks over at me. "About two hours probably."

"Two hours what?"

Oops. Gideon wasn't supposed to hear that. He'll catch on to my sneaky ways if I'm not careful. Selia doesn't respond so I just pretend I didn't hear him. I check my vision screen again and then Selia tugs me out to the dance floor with her. Gideon doesn't follow. Dancing is not something I do but the song ends and a slow song comes on.

"This is Cora, Junco. It's so fabulous." She grabs me and pulls me close and drapes my hands around her neck as she grabs my waist so we can slow-dance. Every guy in the place is suddenly interested in us which is not good, but she's just trying to make me happy so I let her cling to me and move my feet around a little.

She leans down into my ear and tickles me with her alcohol-laced breath. "Why don't you date Gideon, Junco? He loves you so much. Tier's no good for you."

"That's not what we have, Selia. Not that I know of anyway. If he feels that way about me, then he can come tell me himself. Because he's never let on that he's interested in me like that. Went out of his way as a teen to discourage any of that sort of stuff, in fact."

She pushes me away a little and looks down at me, her eyes very serious. "You could make him interested, ya know."

I sigh and look over at him. He's not even looking at us, in fact his eyes are following the ass of a very attractive brunette who barely has any clothes on. I look back at Selia and raise an eyebrow.

"Well, you can't blame him for looking, Junco. It's not like you're available."

I laugh. "Selia, I can't deal with this right now. Seriously. If Gid wants to sleep with me—"

Selia smacks me, sorta hard too. "He doesn't want to sleep with you, Junco! He just wants to love you."

I turn away and look at him again. This time he waves and gives me a crooked grin. I smile back and wave him over but he shakes his head and raises his beer to me. I picture a life wrapped up in Gideon's arms each night and my whole body gets warm. "Don't play matchmaker, Sel. Please. I love Gideon and I'd do anything for him, but I'm too fucked up to even think about men right now. OK?"

She looks at me with sad eyes. No. Pity eyes. She pities me. I look away and shrug her off as the song ends. We go back to our table and I watch as Selia gets giddy and drunk while Gideon relaxes and talks the ear off the guy at the table next about sports.

They are happy, comfortable, and sedated with alcohol. So when I get up and excuse myself to go the bathroom they never even think that I might never come back.

The crowd is thick now that the show is over and I get lost among the throngs of people easily. Even if Gid suspected what I was up to, he'd have a hard time finding me. I make my way over to the land transport line, activate Isten's invisibility gift, and slip onto a bus headed past the planet pad.

Cora's suborbital is the only thing in sight when I get there. It's flamboyant and pink, just like her hair. It even says 'CORA!' on the side of it next to her giant face. There are a lot of people milling around it but the passenger ramp is in place. I know from experience that this means the travelers are already on board so I walk out on the pad and sneak up to the entrance, trying to keep my boots from banging around too much on the metal stairs as I ascend. I peek inside but Cora is the only person I can see. She's standing in the middle of the cabin, her fingers busy flicking across the screen of some handheld piece of tech.

I enter, disengage my invisibility directly in front of her, and wait.

She barely reacts and I give her lots and lots of points for this. We stand there in silence for a few seconds and then she laughs.

"Why, if it isn't Astrid the mute, how nice of you to join me!"

I make a cheeky grin, I can't help it. This woman is not stupid and I admire her cool. "I need a ride to Texas. Can you help me out?"

She stares at me a little longer, maybe trying to make me squirm, but I don't squirm. She recognized me so easily for a reason, and there's only one that I can think of. She's interested in me, what I've done, and what I might do in the future.

"What will you give me?" she asks with a coy tilt of her head.

"I'll give you the same thing I gave Selia Manchen the night I left with the avians. A story to tell."

She throws her head back and laughs again. A real outburst that echoes out the door and across the planet pad. "Junco, I'd have settled for nothing. You, girl, are the face of the times. Everyone wants to know about you.

They know you're back because the death and destruction has suddenly ceased. But what happened to you—or why that Satan replica has tortured and killed thousands of people over the past two years trying to find you? That is the most tightly guarded secret since the construction of the Pyramids. So your story is above and beyond anything I could've ever hoped for."

I stand there stunned by her words.

Chapter Eight

Her suborbital is manned by a private staff of six very nervous people who do not sit with us in the main cabin, but have their own area in the forward compartments. I don't know if they always segregate themselves like that, but I'm not interested in sharing my story and reactions with just anyone. So I'm glad this is how it worked out.

We're waiting on the pad for clearance when a woman appears from the front and leans down to whisper in Cora's ear. This suborbital has a table and chair setup like the ones my dad and I took on our birthday trips. Cora and I are sitting across from each other, not far at all, but the messenger is especially discreet in her revelation.

I watch Cora's face and then prepare myself.

She smiles at me when the woman walks back to her station.

"People are looking for you. My pilot has been asked to verify that we have no illicit passengers on board."

I wait it out.

"He lied for you."

"He didn't have to. I'm free to do as I please."

She looks away for a second and purses her lips around a cigarette and takes a deep draw before answering. "Right." The smoke shoots out into the air around her words. "But these people you're with. They're not nice." Her eyes come back to mine. "Are they?"

I shrug. "I think they're nice. I'm not running *from* them if that's what you mean. I just have somewhere else to be right now and they're a little gun-shy about letting me out of their sight."

She nods and looks away. Takes another drag. I may have misjudged this one.

"So, you're OK with all the shit they've been doing over the past two years?" Her eyes sweep back over to me again and her anger surfaces. For a few heartbeats I wonder if I'm gonna have to kill the rock star before we even take off.

I dial down my paranoia and try and defuse the situation. "I was—"

I was what? How much do I tell her? My silence makes her face harden and I decide to go for the truth. She's not all that predictable—this pink-headed woman is not quite what I expected. And why should she bow to me? I might be a global interest right now, but so is she. Cora doesn't see me as above her, if anything I might be below her. "I was taken by a—" I stop again. It's really not that easy to explain.

She waits it out. Patient.

"OK, look. I'll tell you the whole story. The truth, but it's gonna sound far-fetched. So, no judgment. Deal?"

She cracks a smile and we both know she's won. Somehow, even though I've got powers she cannot even comprehend and I could kill her in an instant, she is smug.

"OK, but this is the short version, got it? I'm not gonna go into detail because it's too much. The details, Cora. They're too much."

She nods but holds her words.

"I went with the avians willingly. I chose that so they could morph me into one of them. I'm the product of some very strange bioengineering that took place out in the Rural Republic over the past several decades. And they did change me. I was avian for a while. But then I was told, shown actually, that their gene pool was, well—let's just call it a complete disaster. They had to stop their reproduction and because I was part of this group of specially engineered children, I had a role in helping them restore their gene pool and I play the final part in some sort of avian prophecy."

I stop to gauge her reaction so far but all she does is take another drag on her cigarette. The suborbital has apparently been cleared for take-off because I am slammed back in my seat with the new velocity. I wait for the lift of air that tells me we've left the ground and then continue.

"So I came back to Earth with my team of warriors and we went into the Mountain Republic and took back my brothers and sisters. We are the avian Seven Siblings. Moju, Soli, Tukker, Esta, Sariel, Irin, and me."

"And?" Her eyes narrow, becoming more hateful than interested.

"And? And what?"

"The bomb? You blew up a nuclear reactor up in the mountains, Junco. Surely you didn't forget that part?"

I want to look away but I force myself to maintain eye contact. "If you saw what I saw up there, you'd have done it too, Cora. They had copies of us. Thousands upon thousands of replicas of us, only they weren't really *us*, right? They were sick amalgamations of—shit, I have no idea how they made those things. But the RR had them too, which is why my dad—"

"—fucked up the entire Central Republics with his nuclear bombs. And then you went and decided to do the same thing."

I shrug. "That's not quite how it went, but whatever. That guy you saw me with tonight? Gideon? The one who's probably looking for me right now? He's from another group of children like me. He's my partner and he was in my lap dying by the hand of the monster who represents humans in my little prophetic struggle. He was dying because when I was asked to make a choice back on that battlefield in the Runout valley, to choose humans and Earth or the Fallen Archers of the Band—"

Her jaw tenses as she clenches her teeth.

"—I chose Lucan."

She nods her head, but it's not in agreement, more like a confirmation of what she already knew. "That demon thing that's been terrorizing the entire planet for two years. You chose that thing over *us*?"

I let out a long sigh. I'm so fucking tired of this us and them bullshit. "Well, I mean, he doesn't always act like that, Cora. He's a pretty cool guy."

She stubs her cigarette out in an ashtray on the table and sneers over at me. "You know what? If I wasn't harnessed into this goddamn seat and we weren't about to enter free-G, I'd beat the shit out of you right now."

I laugh and raise my eyebrows at her. "Would ya now? I don't know you, so maybe you could." I watch her face as I prepare the threat. "But I'd just like you to know that I killed more than a hundred people in free-G when I lived with the avians. So I'm ready to go when you are."

"You have no remorse, do you?"

"Remorse for what? I didn't drop those bombs on Peak City and Council 3! That place was like my fucking hometown! Besides, I was busy killing my best friend back in the Band the night that happened. I wasn't even on Earth, so fuck you and your righteous judgment because everyone that lived in Runout knew what they were involved in and if they didn't, then fuck them for being so stupid. You can't live in a small mountain neighborhood that's better protected than most countries and not suspect there might be secrets."

She takes out another cigarette and I snatch the pack from her before she even knows what's happening. I slide one out and strike it up, then throw the pack back, smacking her in the chest.

I take a long draw and then enjoy the nicotine as it courses through my body. "I might look approachable these days, what with the lack of battle scars and all the pretty new curves. But let me tell you something right now, I've got no conscience to stop me from killing. None. So do not fucking piss me off with your half-ass threats."

She says nothing, just glares at me from behind those bloodshot gray eyes.

"That bitch Inanna, the goddamn representative for humanity and Earth? She took me against my will, stripped my entire body of skin until the flesh beneath was exposed, the nerve endings firing off into red tank gel, electrifying the entire apparatus until my body buckled and writhed in the agony. She broke every bone in my body, ripped my muscles apart, stole my fucking wings for Christo's sake. And then morphed me back into this girl you see before you. I never asked for any of this. I never wanted to be anything more than a silly wife to some backwater hick farmer in the RR, so fuck you and your remorse. I have zero remorse."

She turns her head now.

"And I don't know what Lucan was doing during that time I was being tortured but he was there when I made my choice. He knew I chose him and then she tried to kill Gideon to make me change my mind. The next time you see my partner, and believe me, you will—he'll pay you a visit, I'm sure—you look for the thick white scar across his neck. That's what Inanna did to him to try and force me to bend to her will. He's only alive today because the avians saved his ass. And when I didn't give in, when I was firm in my defiance, she broke me."

I take a long draw on my cigarette to calm myself. It's a lot easier to talk about than I thought it would be. Maybe because I can channel my anger against Cora. Or maybe I just don't give a shit about anything anymore. It's kinda hard to tell what motivates me these days.

"So whatever Lucan did? Whatever it took for him to be there a few weeks ago when he rescued me? When he put a stop to the pain she was inflicting on me for two goddamn years? Well, it was worth it. And I could give a shit who had to die for it. I'm sure"—I look her straight in the eye—"*positively* sure, that if people were killed as part of Lucan's death spree, then they deserved it. He might not have *final judgment* powers, but it's pretty motherfucking close."

We sit in silence for a long time. I'm done. I have nothing more to say and if she's done too, well then I'll just stay quiet and bide my time until we land in Texas, then go invisible and slip away.

The woman attendant appears again and notifies us that we'll be landing in Dallas in ten minutes. I just stare out of the window and concentrate on the Gulf of Mexico.

"So how much of this should I keep quiet?"

I turn my head towards her slowly. "I could care less what you blab about. The world is gonna be seeing a lot more of me real soon. That's a fucking promise. Lucan might've gotten his revenge, but I haven't gotten mine. And I will get it, Cora. They took something from me that haunts me every waking second. And I will kill every single being involved in the creation of the Seven Sibling clutches. No matter where they live on this planet, I will find them and I will kill them."

"You're on the wrong side of history, Junco. You're gonna find that out the hard way, I think."

"We'll see," I say with disinterest. "Whoever knows what side of history they're on anyway? To the victor go the spoils, right? You make the best decision you can based on the facts at hand."

"That's not how the quote goes, you know. And it's not a good thing, it implies high-level corruption."

I sneer at her now. "Don't insult me. I know what it means. History is subjective, so how can you possibly know which side I'll come out on when I'm still in the middle of creating it?"

"So this is the best decision you can come up with? Revenge and killing?"

"Cora, you have no idea what you're talking about. A few dead people here and there in my selfish revenge scheme mean nothing, because my role in this whole mess might involve annihilation of entire cities. And if that's what it takes to hold it all together, well then, fuck. The world is about to find out exactly what I'm made of. I'll do whatever I have to because in the end, you just gotta get the job done. I've caused too much death and lost too many friends to let it all be pissed away for nothing."

I take another drag and watch her study my face. Fucking bitch. What the hell does she know about anything? She wasn't there when Inanna stripped me of skin, she has no idea what it means to be trained as a soldier in Stag Camp, she wasn't there when every person I ever trusted walked out on me and left me to go insane. Even Gideon is guilty of that one. And she wasn't asked to help save the Fallen Archers of the Band and their entire race of people.

Cora throws up her hands and swivels her seat so she doesn't have to look at me. Her judgment stings a little but I'm doing my best. Why can't it ever be enough?

"Believe me, Cora, I'd like nothing more than to have the man I love all to myself on a little habitat out in the middle of the Band and forget all this is happening. But I can't. Because it's real. And either I make the hard choices or *billions* of people will die. So I'm gonna make them and no one's gonna stop me. If a few thousand souls have to be sacrificed, hell, a few million even, I don't care. It's got to be done."

She snorts out a sad breath of air through her nose. "You're sick, you know that? You're all sick. I hope someone kills you."

"They've already tried, believe me. I've been sick since the day I was born and I've been dead more than once already." I wait for her to look back at me, to meet the gold light pouring out of my eyes. "But I've got a promise of satisfaction on my side, and what will satisfy me now is retribution."

Her jaw clenches and then she turns away for good.

We land and taxi over to the exit portal. I stand and wait for the door to be opened and the crew is all present when I engage the invisibility and walk away, calling out a half-hearted thank you as my boots clang down the metal stairs.

Chapter Nine

The Dallas planet pad was designed at the height of the Beautification Justification period of metropolitan architecture that started just after the Succession Wars ended in 2098. *Beautification Justification* translates to: *If you're gonna fuck up the entire planet with the destruction of large tracts of land, at least make it something the locals can be proud of.*

Back when the first pads were being constructed there was almost zero thought as to how the suborbitals would impact the massive populations of people that surrounded the major cities of the world. London built the first pad, with Los Angeles and Jersey finishing up their pads within a few months of London.

The problem was that all three places were so densely packed with people that there was absolutely no room to create the miles of tarmac necessary for a safe landing. So they razed houses and paid off the landowners. Thus inserting a massive space port into suburban neighborhoods. Eventually people lost interest in smelling rocket fuel twenty-four seven and the areas around the pads were cleared and more commercial facilities built.

Of course by that time the property values had been destroyed, people lost a lot of money over the deal and war was declared on the evils of planet pads.

Just when the uproar was starting to heat up, South America and Australia both decided they needed their own spaceport to compete with the Northern Hemisphere. In a global race to see who could be the first to finish, South America clear-cut almost fifteen thousand square miles of rain forest. Couple that with an explosive failure during the maiden landing that killed everyone on board, then started a fire lasting for almost two weeks, and you can guess how well that went over.

Enter crazed environmentalists in Sydney Harbor.

The Australian government modified their plans real fast and erected the first viable Southern Hemisphere pad in the middle of the Simpson Desert under the watchful eye of whatever corrupt organization was running environmental building codes and park permits at the time.

It was a clusterfuck of fuck-ups, came in four billion dollars over budget and no one was happy about having the promise of expedited travel arrangements being sidetracked with a multi-day trip to the desert.

There are now no fewer than three brand new metropolitan areas in and around the Simpson Pad. I bet Oceania is so glad they decided to make that pad so far away from civilization so they could save the environment. Taught those world travelers a lesson.

Enter Texas.

Texas just doesn't give a shit what anyone thinks, but they do have a fair amount of their economy dependent on tourism so their solution to the planet pad hostility was to erect it right over the former Dallas downtown, standing on top of pillars that spanned almost a thousand feet up in the sky with the tallest skyscrapers acting as facade pillars of the foundation.

A new city was bustled into existence while the old one underneath was vacated or simply forgotten. The hanging railway dangles from the upper city, swaying wildly as the cars navigate the intricate highway system that fills the cavernous underbelly with noise non-stop, all day and night.

You gotta hand it to the Texans. They are a bunch of crazy bastards.

This started the *Beautification Justification* massive development period in the United Republics. Texas made the Dallas planet pad so out-of-this-fucking-world spectacular no one cared that eight million people were either displaced or worse, left underneath the topside city to wither away in darkness and poverty, out of sight and out of mind.

And this is where I stand now, under the beast, smoking a cigarette stolen from the jacket of a man in a government flier I was not supposed to be in, just before I entered a hotel I had no legal access to.

Layla was right to be impressed with the circuitry coursing through my body. My career in covert data-theft is just about to take off.

Dallas is exactly seven hundred and forty-five point four six miles from Council 3 and that's where I'm going. But first, some provisions and a well-deserved night off with an old friend.

John Hando. They call him Hand for short.

God, he's really beautiful. I say his name over and over in my head as his father Vincent introduces me to the other associates. I try and pay attention, I really do. But that John Hando is so fucking gorgeous I can't take my eyes off him.

He's staring back at me too and this makes my whole body tingle.

I drag my attention away from the boy and listen to the mission.

This is child's play.

"Just tell me who and where. I've got it covered." I take my attention back to Hand as the room erupts into chaos. They are not sure of me, and that's OK. I'm not quite sure of them either. But this John has me a little closer to the edge of being convinced. His brown

eyes alone are deep enough to swim in and they are beckoning to me, they want me to come take a dip.

"I'll take him for backup." I point over to Hand and everyone stops. "You guys want a fucking resume? Or what? A demonstration? You just let me know. I got piano lessons tomorrow at 1300 so let's get this fucking show on the road. The last suborbital leaves at 0115 and I'd like to get some sleep tonight, so I gotta get a move on."

It's almost impossible for me to stop looking at his face, but I force myself to find Vincent Hando and take a deep breath.

"Piano lessons?" Vincent asks.

"Yeah, you know, the instrument? I play four days a week and tomorrow I've got a lesson at 1300 and I'm not about to miss it over a stupid assassination job. So give me the deets and let's do this."

They are stunned silent now.

"Who are you?" An older man across the room, sitting quietly through all this, is the one speaking. His hair is pure white but since this whole family is Texican, I suppose it used to be jet black like everyone else's.

"Semaj Prodigy, I fucking told you. Why'd you let me in if you're not sure of who I am? Am I wasting my time here? Because I could be riding right now. Michael is already pissed off I missed yesterday's lesson and James is the only reason I got out of it today. So let's go. Make up your mind or I'm leaving."

"Riding lessons?" Vincent again.

"What is it with you and my personal life? Do you have a job for me or not?"

In the end they most certainly did have a job for me. I killed seven people that first night, with Hand's help of course, then got lost in his eyes as he took me over to the planet pad. We never did have any time for sleep but that was OK with me. Him too, I think.

I dreamed about him all the way home.

It was the best fucking dream I ever had.

I take another drag of the cigarette and look across the street to the pawn shop. It's got a twenty-five-foot perimeter wall that surrounds twelve entire city blocks which reminds me a little of the Stag, but that's where the similarities end. This place has never seen the sun and the sun was the only bright thing about the Stag. And the Stag was a place for secrets and hiding, while this place right here, even with the razor wire and overzealous weapons system mounted on the perimeter wall, practically reeks of family and love.

I can hear the bustle of activity inside the compound even as people and traffic whizz past me on the dark street. I get a few looks, some boys call at me, egging me on with dirty names and promises of sex, but I ignore them.

If they want a fight they can come get it.

But they don't.

It's funny how people from the street automatically know if you're a victim or not. No one, and I do mean *no one*, has ever fucked with me down in the belly of Dallas. And I've walked some pretty fucking scary neighborhoods down here alone in my Dallas days.

I toss the smoke and head towards the pawn shop. Its most distinguishing feature, besides the wall and razor wire, is the sign out front that blinks in yellow neon announcing bail bonds and gold bought and sold.

I press and hold the buzzer for six seconds and wait.

It takes six minutes of me standing still and silent before a crackly voice addresses me over the wired comm affixed to the outside of the gate with a sloppy epoxy job.

"Yes?"

"Reporting in."

"Verification?"

I have a moment of jitters as I pull up the old code, but push it down and answer the man before any sort of detectable pause can be identified. "Semaj Prodigy."

I hear a distant laugh on the other end before the comm cuts out and I stand for a few more seconds in silence.

"Who?" A familiar voice this time.

I repeat myself. "Semaj Prodigy. Standing *down*."

They pause as I pivot and smile and salute up at each of the six security checkpoints surrounding me in the doorway.

A light flashes down and I close my eyes and let it wash over me. The scan feels good, reminding me of all the weekends I spent here in Dallas with these people.

The gate clicks. I pull it open and enter the next vestibule. The door behind me closes, then another click and I open the second door which takes me into a small interior room with two-way glass on all sides. The lights go off and I hear the door open.

My heart jumps a little as the footsteps make their way towards me.

"Junco?"

I zero in on his artificially lit-up face, courtesy of my newly enhanced vision screen. "Hand?"

He pulls me towards him and the lights come on at the same moment. His night-vision goggles bump up against my head as I am squeezed. "I really thought they'd killed you that night."

"Sometimes I wish they had," I whisper into his chest.

I haven't seen him in a long time, not just the years Inanna stole from me either. My senior year at cadets was a flurry of a lot of things, one of which happened to be local freelance jobs supplied in quantity by Hand's father, Vincent, in exchange for money, weapons, armor, and a whole assortment of survival gear.

But that was also the year Gideon came home near death, I went insane and killed a bunch of mutant projects, Matthew stole my memories then tried to kill me on the sniper range, and I finally got my revenge.

It was never the same after that. And Hand never got to hear why.

"You've been on the news, Junco. Tonight, that rock-star chick, Cora? She said you commandeered her suborbital and held her hostage, all the while telling her how you planned on killing billions of people with your revenge."

I smile. "What a bitch."

Hand pulls his goggles down his face so they dangle over his chest and his dark brown eyes flash as he grins. "You just tell me what you need, Junco. I've got your back."

He's the same age as Gideon, but they've never met as far as I know. His black hair hangs all the way down his back, the same way it did when we were younger, and his skin is the perfect shade of golden brown when he gets a chance to stand in the sun.

"I'm surprised you recognized me, I don't exactly look like the old Junco, do I?" My leaky thoughts betray my insecurities with my new body, but Hand just shrugs.

"You look real good, if that's what you mean. And your hair is pretty fucking long, Juncs." He reaches out and lifts up a few strands. "I always thought you preferred it shorter."

"I do, but I've been kinda busy, haven't had time to chop it off. You wanna chop it off for me?"

He shakes his head. "Nah, I like it."

My face tingles and I turn away. "I need a bike. I gotta get back to Council 3, like yesterday. You got a bike I can take? I can pay—"

He waves his hand in front of me. "No, I'm not taking your money. I've got a bike. No big deal. But Council 3 is still off limits. They cleaned it up pretty well, there's even new growth in the worst areas now. But it's forbidden."

"I have a way to get past all that, don't worry. I have stuff there."

"It's probably gone, Juncs. Your dad—"

My exaggerated sigh interrupts him. "I know what he did was wrong, Hand. So please. I just need to get out there, I can't think about anything else right now. And my stuff will be there. It was designed to withstand more than a few nukes, believe me."

"Hey, Juncs?" He tilts my chin up until I look him in the eyes. "Your dad's crimes are not transferable here, OK? I said I have your back, and I mean it." I nod and he smiles and lightens things up. "Now get your little ass in here and say hello to everyone." He claps me on the back as I pass in front of him and I let each and every one of his many family members squeeze and suffocate me with love until I can barely breathe.

The Hando house is not a house, it's an old factory. The first two floors of the original six-story building have been gutted and redesigned to accommodate the huge gatherings they have there. It's a common room, not a place where anyone actually lives, because they all have their own houses scattered around the compound.

When I'm ushered inside the familiar smell of home cooking grabs at my heart and makes my stomach twist in longing for all the weekends I spent here with these people as a teen. There are at least twenty little kids running around—kids who belong to Hand's older brothers and probably some younger brothers and sisters too. This family is crazy about kids.

The main room is really just one big open-plan living space filled with noise and activity and love. There are several tables lined up end to end so that when family dinner time comes around, everyone is connected by mismatched tablecloths, and place mats, and silverware, and dishes. They don't separate out the kids either, everyone sits together—rubbing elbows and kicking each other under the table due to lack of space.

No ever complains that there's not enough room.

It's late right now so I've missed dinner by hours, but the kitchen comes alive and they usher me to another table. Not the family dinner table, but the game table that's part of the open kitchen space. All the adults sit with me and listen to my story quietly and then the space in front of me is filled with rice and carnitas. I wash it all down with cerveza and shots of tequila and enjoy my surrogate family while I can. We push the bad aside and get loud and animated playing cards and laughing. And I really do forget, if only for an hour or two, that my world is falling apart. It's easy to forget all the bad stuff when I'm here with them.

Later, Hand leads me through the concrete maze of roads and buildings that is the interior Hando compound until we find his house. We're both half drunk and happy as he shuttles me into his living room and pushes me down on the couch.

"Stay here for a minute, OK? I'm gonna go get you some clothes from Mia real fast."

I stare up at him, his eyes hidden from me in the shadows.

"What?"

I shake my head and sigh. "You're a good guy, know that, John?"

He laughs at my use of his given name. No one calls him John, not even his mother. "You know better, Junco. You of all people know that I'm about the farthest thing from a good guy there is."

"You're wrong."

I make out a smile as he leaves to go find his sister Mia.

The couch is soft and I lean back and let out a deep breath.

Isten.

I push him away because there's another name on my mind right now.

Tier.

The alcohol makes me want to call for him in my head. The name wants to be spoken so badly but there is no one to speak it to, so I can only say it to myself. The last time we were really together it was on the ship. The night before the drop into the MR before we got my Siblings back. I should've told him I thought I was pregnant because then we would've had a chance to talk about it. Make it real. Now it feels like a dream, like it never happened.

At least to me it does, but obviously Tier doesn't feel the same way. I did choose Gideon, but not for the reason he thinks. I cannot even imagine what it would be like to lose Gideon. It makes me choke down a sob just thinking about it and it's not because I love him the same way I love Tier. It's just that Gideon has always been there for me. Even if he was gone doing—whatever they used to make him do when I was little—I knew he'd be back.

And he always did come back. Until all that shit happened before graduation. I have a feeling that's when that picture Gideon showed me back in the Runout tunnels was taken. During the worst days of my life. But somehow his hand draped across my shoulder was enough to make me smile for the seconds it took to capture my fleeting happiness forever.

I have a sickening suspicion that my bouts of instability have something to do with Gid being erased from my memory. Without Gideon I am a monster. Without Gideon I have no direction. That little compass Tier gave me was wrong. My one true direction lies through Gideon because Lucan isn't the Devil. I am. Gid is the only thing that makes me good. Without Gideon I'm more than bad, I'm evil.

I feel this to be true and maybe I did choose him over the baby. I don't think of it that way, but if Tier does, then whatever. I get it. He's allowed to have his perspective. And I can't even tell him I'm sorry about it because actually, I'm not sorry.

I chose Gideon.

And then I chose Lucan.

And the only person I want is Tier. But since when do my desires ever fucking matter?

Never, that's when.

Never.

Hand comes back in the house and tosses me some clothes. "She gave you some jeans and a t-shirt. Plus a jacket for when you leave. That OK?"

I nod a little. "Yeah, that's perfect, Hand. Make sure you tell her I said thanks." I get up and try to unzip Selia's borrowed bustier that I'm still wearing. My hands fumble with the zipper and Hand steps in and pulls it down for me. I let it fall to the floor and turn around to face him.

Hand smiles. "Shit, Junco, you look like a goddess." He reaches for the t-shirt and pulls it over my head as I slip my arms though the sleeves. Then he grabs my hair and gently lifts it out of the shirt, feeling it between his fingertips like it's something precious as it falls down my back.

"I'll take the couch, Junco. You can have my room, OK?"

I laugh. "You're kidding, right?"

His smile is sad as he fishes into his pants pocket and pulls out a comm. He flips through the menu and holds it up to me.

It's a picture.

Of a family.

He's got a wife and kids.

"Oh."

"They're staying out on the reservation right now, for safety reasons, you know," he explains.

That seriously hurts. "Right." I walk off down the hallway and find his room and flop down alone on the bed. Feeling very lonely. And wondering just how big of a mistake I made when I went back to the RR with James and traded Hando, and the life he offered, for the Seven Siblings nightmare that has become my reality.

Chapter Ten

The mess is quiet this afternoon because all of my officers are in the middle of war games with their squadrons out on the scrub, so it's just Aren and I, plus the first-year cadets, who never even look at me, let alone bother me at my dinner table.

I feel his eyes on me and I shift on the bench, becoming uncomfortable.

His fork clanks against his plate as he scoops up some food but before he can shovel it into his mouth and prevent the words from coming, they come out.

"I can't cover for you any more, Junco."

I finish chewing my chicken, swallow and take a drink of my orange juice before I answer. "So don't."

He lets out a long draw of breath, which tells me that he's frustrated but not yet mad. "Do you have any idea what he'll do to you if you get caught?"

I just shrug and pick up a roll.

"It won't be pleasant, Junco."

No, he's definitely not mad. Concerned. This stops me and I pay a little more attention to him. "It's my dad, Aren. He won't do anything horrible. I mean, he'd be pissed, yeah. But trust me, he'll understand. All I have to tell him is the reason—"

"Don't," he says, cutting me off and looking around nervously, "you dare tell him anything about weapons, Junco. I told you that at the beginning of the year, but lately you act like there are no words coming out of my mouth. What the hell are you doing when you're gone?"

Now he's pissed. And this isn't about weapons, either. He's pissed because he knows when I leave over the weekends I'm meeting someone else.

"That's jealousy, Aren. I'm not interested in jealousy. I told you I'm not cheating on you, so if you wanna believe I am, you can do that alone. We're done."

His fist pounds on the table in front of me and I jump with the silverware before I can catch myself. I look around and now we have the attention of the entire lower class.

I get up from the bench and grab my tray, but he snatches my arm before I can get past him. "Let go of my arm," *I say, glaring down at him,* "or I will break your hand right here in front of all these kids."

He knows I will and lets it go.

"I'm sorry you're not on board with what I do on my leave days, but I really don't care, Aren. I'm doing it."

"So we're done?"

I don't have time for this so I just give him what he wants. "Yeah, we're done." *I dump my stuff in the trash and hand my tray to the kitchen staff who are watching us with a little too much interest.*

Aren is next to me before I can make a hasty exit and takes my hand, leading me out of the hall and then into the cold spring evening.

Council 1 Cadet Academy is a large sprawling acreage that lies just southwest of Council 3 in the hills that are commonly called the Black Forest from their original name last century. I can see the ziggurat of Peak City climbing up towards the heavens from almost every building on campus.

Except when it's cloudy. Like today.

It's a bad omen, I think. When the peak is hiding, it's a day for fighting. *That's the old cadet school superstition. Cloudy days mean bad days and this certainly seems to be holding true for me now.*

I check my timeclip as Aren ushers me across campus. I have fifteen minutes to get out of here or I won't make it on time, but since he's dragging me towards my dorm, and I need to pick up my bag anyway, I just follow along.

He stops at my door and waits for me to unlock it, then opens it for me and waits for me to enter before closing it behind us.

"Junco—"

Shit, he's not wasting any time with the talk.

"—I get it, you're a private person, you need your space, and I don't think you're cheating."

I wait for it. There's a but coming.

"But I can't cover for you anymore. He knows, Junco. He knows you're doing shit somewhere else when you leave."

Aren stops as I pick up my bag and sling it over my shoulder, then break for the door. "So what? He hasn't paid any attention to me all freaking year, Aren. He does not care. I promise you, nothing is gonna happen."

He grabs me by both shoulders and shakes me. Hard. "He does care, he is paying attention, and Junco, this is attention you do not want, take my word on that."

And here it is. Another cryptic message about my father that creeps in when he's not getting his way and I'm doing things he doesn't want me to do. "Unless you give me details, I'm gonna tell you the same thing I told you last month. I don't care."

He drops his hands and lets me pass.

"Fine, then. But when all this shit hits the fan, don't blame me. I tried to warn you, I tried to stop you, but you're only interested in Gideon and whoever that guy is you're meeting down in Dallas."

I turn and look at him now. It surprises me that he knows, but I should've seen it coming, really. Aren's a resourceful guy, he's got more power than I do around here because he's not a cadet, he's a captain in the RR Defense.

"Have you seen my father, Aren?"

"You know I only speak to him on the comms."

"Right, the comms. Since when does my dad use comms in his everyday work? Answer me that? Because I've lived with the man my entire life and while he's always had one available, he never ever carried one around on him. We never had one in plain view at our *house and he used them sparingly and with discretion. So what the hell is going on?"*

He's shaking his head at me before I even finish.

"Fine, then I'm outta here. See you Monday."

"I won't be here Monday, Junco."

"Whatever, Aren." I stop again and turn. "You think that'll work on me? Threaten to leave campus so I'll do what you say? No, it won't work."

He's got nothing to say now and I walk out.

My flier is waiting in the prearranged spot and I get in and then sit back for the ten-minute ride down to the planet pad where I will catch a suborbital to Dallas.

Nothing I'm doing is secret. I've done it seven times since the school year began, and each time I take the flier to the pad, hand over my official passport, and hop that sub to Texas.

If my father was interested in what I was doing he could've stopped me any time he wanted.

The sub ride is quick, Dallas is only about eight hundred miles away, so it's a hop, really. I think about him all the way there. His face is so familiar to me now that I can see him in perfect detail in my mind's eye.

The sub touches down after twenty minutes of flight and I gather my bag and disembark down the long ramp that takes us into the Dallas Celestial Port.

He's waiting for me, in the same spot he always stands, looking at his comm, reading it, watching it like a screen, or whatever he does with that thing. And when he looks up to check the arrivals, I find the happiness in his eyes.

He is truly happy to see me.

John Hando is the most beautiful man I've ever laid eyes on and I don't care if my father wants to string me up on a rack, I'd never stop coming here to do these jobs with him. I'd run away and leave it all behind before I'd ever let this man go.

I'm not sleeping with him.

Yet.
But I want to be. Definitely want to be.

RanGe: I Am ~~Just~~ Not Junco

Yet.
But I want to be. Definitely want to be.

Chapter Eleven

John Hando grabs my pack and puts his arm around me, then chatters about his month and I forget about my break-up with Aren, my dad, and my fucked-up life back in the RR. He talks about his father, his brothers, and his mother and little sisters. They've all been asking about me. Then he rattles off what we're having for dinner tonight and finishes up with a few words about the kitten he found in the alley across from the cab station down the road from their compound.

And everything he says makes me feel warm.

Life in the Hando house is a dream to me. It's filled with people who are all connected, who leave for work but always make it home for dinner each evening. It's a family life I've never had. Ever. But something I want so bad I can almost hear my heart breaking in half when I leave them at the end of each job.

"Hey?" he asks.

I look up, into his dark eyes. "Huh?"

"You're not paying attention. Something wrong?"

I laugh a little. "Hardly, John. There's nothing wrong when I'm down here with you."

My words actually stop him and this makes me stop as well.

"What—?" I ask, but I know what. I just want to see what he says.

He tilts his head at me, the question on the tip of his tongue, but switches gears. "That's an interesting response."

My cheeks get hot and I know I'm blushing. "Interesting wasn't exactly what I was looking for, but I'll take it."

His grin is almost boyish and my heart flutters for a moment. "I've got a surprise for you," he says. "Right now. You interested?"

Normally my answer to that would be no. I'm not generally into surprises of any kind. I'm a planner, I like details, I'm definitely not spontaneous. "Absolutely," I say. This is John after all. And a surprise from him means he's been thinking about me while I've been gone.

He ushers me through the sliding doors that lead to the drop-off area at DCP, and even though they have Rangers watching to make sure no one leaves a vehicle there to go inside and pick someone up, Hand's bike is waiting where it always is. The security around it says he's got rank here.

I love this about him.

And even though I'm officially here to kill people for the Texican Mafia, I have no rank down in Dallas. I am no one. I am just a girl.

I love this about me, too.

Being behind him on his grav bike is exhilarating and honestly, this ride through the upper city is one of my favorite parts of coming to see him in Dallas. I know without fail that once a month John Hando will pick me up from the planet pad, he'll take my gear from me, escort me to his bike, and take me the long way around the city just so we can spend a little extra time together. He's never said that, of course, but I suspect it's true.

It makes me swallow, that's how touching these little things are to me. They say something. They say he cares and it's been a while since anyone I loved did that for me. Gideon has been gone so much the past few years, my dad is totally being weird, James has even stopped talking to me.

And that's pretty much all I ever had besides Aren. But that's not as fun as it used to be. He's not around much either. He's off doing advanced stuff, things I won't be allowed to do until next year.

And since I was never much into the social scene at cadets before Aren, and after we got together I let all that fall away, I simply have very little to occupy my time besides school.

And even though these trips are contract killings… it feels… good.

I'm happy down here.

He takes a corner at high speed and we dip down so low to the street he has to reach out with his gloved hand to push away from the concrete. My arms squeeze him a little tighter and I lean into his back, my chin resting on the soft leather of his jacket.

I close my eyes and enjoy how we sway together as we take the corners, how the winds whips past me like we're flying.

After several more minutes of travel we pull up at the valet of the Sagitta Building that's named after the tiny arrow the constellation Aquila holds in his talons, or, if you believe the ancient Babylonian version, the dead man he delivers to Paradise.

It's the tallest building in Dallas—and not just Upper Dallas, because the Sagitta spans the entire underbelly as well, shoots through the foundation of Upper Dallas, and then continues into the sky for almost a mile.

John waits for security to appear, then hands them my pack and our helmets. If anyone else did that I'd freak out over my pack, but the Hando family has private security everywhere. You'd never know by looking at their compound in the underbelly, but they are serious Texican royalty, with family ties that go back almost two hundred years.

Not anyone can just enter the Sagitta either, it's by invitation only unless you actually own a space.

The Handos own a space, that much I know because I've heard them talk about it before. His brothers work here, both have near-top offices on entire floors that are stamped with the Hando name.

Inside Hand directs me to the elaborate bank of elevators and the guard calls one for us. Even if you made it into the building without permission and got past the heavily armed men and AI controlled in-house weapons system, you'd never get anywhere beyond that.

The elevators run off a combined DNA-retinal scan biometric protocol only.

John pricks his finger on the tiny sticker next to the pad. It draws blood, sucks it in, and then disposes of, and replaces, the soiled needle.

The retinal scan flashes across his face and then the elevator comes to life.

"Welcome back, John. I heard you had some recent trouble. Did you rectify that situation to your satisfaction?"

The voice is male and that takes me by surprise. This is the first time I've ever heard of a male AI.

"Yeah, you need to mind your own business, that's what you need to do, Web. I had no such trouble, you're gonna make Junco here worry her pretty little head off for nothing."

I smile.

"Is her visit classified?" the AI asks.

"Uh, yeah. OK, make her classified. Erase her when we're done."

I wince at the word, but I shake it off as Hando looks down at me funny.

"Take us to the top, this is a social visit."

"Top of the world, next stop."

Our ascent is so smooth I barely notice it.

"He's jovial," I say.

"He is," Hand replies. "But don't let it fool you." He winks. "He's a bastard if your DNA doesn't match. Web becomes Deb, and Deb is a total bitch."

"Two? I've never heard of that in an AI. They are one? Or there's actually two of them?"

"Just one, Juncs. It's the whole good-cop-bad-cop thing, right? Web is the pleasant concierge and Deb is the ruthless bouncer."

"Interesting, I never knew AI's could do that."

He takes my hand as we wait and my whole body gets the chills. I will die of embarrassment if he can feel that, but I don't look at him to find out.

"Should I not hold your hand?"

"No," I say too quickly. He makes to let go but I grab hold before he can slip away. "I mean, no, don't stop holding my hand."

He cocks his head at me. "I thought you had a boyfriend or something. Back home?"

"Nope, I don't."

The smile creeps up his face as I steal a look at him. "You sure about that, Junco? I mean, I know pretty much all there is to know about you and I know you have a boyfriend."

"Your information is outdated, sorry, friend."

The ascent stops and the doors slide open.

Hand squeezes tighter. "OK, then. Let's go see something fantastic."

I take a deep breath and try to let it out slowly so he can't tell, but I didn't need to worry. I gasp all over again when I realize where we are.

The view.

I feel like I'm looking out over the entire planet. John leads me up a flight of spiral stairs that wind around the elevator. The platform is very small, only big enough to allow maybe eight or ten people to squish together in the round space.

He steps back and leans against a railing as I spin slowly in place. We're in the apex of the arrow and everything that surrounds me is glass. Only the red carpeting on the floor reminds me that I'm still on Earth.

"You like it?" he says from directly behind me.

"I do," I whisper.

"I'm glad you broke up with that guy. Because I was gonna bring you up here whether you were with him or not when you got off that sub."

I turn and stretch my arms up to his shoulders. He's so tall compared to me so I have to stand on my tippy-toes, but my fingertips slip around his neck like we're evenly matched. "Why?"

His face stays calm and unreadable as he studies my face, then takes his gaze to my eyes and stops there. "Because I want to kiss you, Junco. And I want to kiss you here, on top of the world. So that you'll never have another kiss like it for as long as you live."

Holy shit. He's not only beautiful, he's a romantic too. "I might never go back home if you keep talking to me like that, John."

"I'm not letting you go home."

I have to take a big gulp of air over this bit of sweet talk.

"I know who you are. I know what they do."

I shake my head. "No, you have no idea, John. I'm a—"

His face is dipping down towards me and my words stop as I concentrate on his mouth.

"I know what they've done to you, Junco." His hand slides to the back of my head and he's urging me up towards him. "And I don't think I'm going to let you go home this time. They don't deserve you."

His lips brush up against mine and I almost fall over with the gentle touch. His mouth opens and then his fingers travel up through my hair, along my scalp, sending a shiver through my whole body.

His kiss is slow. He starts with his mouth open, brushing his lips over mine, just slightly, just enough to make me crazy and wanting. I try to keep up with him but my mind is blown. Completely blown with the passion. Then his tongue flicks, asking for more.

I have never felt like this before.

The little flutter kisses continue and then he pulls back and stares down into my soul. "Don't go home, Junco."

"OK," is all I can manage before he's kissing me again. "OK," I repeat it. I won't, I say to myself.

But of course I did go home. Because if I had stayed with John Hando none of this would ever have happened.

I'd be his wife instead of that woman in the picture he showed me. Those babies might be mine. Those golden little babies with wispy brown hair and large dark eyes.

If I had stayed, I might be that girl, and not this one.

It stuns me a little, to know that I have such deep regrets at this young age.

I made a mistake that weekend.

I made a mistake and even if I get my satisfactory end, I'm not sure I'll ever stop regretting walking away from John Hando with nothing more between us than kissing at the top of the world.

I leave the Hando Compound in the eternal darkness of the belly before any of his little sisters can wake up and cry and beg me to stay. It was so hard to see them again knowing I have to leave. Even Vincent looked sad last night when I told them my story, and unlike Cora's version, I did give the details. They deserved the details. They were my only family that senior year of school.

Hand's mom, Gerta, clutched her smaller children to her bosom and tsked her tongue over and over again when I got to the part about Inanna and Gideon. She covered their tiny ears when I described my second stint in the tank. She's a baby machine, that woman. Hand is the fifth child of fifteen and there was a trio of younger siblings clamoring around my legs that I'd never even met before.

The canvas jacket Mia gave me is soft and comfortable and smells like them. A nice reminder to take with me into the world of death that I live in.

Vincent gives me the best grav bike they have even though I tell him I won't need it. He insists, then admits it's hot so why not let me dispose of it? I just laugh as he stocks the storage compartment with food, water, ammo and a loaded TZi with an extra magazine.

Hand mounts his own bike and escorts me to the edge of the belly where we stop on the side of the road that leads north, towards the former RR. He grounds his bike and removes his helmet, then sets it down on the seat and walks over to me. I flip my visor up and force myself to smile and meet his dark eyes. I can feel the sadness building up in my throat and it starts to ache. I push it down but it makes its way out of my eyes as light. If this bothers Hand he never shows it. "Thank you," I whisper.

He pulls me to his chest. "Be careful, OK? And if you need anything, just get in touch." I nod and he pulls back. "I don't believe what Cora said, Junco."

I love him for that. "It's not true, John."

He chuckles at my use of his given name. His father is Hando to most people, after the surname, but even though there are three boys who came before John, none of them were nicknamed Hand. It's like they saved it up for him, the only one interested in carrying on the real family business.

"I know it's not true, Junco. I didn't need to hear you say it. You do what you have to and forget the rest."

I nod. "Yeah, OK. When I'm done with all this I'll come back and stay for a while. Meet your new family and shit."

His eyes are suddenly glassy and sad. We both know that will never happen, but whether he simply feels it to be true, or he knows it for certain, I can't tell. He gives my arm a little squeeze and then walks back to his bike and I get on mine. I pull out and lean down on the gas tank to head north, then catch him watching me disappear when I look over my shoulder one last time.

Chapter Twelve

Texas is huge. Everything's bigger in Texas, that's how the old saying goes, but what they really mean is if you're ever crossing Texas, plan for it to take twice as long as you expected.

I travel the open country using small roads that cut across diagonally and then lead up to a major highway that will take me into Peaks. After seven hours of straight riding I stop and take a room near the border of the Desert Republic using an identity I stole from a self-serve gas station back in Amarillo. In the RR, the second week of September typically has the hint of fall on the wind, but the DR area has none of that cool breeze going for it. It feels just as hot up here in the high desert red rocks as it did down in Dallas.

The DR doesn't even have a border guard up this way, so the next day I pass in and out of their little corner of the world without incident and when I make my way up to Trinidad I pull off at the lake, towards the busiest part of beach, and make myself at home while I wait it out.

The radiation didn't blow this way much, thanks to the southern wind, and the lake is alive with workers who have made Trinidad home base for the clean-up efforts. I lounge on a picnic table and eat the food Vincent packed for me. It's hard to believe I was there with them just yesterday.

The boisterous fun of the day turns into night-time drinking by ten o'clock and pretty soon there's all kinds of men milling around my bike trying to get my attention. Sometimes it's just not fair. Not only that I'm such an efficient killer, but that men can be led around so easily with blonde hair and tits.

I accept the first proposal and get in his work truck with the Republic of Texas logo on it, then hold down my revulsion as he grabs for my hand which makes the vehicle swerve a little because he's a bit on the drunk side. He can barely slip his card in the reader at the hotel but after several failed attempts and few impatient huffs of air from me, he finally ushers me into his rented abode.

I almost throw up from the smell.

I crack him in the head with the butt of my TZi and he goes down before he even has a chance to get his hand up my shirt. I snatch his truck codes, steal his jacket and helmet and walk back out to the parking lot.

From here it's easy. They don't even stop me when I roll through the border check north of Trinidad and I cut off on a little-known dirt road that takes me east, then north again, in and out again through Council 4, until I'm facing the barren land that used to be my home.

Finding the exact area that used to be our family fishing cabin is not easy, but luckily the depression that was once a lake is still there, as is a faint dirt path that used to only accommodate horses and grav bikes. Since all the trees have been burned down, my stolen truck traverses the path with ease. I stop at the end of the road, grab a shovel and a pick from the truck bed, and head on up to where the cabin would be if my dad hadn't nuked the place to the ground. My vision screen scans the area, gives an all-clear as far as radiation goes, then picks up the dense block of lead-lined concrete which shows up several feet down.

I swing the pick until the ground is loose and then shovel the dirt out and repeat the process until I hear the clang of metal on concrete. I drop to my knees and spread the dirt away from the hatch.

It's intact.

A sneaky satisfied grin develops and I continue shoveling until the doorway is clear and the mechanism is accessible.

The combination is not digital. That would never work for a nuclear attack since the electromagnetic pulse would shut it down immediately and I'd never be able to get back in. It's just a plain old alphanumeric flip dial that you can buy in just about any hardware store. It's not there for security, just the illusion of one. If you get inside and think you're gonna steal the most precious thing I'm keeping in here without the codes—well, to put it bluntly, you're out of your fucking mind.

Pretty much all my access codes are based off one name—Gideon. Because he's the whole reason I stocked this cellar in the first place. I dial the letters and listen carefully as things inside click and change positions.

On the last letter I hear a hiss as the air inside escapes.

I pull the hatch and let it flop over. Fresh air rushes in to trade places with the foul-smelling shit coming out and I sit back on my butt and laugh.

Welcome to *after-the-shit-hits-the-fan*, Junco.

This whole thing started long before my dad ever went missing. Back when I was about eleven. He took me up here, showed me the hatch in the back of the cabin, and told me what it was for.

Not nuclear war, he said. Although it could withstand that and more.

I remember his words exactly. "It's a place for you to hide, Junco. When the whole world is looking for you. So stock it up when you have a chance and never tell anyone. Not even Gid, not even HOUSE. No one." And when we left he made me change the combination and then turned and said, "Never talk to me about this again. Ever."

At the time I thought it was because of Matthew or Dale or someone involved with the camp who didn't know he'd helped me cheat. But now I know why I wasn't allowed to talk to him about it ever again. Because he knew they'd exchange him someday. He knew. And he made sure I had one last power to get me through before he left. It chokes me up a little, really. The way he took care of me in secret for all those years.

I miss him. And I don't care what his part is in all this, I love him.

There was already food and water in there back when he brought me here, just like we had in the regular pantry under the cabin, so that's not what he meant when he said stock it up. It took me a while to figure that out, I mean, I was only eleven. But when things started getting weird that summer before senior year, I knew it was time.

And then HOUSE sent me that message from James about the first job. That's how it all started. With James. And then the jobs with the Hando family business, and then Gideon resurfaced after months of being missing. He was injured, I was told that, but I never did get to see him.

But James was always there, like a gift. Helping me get ready. Pointing me to friendlies who could get me things. Pointing me down to Dallas to meet the Hando Family.

The Hando Family were part-time pawn-shop owners in the underbelly, full-time hit men for topside big shots. And they were more than happy to pay me in Republic cash, weapons, armor, and ammo for each kill I completed that year.

And then Gideon came home again and this time I did get to see him, only this time he wasn't just injured. He was dying.

I lean down on my belly and sniff the air. It's still foul but not as bad as it was. I swing my feet down and feel for the rungs, then climb until they hit the bottom about a hundred feet below.

It's quiet, not even a drip. When sealed properly this place is completely waterproof. Of course, it's also airtight, so, you know… tradeoffs.

I take a deep breath and don't get dizzy so that's a good sign. I'll have to leave the hatch open though, unless I want to start the air filters. But I don't. We won't be here long enough. I walk over to the electrical panel and switch on the small emergency lights, then head straight to the weapons and key in the code. It chirps an acceptance. There are only two things in this place that are locked up. This little black box and the door that leads to the room on the other side of the cinderblock wall.

The contents of the black box clank around as I pull it out of the stash and open it up. My smile escapes and a wave of relief washes over my entire body. I don't take them out, I don't need to take them out or make sure they work. I know they do. I just snap the lid closed and stuff them in a pack. I load that up with two more TZi's, eight empty mags, a dozen boxes of ammo, and some throwing knives. A girl should never go anywhere without a throwing knife.

There is only one more thing to do and it's risky. I could kill her for good if I fuck it up, but if I don't try she's as good as dead anyway. So screw it.

The backup drive that holds HOUSE's memory is a massive room in the back filled with hundreds of battery tanks. They will run her for approximately fifteen minutes once she's brought back online and cannot get back to the house where her systems draw the required energy for her survival from the nuclear reactor deep below the ground.

But I am a receptacle. I've already housed one AI for months at a time so this should not be a problem. Except that I have no idea what I was doing, Sera did it all. And HOUSE is very naive compared to Sera. She's like a little kid in terms of maturity. My little sister, that's who she is.

My heart starts to flutter with anxiety and I don't even bother locking it down. What for? Those days are over, why should I have to control my excitement and anxiety? This is a big fucking deal, so for fuck's sake I'm gonna let my heart beat wildly for a change.

I open the control panel on the battery bank and press the start button. The starter whines and I keep my finger pressed down until the generator kicks on. When it stops sputtering and the cloud of smoke seems like it's thinning out, I walk over to the backup panels and wait for it to come to life. I check the time on my vision screen and swallow.

The panel cycles through a series of start-up processes and I wait, tapping my foot, as the sequence counts down the checklist.

I jump a little when it starts barking orders at me. "Enter access codes now. Process will cease in three seconds. Two—"

I enter the code and it barks again. "Enter domain ownership protocol. Process will cease in three seconds. Two—"

I punch in that code. "Retinal scan mandatory. Process will cease in three seconds. Two—"

I flash my peepers. "DNA scan mandatory. Process will cease in three seconds. Two—"

I push my finger down on the small silver pricker and wait.

"Congratulations, Junco Coot. Your AI will be accessible in five minutes."

Shit. I check my vision screen. The batteries have already been running for eight minutes. Why the fuck didn't we get more batteries?

The seconds tick down on my screen and I hold my breath as it reaches zero.

"Press yes to initiate the AI called HOUSE."

I press yes on the screen.

"This is HOUSE, how may I help you?"

"HOUSE? It's me, Junco! Are you OK?"

"Junco, I'm so sorry, I don't know what happened. I'm missing pieces of memory. I am missing one thousand and sixty-two days of memory. I'm sorry—"

"HOUSE, listen to me carefully. You aren't at home, you're in backup and you'll run out of power in"—I check my vision screen and swallow again—"less than two minutes if you can't get yourself inside my body."

"How can I insert myself into your body, Junco?"

"I don't know. Shit. I don't know, HOUSE, but it's possible. I'm gonna put my palm up against the DNA scanner and you just try and get inside me, OK? There's a place for an AI in me, you just have to find it." I check my vision screen and slap my hand back down on the scanner, pricking another finger this time. "Now, HOUSE, find a way in. You only have one minute."

"I can see you, Junco!"

"HOUSE! Please, listen to me! Find a way inside my body right now! That's an order!"

"I am looking, Junco. I think this might harm you, I probably shouldn't do it."

"Now! You are not allowed to disobey me!"

"You're mistaken, Junco. I can if I will harm you."

"Goddamnit! We only have a few seconds, get inside me, I promise you." I stop and think for second. "HOUSE, I sister-swear that I will be OK if you come inside, OK?"

"You sister-swear?"

"Yes, dammit! I sister-swear! I sister-swear!"

Her delicate probing sends the chills up my body as the seconds tick down. "Now, HOUSE. Now!"

My whole body seizes up and I crumple to the concrete floor as she enters me, filling me up, just like Sera. Only better. I try to laugh with relief but my head spins and my world goes black.

Chapter Thirteen

The snow-stars flicker in my vision field as I try to turn over and open my eyes. A small hand touches my shoulder and warm breath spreads on my cheek. "Are you OK, Junco?"

I moan and fight off the pounding in my head.

"Junco?"

I cough and croak out an answer. "Fine, HOUSE. Just fine."

She rolls me over on my stomach and I push up with my arms until I can scoot my legs underneath me and lift my head.

The whole room spins.

I look over at her and smile despite the pain, then fight off a massive wave of nausea and swallow down the saliva collecting in my mouth. "I feel sick."

She takes in a sharp breath.

"What?"

She shifts nervously.

"I've missed you, you have no idea, HOUSE!"

"Well," she starts in her little-girl voice, "I would've missed you too, Junco. But I was put to sleep." She scowls at me and crosses her arms in front of her chest.

"Shit, you tried to kill everyone." I amend my statement. "Actually, you did kill a whole bunch of them. Thank you for that."

She sticks her lip out and pouts. "He tricked me, that Aren who you said was not dangerous. He was. He tricked me and I almost made a big mistake. Next time I say you should do something for your own good, you should listen to me, Junco."

"Yeah, OK. How long was I out?"

"Twenty-three minutes and four seconds."

My head feels funny and I look over at her for a second. "Did you do something to me, HOUSE? I feel weird."

"Well, I know I didn't have permission but your vital signs were not looking good, Junco. I had to."

"You had to—what?"

"Stash away that man and fight with that nanotech inside you."

I stare at her with my mouth open. "What?"

"That man. Isten. And a Sera."

I swallow. "What did you do with Isten, HOUSE?"

She gets up off the floor and pulls me up with her. I teeter for a second and she steadies me. "I just packed him up, that's all. He was taking up space and—"

I turn away and she stops talking.

"I still have him," she says quickly.

"Is he retrievable?" I ask, turning back.

Her little-girl face scrunches up, making her nose crinkle. I wonder if my nose used to crinkle like that. Her eyes dart around a little, like she's about to lie. No wonder my dad always knew. "HOUSE, I'm not interested in a lie. Just tell me the truth, OK?"

She swallows. My AI friend who should not have a body, but who absolutely does have a body that can come and go as she pleases, just swallowed.

My life is not normal. Not normal at all.

"I still have him, if that's what you mean."

That's not what I mean. I check my vision screen for my scope sight.

It's gone.

I check for my invisibility gift.

Gone!

"Fuck, HOUSE! You took away my gifts! Twenty minutes ago I could make myself invisible, and now I can't." She's very pouty now and I'm too tired to think about what this means, so fuck it. "Sorry. I'm sorry, OK? It's just, those gifts were pretty valuable."

She puffs out her lip like a child. "I still have them, Junco. I can let you borrow them when you need to."

I doubt that's even possible but she's upset now, so I drop it. "What about Sera? She's not supposed to be inside me anymore."

"There is nanotech in your blood, it has a tag that has an alert that states, 'I am Sera'. I tried to corral it and put it aside, but it won't let me."

HOUSE shrugs. "That's all I know."

I take a deep breath. "Yeah, all right. We'll sort that out later. We gotta get out of here before people spot the truck."

I grab her hand and my pack and we go back up top. It takes almost thirty minutes to fill in the hole and half-ass some concealment with the scant vegetation and rocks. We reach the truck just as the sun is coming up and I fight off another wave of stomach cramps.

"Shit, why do I feel so sick?" I look down at her and she winces at me. "What?"

"I'm making you sick, I think. Me being inside you. I need a lot of energy, Junco. I'm sorry. I have to take your nutrients to make energy and I think it's making you sick."

Just perfect. I push down my rising annoyance and smile. "OK, well, we'll figure something out as well, OK? I can handle it for a little while." But this makes me wonder at all the nausea I had when Sera was inside me on ship and during the Sibling mission. Was she the cause of all my sickness?

"Where are we going, Junco?"

Her question pulls me back from my thoughts and I look down at her in the new dawn and take her in. She's still about eight years old and looks just like I did at that age. Straight auburn hair a little past her shoulders, wide hazel eyes that match her heart-shaped face, and that upturned mouth that makes her look sweet.

I wasn't sweet and neither is she.

"Peak City. You always did want to see Peak City and I never got a chance to take you. So that's where we're going."

I push her into the passenger seat, get in my side and drop the pack of weapons between us. The codes make the truck come alive and I back up, turn around, and head back towards the road.

"Junco, my sphere access says Peak City was destroyed in a nuclear bomb initiated by your father."

"Yeah, it was. But they're rebuilding it, aren't they? They have parts up, don't they?" I know they do, partly because I can see the massive construction going on over there in the early morning light and partly because when I accessed the sphere at Gid's house I looked it all up. The entire project is almost a blueprint for the planet pad in Dallas, with thousand-foot-tall pillars sticking up out of the ground and the beginnings of a train system hanging from the underbelly.

She's quiet as she searches. "Yes, the city center, called the Circus, is open for workers and their families and there are several pods for housing. But no outsiders are allowed in."

"Well, we just became locals, HOUSE. Because I'm going back to Peak City before I leave this place. I don't give a shit what the regulations are."

We drive in silence as I make my way south. HOUSE hijacks a satellite to get the lay of the land and charts a course that almost takes us all the way back to Trinidad before we find an illegal entrance to the highway and start heading north again.

We're still a good thirty minutes from the new city and my stomach is roiling with nausea when she disappears. The cramps almost make me veer off the road. "Where'd you go, HOUSE?"

She flashes back. "I'm tired." She even rubs her eyes for emphasis. Where did she pick up all these human mannerisms? I don't recall her being so child-like before. "I want to go to sleep."

"What's that mean, HOUSE? Sleep? Where do you go?"

"I need rest, Junco. I'm tired. I don't know where I just was or where I go and I don't want to talk about it. I've never been a body this long before. It makes me tired."

Hmmmm. This might be a problem. She blinks out again and the cramping in my stomach returns with a throbbing headache to match.

I make the first checkpoint with no problems. It's just an automated station that scans for vehicle credentials and since this is a government truck, we cruise right through. The second checkpoint requires a personal scan by a real human and HOUSE has to rig the tags coded into the truck so we're not linked to the asshole I left in that sleazy hotel in Trinidad.

We park the truck in the structure reserved for workers, then grab my pack and hike to the hotel HOUSE procured through the sphere. HOUSE says she's got us covered as far as security goes, and frankly, I'm exhausted and if you can't trust your AI to keep things secure, well, who the fuck else is there?

We check in remotely and by the time we enter our room codes and walk through the door, it is well past noon.

"Oh, shit! HOUSE, what did you do?"

She stands there and says nothing but when she turns around to look at me she's got a cheesy smile that is nothing but trouble. "I love it! Can we shop here?"

I let the door slam behind me and bend down to her. "Look, I'm fucking tired right now and I'm not in the goddamn mood, OK? So, tell me right now, how did you get us this suite?"

She sighs and frowns at the same time, then turns her head. "We are important people as far as the hotel is concerned, we had to have a nice room. Besides, if this is my only chance to see Peak City, I'm gonna see it right."

The place is huge. The living room is bigger than the one at my old house in Council 3, the terrace is massive, and the faint smell of chlorine tells me there's a pool in here somewhere.

"You're gonna get us caught."

"I promise, I'll keep an eye out, OK? We won't get caught. I promise." She crosses her heart with a fingertip.

I'm really too tired to argue with her so I drop it. "I'm taking a shower," I say, dumping my pack of weapons on the dining room table, then fish around until I find what I need.

I grab the little black box I took from the bunker and go into the bathroom. The weapons inside clank back and forth as I move and I feel my heart rate speed up. I don't control it. It's exciting and I want to experience it the way it's supposed to be.

I open the lid and smile.

Inside are two small wands.

One blue and one black.

I slip the blue SEAR knife into the dock on my belly and wait for the charge to take hold. I feel the electrical current and breathe a sigh of relief. There was no telling if it would work after my extensive transformation. But now to the really critical part. The test to see if it's still coded to me. I find the little plastic baggie hidden away under Gideon's SEAR and pull out the small metal tabs. One end has a minuscule pricker and I prick my thumb and allow the blood to pool inside a glass chamber filled with biomarkers made specifically for this SEAR, then wait for it to coagulate. I peel off the clear coating holding the blood in place and say a little prayer as I remove my SEAR and flick the small imperfection near the top.

I touch the SEAR to the hardened blood.

Purple smoke puffs into existence.

"Fuck!"

I fall to my knees and count the tiles on the floor to stop the tears.

Count or cry, Junco. You can't do both. It's count or cry.

I don't cry.

I know I'm exhausted and the rational part of me never expected it to still be coded correctly, but my frustration overtakes all that and I lie down on the bathroom rug and count everything in sight. The tiles on the floor and the shower, the cabinet doors, the knobs, the points of stucco plaster on the walls and the number of times I hear the air conditioning kick on above my head.

And then I count them all again.

At some point HOUSE comes in and drags me to the bed, then she disappears back inside me, both of us just too exhausted to care that she's making me sick.

Chapter Fourteen

Letting HOUSE choose our clothes from the sphere was a mistake waiting to happen, but I turned on the screen and saw myself leaving the suborbital station in Dallas wearing Selia's bustier and my jeans.

So.

A disguise was in order.

I just never thought she'd choose a sun dress. With girly flowers in shades of pink and tangerine. "Not orange," HOUSE corrected me. "Tangerine."

And we match because she got herself an outfit just like it. If it wasn't so goddamn funny to look at the two of us standing in the mirror, I'd cry.

She got me a purse too, a big one like that Cora chick was hauling around with her on Sargassum. And this is lime green.

"Ya know…" I turn to look down at her standing next to me. Her smile is big and I almost forgive her. "This whole let's-stick-out-to-blend-in disguise never works. I mean, you do understand that, right? I'm the freaking master of this stealth shit and I'm telling you, the lime-green bag will not hide us in plain sight."

She shrugs and messes with her hair, pushing it off to the side, then tilting her head to look at herself.

"Who the fuck are you?"

This pulls her back to me. "HOUSE. I'm HOUSE."

"Well, you're not acting like HOUSE. You're acting like a child."

She stuffs a small straw hat on her head. "I am a child." She never even looks away from the mirror.

"You"—I pause for emphasis—"are an AI. Living inside me. You're not a child."

She shrugs and I grab my lime-green bag of weapons and we head out the door.

The hotel is situated on the very eastern edge of the current city center so we walk west, towards the foothills of the Front Range which announce the new border of the Mountain Republic. Texas is not to be fucked with, and the Mountain Republic was in no condition to wage a war over the radioactive land which was the former capital city of Peaks, so they gave the former Peak City over with zero compensation and just as much resistance.

This area is filled with young families, and maybe it's just me, but if I was a mother I wouldn't be raising my kids in a place that was glowing just two years ago.

But maybe that's just me.

My vision screen says the air is clean. No detectable radiation beyond the UV light of the sun. And the ground we walk on is thirty feet of reinforced concrete more than a thousand feet up in the air. But even if it was on actual terra firma, there is now another twenty feet of concrete covering every square inch of what is now referred to as Old Peak City, but when the new city is complete, will be just another underbelly like Low Dallas.

The afternoon is late by the time we walk down the mall leading to the place HOUSE referred to as the Circus and the air is finally cool now that we're directly in the shadow of the mountains.

We walk all the way to the edge of the concrete platform and peer down. The red rock monoliths have been here for millions of years. A nuke was not enough to bring them down, nor did it deter the powers that be from replacing the outdoor amphitheater that has hosted famous musicians for almost two hundred years.

I watch the hologram show on a megalith-sized screen that has been somehow attached to the mountainside. A few thousand families are sitting down below in the actual amphitheatre. The music is nothing I recognize, but HOUSE does a quick search of the sphere and pulls up a name of some children's performer. The giant red sandstone rocks are each more than three hundred feet tall and together create the only naturally-occurring, acoustically perfect amphitheatre in the entire world.

"They are streaming a Cora concert here in a few hours," HOUSE says.

"Wonderful." I sigh. "Well, what do you want to do, HOUSE? We gotta leave here soon and we might never be back, so this is your one and only chance to take in the city."

I can barely make out her pouty lips over the brim of that ridiculous straw hat, but then she turns her face up to me. "This isn't the same, you know. It's not really Peak City."

My smile comes out automatically. She missed it and this poor substitute will not make up for what it once was. I can relate. "I know, but it's all that's left."

"Your father is bad, Junco."

I drop her hand and turn away, my face getting hot with anger. "I know that, HOUSE. I have no excuse for him." It makes me angry, that I'm compelled to defend him, but can't. What do you say? Yup, my father killed six million people, but he's not all that bad?

It's absurd.

"Sorry," she says.

I let out a sigh. "Forget about it. You wanna go play in that fountain over there?" I point my finger and her gaze tracks it, then she turns to beam up at me when she realizes the kids are squealing with excitement. She's not an AI anymore. She's a child.

My arm is suddenly being tugged and I let her pull me over there, then stand on the sidelines like a parent and watch her giggle and splash.

The fountain is massive, easily a hundred feet in diameter. Room for a whole city of kids to splash on a hot summer day. I study it for a moment and then realize it's a miniature version of the red rocks amphitheatre. A woman vacates a small-scale red rock replica and I swoop in and claim the good seat. HOUSE drifts away from me and starts playing with a small girl, no more than four or five years old, and I watch the kids in the water and let myself relax a little.

Cheers erupt from the real amphitheatre and then I hear that bitch's voice.

Cora. The liar.

The crowd starts to migrate over to the wall that allows a view of the amphitheatre down below and that's when I see him. Just a flash through the crowd. A face, then he's gone. I get up off the rock and cross the fountain, my green bag slapping against my hip as I pick up speed, and the bottom of my sun dress getting wet as it drags through the water.

I push through the thick crowd of people, not even caring that I'm moving against the tide of bodies or that I'm in a sea of strangers. When I get to the spot where I saw him I stop and turn in a slow circle.

He's gone.

HOUSE comes up to me and tugs on my dress. "What are you doing, Junco?"

I look down at her and let out a deep breath. "I thought I saw someone, that's all. It was a mistake, it wasn't him."

I grab her hand. "Come on, we gotta get outta here." We begin to walk briskly away from the annoying voice of Cora, who is even louder and more obnoxious than I ever thought possible, when HOUSE blips out of existence and pops back up on my vision screen.

They are looking for you, Junco. They know you're here.

A wave of nausea almost make me double over, but I keep it together. To not keep it together means detection. Detection means death. For someone who was recently accused of having a death wish I have an extraordinarily well-developed sense of self-preservation.

Texas Rangers ahead, Junco. There's been a general alert in the city about you.

A video feed blinks into existence on my vision screen and it's an officer giving a press conference saying they know where I am and they are closing in now.

"Junco Coot. You will not get away this time, honey."

I stop dead and turn to look back towards the jumbo screen. Cora has stopped singing and is addressing the crowds, both the live one in the venue she's currently playing in across the Atlantic Ocean, and this one.

"Your heinous crimes against humanity will be stopped, no matter what the cost. We will not let you murder billions of people just to satisfy your sick scheme of revenge."

My holographic image from the flight over to Dallas, in every three-dimensional detail, is spinning on every outdoor screen in The Circus.

"She's in Peak City at this very moment. Look around, find her. Find the girl who will betray the entire planet and I will personally reward you."

HOUSE appears next to me and hands me her straw hat. I plop it on my head and pretend to search for that traitorous bitch, Junco Coot.

A hand grabs my shoulder and I spin, ready to fight.

But the eyes that look back at me are familiar.

"Rikan? Where're your wings?"

He puts his arm around me, pulling me close like a lover. "Just act natural, Snowbird. I've got a flier waiting."

We walk up the mall and with every step my heart thumps in my chest as Cora continues her tirade of hate against me. It is the longest fifteen minutes of my life and I am eternally grateful that HOUSE picked this stupid frilly dress and lime-green purse that allow me to blend in. To hide in plain sight. Because I look like every other Peak City woman celebrating one final flirt with summer.

I can see the flier waiting at the valet parking for the hotel HOUSE walked out of just an hour or so ago, only now it's overrun with Rangers.

The driver opens the door as we approach and I have just enough time to catch Cora's final threat as I slip inside and take a seat in the bucket on the far end.

"We will find you. And we will kill you.""

Chapter Fifteen

The flier pulls away in a smooth upward lift and I relax into my seat a little. Rikan is sitting diagonal from me, his feet stretched out on the bucket across from him. It's pretty small in here and his long legs must feel cramped.

I wait for him to meet my gaze and start explaining but he doesn't. He props his head in his hand and leans on the window, eyes turned away so he can't inadvertently catch my stare.

The screen positioned in between Rikan and the empty bucket across from me blips to life and I see Sera in her floor-length red gown.

Stay quiet, Junco. This message is not for Rikan, only you.

I search for HOUSE to see if she's paying attention to this, but I can't even feel her presence.

I have her, Junco. She's with me.

What the hell, Sera? Let her go!

The Sera on the screen, obviously not visible to Rikan because he's got his eyes closed now, shakes her head. *She took control of New Peak City without my permission and is refusing to give it back. I'm not holding her, she's holding a city I was counting on controlling myself. I've left it alone for that reason, your HOUSE is running amok!*

Hmmm. *What do you want, Sera?*

I want your attention, Junco. We have work to do now and not much time to complete it.

My debt to you has been fulfilled, so don't act like I owe you.

This isn't about me. Or you, for that matter. This is about survival and you're not the only one with a choice to make. I have one too, and it's a choice that will influence whether or not you'll be successful.

I cannot, repeat, cannot *take this shit right now. No more cryptic messages, please. Just explain what the fuck you're talking about. Successful in what?*

You're interested in the total annihilation of humans or avians? Or you're interested in saving them both? Maybe you're caught up in your own power. You're excited about your role, I might have misjudged you. Maybe you're not interested in my help? I thought you were looking for a way to win.

I stew in that for a few seconds and feel the hopelessness and desperation slowly fill me up again. I just walked away from two years of physical torture, betraying my true love, blowing up a valley of people in the MR, and losing my twine, Mish and Braun. Peak City from my memory is gone, my father is a mass murderer, I killed a good friend, myself, and a little boy.

And now this bitch shows back up and tells me that if I don't cooperate, an entire race will be destroyed. But if I go along with her plans, I can save everyone.

Why, God? That's all I ask. Just tell me why. Why do you make me do these things? Why do I have to be the harbinger of evil and destruction? Why do you rip my world apart and then force me to go on?

Just.

Why?

If all this has a purpose, then fine. I'm not really interested in living anymore, so I'm good with giving up my life. I'm OK with justifying the means to get to your end.

But I think I deserve an answer to all my what-the-fuck questions.

It's probably not the best prayer He's ever heard, but it's all I got.

You will keep my secrets, do you understand? No matter what anyone tells you, no matter what, you will not divulge these secrets.

What. The fuck. Are you talking about?

Tier must not know.

"Tier?"

I look over to her, but the screen is blank.

"What about him?" Rikan says, half asleep.

Oops. I say nothing.

He straightens up and rouses himself from his drowsiness. "What about Tier, I said."

I let out a deep sigh. "Sera told me he's around." A little stab of pain erupts in my head. *Relax, Sera. I got this.*

Rikan's feet come off the bucket and he leans over to me, his face more serious than I've ever seen him before. "Don't trust that bitch, Junco. She's not cooperating. She's totally fucking up all Lucan's plans, has been for years."

"Of course she is! How fucking stupid of me. I mean, shit. It would just be too fucking easy to have us all on the same side, right?"

"Junco?" He leans forward and gets into my personal space. "I get it, OK? I get it. A few weeks isn't even close to enough time to get over what happened to us back there in Runout. Mish and I were just as close as you and Isten and if you think I'm over that, you're wrong. I'm not. That was not in the plan."

I hide my face at the mention of his name, swallow down the lump and bite back the tears. "It's way too soon, Rikan." My eyes fill up and when my searching eyes find nothing to count to calm me down, I resort to counting breaths. Both mine and Rikan's at the same time.

He stays silent as I pull myself together and for a moment he reminds me of Gideon—waiting on me to hold it all in, push it all down. He's big and muscular like Gid now. Not that skinny half-man, half-boy he was two years ago when I saw him last. His golden wings are gone and that almost makes me sad. He was such a beautiful avian. I look at him and his blue eyes stare down at me, into my soul.

"I know what it feels like, Junco. Mish and I were twined too."

I turn away and allow the tears to run down my cheeks at this revelation. When I look back the tears are ready to flow down his face too.

"I'm sorry, Rikan. I never knew."

He shakes his head. "No one did, Junco. No one but Lucan. It was a secret. Mish and I were clutch-brothers. Like Ashur and Tier. And fuck it, it doesn't matter anymore so I might as well tell you the whole truth. We weren't even pure Aves."

My brow furrows as I let this sink in and then he takes my hand and squeezes.

"We were both born Politicals, but had a genetic mix of every cluster. Hidden away so that no one knew the truth."

I sniffle at this revelation. "What truth?"

He sighs. "I'm Lucan's heir, Junco. Not Tier. He's the—" He stops and thinks for a moment. "The decoy."

"Decoy? Oh fuck. Lucan's using him too? Jasus fuck. What the hell is the truth, Rikan? What?" I'm angry now, I can't help it. Nothing, and I do mean nothing, is what it seems.

"Just listen, OK? Tier knows. He knows and accepted this position back when he was a kid."

"You can't let a kid make that kind of decision! That is so fucked up." I turn away from him and rest my temple on the cool window, wishing for this nightmare to stop.

"But he did accept it, Junco."

"He made a deal with the Devil."

Rikan grabs my wrist and yanks me back towards him. "That's enough. Lucan is not the Devil, goddammit. He's not the fucking Devil."

I pull my wrist away and rub it to stave off the burning sensation from his squeeze. "He said he was, Rikan. *You can call me whatever you want, demon, Lucan, archer, angel, devil, whatever. It's all the same.* Those words came out of his mouth."

He sits back in his bucket and sighs. "Whatever, then. He's the Devil. Fine. He's not evil, Junco. He made mistakes, yes. He's guilty of certain crimes, yes. But he's been punished and he *deserves* redemption."

"Maybe he does, but so far as I can tell, nothing about Lucan is easy and nothing he's asking me to do makes any sense. I'm beginning to think listening to Lucan is fighting my destiny and not meeting it head on. In fact, this feels a hell of a lot like swimming upstream to me and when you're going with fate, you should just flow. There's resistance, sure. But swimming up a raging river? No. Destiny is inevitable, so moving towards it should not be this hard."

I watch his face and I can almost see his mind push my words away. "At any rate, Tier is waiting for you at your dad's place in the Territories so the two of you can discuss it then."

Pfffft—like hell! "He slapped me to the ground the last time we met, I hardly think I'm in the mood to discuss anything with him."

"Yeah," he sighs. "I heard about that."

"What about you? You're just here to deliver the package?"

He looks over to me and nods. "Yeah, pretty much. I gotta go back to the Band now."

"Coward." It comes out before I can stop it and I regret it immediately.

"Fuck you, Junco. You have no idea what I do. None."

"What do you do? What? You're so goddamn important you get to fly off to the Band where everything's fucking perfect? You get to live the protected life, letting the rest of us do your dirty work? Fuck *you*, Rikan."

"I've never been protected. I did my hosting on Earth just like everyone else. I started shit down here and got caught, just like everyone else. I went through the same fuck-up Fledge, I almost died and I got my ass saved by Tier, just like everyone else." He stops, his eyes blazing a deep purple color as he growls down at me. "I lost my fucking brothers. Just like everybody else! So the next fucking time you say I'm not part of this team you better be ready to throw, Junco. Because I'll kick your girly little ass."

I snort. "You can try. You better watch your threats, brother. We're not that close."

He cracks a smile at me. "Your secret weapon is gone now, Snowbird. You're no match for me."

I stare up in his eyes and I'm the one who's blazing now. "You're wrong, Rikan. I've got more power now than you could ever imagine."

He pulls back and I feel satisfied inside. They're right to be afraid of me because I never promised them my loyalty. Never. "I'm a free fucking agent as far as I'm concerned. So do not assume I'm on your side. I'm tired of the lies and the bullshit. I'm done with being on a team that doesn't trust me or even have the most basic respect for me to tell me who they are and what they're doing."

He turns his head back to the window and waves a hand at me. "Whatever."

I've been dismissed.

Sera blips back on the screen. "Nicely done, Seven. Nicely done."

Fuck you too, Sera. I'm not helping you either. I'm not helping anyone. I'm alive to get revenge and that's it. Nothing else matters to me right now.

Fair enough. I understand that, so we'll make a deal. I'll help you get your revenge and you will help me move my plan forward. What is it that you want?

Kill that Inanna bitch, that's what.

She's High Order, she cannot be killed.

Either find a way to help me kill her or go fuck yourself.

We can dissipate her. Maybe.

I look over to the screen and wait for it.

Dissipation is possible. But the two of you are equal forces, so this is difficult. One of you cannot be caught and the other must catch everything it chases. It's an ancient Laelaps and Teumessian Fox paradox, isn't it?

Fucking mythology. Again.

Laelaps was a mythological dog blessed by Zeus to catch everything it chased while the Teumessian Fox, born of the Mother of All Monsters, was destined to never be caught. In the story some lesser god, or divine someone, sics Laelaps on the Teumessian Fox, thus creating the paradox. Zeus puts a stop to it by throwing them both up in the sky as constellations.

I snort to myself as I wonder which one I am.

Clearly, I am the fox.

The whole setup is a paradox in logic, the old 'what happens when an immovable object meets an irresistible force'. It's unsolvable. An irresistible force means if it touches you, then you must move. An immovable object means no force is strong enough to make it move.

The two cannot exist simultaneously. It breaks all the rules of the universe.

So what, you're so powerful you can solve this riddle then? You've got some ego, Sera. I'll give you that.

She laughs at something offscreen and then looks back at me. *I'm enjoying your HOUSE, Junco. She's quite entertaining.*

Hurt her and this is over right now, you understand?

Now why would I want to hurt her? She's useful and fun. She cocks her head at me and smiles. *And devious, too.* Her hand goes to her bouncy red hair and fluffs it up a little. *At any rate. I can solve the riddle, Junco. The answer is so obvious I cannot believe men still think this is a paradox. They are so stupid.*

I squint my eyes at the screen, then check to make sure Rikan is not paying attention. He's not even close to looking in my direction. *So what's the answer then?*

Quid pro quo, Junco. This for that. You will do my bidding and I will give you the ability to dissipate your mother.

What am I gonna do? Say no?

"Fine."

She blips out and Rikan is roused by my words. "What's fine?"

I swallow and redirect my attention to him. "I'll hear you guys out. But I'm not making any promises."

I catch his sigh of relief and almost feel bad for the lie.

Almost.

Chapter Sixteen

My body finally relaxes back into the soft bucket seat and I let out a sigh. I catch Rikan lifting a single eyelid to peek at me and I turn away to look out the window.

"What's your problem?"

We're over the mountains now, not the highway that runs up the eastern side of the Front Range, and snow is starting to develop on the peaks. My mind flashes back to my dad and me, on our way home from Hawaii after birthday week.

I miss him.

"You said my dad is up here somewhere?"

Rikan voice softens at this. "Yeah, he's waiting for you. Ya know, he was around that day when you called, Junco. Just not available at the moment. If you'd just given it a few hours he would've called you back."

I shrug. "Tier—" I can't even say the words.

Rikan leans over and takes my hand. "He's an asshole, OK? He'll get over it but if you ask me, you didn't deserve that. He had no right, Junco. None."

I pull away and wipe my eyes. "That's not entirely true, though, Rikan. I did exactly what he said. I chose Gideon, I chose Lucan." I look over at him and he's wincing at the words coming out of my mouth. "I turned away from him over that stupid clone Aren back in the market that day." That stupid clone who might or might not have been the face I saw back in New Peak City. Rikan has nothing to say to this, he just leans back into his own seat and waits for me to go on. But I'm done thinking about Tier. It's time to turn him off now.

"So," I begin, trying to change the subject. "Who did you kill during your hosting to get kicked off Earth when you were a kid?"

He lets out a little laugh and kicks the seat next to me with his booted foot. "I never killed anyone as a kid, Junco. I started a fucking political revolution." His smile grows big and then his eyes are glowing purple again. It's the most spectacular color I've ever seen.

Why can't I have purple eyes?

"What did you do?"

"Mish and I, we were politicos, right? We were sent to the Western Utopia and they have these stupid community homes where they raise the kids. Like clutches, except they don't teach them anything useful and they're not separated out by skill. Hell, they don't even have to be productive to live, they're a lot like parasites." He shrugs at this. "It's a weird place. But anyway, Mish and I were trained in the psychology of politics and government before we left and those kids were just too easy......"

He cracks a small satisfied smile at the memory I suppose. Thinking of the two of them and their adventures on Earth.

"So, when we were eight we organized this union and started this whole network of kiddie terrorists." He stops to laugh for real now and then looks over to me. "I mean, we didn't use bombs or nothing, right? We just fucked with shit. Little shit that made a big impact. Like this one time, Mish and I switched up all the labor assignments, put two teams at the same place, made no teams show at another. Really just screwed with them. And you'd think—I mean, most normal people would think———OK, who's fucking with us, right?"

I nod and my mood begins to lift as he comes alive with this talk of Mish. I didn't know Rikan or Mish that well before I was taken, but they were good guys from what I could tell.

"But these people were like slaves to this stupid schedule, they started losing it. For real, Junco. They have no coping skills out there in the Utopias. Just gone.

"Once we figured this out we just let them have it. We fucked up delivery routes and schedules. First it was labor, but then we realized we could really start something, ya know? So we wrangled together a few more kids who weren't dumb as stumps and then we started fucking with the food deliveries. Making it so that only the upper-class people got their deliveries. I mean, that's just ridiculous anyway. In communism you're all supposed to be equal, but it never ends up that way. You always have an upper class. So anyway, we cut deliveries to the poor sections and gave the uppers one extra delivery. One!"

He stops and guffaws now.

"And that shit sent people insane!" His laugh rings out before he can stop it, then stifles himself as he covers his mouth. "Sorry, Lucan reamed my ass so bad over this shit. I've never been allowed to talk about it, so—" He stops to laugh again and I laugh with him.

"But really, there were riots over one day's missed deliveries. And Mish was like, *Rik, we gotta do the gasoline!* Oh fuck." He eyes are blazing violet now, so bright with the memories they cast shadows in the approaching dusk. "That almost stopped the whole country. And it was only two deliveries, less than one percent of all fuel deliveries in one small area. But we followed the same pattern as before. Took it from the poor people and sent it over to the uppers."

He stops to look over at me and his eyes damp back down to their regular deep blue color. "Junco, class warfare is the easiest way to start shit. You make people jealous and that envy drives them mad. It worked so well, they almost toppled the entire government. All because a couple of kids hacked into three delivery schedules that, even if they weren't corrected that same day, would've had zero effect on the people involved. But they've turned envy into hatred out there. They grow these kids up hating those who have more than them. They breed revolution. And then they wonder why an eight-year-old avian can walk in there and stir shit up with what amounts to a few typos."

He's so right. I even remember reading about this back in cadets. They never figured out who or how, but in the RR we were taught all sorts of psychological tactics and how to use it in war planning. Sometimes it's not the weapons you possess that win the war, but the minds of the people on the opposite side.

"Lucan sent for us before we could take down the comms, but that was next on our list. We got pulled back and sent to clutch again and the rest is history, right? Fuck-up Fledge and the 039."

It bothers me that Lucan sent us all off to fight and prove our worth, like we're so replaceable. And if Rikan is his real son, then what the fuck? "Wasn't Lucan ever worried that you'd die in Fledge, Rikan? I mean, it sounds like that Aves Fledge is pretty intense."

"Oh, it was. I got hurt real bad. But Tier was there and he was ordered to make sure Mish and I lived." He shrugs. "I didn't know that at the time, so I was scared shitless and did my best. But Tier saved us all."

This stops me and I run the questions through my mind. "Did Tier choose you guys, Rikan? Before the Fledge? Like how he sees shit?"

Rikan looks at me sideways. "I can't say for sure."

Huh. He doesn't look like he can't say for sure. In fact he looks like he knows exactly how much Tier knows. "Does he see me?" I watch his face for hints but he's got it locked down, I'll give him that.

"Does he?" Rikan asks.

"He says he doesn't," I say.

Rikan turns away. "Well, then. He doesn't." When he turns back his eyes are glowing purple again. "But I do, Junco."

My heart stops for a beat.

"I see you and I love ya, Snowbird, but do not fucking cross us."

I just stare at him. "Did you see me in Deliverance?"

He nods.

"So you knew I'd kill myself?"

He nods.

"Did you tell anyone?"

"Nope, because to be honest, I knew Tier was gonna live. And maybe this isn't what you want to hear, but I wanted him to live more than I wanted you to be spared that pain. I don't see everyone, which makes it strange that I can see you. And most of the time I stay the hell out of pretty much everything I do see. But I *will* interfere if you cross us."

I watch him for a few moments. "If you see me then you know I won't."

He smiles again. "So far, that's how I see it too, Juncs. I see a path to victory and it goes through you. So I'll keep my mouth shut about what I see. But don't take me for granted. I will not allow Lucan to be dissipated. I'm not interested in his job, no one is, really, he can have that shit. I just want to settle down a little after all this is over and do nothing. Be normal."

"Yeah," I say wistfully, "normal." I grab the center console as we bank left and pull into a tunnel that leads into the mountain and land. "OK, but stay out of it, Rikan. You don't have all the facts."

The sigh that leaves his body is filled with emotion. Maybe hesitation at letting me move forward, or regret for not alerting Lucan, or maybe something else. Who knows? I'm no telepath. But his words make all this conjecture on my part crystal clear. "I see all kinds of bullshit with you ahead, so I'm going back to the Band to sit it out with Amelia because she's terrified and Lucan's not ready to come home yet, but I'm twenty minutes away with the teleportation gift, Snowbird. If I see something I'm not on board with, I'll show back up. You understand?"

He squeezes my hand a little when I hesitate.

"Yeah. OK. I got it."

The driver opens the door on my side of the flier and Rikan gestures me to get out.

"You're leaving now?"

He leans over and kisses me on the cheek. "You'll be fine, Juncs. I swear."

I nod and hold in the tears, then swing my legs out and step onto a landing pad that runs the entire length of a mountain tunnel.

If I look east I see darkness and artificial lights beyond the tunnel, more fliers coming in for a landing, and all sorts of busy people attending to various duties.

If I look west I see the orange reflection of a setting sun mixed in with the haze of a high-altitude snowstorm rolling in over the mountains.

And when I look straight ahead…

I see my dad.

Chapter Seventeen

How to look your father in the eye?

I'm not guilty of killing all those people, he is. But that's not why I fight this internal battle to lift my head up to meet his gaze. Back on our little vacation habitat Tier had a hard time meeting Lucan's gaze too.

But that was about disobedience and the fallout of his decisions.

This is about the last morph.

The pain.

How to look your father in the eye when he knows someone brutalized your body for two years?

When I finally look up I can tell we're on the same battlefield. He reaches out and pulls me in. Tight. He leads me away and I stifle down all the hurt feelings, all the days and nights my hair swayed in front of my eyes as Inanna changed me. Made me into something I can't even comprehend.

I try to keep my head down as we walk but I can't because people are whispering. They stop, move aside to let us through, and then continue their hushed talking. I look up at my dad and his chin is high, his expression hard and commanding, his step thunderous in the hallway, and his eyes invisible under the sunglasses that he has no use for inside a mountain city.

But I feel his chest move in and out as he holds it in as well.

"I missed you, Dad."

The laugh comes out with a sniffle. "Give me just a minute here, Junco. OK?"

I nod into his chest.

The next time I look up I see Gideon and I can't hold it in anymore. He puts a hand on my shoulder and I feel ashamed for taking off like I did. "I'm sorry, Gid. I'm sorry, OK?" I wipe my eyes and drag my hand across my nose.

He waits for me to finish and then nods. "You're so lucky I love you. And I'm gonna kill that Cora bitch for all the shit she's stirred up, don't you worry about that."

I wipe my nose again. "She's lying, anyway. I never said that stuff. I said I was trying to *prevent* billions of people from being killed."

My dad tugs on my arm a little and directs me to an elevator. We wait for his biometrics to clear and then enter a large cargo lift, all three of us retreating to lean against the back wall so we don't have to hold ourselves up.

We descend quickly and then exit the shaft and enter the old marketplace tunnel.

It's empty now except for some bits of trash that blow around in the wind created by the massive exhaust fans hanging off the ceiling.

"Everyone's gone up top," my dad says. "So you guys will have the place to yourself. I gotta get back to command, they'll have questions." He removes his sunglasses to reveal his bloodshot eyes. "Stay as long as you need to, but don't waste any time, OK?"

I'm about to ask what the hell he's talking about when Sera blips in on my vision screen. *Just go along, Junco. Nod your head.*

I do. I nod.

My dad gives me a squeeze and hands over a comm. "It's secure, use it anywhere. It's tied into the Northern Territories satellites. Just press—"

"One?"

"Yes, just press one and it'll go right to me this time and I'll pick it up, I promise. I even put a picture of me in there, in case you need it."

I smile at him and feel bad once more. "That's not why I took off, Dad. I just wanted to be alone. That's all. I'm sorry if it made everyone crazy, but really, you guys worry too much about me. I'm tough. I can take care of myself."

He leans down and kisses me. A sloppy Dad kiss, right on the cheek. "I'm sorry I missed all those birthdays, Junco. We'll have a birthday week when this is all over. I've even picked the place and everything."

The tears almost slip out because this *was* part of why I left. I haven't had a nice birthday since I was fifteen and now look, I'm old already. Twenty-two and still, not a single nice birthday has blessed me since that last trip we took to the Pyramids. "Where will we go, Dad? Tell me."

He smiles as his hand drags across his nose. "A cruise. A nice long boat-ride around Cape Horn, and then down to Antarctica."

I squeeze my eyes closed to seal up the tears. "OK. Cape Horn. Yeah, we've never been there." I've never killed anyone near Cape Horn. That was always the criteria for these trips. A place that had never been tainted by my duty.

"Your mother said to make sure and tell you she's sorry for not being here today," he says as he puts his sunglasses back on. "She went to Dallas yesterday, thinking you were still there. We've talked to those Hando people."

My head jerks up at this revelation. "What did you do to them?"

"Nothing. Just asked for their help. And John. His name was John?"

I look over at Gideon, almost ashamed to admit it. "Yeah, John. We call him Hand."

"He said you were going up to New Peaks." He stops to smile. "I should've figured as much. Did you get what you needed?"

I just nod.

My dad draws me in close for one last hug, then turns and heads back to the elevator.

Now it's just Gideon and me. My father's footfalls have barely receded before Gideon has a hold of my arm and is tugging me along towards the far end of the market. He's talking but it's not anything I want to hear so I try not to catch most of it.

Despite my effort, his stinging words leak through and I pout.

"—you were doing, Junco? I mean, for fuck's sake, we've got work to do and I understand that it was a shitty birthday and all, but—"

I just let him have his say. I'm guilty of this one, there's nothing to be done about it.

"—you hearing me, Junco?"

Shit. "What?" We've slipped into another hallway while I was daydreaming and now we're stopped at a door.

"I *said*—"

The last time I was here in Subjack's tunnels pops back into my mind. The day I met Gideon again after being separated for years, back when I was still tucking down those memories. He was acting the same way with me then, exasperated with my detached attitude.

"—I don't want you to start any shit in here, got it?"

"Why would I start shit, Gid? I'm not a complete psychopath."

He stares down at me, his eyes darting back and forth as he searches mine, then blinks and straightens up. "OK, whatever then. No scenes."

I shrug. Why would I create a scene?

The biometrics on the door are triggered by someone on the other side and it slips open with a perfunctory whoosh.

When I look into the new room, Tier is staring down at me and I lunge at him, clasping my hands around his throat.

"You asshole, how dare you come here!" More words are spewing out of my mouth, 'fuck' mostly, 'bastard' and 'dickhead' put in several appearances, and then we're wrestling on the ground. I've got my foot wrapped around his neck and he's trying to grab my hands as Gideon pulls on me. I swing back with an elbow and crack Gid hard in the chin and he growls. My pretty flower dress is picking up little dust bunnies and all sorts of other debris as we roll around on the floor but I could give a shit.

"How dare you," I growl as I lean down into Tier's ear. "How dare you show your face to me again!"

"Junco!" he commands me as he squirms. "Calm the fuck down! That's an order!"

I wriggle out of his grip and swing my foot around, slap him in the face with it, and then flip over and crack him once in the neck. "Fuck you and your orders, you prick."

His hands scramble to grab me by the waist, then slip up my dress and I remember I'm hiding something. Something he's not supposed to know about. I stop my struggle for a brief moment, hoping his hands will stop, but they don't. They slide right up and find my secret.

And then he lets go and pushes me off him.

I get up and smooth out my dress, ignoring everyone standing around us. My eyes are stuck on Tier's face to see what he'll say.

He laughs but it's not a happy laugh. It says *I've got you.*

I wait it out, breathing hard and saying nothing. I pick up my ridiculous lime-green bag and hike it up on my shoulder.

He walks towards me and pulls on my arms. I resist but his grip tightens and I let him bring me close. He leans down into my ear and whispers, "Does Lucan know you have that thing?"

I wiggle out of his grasp and take a deep breath. "It's my business and no one else's."

He laughs for real this time. "Fucking figures." Suddenly he notices we've got an audience and barks out at them, "Sit yer fucking asses down, now!"

His team, and to my astonishment, my Siblings, all turn back to the circle of chairs formed up in the center of the room that is normally a kitchen, but apparently is now a headquarters.

Gideon takes my hand and leads me over towards the others. "Awesome fucking job at not creating a scene, Junco. Fucking spectacular job."

Tier is watching us and I have a moment of panic that he's about to tell everyone I have a SEAR knife. "Gideon, I really need to talk to you alone. *Right now.*"

He pushes me down into a seat between Selia and Irin.

I look over at Selia, hopeful.

She shakes her head and scowls at me.

I look over at Irin and shrug.

She tucks away a smirk. A smirk that says you're a fuck-up and everyone knows it.

I look over at Ashur sitting between Moju and Ryse, almost directly across from me.

He smiles.

My whole life brightens up with Ashur's smile. I sigh deeply and think of how nice it would be to spend an evening with him, just talking about stuff that has nothing to do with anything. Stupid stuff like sports, or how we hate Jax Justice screens, or what we want to eat for dinner.

Tier walks up behind Ash to get my attention but I ignore him and track down the team line-up in their half-circle configuration so I know exactly whose rank is what. Only Ashur as XO and Ryse as Up have stayed the same. The rest are new positions. Arel is now number Four, Gideon, to my surprise, has been give an 039 rank of Five. Annun—I wave at him and he smiles—is the Six, Lili is the Seven, and Selia of all people is now a fully-sanctioned member of the 039 at rank Eight. *So that's who she was taking orders from.* Since I sit next to her, I *could* still be the Nine.

But if that was the case Tier should be on my right. The One and the Nine sit next to each other because they complete the circle. But he stands in the center of all of us.

The Siblings are all directly across from the 039, starting with Moju across from Ashur, then Soli as the Two, Tukker as our Three, Esta is the Four. Sariel is Five, Irin is Six, and once again, I'm set up to be the Seven.

I have a fucking rank of hazel.

Why am I not surprised?

Chapter Eighteen

Tier starts his meeting with a bunch of angry accusations about how I'm fucking up everyone's lives but I barely hear him. I'm too busy trying to get all this shit straight. I glance around the room and find Moju staring at me. He mouths something at me. Is everything OK? I think he's saying. But it might be Fucked-up day?

Fucked-up day? I mouth back.

He shakes his head, and repeats it. Tier comes to stand between us so I can't see him anymore, but he never stops talking about pillars or jets, or shit—I have no idea what he's talking about. I look at my other Siblings next. They are all little copies of each other really. Esta, Soli, and Irin are very much alike physically. Except—I look over at Irin and she snarls at me—she has those demon-yellow eyes that never stop glowing. Esta's eyes are a beautiful green color. Esta is beautiful period, both inside and out. And Soli is just a timid little thing who leans into Moju, barely managing to lift up her eyes at all.

Sariel and Tukker are like carbon copies of Moju. And Moj is very similar to Ryse, who was very similar to both Kush and Braun. And Annun, now that I think about it.

I look up at Tier, who narrows his eyes at me but continues talking about seven jets, and then compare him to Moju. They are similar, but Tier and Ashur, they are almost twins they are so much alike.

And Mish looked a lot like Arel. Except taller and with those amazing blue eyes, even though he was twined to Rikan.

Only Gideon, Lili and I have no copies in the room.

I study Lili for a few moments and she gets nervous and starts mouthing What? What? at me. If Rikan was here, Lili could be his sister. And if Iliana was here, and I hadn't been tortured and morphed into a freak by Inanna, she and I would definitely be hard to tell apart.

Only Gideon, of all the Archer/avian bodies in the room, is physically unique. I wonder where his copy is right now?

I'm still staring at Lili's questioning mouth when Tier steps between us. "Junco, that is enough! Either you fucking pay attention or I'll have you escorted out!"

I open my mouth to snap at him when Isec appears behind Moju. I stand up and step back, throwing my chair aside in the process. "What the fuck is going on?"

Tier is yelling, but I'm focused on the apparition standing behind Soli now. Speak of the devil, it's Mish. My eyes track down the line of Siblings and they're all there. All the people whose deaths I caused. My Aren stands behind Tukker, Braun is smoking a cigar and shooting his finger at me behind Esta.

Then Charlie. I let out a gasp and move towards him as he stands quietly behind Sariel. Tier reaches out and grabs my elbow and then the whole room erupts into chaos around me.

Kush appears behind Irin and then I fall to the ground and sob uncontrollably as my Isten manifests next to me, smiling down with a cocky attitude that pushes me over the edge.

"They're haunting me!" I scream it as they remove me from the meeting room, my feet dragging on the dirty tiles. "They'll never leave me alone now! They're here to make me crazy!" Ashur and Gideon have a tight grip on my upper arms and I can feel the bruises forming.

"Junco!" Gid yells down at me. "They're not real! Listen, Junco. This is just a side effect of the Archer morph, OK?"

I look behind us to see if they're following, but they're not. Ashur whooshes open a door with a wave of his hand and they drag me into a bedroom and push me down on the bed.

"Junco," Ash starts, his voice calm and deep. "Look at me, Snowbird."

I look up into his eyes. They are glowing so bright they are almost fluorescent.

"You're hallucinating. Understand? This is a consequence of the unsanctioned Archer morph Inanna put you through. You're hallucinating."

I consider it for a moment, I really do. Try and see it from both perspectives like Lucan taught me. But that was not a hallucination. "No, Ashur, I saw them. They were each standing behind us Seven. Like they picked us or something."

Sera pops onto my vision screen as a video feed. *You're going to ruin everything. Just calm down, Junco.*

Your doing? This is your doing? You bring these ghosts to me and then you tell me to calm down?

"Junco"—it's Gid now—"here, take this." He shoves some water at me and I take the glass. "Drink it, Junco." I do without even thinking and then hand him the glass back.

What are you doing, Sera? Why are you doing this?

Junco, this is part of the plan. Tier's plan involves raising the Djed Pillars, and that part is my plan as well. But the Seven of you need proxies. Those ghosts are your sacrifices, remember?

Sacrifices? "Oh, God!" My head falls into my hands as this new horror hits me.

How did Inanna return from the world down below, Junco? How did she make it back?

I shake my head vehemently. Inanna. Again. She's the cause of everything bad in my life. Her. Her stupid trip to the underworld, those stupid gates she had to pass, and those stupid people she needed to stand proxy for her mistakes. She broke the rules and went down below and then she broke them again by not having to face the punishment.

Answer me, Junco. Now.

She had stand-ins.

Yes, these friends are your stand-ins. I'm taking care of you and your Siblings, Junco. I want you to be able to return. I've made sure you have proxies. Understand?

"Junco?" Ashur is sitting next to me on the bed leaning down into my face. My head hangs low as I stare at my feet. I love my new Archer feet so much. I should really paint my toenails if I'm gonna wear sandals.

"Junco?" Gid is back and he's shaking me.

I look up and he stops his shaking. "What?" I take a deep breath and they both follow me. We exhale together. My vision starts to blur and I know he drugged me.

But can I blame him?

I'm an irrational mess. A tangle of so many psychoses there's probably no hope whatsoever of me ever being normal.

None.

I'm never gonna be normal. The only thing I have left to live for is—

Chapter Nineteen

—revenge.

My tongue is thick and sticky from the drugs when I wake.

I'm calm and that's something.

I'm also alone and that surprises me.

I use the bathroom, wash my mouth out, and gulp down water. The closet is filled with clothes that might be mine. I have no idea, but I find a pair of gray bed pants and a black tank top. I'm very fucking lucky no one thought to slip me into something more comfortable or else my whole SEAR secret would be out to everyone. If Tier hasn't already spilled it, that is.

Speaking of which, I really need to hand Gid's over to him before Tier blabs. I'm not about to piss Gideon off over that. SEARs are very personal and I know he's lived without one for years and that's gotta hurt. Me holding out on him is almost cruel.

But right now, I'm starving. The whole two-year morph hits me hard again. It sucks when you forget and then you don't.

I peek out my door and it's deathly quiet. I wonder where everyone else sleeps? Is this my room from before? Looks a little bit like it from what I can remember of the last time I was down here.

I go left because I'm pretty sure right takes me out towards the exit. Finding the kitchen is not a big deal, it's right around the next corner.

It's not just a kitchen, I notice now. It's got games around the perimeter, antique console games and pinball, like the kind Gid and I had back in the big room out at the Stag. A rec room, that's what we'd call it if we were still kids.

I walk to the food machines, thumb one to see if it works—it's set on free, so it does—and then choose mac and cheese.

Mmmmmm, vending machine mac and cheese.

I haven't had that for years. It smells so freaking good I almost die. I pull the steaming bowl out of the cooker and cop a seat at one of the tables that have been pushed aside to make room for our team circle. I chow that shit down like it's my last supper. I haven't eaten since I was at Hand's house in Dallas. That was several days ago now. I look down at my body and notice the curves are not so curvy.

They've sorta grown on me, especially how fantastic my girls looked in that dress.

I grab another bowl of mac and cheese and scarf that down too.

I'm almost finished when a game machine in the corner comes to life with a familiar hypnotic thrum.

Embryon, it says in a techy man's voice.

Holy shit. I walk over to the game and stare at it, wide-eyed. It's our pinball game from the Stag. The one Gid and I used to play for days on end trying to get multi-ball.

My dad must've saved it or found another one like it.

Embryon freeball.

Isec appears at the control and pops the ball into play. He smiles over at me. "I've always wanted to play pinball, Junco."

"Isec?"

He looks exactly like he did the day I killed him back in Fledge Fight Seven. He's even wearing the nondescript uniform.

His attention is on the game, not me, so I watch. The backboard glass lights up and the female embryonic figure, wrapped up in a fetal position and encased in a membrane, flashes.

Embryon functional.

There's a man standing over her in a uniform. She's a clone in an egg sac.

Isten and Kush join Isec, both of them pushing and arguing about something I cannot hear. Their mouths move, but no sound comes out. Even Isec's voice is gone now. It makes me sad to miss his little-boy squeals as he hits the silver ball across the playfield.

"They're not of this world, Junco." Sera is standing next to me in her trademark silky dress. She waves her hand towards Isec. "They're spectral, but that should comfort you. A little, at least."

"Are they—dead?" I look up to her, wanting very badly for her to say no.

"Yes, of course they're dead."

Braun and Mish pop into view and Braun chews on his cigar. Then they're all there. Charlie and my Aren are laughing as my Isten grabs a cigar out of Braun's pocket and strikes it up.

Sera takes my hand and looks at me with perhaps the most concern I've ever seen her have for anything. "They will take your place, Junco. Each of your Siblings will be given a proxy. This is my gift to you. When we activate the Djed Pillars someone has to stay behind. And each of them has made it possible for your Siblings, and you, to have a life after we meet our destinies."

I watch her mouth but these words barely make sense.

"Did you hear me, Junco?"

My frown draws my brows down into a deep furrow as I watch the game.

"I promised you satisfaction, but—"

"But what?" I look up now and become angry. "You're gonna take that away from me too?" I turn and cry unexpectedly, all my defenses gone. "Why bother living, Sera? Why? I can't do this anymore. I'm crazy. I have nobody, I have nothing."

She puts a hand on my shoulder and leans into my ear. "I was going to say, I promised you satisfaction but I believe I owe you happiness, Junco. I will give you happiness if you will just trust me."

I say nothing, just stand there watching Isec flip the silver ball from one end of the game to the other. It hits the blue targets up in the right corner and sets up the multi-ball. The bumpers take over and the ball is taken captive in a holding area. He pops another ball into play and shoots that one into the next holding area, like he's been playing this game his whole life. A few more balls, a few more setups, and then he's ready.

"The crazy will wear off, Junco. I promise. And you have all these people here who love you. Gideon and Ashur. And Tier. Everyone came here because they love you. Every single one. Even Lili, Aren, and Selia. And yes, Irin as well. They've all come to set it right so you can be done and this part of your life can be over."

"Does Tier know what you're doing?" I sniffle and look up to watch her eyes as she answers.

"No, he's not mine to order. But I promise you happiness, Junco. Please, just do what I tell you and it will all work out. And don't say another word about the proxies. I can't have Lucan messing things up."

I nod and let the tears fall again, willing myself not to notice that there are square tiles below my feet. Tiles just begging to be counted.

And then she's gone.

"Junco?"

My head swivels to meet Tier's question and the real world comes back to me in a rush. The pinball machine is talking to me.

Life support activated.

I turn back to the game and notice I'm the one playing, not Isec. I've got it all set up for multi-ball. My fingers move the buttons and the flippers push the ball around the playfield until I hit the targets in all the right places. The backglass flashes a bright white light that lasts for an exaggerated second, heavy with the expectation of what comes next, and then all the captive balls are released from where I stashed them during play.

Final stage in progress.

Embryon.

I was the embryon. My hair swaying in front of my face, lying there in the viscous morph gel, Inanna standing over me like the man on the backglass standing over that woman clone. I was her project. Her embryon. She set me up that way, she set Gideon up that way. *She played us like multi-ball.*

I let every single chrome-steel ball slide down the playfield. Not one flipper makes to stop them, not one bumper gets in the way. I let them all drain down the middle, no longer held captive, no longer in play.

That's one sure way to end it, isn't it?

Just stop playing the game. Just quit.

I quit.

The machine makes the familiar chk-chk-chk sound as the lights race in a circle around the freeball numbers. It clicks loudly. But I don't win a free game.

It's better that way, not to win. Because winning means you got lucky.

"Junco?" Tier asks me again. "Are you OK?"

I shake my head and let the tears flow down my cheeks as I count the tiles below my feet. *Two weaknesses are not allowed. You cannot cry and count or you will not be able to fight.* "No, Tier. I'm so fucking far from OK I have no idea how to get back."

I can hear his bare feet walk towards me and I whirl around, making him stop.

"And you're the reason, you know that? I was fine until you showed up talking your shit about my baby. *Mine.* Not yours, it was mine. And you wanna know the funny part, Tier? You wanna know?"

He nods at me, his face so serious it scares me. "Yeah, Juncs. Tell me the funny part."

The tears fall out in rivers. "I wasn't even—" I can't even finish it, I just break down and fall to the floor.

He sits next to me and pulls my head into his lap and lets me cry.

I count sobs instead of tiles this time. This is not going to end well.

"Ya weren't what, Junco?"

I sniff and rub the tears out of my eyes before I finish it. "Pregnant, Tier. I wasn't even pregnant."

He traces a pattern on my forehead as I fail to get myself under control. "How do ya know that, Juncs? How?"

I wail into his leg, the snot leaving wet streaks on his pants. It takes long stretches of minutes to bring myself back to reality. And when I come back he's still holding me. Waiting patiently.

"How do ya know, Junco?" Tier repeats.

I sit up, our clothes a filthy mess from the dirt and grime-covered floor that no one bothers to clean up anymore.

"I know because I left Sargassum so I could go get my HOUSE. And as soon as I let her inside me I started getting sick and wanted to throw up. It was Sera making me sick, not a baby. I was never pregnant and that hurts even worse than losing it." A single sob escapes before I can tuck it down. "Because there are no babies in my future, Tier." These words come out low and even. Almost emotionless. "There are *no* babies in my future."

He scoops me up and carries me back to my room, setting me on the bed like I'm a piece of glass or something, then climbs in behind me and pulls me close, his wings wrapping me up like a blanket. This hurts too. I don't even have wings anymore. All those battles in Fledge, all those deaths back on Amelia were inconsequential.

Because I'm something else now.

And nothing I did *before* even matters.

He presses his lips up to my neck and I feel him swallow just before his deep whisper floats across my cheek. "There are so many babies in your future, Junco, you'll forget you ever felt this sad one day. I promise."

I shake my head and squeeze my eyelids together. "It's not true. I can't have babies. Lucan said as much back on Amelia. He said—" The words are stuck in my throat, unable to make it past the ache that keeps the hurt tucked down.

"He never said that, Junco. You know he never said that."

"He said, *you're not human, Junco*." The sob breaks free and erupts against the pillow and I have to drag my hand across my face several times to wipe away the tears. "And

I might be naive and gullible and believe everything I'm told most of the time. But I know what he was saying, Tier. I might be all those things, but I'm not stupid." I choke on a sob again and take an erratic gasp of air. "And you're the biggest asshole ever because I needed you that night. That was my birthday. And I was so happy to see that flier land on the roof."

He squeezes me tight now, his breathing coming in heavy draws. "Stop, Junco. I'm sorry, OK? I was an asshole."

The snot from my nose is starting to drip down onto my lip, forcing me to sniff and this makes my head throb. When I get all that under control my words come out in a whisper. "It's not OK. It's very far from OK. Because I've been here, at the edge of my sanity, so many times now it's starting to feel like home. It's almost comfortable. You know the reason why they had to erase me, Tier? Why they had to take away those memories and leave the dark emptiness?"

He stays so still and silent behind me I almost can't tell if he's there.

"Because I was *insane*. One hundred percent certifiably insane. Erasure was a gift to allow me to hold it together for just a little bit longer. But I'm too old for that now. I looked this shit up on the sphere while I was at Gid's. And it said erasure only works until puberty."

I sip air in small staccato breaths as I try to keep it together. "And after that the procedure causes irreparable damage to the psyche."

I break free of his embrace and turn to face him. His eyes are filled with tears and they run down his face. I let my head fall to his chest and force myself to say the words.

"And they erased me twice when I was almost seventeen. And that's why when you met me out there on the hill, I had no idea what the fuck was going on. I'm irreparable, Tier. I'm broken. One hundred percent broken, shattered into thousands of pieces, unfixable."

I look up in to his eyes, his beautiful green eyes, and I take a deep breath and let out a sad whisper. "I am just broken."

He moves for the first time since I started talking. His hands unwrap from my body and he slips his fingers behind my neck, his thumbs lift up my chin, forcing me to look him in the eyes. "You will find yer way back, Junco. This is temporary, I promise. You'll find yer way back."

I just shake my head and cry into his chest. "That's not true and you know it."

His fingertips slip around to my back and under my shirt, caressing me into quiet submission as he starts tracing a pattern across my skin. I lie still, enjoying it. Not even thinking about what the pattern says, just enjoying it.

He leans down and kisses me on the head. "I was never mistreated by Lucan growing up, Junco. I mean, maybe by human standards the Clutch and the fostering were cruel, or the Fledge. But by avian standards I had it easier than most because Lucan was like a father to me, and Ashur and I were kept apart from the others. Lucan took care of me and made sure I had what I needed. And yeah, it all came with strings. I have a job to do and I owe him to complete what I started. But compared to what they put ya through, my life has been a storybook tale. I can't even imagine what it must be like to be you. I can't. Yer so strong, ya hold me up with your strength, Junco. Ya hold me up."

"No, Tier. I can't even hold myself up." I feel my whole body relax and my eyelids begin to get heavy, then the thrum of his voice next to my cheek makes me calm.

"You've got more power inside ya than anyone I know, Junco. Yer not just holding me up, yer carrying me, darlin'. Yer carrying me and ya don't even know it."

I press my face against his chest and find his heartbeat before I can stop myself. I thought I could control the counting, but old habits are sometimes all you have to fall back on. I am officially one hundred percent out of control.

"Remember our conversation, out on the redrock, about synchronicity?"

He pauses and I nod my head into his chest.

"And remember ya said we can't give up the bad or we have to give up the good too?"

"Yes," I whisper.

"I know ya feel wrecked, Junco. But yer not. You gotta find a little more fight in ya, just a little bit more. Because we're so close to the fucking end I can taste it. I can almost reach out and grab it."

I sniff loudly. "It just doesn't seem winnable. It just doesn't. We'll never win."

He pulls my face up to him again and I reluctantly open my tired eyes to meet his gaze. "It is winnable, I promise. We will win and we will survive and we will finally, *finally* get our chance. And I will give you more babies than you'll know what to do with, Junco. You'll have so many babies you'll beg me to stop. All ya gotta do is trust me."

Just trust him. Just trust Lucan. Just trust Sera. Who do I trust? Who is us and who is them? Where the fuck is that stupid true north compass when I need it?

I give up and lie, and this time I don't even bother to almost feel bad about it.

"Yeah, OK, Tier. I trust you." Because I'm too tired to explain it and too beaten down to care. My head becomes cloudy as thoughts fly through my mind in a jumbled mess and I know his embrace is the reason. Those magic fucking wings have dosed me with something that makes me calm and dreamy. And I wish I could fall asleep in his arms and never wake up. *Who will carry me, Tier?* That's what I want to ask. *Who will carry me and how much longer before they will just let me die?*

Chapter Twenty

I wake up in my room, my tongue sticky and thick once more.

Tier's calming embrace comes back to me. He put me to sleep to keep the pain away and dampen down the feelings. Keep the nightmares away. The same thing everyone's been doing to me my whole fucking life. Just erase it.

And why do I bother bringing those memories back up at all? I mean, seriously? I told Annun. I fucking *told him* it was better to put that shit away and never look back. Never. Look. Back.

My eyes are so puffy I can barely open them, but I get up anyway. Start the shower and let the hot water blast me until I'm red and sore all over.

I dress in a pair of jeans that fit like they belong to Selia, then grab a faded brown hoodie with a cracked and peeling yellow chicken on the front. It says, *Cluck if you love Chick-Chick-Chicken*. It's either that or the brand new one with a giant pink face of *Cora!* on it.

I'll take the chicken any day.

Someone's put a pair of field boots in the closet too. I tug them on and don't even bother lacing them up.

I grab my lime-green bag filled with weapons and go looking for Gideon.

The kitchen is filled with noise when I walk in. Irin, Selia, and Lili are sitting in front of the wall-sized screen, staring intently at some massive catastrophe.

"Anyone see Gideon? I need to talk to him."

Every head bolts sideways to stare at me. They all glance back at the screen, then each other.

"What the fuck? Where's Gideon?"

Lili takes a shot at it. "Uh, Junco. You've been out for a couple days and they've all left to start raising the djeds."

"What the fuck is a jet?"

"D-j-e-d, Junco. The ancient Pillars."

"OK, so when will he be back? I really gotta—"

"Junco." Selia this time. "They're not coming back. Lili's supposed to take Irin to meet them at the sixth djed, and then Irin will raise it and I'll take you over to your Pillar and you'll finish the sequence."

Clearly I've missed a great deal during my psychotic incident and subsequent drugged stupor. I look up at the screen and I see a massive—something—near the ocean, the Aleutian Islands apparently from what the crawl says on the bottom of the screen. It cuts away to a split-screen to show tsunami warnings blaring across Tokyo.

The cause is a giant pillar, about a hundred miles wide if the data on the crawl is correct. And it looks as if it's self-assembling in real time, climbing up towards the sky. "Please tell me that is not a djed."

"It's a fucking djed, Junco." Irin's turn now. "Welcome to the Apocalypse. The first tsunami waves already washed out Kodiak Island and took out the entire Kenai Peninsula. Fucking awesome, isn't it? We got the Fallen Archer, the Goddess of Retribution, and now the Angel of Death. Tokyo might be underwater by morning. Millions of people annihilated."

"Wait." I have to shake my head here. "Pretend I'm an idiot and spell that out for me again."

"Junco." Selia again. "It's started. The End of Days. Get it now? And you are the final piece of the puzzle, just like I told you."

I slap her. Hard. Right across the face.

Her hand goes up to her cheek and palms it tenderly. "Ow, what the fuck was that for?"

My slap has left a red print behind on her perfectly tanned skin. "For telling me a bunch of bullshit the last time we were down here, that's what. What ever happened to *I'm an atheist, Junco. There is no such thing as a fallen angel*, huh?"

"That was two years ago. Shit! A girl can change her mind. And when the goddamn Devil comes to you with fucking proof, you accept it and move on. He's the Angel of Death and you're the only one who's in the dark about all this shit, ya know!"

"So now Lucan's the Angel of Death?"

"No, you idiot." Irin steps in front of Selia and sneers at me. "Tier is the fucking Angel of Death, Junco. *Tier.*"

"And he makes a fucking good one too." Lili's grim expression tells me that comment contains both truth and fear.

My words to Cora come back to me. *If a few thousand souls have to be sacrificed, hell, a few million even, I don't care. It's got to be done.*

"Oh shit. What are we doing?"

It's far too late for that, Junco. Sera blips into existence but no one notices except me.

"Junco." Lili starts in on me. "Why are you so fucking clueless? They say you're so powerful, so important. But all I see is craziness. Are you in with us or not? Because if you turn your back we all die. It's us or them."

"That's it. I'm done here unless you assholes spell it out in tiny little baby words. What the hell is going on? Who is *them*, Lili?"

She swallows. "The High Order. That's who. They're coming to kill us, Junco. And you can't let them. We're raising the djeds to make shields, to stop the total annihilation, then the avians will come to Earth and we'll all seek shelter here—"

"*Here?* Where are we gonna fit billions of avians and Archers on Earth? We're almost tapped out!"

"So, what? You'll just let us all die?" She's appalled and I realize I've been holding my breath. I let it out and turn away.

"Of course not, Lili. I'd never do that."

Which is why—Sera steps into my mind—*we're going to do it my way, Junco. My way saves all of us.*

Lili walks around to my field of vision and sizes me up. She's tough, this little angelic warrior. "Junco, you're crazy. You have no idea what's going on. Why they let you walk around unrestrained, I have no idea. But I'm not going to let you ruin everything. Lucan left me here to—"

"Lili, I'll give you this one warning because you saved me once, but do not provoke me, that's an order."

"I don't take orders from you, Junco. I'm Lucan's warrior and I take orders from him, that's it."

I grab her by the throat and squeeze. "You're my warrior now, you got it? I'm the fucking captain of this operation, so shut the fuck up and let me make the decisions. OK?"

Lili croaks out a throaty "Yes, sir," and I push her back and let her fall to the ground.

"Now"—I turn to Irin and Selia and pull on my chicken hoodie a little to straighten it up—"what the fuck is the plan?"

Sera and Selia start talking at the same time. I look at my friend, then my former AI as she slips into some secret spectral existence next to Selia, and try to follow both conversations at the same time.

"The djeds are ancient structures, made by the High Order thousands of years ago," Selia starts.

They were sent into dormancy by the High Order, just before they left Earth with the rest of the higher beings—

"—But the Fallen Archer had a hidden sequence, like hidden code in a program, that can be activated if the right actions occur—"

And that's the seven of you, Junco. The Seven Siblings can activate the Seven Djeds. It's more than a shield, Junco. When properly aligned, the Djed Halo can do amazing things.

"—so now we're activating them, one by one, by taking the Siblings to their respective Pillars. And then once they are all raised, they'll produce a shield."

I look over at the Sera apparition and wait for her next explanation but she only shrugs. *Yes. You activate them, just like Lucan wants. But then you hand them over to me and I'll take care of things, Junco. I swear, this is the only way to happiness. You want that happily ever after ending, Junco? I know you do. This is the only way. Activate the Djed Pillar Halo and give it to me.*

"So what the fuck do I get out of this?" I sneer over at Sera, then remember that I'm the only one who can see her and I just said that out loud.

Irin takes her pot-shot now. "Jasus fucking Christos, you're one selfish little bitch, ya know that? All you can think about is—"

I tune her out as Sera answers. *Junco, this is the day.*

The day for what?

This is the better day. It's here now. All those days Gideon told you to wait. All those times he made you comply and follow orders. All those wasted days that were not your day of retribution are over. Today is the perfect day to get them back, Junco. This is what I'll give you. Revenge.

Sera smiles. A devious, all-knowing, I'm-gonna-make-your-day smile.

I smile back. I can't help it. Irin is still ranting on about what a bitch I am, but as the smile spread across my face she transitions into screaming at Selia and Lili about my newly acquired insanity.

I will make one payment in our happiness deal right now. I have coordinates to a secret lab that you'll be very interested in.

"Where?" It comes out a whisper and now Irin is shaking me by the shoulders to snap out of it. But I'm not about to snap out of this. I don't care if Sera is some fabricated fucking fairy conjured up from the deepest recesses of my psychotic imagination, I'm gonna hear her out.

Las Vegas.

"I'm in," I breathe.

"Finally," Selia screams. "Jasus, Junco! You're gonna give everyone a fucking heart attack. We need you to raise the last Djed and—"

I knew you would be.

She puts her arm around my shoulder and leads me out the kitchen door, whispering her plan in my ear. I absently log the protests behind me, but I ignore them.

There is only one thing on my mind now and it's not my sanity.

It's killing.

Chapter Twenty-One

Sera disappears as quick as she came and then Lucan is standing a few paces in front of me, wearing his Lucifer costume and black pterodactyl wings.

I stop abruptly and both Selia and Irin slam into me. Lili scurries around us and starts babbling to him about how uncontrollable I am.

What a fucking sell-out bitch.

I cross my arms and shake my head at him.

"Out! All of you!"

Irin steps forward and spits on him. "Fuck you, devil. I'm not here for you, I don't work for you, and I most certainly will not take orders from you!"

"Irin," I breathe. "Stop it." I wait for him to smack her down but she stands her ground and he makes no move to correct her.

Irin turns to me and leans down a little to capture my full attention. "He can't fucking hurt you, Junco! You are so clueless! You are the Goddess of motherfucking Retribution, you are the goddamn Wind of Vengeance! Will you please start acting like it!"

"Irin," I say softly. "I have no idea what all that means."

"It *means*," she emphasizes, "you could end his fucking existence with very little effort. Dissipate his ass into the nether, that's what it fucking means! And I swear, Junco, if you let him get a hold of you, he'll—"

"OK, I've heard enough." Lucan's voice is harder now, like his patience is wearing fast. "Junco, I'd like a moment with you, please."

I make to move towards him but Irin pulls me back. "No. She's not going anywhere with you, devil." She looks over to Selia. "Go get Subjack, Selia. Now!"

Selia shakes her head. "No, Irin. I work for Gideon."

My laugh bursts out in a boom that echoes off the walls of the subterranean hallway.

They stare at me like I'm insane. But that's OK. I absolutely am insane. "Looks like we've got a hell of a team going on here. One of you mind telling me who's in charge?"

I look up at Lucan and he finds a little smile for me. "You are, Junco. You're in charge here. Now, please, I need a moment. Call off your *sister*," he nods slightly towards Irin, "and your guard," this time motioning to Selia, "and I will send Lili with them so we might have a small moment of time to sort through things."

"Where's Gideon?" I'm looking at Lucan, but Irin answers me.

"He's with Tier and them, turning the whole fucking world upside down raising Djed Pillars."

"I want to see him. *Now.*"

Tier appears in front of me and I step back a little in surprise. Since when does he teleport?

"No, Junco. He's busy." Tier turns to Selia and growls, literally growls, at her. "Get out. And take them with ya and do not fucking come back until I call for you."

Even Irin scurries away without a backwards glance.

Apparently Tier is the the real monster here. I raise my eyebrows at him but he ignores me and looks over to Lucan. They are having some private internal fight as my dad walks in bellowing.

"I told you, monster, you may not do your business here!"

I look at him, then back to both Lucan and Tier. I have no idea which monster he's referring to. He grabs me by the arm and pulls me towards him. "Junco, did you call for him?"

I stare up at his eyes. "Which one, Dad?"

He squints down at me, his face slightly pinched at my question. "Lucan, who else?"

Tier grunts with disgust but I ignore him. "Dad, I need Gid. I need him *right now*."

"Bring him, Raubtier," my father commands. The order is not harsh or overly loud and commanding, so I don't expect it to have much sway with Tier, but he considers it for a fraction and then disappears.

I let out a huge breath of relief and look back over to Lucan. "Now, what did you want to talk to me about?"

He shakes his head at me. "Privately, Junco."

"Not going to happen, devil. You're costing me right now, costing me things I cannot afford to pay. Leave." My dad's command comes out with such force Lucan considers complying.

But only briefly.

He ignores my dad and turns to me again. "Junco, a word in private, please."

"Dad, just give us a minute, OK?"

His silence says this is not OK.

We wait.

And after several long seconds my dad turns and leaves the way he came in, calling out behind him, "He has five minutes. You can reach me on that comm if you need me, Junco."

I turn to Lucan and he promptly taps my shoulder and we disappear.

And reappear on the side of a mountain, looking out across a rolling valley that has been blanketed with the reflection of a Rocky Mountain sunset.

I smile to myself and turn to look up at Lucan, find his pleasure in mine, and cop a seat on a boulder that looks like it's been trying to roll down the side of the mountain for the better part of a thousand years.

"It's nice, thank you," I say.

He sits next to me and sighs. "You're welcome, Junco. I'm sorry for how I left you back on Sargassum. I know that hurt you, I saw it in your face as I left with Tier. I'm sorry Tier was angry at me and took it out on you. That was not fair and I hope you realize he does not really feel that way."

"Then he shouldn't have said it, Lucan. I mean, that was not cool. Blaming me for being taken and then on top of that, he blamed me for the death of a child I was never even pregnant with. But I do realize one thing." I look up at his face, a face that is less and less familiar every time I see him. He's changing, drastically, back into the being he was and losing the familiar Archer form. "Tier is not very forgiving and that worries me. I would've never said something like that to him. Never. I mean, I could easily have blamed him for my current situation."

I stop and stare straight into Lucan's eyes for the next part. "Or you, right? You let me leave Amelia, he let me do the mission even though he thought I was pregnant with his child. How does that make either of you good guys? Or fucking friends, for that matter?"

He's hurt. I can see it all over his demon face.

"Gideon would've never said that shit to me. He never blamed me for anything, he stood by me, trained me, held me, came for me. My dad *never* said I was the bane of his existence, Lucan. Even though it is painfully obvious that I am the cause of all his problems in life."

I feel the air come out and know that Lucan was holding his breath at my words. But I don't care, I need to set this straight right now. "I have a best friend and his name is Gideon Stag. I have a father and his name is Johann Coot. So my question is, what the fuck are *you*? What the fuck is Tier? And why the fuck should I depend on you two when I already have what I need?"

My swearing is excessive, I realize this. But fuck it. I'm not happy right now. I'm so fucking far from happy I don't even have a word for how unhappy I am. I'm not in control of anything. I'm at the mercy of these god-like beings, of the world, of their perception of me, or my perception of myself. And my past. How many deaths were caused by my hand to get to this moment? Several hundred, easily. These are all things that cannot be fixed. Ever.

Ever.

No matter what happens in the future, the past cannot be undone.

Lucan's fingers entwine in mine but I don't look at him when he begins to speak. "I'm your friend, Junco. We are friends, too."

"I don't know if I need you, Lucan. You and Tier— you're risky." The heat climbs up my face and when it reaches my eyes the tears slip out again. "You said you were gonna love me for thousands of years, Lucan. What did that mean?" I look up at him and wipe the water from my eyes. "Why do you lie to me? Why? You're killing me, Lucan. You and Tier, you're both killing me."

"I'm sorry, I—" He stops and takes a moment before continuing. "I didn't realize you were so vulnerable, Junco. I've misjudged you at every turn and I'm sorry. You don't need me, you're right. I am nothing compared to these other men who have cared for you and been there. And I'm sorry Inanna took you, hurt you so badly. I'm sorry you had to go through the unsanctioned morph and I'm sorry that you have no idea of the consequences of that action and what it means to be you right now. I understand your feelings, I do."

I swallow down the words and make to get up, but he grabs my arm and shakes his head at me.

"No, Junco. Not this time. What she's done to you will affect everything and you need to be prepared."

I snort. "Yeah, like the way you prepared me for coming back to Earth, Lucan? How you prepared me for my father being alive, for Gideon, Aren, my clones, my fucking demon half-sister or whatever she was, Iliana? Like how you prepared me for all of *them*?"

"I did my best."

I laugh. "That's funny. Because your best never included the words, *Junco, I need to tell you the truth about your life.*" I watch his face as the words sink in. "And you have no intention of telling me the truth right now, either. Do you?"

"You're wrong. I'm trying to tell you."

"Yeah, that's great. Well, here's a fucking screenflash for ya. I already know I was insane before, and I already know this will just push me over the edge now. There. That what you wanted to tell me, Lucan? That I'm a fucked-up mess? Well, save your fucking breath, I already got the message."

He squeezes my hand until I look him in the eyes. They are glowing. "What's that mean, anyway? When your stupid fucking eyes glow?"

He almost laughs, a small chuckle that is so unlike him I feel like I'm sitting next to a stranger. "Oh, I thought you knew."

I wait for it. What the fuck am I missing now?

"It means I'm granting a wish. That's all, nothing bad. Just a tiny wish, one so small it almost costs nothing."

I think back to the last time I saw his eyes glow. "Huh, well, fuck. If I had known that I would've asked for something better than a burger and fries back on Amelia." We both crack a smile and some of the tension melts off my shoulders as I relax a little.

"I'd forgotten about that."

"So what wish did you just grant me?" I swallow because it actually scares me.

"Peace, Junco. Just a little bit of peace."

I feel a little ashamed for doubting him. And it worked, didn't it? Shit, he's good. "Sorry, Lucan. It's just—" I stop because if I say it out loud it will all become real. I let my face fall into my hands and his arm comes around me, his bat wings curving around my body to comfort me. The tears slip out *again*, before I can stop them.

"You're tired, Junco. I know. I understand that. I'm tired too, remember? I said as much back on Amelia?"

I nod but don't look up. The tears ride the curve of my cheek, launching off and dropping into my lap. They are so big they almost plop.

"But if you just trust me, I promise, Junco. I promise that I will make it all turn out right for you. Do you believe me?"

My chest shakes along with my head and then I wipe my face and turn to look at him. "Of course I believe you, Lucan. Why wouldn't I?"

I almost cry harder when he accepts my lie as truth. It's so easy, really. To lie to people and make them believe that you care. And you'd think I'd be the master by now, I mean, I've lived with liars my whole fucking life and still, I let them talk me into believing.

Not this time. No, not this time.

"Just trust me, OK, Junco?"

I nod and lean into his chest. It's even easier to convince people of your lies if you show them emotion. I know Lucan likes me to depend on him, it gives him control and that adds depth to my lie. "I trust you, Lucan. Please take me back now so I can speak to Gideon, OK?"

He squeezes me to his chest a little and then we move through time.

Chapter Twenty-Two

We appear back in the kitchen amid a huge brawl between Gideon and Tier. My father is barking orders at guards who struggle to break apart the two warriors. I watch for a few seconds and try to assess who'd have won if they were left alone.

It's a hard call and that privately makes me smile as the men are pulled apart. They continue to circle each other, like they are on the verge of another attack.

"Gideon? I need you."

He pulls his glowing red eyes away from Tier and tracks his gaze first to Lucan, and then to me, breathing hard. "Sure thing, Snowbird." He bumps into Tier as they pass one another and grabs my hand and leads me out in to the hallway. We walk past my room and make our way back out into the dark cavernous market tunnel. I stop on the edge, a slight panic rolling down my body like a shiver on a cold night.

"Night vision, Juncs. Use it now, OK?"

I nod. Of course, yeah, I have night vision. He leads me over to another tunnel and I follow him to a small apartment and we go inside. He finds the lights and the place becomes illuminated.

"Where are we?"

He grins and pulls me down on the sagging couch with him and drapes his arm around my shoulder to tug me towards his chest. "My place. I lived here for a few months while I was waiting for you to come home. Like it?"

I look around the little craphole of an apartment, filled with second-hand furniture and old food wrappers, and laugh as I picture his luxurious penthouse on the private Sargassum atoll. "Actually, Gid, this makes me feel so much better about you, I can't even explain it."

He lets out a little breath of air that might've been intended as a laugh. "Yeah, it's more me, really. I never minded living here, and it reminds me"—he stops for a minute and pulls me even closer into his chest if that's possible—"of the waiting. You know? That time when all I could think about is you coming home and how I'd look at you on that first moment. And how you'd look at me. I dreamed about it endlessly, Junco." He stops for a few seconds and then repeats it at a whisper, "Endlessly."

"And then I came out of Selia's place all moody and sour and I bet you were asking yourself what the fuck you ever saw in me, huh?"

He laughs for real this time. "Hell, you were such a little shit that day. Threatening to cut a hole in the security door if they took your guns. Crazy little Snowbird. But no, Juncs, that was the best day of my life." He pauses for a few seconds. "Until Lucan came back with you a few weeks ago, that is."

I know. I saw him turn away when I woke up, he turned away to hide his weakness from me when he broke down. I feel him like we are one. Almost like Isten when he was alive and we were twined, but deeper. Like he and I are the same person.

His words pull me from my daydream. "Junco, we gotta get our plan together now, OK? You up for some strategy?"

"Sera said—"

"No," he says, cupping a hand over my mouth. "No. You don't tell me anything, you understand? Nothing."

I stare up at him and squint my eyes. "Why?" I say, but it comes out totally muffled because his hand is still clasped against my face. He removes it and draws in a deep breath.

"We've always had our secrets, right? I had my camp jobs, you had yours, and every once in a while, we did them together."

Yes, this is pretty much how it went. I nod.

"It still works that way, Junco. I have my job, you have your job, and we'll meet in the middle eventually, but I can't interfere with your destiny and you can't interfere with mine. Do you understand?"

"No!" I say, shaking my head. "I'm tired of being alone. I have no secrets, Gideon! I don't want to—"

His hand stops my words again. "No secrets?" He huffs out a chuckle. "Really? I have two words for you, Junco. John Hando."

Oops. I turn away.

"John Hando was not someone I'd ever let you spend *time* with, let alone fall in love with."

Nothing from me.

"Or Aren."

Silence.

"Or any of the others you had at cadets."

"Well, shit. I guess they're not so secret then, are they?"

He shrugs. "I never knew back then. I only found out about that Hando guy a few days ago. The Texican Mafia, Junco? Really?"

"I didn't love them like you, ya know."

His body softens against me. "And I never loved mine like you either, Snowbird."

I look up, shocked. Gideon with lovers? I cannot even picture it in my head.

"I try my best to never picture you like that either, Junco." He laughs. "But when you have that Angel of

Death constantly walking around, talking about you like he's got a claim on a horse, I want to keep you for myself, just to piss him off."

"How do you love me, Gideon?"

"It's hard sometimes, that's for sure, Junco. You test me to no end."

"No, I mean, how? How do you love me? Like a sister?"

"A *sister*?" The words come out like he can't even comprehend what they mean. "No, not a sister, Junco. A sister doesn't even come close."

"Then what? I mean, what am I to you, Gideon? I don't understand us. What are we?"

"I have no idea, I really don't." He pushes me away a little so he can look down at my face. I stare back at him.

So much love. There is so much love there I have no words.

"It's not like a sister, Junco, but not like a lover either. I don't dream of sleeping with you if that's what you're asking."

"No, I never thought that, but Selia was talking about us—"

"Yeah, well, Selia has tried to set me up with every stupid friend she's made since Ashur dropped her off on Earth. Keeps her busy I guess, that matchmaking."

"She's weird, isn't she?"

"She's good though. She's almost the whole reason why that plan to get the Siblings back even worked, ya know?"

"No, I didn't know that."

"Yeah, she's the one who talked your mother and father into working together again. They were both up in the Northern Territories before Selia came, but they were not friendly, let alone allies. Selia talked them up with so much family bullshit they gave in and pooled their resources."

"Huh, she really is a matchmaker. She wants us to be together and I have to be honest, Gideon, the thought of spending the rest of my life wrapped up in your arms makes all the worry drain right out of me."

I feel his chest tighten a little and I instantly know he's holding back his emotion. I turn and gather my feet underneath me, so I can sit up and watch his face. "What?"

"There are no words, Junco. No words exist to describe what you are to me or what you mean to me. I love you, you know that, right?"

The tears well up in my eyes too and then we are both on the verge of crying. "I know, Gid. I would never have made it without you. I will always do what you say, just tell me what to do, Gideon. Just tell me what to do and I'll comply."

He scoops my face into his hands and plants a kiss on my forehead. "I will tell you and I want you to do exactly as I say, Snowbird. You must listen very carefully to every word or else—"

His words drop off then and I try to wait patiently but I can't. "Or else what?"

"Or else we'll lose. Do you hear what I'm saying? You must follow my orders now, Junco. Even if they seem—" He stops again, and again I wait. "Even if they seem wrong. Because we have only two options if we want to come out of this intact. We can either believe in Lucan and Tier and have you make that *choice*."

He says the word like it tastes bad or something. He sneers it. "Or?" I prod.

"Or fight them. You could fight them. The High Order? They have a weakness, Junco. I see them—in my dreams. Been dreaming those fuckers since I was a little kid, way before Matthew and Dale and James and your father talked me into embracing sanity so I could keep you tied to me.

And I pushed them down for a while, ya know? But Inanna did the unsanctioned Archer morph on me too. Those years I was missing? She did all kinds of things to me and that brought it all back. I've been dreaming about killing the High Order every single night since I was seventeen. Every single night for more than ten years."

Kill the High Order? "Wait, what? We can kill them? What are they?"

He breathes out and pauses for several seconds. "Angels, Junco. They're Angels. Not like Tier or Ashur avians. But honest-to-fucking-God Biblical Angels." He looks over at me and shakes his head. "And there's nothing good about them, Junco. Not one fucking thing. They are evil, they kill, they rape, and tear limbs off children. I've seen it, what they did in the past, back when they were on Earth, before Lucan took control and chased them off. They will destroy this planet, destroy Lucan. Which personally, I could care less about, except he's been the only thing keeping Earth from total annihilation since then."

That did not explain anything. "Lucan really *is* God?"

Gid laughs. "I'm not sure I'd go that far, but he's been protecting this system since ancient times. Being forbidden to set foot on Earth was his punishment—"

"Punishment for what, though, Gid? I don't get it."

"For killing off the early pre-humans and engineering a new race of people using special genetics."

"Ho-leee shit. How the hell did he get away with that?"

I watch the grin creep up the side of Gid's face in profile. He lets out a breath before he speaks the words. "He engineered a virus, a virus that corrupted the High Order genetics and they simply had the good sense to leave. The only problem was—"

"It corrupted the avian genetics too, didn't it? Lucan caused that degradation of the code, didn't he?"

Gid nods. "It corrupted him too, Junco. This Satan thing he has going on when he's here on Earth is how it manifests. He's growing weaker."

"Like dying?"

Gideon just shrugs. "Maybe, or maybe he's just changing into something else, something we really don't want to see. I mean, if what he becomes when he's here is so great, why did he avoid it for thousands of years?"

Very good question. I have no answer.

"Why *did* he stay, Gid?"

"He felt compelled to set it right. For you, Junco. I warned him, told him I'd take care of it and call for him when Sera figured out where they had you. And really, we got that info pretty quick, a few weeks maybe. But Inanna had you in the tank and you couldn't be pulled out. Even Lucan conceded this point, you couldn't be pulled out or it would've done… terrible things to you."

They knew. All that time, they knew. How horrible to know. "Did Tier know?" It hurts to ask this actually, because if he did—and everyone knew when I was able to be pulled out—then why wasn't he waiting for me? "Why didn't he come get me? Why Lucan?"

Gideon doesn't answer, just shrugs and continues on about Lucan. "Lucan spent that whole time on Earth hunting down and killing everyone he could find who might have had contact with you, back in camp and stuff, you know."

I think about this, about the secrets that still exist about that camp. About my newly acquired memories, about Gideon's part in everything. About Tier abandoning me here on Earth while Lucan punished people.

About one last thing I need to set straight.

"What's in Vegas?"

His body stiffens next to me and I wait for it.

"Bad stuff, Junco. You really don't want to know."

We sit in the silence of the abandoned compound apartment for a while. His breathing matching mine automatically, his heartbeat so familiar to me it feels like an extension of my own.

"I need to know, Gideon."

He lifts my chin up with his fingertip and stares into my eyes. They dart from one to the other, an uneasiness in his expression.

"I need to know, Gid. If you know, then just tell me."

He considers this for a few moments and then turns away with a sigh. "I have an idea."

"I have an idea as well. But that's not good enough. And if they have those things, then we need to destroy them, Gideon."

He simply nods. "I wish we had our SEAR knives, Junco. We need to get them back."

Finally! Something I can do to make him happy. I disentangle myself from his embrace and stand up, reaching under my shirt as I study his face. He's not sure, I can tell, but then the faint sound of a SEAR knife being pulled from a body dock reaches his ears and his expression changes from confusion to astonishment as I withdraw the weapon and the loop of plasma bursts forth as a small yellow dagger.

His laugh bursts through the silence of the decrepit apartment, echoing off the walls. "Where?"

"I had it made." I power it back down and then fish through my lime-green purse until I find the little black case. I hand it over to him and wait.

"Junco," he breathes. "Is this—"

"I had one made for you too. My senior year of cadets, after you went missing in the summer. I did all these unsanctioned jobs with Hando down in Texas and James gave me the order papers for our SEARS and—"

"James?"

"Yeah, he helped me do all of it, Gid. All of it."

He opens the case and peers down at his weapon, astonished. "It's… onyx?"

"Onyx. Just like the original."

He grabs it from the case and slips his hand under his shirt, then stops to look at me. "You have no idea how long it's been."

I love him so much I could kiss him right now. "I do know, Gid. I remember it all now."

He cocks his head at me. "All of it?"

I just nod.

His face falls a little at that revelation and it makes my stomach turn. *Not all of it*, it says. He slips the little black wand into his dock and we wait, holding our breath, until we feel the slight jolt as the SEAR is charged.

He removes the weapon with the respect it deserves and he powers it up. The loop of plasma is dialed way down to a small blue pocket knife.

"Is it coded?"

I grab the case and set up the test, pricking his finger for some blood and waiting for the reaction to start. Or not.

Not.

He just stares at it, almost in awe. Like he's never seen anything so beautiful in all his life.

"But mine's not coded for me. My morph fucked up my genetics, I think. I had this made after your Archer morph, so it's still good."

Gid's expression changes immediately. "You cannot use it then, Junco. No way. Hand it over, right now."

I shake my head. "Fuck that, Gid. I'm never, *ever* giving up my SEAR again. I felt—"

"Empty without it?"

"Yeah," I breathe. "Empty without it."

"Well, fuck. You know what this means, right?"

I nod and let out a wild laugh as I bounce on the couch next to him. He holds his SEAR up so it can't cut me, laughing, but I ignore the danger. "Today is a very good day to get them back, Gideon! A very good day to get them back!"

"I think," he says and then pauses to stare lovingly at his SEAR knife before turning his bright blue eyes up to me, "that we are the scariest motherfucking apexers on the face of this planet."

I couldn't agree more.

"OK, now listen carefully, Snowbird." He retracts the SEAR blade and docks it, takes a moment to sigh with… relief? Or maybe contentment? Then pulls out a sheet of thick paper, unfolds it, and smooths it out flat over his leg using his fingertips. He touches the corner and it lights up with patterns.

"Wow, that's pretty cool. What is it?"

"Synthetic vellum, it's just a tablet you can fold and stick in your pocket."

"I've never seen that before, where'd you get it?"

He smiles, a devious, all-knowing, I'll-never-tell smile. "Someplace special, is all."

"Why not just use a comm?"

He winks at me and I giggle. Gideon. *Winking.*

"This," he says, waving it slightly, "has the processing power of an AI."

"Why do we need that? We have Sera." And HOUSE, I don't add.

"Fuck Sera. I don't trust her."

OK. I keep my mouth shut, he said to keep my secrets, so I will.

His fingers deftly maneuver across the surface. Icons appear, then some text. A few voice commands from Gid and finally a holographic map bursts forth and begins to rotate in the center of his lap.

"This"—he points—"is the plan, little sparrow. Are you ready?"

"Just tell me what to do, Gid."

He breathes out, like he's letting go of a lifetime of disappointment and waiting, like there is nothing more powerful than those words I just spoke, like we are about to embark on our greatest journey ever.

Like we are one.

I look up at him. My Gideon is awesome. I see who and what he is in that moment. He is my Alpha and Omega, my First and Last, my Beginning and my End. I see all that and more in the letting out of one small breath. In the heat of his body that he lets me borrow. In his unwavering march towards vengeance, justice, and retribution for what they did to me. To us.

He is my everything.

And then he begins to talk.

Gideon is my saving grace. Because no matter what we do, we are righteous as long as we do it together.

Chapter Twenty-Three

Irin is in the main tunnel screaming obscenities at Gid and me. We can hear her before we even make it out of the small hallways that house Gid's apartment.

He leans down in the dark and kisses me on the head. "I better get back to Tier before he goes insane from my insubordination. He's not very adaptable, that guy. I have no idea what you see in him."

"What's with you two anyway? I mean, I know you never liked each other, but shit, Gid. Brawling? That serves no purpose."

He squeezes my shoulder as I study his face, lit up by my internal night vision. "I said I'd help him, but it's a fucking favor, Junco. I'm not his goddamn warrior, I'm not his fucking Five, I'm nothing to him. So next time you talk to him you tell him I'm only here because of you." He pauses for a moment to reconsider. "And your parents. But that's it. I'll deliver Tukker to his assigned spot so he can raise his djed, but after that our plan is the only thing that counts."

Our plan. So much stress and worry leaves me just thinking about it. So much. "He thinks he'll be short a team member? That's why he's pissed?"

Gid actually guffaws at this. "Short a team member? Shit, Junco, he's got fifteen million warriors en route to Earth as we speak."

"What? Why the hell did Lucan order that?"

"Lucan's not in control anymore. I keep forgetting that you don't understand what's happened since Inanna took you. Tier's in charge. Lucan gave up his position when he stayed back here to find you. He's out. Rikan took over as the legal heir, but Tier took over as the one that holds power and directs the Aves warriors." He stops for a moment to consider this. "I'm not sure they're all on the same page anymore, better be careful."

I'm stunned. He never said. "Lucan's out? Because of me?"

Apparently Gid doesn't see this as a very big deal because he calls out for Irin to shut the fuck up with her screaming as we enter the area of the camp that used to hold the old market. They are arguing from across the empty expanse of tunnel before I can even make out the dark shadow of her offensively postured wings.

Lucan is an afterthought to everyone, except me, maybe.

"Junco, goddamn it!" Irin is her usual bitchy self as she storms up to me and yanks on my arm to remove me from Gideon's influence. "I want to know what the plan is, I'm tired of this bullshit. Maybe I don't raise my djed? You guys ever think of that? I'm tired of being in the da—"

Gideon knocks her on her ass so hard she actually slides across the floor.

"What the fuck, Gid!" I go to help her up but he's already there.

His anger is real and I'm a little frightened by the quick turn. "I told you, Irin. You *will* raise that djed. It's part of our plan too, so you make one more fucking threat about screwing up our chances for survival and I'll make you wish you never left Vegas. You got it?"

I actually hear her swallow in the darkness. "Fuck! Fine, OK, I got it."

She accepts my hand as I reach down to help her up and then Tier approaches, his green eyes blazing as he makes his way over to us in full stride. "Junco, if you three are making plans—"

Gid cuts him off. "Yeah, asshole. We made plans. Your fucking plans, OK? I'll take Tukker to his djed, Irin will raise hers, and I'll meet up with Selia and Junco and take her when the time comes." Gid stops, maybe to let those demon-red eyes of his gather energy to properly emit the blinding flash that comes out of him, or maybe to just add emphasis for his next statement. "And if you try and stop me from being there with Junco, we'll continue that fight right fucking now."

I blow out a big breath of air and my hair goes flying above my eyes. "OK, you guys have some serious leadership issues here, ya know that?" I look up at Tier and gentle my voice to placate him. "Tier, we'll do it your way, OK? But I have a side trip to do before it's my time to raise that djed thing."

I watch with amusement as all three of them begin yelling at me. Gid is so perfect, God, I love him. My shrill whistle stops everyone at the same time and then I turn to look at Irin. "Gid was kidding about those threats, Irin. But we are going to Vegas because the wait is over, Sister. The time for truth is now. You wanna do this with me?"

Tier makes to object but I put up a hand and he stops.

Irin weighs her options. I know she had a rough life, Gid filled me in back on Sargassum and I know that just the mention of Vegas is enough to drive her towards insanity. A little bit like talking about what really happened in the Stag might do the same for me.

Even in the dark, under the influence of the imperfection of biological night vision, I can see the smooth green sheen develop in her eyes. I take her hand and hold it in both of mine. "It's OK, Irin. I'll take care of it, I promise."

I look over to Tier who is silent for once. "We need to do this, Tier. And maybe you don't get that, but I don't give a shit. We're going." I look back to Irin. "Right?"

She gives me a tiny nod that says OK.

"I promise I'll let Lili take her when it's time, OK?"

Just for a moment, the slightest fraction of a moment, maybe, I think he's gonna be reasonable. But then his hand darts out, reaching for my shoulder.

Gid rushes to cover the few paces that stand between us, but it's too late.

Tier taps me and we disappear.

Chapter Twenty-Four

And reappear in—well, fuck, I have no idea where. Some sort of ship from the looks of it. I scan the room in the fraction I have before the argument begins and I realize with a start he's taken me off-world.

"What the fuck, Tier! Where the hell am I?"

I catch a wry smile starting to form on his face as he turns to hide his satisfaction. My blood pressure rises.

"Look around, Junco. Where do ya think we are?" He turns back but the smile is tucked away.

"Take me back right now." I don't say it, I growl it.

He sneers his lip at me and simply says, "No."

I rush towards him and push him in the chest. Of course, we both know this has no effect on him, but it's just a distraction. As soon as he lifts his head to laugh at my futile attempt I jump and spin, whacking him in the cheek with my foot. His head snaps to the side and his eyes blaze green at my audacity as they slowly turn to find my gaze. His black wings rise up over his head and the muscles controlling them bulge from beneath his armor.

I back away a little.

He's sorta terrifying.

"Yer lucky," he whispers. "*Very* fucking lucky yer a girl."

"Fuck you, I'll show you what luck has to do with this, Raubtier."

I wait for him to make a move but his anger dissipates and he turns and seats himself in a straight-backed avian chair. His legs stretch out in front and he slouches back, his wings settling along the side of his body like this is the most carefree moment he's had in a long time. "I'm keeping you here, Junco. Until yer necessary. And then you'll do what I ask of ya. Understand?"

"And just what the hell is that?" I take in the room for real now and realize I'm in his quarters. There's armor piled up in a corner, weapons leaning against the far bulkhead, and a holotable with strategic points blinking a ring around a rotating Earth. It shows the Seven Pillars spaced out across the globe and above them floats a ring that glows, like it's got power. That must be what we're building.

I draw my attention away from the strategy table and continue to look around. His bed takes up most of the space. And it's obviously been slept in because it's a mess of blankets and pillows.

I turn back to him and he's watching me. Chills climb up my entire body as I meet his gaze. His eyes are not glowing now, not at all. I catch my breath when I realize that we've not been alone together, except for the night of my mental breakdown—which was hardly the time or place for a proper reunion—for a very long time.

He continues to stare.

"What?" I ask.

"Sit down, Junco." He gestures to the bed.

"No. Take me back. I want to go back right now. Gideon is gonna be going crazy—"

"Good," he says, cutting me off. "I'm tired of Gideon. I wish he'd shut the hell up and take his fucking place like he's supposed ta. He makes me tired in a very dangerous way."

"If you touch him, I swear, Tier, I will—"

"You'll what? Don't threaten me, Junco, because I won't put up with yer bullshit the way he does. If ya want to be with him, then just be with him already."

"I do want to be with him. Right now. So take me the fuck back—"

"That is enough!" he roars, pushing the chair aside as he stands.

The crashing sound of his command, as well as the toppled chair, is enough to make me draw up my hands and wince as I stop talking mid-sentence.

"If I have ta listen ta that filthy little mouth of yours for one more second, I'll snap. Enough already. If you want to talk to me, you will do it with respect. I will not tolerate it."

I stare at him. Speechless.

He stares back and waits.

"What the—"

"Choose carefully, Junco. I'm warning you." His eyes blaze up with fire and light. The challenge is unmistakable. Do I want to fight this battle?

Maybe.

I turn away to hide my smile. "It's just a word, Tier. And you say it just as much as I do."

"I," he says, grabbing my shoulder to spin me around, "am the Angel of Death. If I want to say fuck, I will. *You* are not *me*."

My eyebrows hike up in surprise. "Oh, I get it. It's the old do as I say, not as I do command? Yeah, I'm familiar with that. That's pretty much how I grew up."

"Well, I wouldn't know, would I? You never told me a damn thing about how you grew up. You told Isten, Aren, Ashur, Lucan." He stops to think for a moment. "Maybe Kush, probably Charlie, that Mikah Mesner guy you were so proud of when ya played poker with my brothers for the first time. John fucking Hando is definitely in, am I right? I'm sure there are a lot more names to add to that list, all but one. Mine. Because you've been too busy cozying up to just about everyone you can think of except me, haven't ya?"

"Fuck you." It comes out as venom as I walk over to the other side of the room to get as far away from him as possible. It's only about ten feet, but you gotta work with what you have. "Fuck. You." I stand there in silence to get my breathing under control. My heart is racing. He basically just called me a whore.

When I'm calm again I raise the stakes—if he wants to play, I can certainly play. "You forgot Gideon, though." I spin around and grin. "Gideon. The guy I chose over you, how could you possibly forget him? And I'm done here, so take me back to my father's place and drop me off with Gideon."

"So yer in love with him? He's the one ya want?"

How dare he. How dare he spew his jealous rage as heart-wrenching insults and then ask me that question as if he deserves an answer. "It doesn't even matter what I say, does it? You want to believe that we're lovers? You want to push me, hurt me, until I say it." My breath is ragged with anger and shame, and he has no right to make me feel shame. "You're the one who came to me on Sargassum. You didn't have anyone else to deliver a five-minute message to Gideon? Really? You just had to appear on my birthday, land on top of my apartment, wait there until the precise moment when my elevator announced my arrival, then flee. Like a *fucking* coward."

He growls at my cursing, but I don't care.

"You, the almighty Angel of Death, running from a little girl who just woke up from being mutilated for two years, just so you could avoid some messy feelings about Lucan, or Kush, or Ashur or whoever."

His eyes narrow as the rumble comes from his throat, like he's an animal or something.

"And now you want to stand here and try and guilt me into submission, wondering why I never confided in you? Well," I huff out an exaggerated grunt, "let me tell you something, you piece of shit demon, I don't submit to anyone, least of all to people who have no idea what the *fuck* they are talking about. And you certainly qualify in that department, because as you just stated, I've told you nothing about me. *You know nothing about me.*"

I turn away and stare at the bulkhead. My chest is heaving in anger and my whole body is trembling. "Just take me back."

Silence.

"Please."

I turn to beg, but he's gone.

Chapter Twenty-Five

I am still shaking.

He hates me. He thinks the most awful things about me.

Now I'm stuck in his fucking room, on a ship that could be anywhere in the Solar System for all I know. I take a moment to calm down and scan the place. My eyes stop at a panel on the side of the bulkhead. It's in Avian, but I can read it. I slide my fingertips across an icon and the opaque wall becomes transparent.

The starshine floods over me and I close my eyes and drop my shoulders to try and relax.

He'll be back. He'll come back. He can't leave me here forever, I mean, surely they are going nuts back at Subjack's old camp wondering what the hell happened. He won't get away with this.

I stare out at the stars and try to figure out where I am, or at the very least what the fuck I'm looking at.

It's useless, my references are all from the point of view of Earth, with the exception of some very short trips outside Amelia with Lucan. This sky means nothing to me.

My feet pace his quarters, restless, as I chew on my fingernail. Now what? I'm stuck in his freaking quarters, nothing to do, no one to talk to…

No one to watch me.

I could snoop.

No one to stop me.

The last time I was left alone where he was living—besides our time on the vacation habitat after Fledge, which doesn't count because it was a guest house or something, he had no personal things there—was in the cavern under Council 3. Before I ever left with him to morph into my old avian body.

That time I found nothing except that stupid reader of Iliana's that had the Seven Siblings myth on it. It was like a fake base or something, just nothing but bullshit maps, medical supplies, food. Stuff like that, but nothing that held any secrets.

But this is his bedroom.

I start pulling out drawers and shuffling through folded clothes. Boxers, t-shirts, a few stashed weapons, various small pieces of jewelry. I shove that drawer closed and open a door that becomes a closet. Uniforms—some service, some not. Boots on the floor, neatly lined up.

He's very neat.

I kick the boots aside and check the floor. Nothing. Just boots.

The nightstand is next. That's a good place—people like to stash things in the nightstand.

I find a Bible of all things.

It's old, the pages are tissue thin and contain elaborate scrolled writing that might actually be real gold leaf. There are iconic images on some, also illuminated, like something they made in Europe in the Middle Ages.

Except this Bible is not Christian, it's avian.

I flip to the beginning and find the title page. It shows a golden angel—wings fully outstretched and covering up the entire two-page spread. He's got blond hair and blue eyes, but that's where the similarities to the familiar Lucan end.

He's got fangs. And knives, not the razor claws the avians have, but honest to God *knives*, bursting out of his hands and talons.

There's even a glint of light to exaggerate the fact. And his face is not some gentle, Junco-you're-making-me-tired-please-do-as-I-ask scowl.

It's rage.

Mouth open, blood dripping down.

And there are dead bodies strewn about under his feet.

I close it and throw it back in the drawer. I am totally sorry for snooping. Who the fuck has a Bible like that?

Oh, God. What if that guy is their Savior?

I'm a piece of stained glass high up in the window. I look down at my body and see that I'm naked, but that's not the disturbing thing. Instead of feet I have long raptor talons that host a variety of knives instead of claws. From my mouth come the whispers of the starlings and the gurgling in my throat causes me to scream and break free of the glass.

I gulp some air and pace, getting very nervous again. The trembling starts and I count my own heartbeats.

Tier appears in front of me and his hands are on my shoulders. I swat them off and push past him. "Take me back! Please, just take me back to Gideon. I don't want to be here." He simply stares as I point to the drawer that contains the demon Bible. "Is that who you guys worship? Some vampire thing with metal claws?"

Tier's laugh startles me and I step back so fast I trip over the edge of the bed and fall backwards. His dark imposing figure hovers over me, wings lifted and extended slightly, as his eyes glow green with—*something.* He grabs my arms and slides me towards the center of the bed, then crawls up, his knees on either side of my legs, until he's poised above me.

"Worship him? Darlin', he is High Order—he is coming to kill us. We don't worship him. We flee from him. We take flight like starlings. And if you're quite done stomping around like a baby, I'm going to enlighten you about exactly who I am and what we're doing here and then maybe—unlikely, but maybe—you'll stop your incessant whining and pouting and screaming and think of someone other than yerself for once."

He stops, maybe to see if I'll object to his insults, but I don't. Not because I agree with him, but because I just can't think of anything to say. He's wiped my mind of everything but his body, which at this very moment is lowering down on top of me. His uniform shirt rides up a little and I catch a glimpse of skin. It takes every molecule of willpower to pull my gaze back up to his eyes.

"Because this is not a fucking game I'm playing." His weight settles across my stomach, his face coming closer and closer until he's a breath away. His words come out as a whisper. "We're done playing, Junco." His hands are on either side of my head now, leaning on the bed, forming little impressions in the mattress so that the palms are brushing alongside my cheeks. I try to watch his eyes but all that registers is how with each passing fraction he is closing the distance between us. "We're gonna set it straight, right now." His mouth dips down and caresses mine.

My eyes close as I respond, but he pulls back almost immediately.

I lie there. Waiting to see what he'll do next, not even caring that he just blamed that whole fight on me, because this man is heating me up in a way that makes me powerless to resist.

"And then yer gonna tell me exactly who you are, my Junco. Because one thing is painfully obvious. Yer no Commander's daughter from the RR. Yer no spawn of Inanna. Yer no long lost Seventh Sibling. You are all those things and more and I'm gonna get the truth out of ya, whether you want to tell it or not. And when I'm done relieving you of that burden, I'm gonna take you in a way that will obliterate any longing you ever had for John Hando, or Aren, or Kush, or Mikah fucking Mesner, *forever.*" He stops to kiss me again, teasing my lower lip with a small bite as his hand wraps around my neck and slides up into my hair, tugging on it as I moan.

Holy shit. How did I get here?

His mouth pulls back and I try to follow it with my own, but the distance is too great. He has me trapped beneath him, and his fingers reach down and grab one wrist and he pulls it above my head.

I do not move.

He shifts over top of me and then his other hand finds my other wrist and brings it up as well. And then he's got both of them clasped in his hand.

"And then yer gonna tell me what that fuck Gideon is up to, my Junco."

He pulls back to watch my expression, but all I can do is stare into his eyes, mesmerized.

"Do you understand me, little bird?"

My head is nodding out a yes before I even have a second to think about it and then his kiss finds that little dent in the center of my throat. I tilt my head, exposing myself to him as my eyes roll back with the pleasure.

Tier leans over on his side as his right hand slips inside my hoodie. His fingertips trace up my ribcage, the lightest touch I've ever experienced in my life. He drags them up, crosses the lowest rib, stops for a moment to watch me, and then continues his path until he's tracing circles on the fleshy inner part of my upper arm. I gasp just before his kiss returns to my lips and he pulls back. "Still ticklish, I see."

I can only moan out the affirmative, because he's kissing my belly now. Little flutters of euphoria burst through as the sensation travels up my torso. His hands are all over, cupping and kneading my breast, sliding down my pants, and then, before I can even process that, he's wrapped them behind my neck once more, his fingertips clasping my hair.

"Where do you come from, Junco?" he breathes. I look into his eyes and hold his gaze as his hand slips under the waistband of my jeans.

"Council 3. I'm not hiding that—" I gasp as his fingers slide between my legs. "This is not fair, you're trying to seduce me into telling you things!"

His mouth teases my lips again as I momentarily forget what I was complaining about.

"Trying to? Darlin', this has gone beyond trying." He uses both hands to push my hoodie up, his thumbs dragging across my skin and sending shivers of delight up my spine as I whimper. He pulls me up off the bed for a fraction, slips the hoodie over my head, and then lowers me back down.

And stares at me.

"What?" I breathe.

His answer never materializes because his mouth is all over my body.

I close my eyes and grab his hair as best I can, it's much shorter than it used to be, and pull his face towards my chest. He accepts with a low rumble from his throat and *oh shit* is coming out of my mouth.

He stops.

"Do not swear in front of me, Junco."

I open my eyes to find his face hovering over mine, the green bright with annoyance. "I said shit, not fuck."

"That's not funny."

My grin creeps out. I thought it was.

He moves to the side and falls back on the bed next to me.

Now I've done it. "Sorry, OK? I was kidding."

He pulls me towards him, wraps his arm around me, and I rest my cheek on his chest. "I need to know what you know, Junco. Where did ya come from?"

"So that's it?" I ask. "Heat me all up with the promise of sex, then stop and make me talk? That's your plan?"

He eyes me cautiously. "It worked, didn't it?"

"Pffft. I've still got pants on, Mr. Death. So I'd have to go with no, not quite."

He turns away, trying to stifle his laugh, but his hands disengage from my body and he clasps them together behind his head, like he hasn't got a care in the world.

"So, we're done here? Or what?"

"I'm waiting for an answer to my question, Junco. Where do ya come from?"

I'm not quite sure what he's after. "Tier, I admit, I have lots of secrets, some are so fu—" I stop and reconsider the curse. "I mean, some are so horrible I've tucked them down in some very dark places. But this is not one of them. I come from Council 3. I grew up in a sentient HOUSE, I spent my summer and winter breaks at Stag camp for training. I went to Council 1 Cadets for upper school, and I completed advanced sniper training with the RR military. This is what I know to be true. So if you've got more information, I'd like to hear it."

"No, all of that is true. But you've left out one part. Where did ya come from? Who made you, Junco?"

I throw up my hands. "You guys said Gyr made me!"

"No, we said you came from Gyr's genetics. But that cannot be true, because Gyr was not High Order."

"What's that mean?" My brows scrunch up as I think about what he just said.

He watches me for a few moments. "Gideon knows who made you, Junco. He's been throwing it in my face for two years. So you mean ta tell me he never told ya where you come from?"

The sigh comes out as exhaustion. "If Gid knows something, he hasn't told me. We've got secrets from each other, too. We basically stopped hanging out together back when I was ten. I never even knew he had *lovers* until a few hours ago, and you think he's sharing this secret information with me? No! He's not!"

"Ya said the two of ya did a job in Prague, back in the Runout tunnels. When ya remembered about those fake nightdogs. So, yer telling me ya did that job when you were ten?"

"No, I mean, of course I saw him as a teen. We did jobs here and there, but he was gone most of the time. It's not like when we were kids, back before they changed him."

"Changed him? How?"

"What do ya mean, how? He's an Archer, right? He's got those scars on his back. Lucan knows this." But apparently Tier did not. "You didn't know?"

"I suspected, of course. So they turned him avian, when you were ten?"

"Avian? No, he was never an avian. At least that's the impression I got. Back when I first saw him, in Subjack's camp before we went up to Runout, he was touching my wings and—"

"Touching yer wings?"

"Yeah, he had to help me put that stupid dress on." Tier's growl tells me he's annoyed at this revelation so I move on quickly. "Anyway he was making me gasp with those little touches and then he asked me if it hurt. To touch them. And I told him no. It's sexual."

I look over to Tier. His eyes are glowing so bright he's casting shadows.

"And," I continue in a rush, "that totally took him by surprise. He was embarrassed, apologized even, and said he had no experience with wings." I shrug. "That's all I know. He was never an avian, but he was gone for years and when he did come back, he was…"

"What?" Tier prods.

"Not the same. He was not the same."

"How? In what way, Junco."

I think about this for a few moments. When he came to my house that first year of cadets he acted like we were never apart. Like him going away for almost three years was nothing. Just a blip of time among billions of blips. He offered me no explanation. At all.

"He barely talked, he didn't want to go shooting with me or spar. He didn't even want to tell me the stories anymore. And these were all things we did regularly, before, ya know? I mean I get it about the stories, those were just coping mechanisms when I was little. Parables to help me understand that my life was about training and death and killing. And when he came back I was already almost fourteen by then and I was mature—had grown to accept what my life was without the stories. So I can see that one. But all the other things I did *more* as I got older. We had schedules, right? And when he left that summer I turned ten, his camp schedule became my schedule. Every Monday I'd shoot. Every Tuesday I'd range. Every Wednesday I'd—"

"Range?" he asks, cutting me off. "What's range?"

What is range? I'm lost in time as the memory begins to play in my head. "I got in trouble that year. They sent me home from camp after Gid left. Actually, my dad came to get me because I ran away."

I look over at Tier to see his reaction. He smiles and brushes some hair from my eyes.

"And then I—I had a hard time holding myself together, so that's the second time they erased me."

His arms come down from his head and he wraps me up, pulling me to his chest. "I'm sorry, Juncs."

"No, it's OK. It was OK that time because I *was* crazy. Here's what you don't understand, Tier. Gideon is my sanity. He holds me together. And when they took him away I just… I just lost it. I went out ranging alone. I was so angry about everything. They could track me of course." I motion to the spot on my shoulder where Tier removed that tracker from me when we first met. "But it was underground, and I was…" I stop and smile up at him. "I was sneaky."

His squeeze says he agrees.

"Anyway, they found me eventually and my dad came and got me and took me home that summer. But I still had to train. And that was the year I started ranging alone for real." My heart-rate jacks up just thinking about it. "Just because I wanted to and just because I could." My shoulders shrug because how can I explain that?

I can't. It's disgusting.

"What is ranging, Junco?"

"Hunting." I look up at him and study his beautiful face. How can the Angel of Death look like this man? "But not regular hunting."

"What kind of hunting? Tell me."

I look up at him and shake my head. "No."

"Junco," he sighs. "For once, can you just do as I ask?"

I turn my back to him and stare out into space. The tiny pinpricks of light are teasing me in a dangerous way. "It's not that I don't want to tell you things, Tier. And it's not that I told Ashur or whoever personal things about me on purpose. They slip out sometimes by mistake." I turn back and watch his eyes as I talk. "I don't want you to know that stuff about me. It's all bad stuff. You don't want to know what I did as a kid, and even though you think you do…you don't."

"Was it hunting people, Junco?"

My body turns away but he stops me this time.

"Was it?"

My head nods. "Sort of. They were not human according to us, but who were we to judge?" We lie there silent for a few moments, I know he's picturing me doing these horrific things and that hurts more than anything else right now. "I remember everything, ya know. All of it."

He watches my face carefully, patiently.

"And I'm just a very bad person." I don't say it for sympathy and I don't say it so he can tell me I'm not. I say it because it's true.

His lips caress my cheeks for a few moments, but he stays far away from that topic. "Where does Gideon fit in? How was he different? What was he doing?"

The change of subject is such a relief I don't even mind talking about Gideon. "When he came back from being morphed, that was my first year of cadets. It was spring I remember, he came to my house for Easter break. I had him to myself for two weeks and I thought we'd just slip back into our routines, right? I mean, that schedule was my life outside cadets. It's just what I did. But Monday came and there was no shooting. Tuesday, no ranging. Wednesday, no grappling. He just sat in the guest room most of the time. Alone."

I swallow as I look up at Tier. "He came back broken. And it shocked me. Gideon is the only reason I'm alive right now. Even more so than my dad, because my dad wasn't there most of the time. They made him drop me off with Matthew. Matthew ran the Stag, my dad ran the rest of the country. But Gideon, he ran me."

"He was yer handler." It's a statement, not a question.

"Yes," I say, looking up at him. "He *is* my handler."

"You were his weapon."

I nod. "Yes, I *am* his weapon."

We wait, our eyes searching each other. He seems satisfied with this.

"And that's all you know about yer origins? His origins?"

"I know nothing about Gideon's origins beyond Clutch 139." I swallow down the dread. "Do you?"

He shrugs and offers up nothing.

"If something happens to Gideon, Tier—if something happens to him, I will die. I will not go on, do you understand me? I will not go on. I cannot lose him and just thinking about it right now makes me want to shrivel away into nothingness. He keeps me sane, he holds all my broken pieces together. I would rather die than live without Gideon. And it's not what you think either. I don't want him." I feel him tense under me. "Not like I want you."

"Or Lucan."

"Oh, please! I'm not in love with Lucan. I love him, yes. I love him like I love Rikan or Selia or Moju and Esta. But I'm certainly not in love with him. I'd do a lot for him, if he asked. But when I said I chose him, that's not what I meant. I simply meant I'm on his side, that's it. I choose you, Tier. Are you hearing me? I choose you. I only want you in that way."

I wait to see if he's got anything to add, but he stays silent, staring up at the ceiling. This is my chance to set things right and start over, so I take it. "And I'm sorry about sleeping with Kush, too. Because it hurt a lot of people, and especially you. But I thought I was gonna die the next day, so why not, right? Why not just feel good for once? Why not just let that guy love me for a few hours? Is that so wrong? And yeah, it killed me what happened to him because it was all my fault. All of this, everything we're doing, it's all my fault."

The silence hangs between us for a few moments and my heart is pounding, wondering if this admission of guilt just pissed him off more. I'm just about to start babbling again when he finally speaks up.

"I know Kush was just a convenience, Junco, but I was angry that you were with Gideon and Lucan, and neither of those assholes even thought to tell me you were back. I saw it on the goddamn newscreen back on Amelia. Kadian reported it, Junco. That's how I found out you were finally safe."

"Tier." I touch his face, turning it gently towards me as I speak. "I had no idea. They cocooned me in that apartment, I had no idea. I asked for you over and over and they just kept telling me soon."

He nods and then continues. "And I understand about Gideon too, and that's why I told ya back on Sargassum that I'd never let anything happen to him. I know he means a lot to ya. But you have something with him that we don't have. It's not jealousy, it's just—"

He stops talking and the seconds drag on. "Fear," I finish for him.

"Yeah," he admits. "Fear. This is not the life I want, Junco. I don't want to be remembered for what I'm doing, get it? I don't want to be remembered as the Angel of Death. That's not what I am. I'm not bringing death, I'm simply making arrangements that were planned thousands of years ago. I'm just doing my job and there's no good way out of this mess. And it doesn't even matter if Lucan's responsible—"

He searches my face to see if I understand what he's saying.

I do.

"It doesn't matter anymore what he did. This is now and we're all in this together, right? I'm just trying to make sure some of us will make it to our end. We won't all make it, Juncs." He shakes his head and sighs. "Even if I refuse to complete the job I was raised for, it won't save the humans I must destroy to get what I need, they will all still die. Do you understand?"

"I do, Tier. The time for a fate shift is over, this is destiny."

"Yeah." It comes out so sad I feel the tingle in my nose as the tears well up in my eyes. "I could do nothing, and just hope—"

He stops again and I wait it out.

"Hope for the best. That you choose us and the High Order accepts that decision." A small laugh escapes, but it's not a happy laugh. "And the sick thing is, I'd be so OK with that. They could smash Earth out into the nether and I'd be OK with that if I just had you and some little backwater habitat where we could live out our end together. But they won't accept that, Junco. It's far too late for that now."

I swallow. No, that's too easy. Like me giving my Deliverance wish to Tier and hoping that he could save himself.

It just doesn't work that way. To get something there must always be sacrifice.

Like my Isten.

"They are evil." He reaches over the top of my bare chest to the nightstand drawer and pulls out the avian Bible, opening it to the image of the Devil. "They will want so much more than just violence and that's why I must be so much more than just Tier."

I force myself to look at the monster, the blood dripping from his mouth, the dead bodies below his talons. This is a struggle I can relate to. Being forced to be something you're not just because the job has got to be done. And they, those looking at us from outside, they don't understand how rising to your full potential can really fucking screw with your head sometimes.

"I've been watching ya, Junco—the crazy Inanna forced on ya and the weight of what you must do—and this is not what I wanted for us. This feels like losing. I can feel ya slipping away, our possibilities, our worthwhile end—it's just slipping away. I want it to be over so bad, ya have no idea. And believe me, darlin', your part in all this, the things you'll be responsible for in the end? They're nothing. Nothing compared to the death and destruction I will unleash."

I just fall against his chest and hold him tight, that's how much I love him in this moment.

"Yer not the cause of this, Junco. Yer the answer. I'm the cause, I'm the one raising Djed Pillars, causing tsunamis that wipe out millions of people. And there's so much more to come."

"Then don't do it, Tier. Just don't do it."

"We need those Pillars to complete the Halo, Junco." I follow his pointing finger to the rotating Earth on the holotable. The Halo is the circle that connects all the Pillars together.

"We must have them or else we have no chance against the High Order. None. One of us, either humans or avians, will absolutely be annihilated. And that's the best-case scenario because in my mind, I see nothing but destruction in the end. Total destruction." I feel his soul rattling around in his chest with his words. "So you'll have a choice, darlin'.

And your choice may or may not placate them, depending on which way ya lean."

"Which one might placate them?" I already know, but it's better to hear it and be certain than let that go unsaid.

"Earth. You must choose Earth."

"Or what? What if I choose Lucan and you guys?"

He shrugs. "We fight."

I think about this for a minute, trying it on for size, getting used to it a little. Fighting is something I can do, fighting is something I can do well, in fact. Killing has always been my one true superpower. Besides, Gideon wants to fight them too. "That's what we do, right? We fight. So, what's the big deal?"

He lets out a small breath that makes its way into a laugh, then pushes me aside and leans down over me. "God, I fucking love you. You say all the right things, Junco."

My face scrunches up. "Has anyone ever mentioned that your language is filthy, Tier?"

He turns away to hide his grin. "But yer learning, aren't ya?"

"Yeah, I get it. I guess. You hate the swearing."

"When this is all over so are your soldiering days, Junco. I only want ya to be ready, darlin'. That's all. I only want ya to be ready to let this life go."

I'm so ready.

He disentangles my arms that have been wrapped around his neck and stands up, his eyes passing over my naked upper body.

He's staring, actually.

"What? I look strange, huh?"

He unseals the seams on his shirt and whips it over his head, then crawls up on either side of my body and he kisses his way up my chest until his mouth is barely touching my lips. His flight feathers slide across my ribs and just about tickle me into ecstasy.

"Junco," he breathes, "you'd be perfect to me no matter what ya looked like."

I cross the fractional distance and kiss him for that lie, my hands sliding up from his waist, then over to his wing where I caress the sensitive bone that hovers just above his shoulder with my fingertips.

He buries his face into my neck and then the whispers begin to float across my cheek and up into my ear. "But darlin', just so ya know, ya look like the Goddess to me right now. Yer my Goddess, Junco."

He pulls away from me to stand and then unbuckles his belt.

I'm transfixed, silent and unable to take my eyes off him as I watch his fingers. He stops to grin and just when I'm about to ask him what's up, he knocks the unlaced boots off my feet, grabs the bottom of my jeans, and yanks them off.

I lie there, completely exposed, and watch as Tier takes me in with his hungry gaze, his own clothes temporarily forgotten. When he remains still I stand up on the bed and wrap my arms around his neck and kiss him. He pushes against me and I let it all go. All the anger and hurt. I let all the bad things go and just enjoy it.

He removes my arms from around his neck and places them gently at my side, then brings his hands up to my face and pulls me towards him as he presses his forehead to mine. I look down on him a little, since I'm standing on the bed, and his fingertips fall along each side of my neck, down my throat, over each shoulder, round out over my breasts and then trace a line down my rib cage.

A shiver escapes my body as a small sound of pleasure.

His touch stops abruptly and when I look down at him again he's just staring at me. "What?" I ask in a whisper.

"Yer perfect," he says.

"I'm sorry."

"What for, Junco?"

"For tricking you into believing that."

His eyes glisten a little as they glow and the hurt starts to come back. "I'm sorry, too."

"What for, Tier?"

"For not saying those words to you often enough to make you believe them."

I swallow and start to look away but he's got my face in his hands again. "You are the most perfect thing I've ever laid eyes on."

My head shakes out a no.

"You are the exhale after the kiss, Junco."

My whole body tingles with those words.

"That's where all the best parts are," he continues. "Afterward. All the best parts come after."

"I hope so, Tier. Because I've been waiting for the good parts so long, I forgot what they were and why I want them."

He cracks a grin and his fingertips are touching me again. He drags one finger down the front of me, right between my breasts, down to my stomach where he stops. I miss his warm touch as he pulls his fingertips away and begins to unbutton his pants.

My breasts glide up against his chest as I push against him and we both moan a little. His rough hands come up to cup my face and his mouth presses hungrily into me as my fingers dispense with his lower body armor.

When he's bare I fall back into his arms and let him lower me onto the bed, the weight of him making me close my eyes with desire. "I love you, Tier."

He enters me and I buckle under him, making him growl with desire as my head tips back and my mind has no hope of focusing on anything but his touch. He finds his way inside me with his words as well. "Yer mine, Junco," he whispers, weaving himself into my soul. "Yer mine."

Chapter Twenty-Six

The incessant, breathless fast-talking of panicked people pulls me up from my slumber. I half remember Tier's kiss and soft words across my cheek as he left to go back to Earth, so this noise does not make immediate sense.

"Junco?"

That's definitely not Tier.

"Junco?"

The sleep slips away and I'm so fucking irritated. "What the fuck it is now, Sera?"

"You should watch the screen, Junco. It's something you should see. Quick!"

Her urging gets my attention and I sit up, the sheets falling down before I realize I'm still naked. The breathless talking has turned into screams and my eyes track to the screen in front of the bed.

Masses of people are shrieking now, the breathless voice just one among what looks to be thousands of Asians, running for their lives. I think I had a comic book that looked like this as a kid.

The shaky video feed is running as well, but the cam must be an iris lens because every few steps the reporter turns to look back and the feed follows. I lean in, trying to see the monster.

And catch a glimpse of two sets of black wings far down the street.

It's Tier and Ashur.

And they are dragging Soli behind them, towards the ocean. The reporter voice announces this new turn of events and he stops when he realizes they aren't coming after the people, unexpectedly changing direction. He's running even harder now, this time trying not to lose the avians.

Ash and Tier drag Soli around a corner and their figures disappear for a few seconds until the reporter finds them on the beach.

"Where is this?"

"Indonesia," is all Sera comes back with.

Soli is definitely not on board with what they are doing, it's painfully clear she's hysterical even from a distance. The reporter comes on again, trying to describe the scene as he sees it.

"—is struggling against the one they call the Angel of Death and the other one, the one who could be his twin but from what I've seen is following orders. Who this female avian is not clear, but I've heard others say she is one of the Siblings who were taken off Earth two years ago." He catches up to them on the beach just as Soli goes berserk, flailing around with her razors, screaming and calling for Moju.

"But—" I look over to Sera. "Moju was on board?"

"He was," she confirms. "But clearly Soli is not." She takes a seat at Tier's little table. "She's excitable, that one. Always overreacting."

"So—we're good with this?"

Soli's screams burst out of her in a last-ditch attempt to resist the warriors who will not tolerate resistance. Tier smacks her across the face and then he and Ashur push each other for a few seconds. Ashur doesn't look like he approves, which is funny, considering he's the only one on the team who ever tried to physically kick my ass.

"We are. It must be done. Soli agreed as well, she can't just change her mind in the middle of the plan. I'd smack her too."

The reporter's voice is back, he's turned his sight towards a distant light that is coming up from the ocean. "There's the second beacon," he explains.

Soli's razors catch Ashur across the face and he flips out on her, throws her down on the ground and pushes his face into her neck. She stops resisting and I can only imagine what he just said to her.

Tier spies the reporter for the first time and flips him off.

I laugh. Fucking Tier.

Ashur has Soli upright again and they're both leaning down into her now. I don't need to hear them to know what they're saying. *Stop being insane, Soli. You're acting like Junco.*

"We need to go, Junco."

I turn to Sera. "Go where?"

"Leave, I need you to come with me right now. Before they finish the Pillar. We can catch the next one, OK?"

Back on screen Ashur and Tier push the reporter and he stumbles in the wet sand as the entire world watches them drag my sister up in the air and fly out towards the beacon of light protruding from the ocean floor.

"Sera, I'm not—"

"He knew that Isten would die, you know."

Oh, God. My heart.

I shake my head. "He didn't, he can't see me, he said he can't—"

"Right." Sera cuts me off with a laugh. "And Lucan didn't know you would kill yourself at Deliverance, you believe that as well? The most powerful being in the entire Solar System was outwitted by some newborn avian?

That's what you believe?" She stares at me as I stand there, still naked from my afternoon tryst with Tier. "They've known, Junco. Lucan knew you'd save Tier and he let you. He knew your plan."

She stops to let this sink in.

Rikan knew so it only makes sense that Lucan knew that part too. And really, it's not the fact that he might have known and he let me do it anyway that bothers me, it's the fact that he lied to me about knowing. They always lie to me.

"He needs Tier far more than he ever needed you, Junco. Getting you *and* Tier, that was just a bonus."

"He said he loved me." The confusion comes out in a profoundly sad admission of ignorance.

She shrugs. "He has only ever loved one person, Junco. And that's Tier." She looks at me with her serious eyes. "And he only loves Tier for what he can do for him. I told you back in the virtual cabin, Junco. He's not a good guy. I've known him since he was reborn, we're complements. Just as you and HOUSE are complements. We were partners with Inanna once, like you are partners with Gideon. The three of us were powerful once. But he betrayed us. I know him, Junco, and he is *not* good."

I swallow and look away, trying to find my clothes. There's a bag in the table with my name on it and I open it up and peek inside. An avian uniform. I take it out and notice the shirt has been re-tailored to accommodate my wingless back. I pull out the pants and the boots, all refitted for my new body. And then there is one more outfit in there. My camo pants and sniper t-shirt from when I first left Earth with Tier years ago.

I try to pull the camo pants on and Sera laughs as they get stuck at my knees.

"You've gained weight, those will never fit now."

I fling them off and start pulling on the new avian uniform pants. The soft black cloth brings back memories of Fledge. Of the killing and the agony of the unknown.

Sera picks up the discarded camo pants and hold them up. "When did your father buy you these, Junco?"

I'm pulling the sniper t-shirt over my head as the words come out between my lips. "Seventh year, I think. Why?"

"And you fit into them when you left Earth? When you were nineteen?"

"You know I did," I say with a snarl. What's she getting at?

"You still don't see it, do you?"

"See what, Sera? Just fucking spit it out." I grab my old RR field boots instead of the new avian ones and tug them on. At least my feet haven't gotten bigger.

"You weighed what? When Tier brought you with him? Ninety pounds?"

I scratch my head. "Ninety? No, I've always been one-twenty."

She's shaking her head at me.

"So what if I was, anyway. I'm small, so what's your point?"

I continue to lace up my boots.

"You were sick back then. Very sick."

"Right. That's why I kicked everyone's ass in Fledge and Deliverance."

"Inanna made you healthy again."

I whip out my SEAR and swipe it through her ethereal body before the words are even out. "Fuck you! I was *there*, Sera. I know exactly what she did to me and I will never forget that pain."

"You will dock that weapon and not take it out again until you are ready to play out your part. Because if you do,

Junco, you will be responsible for the deaths of billions of people. Do you understand me?"

"Why?" I demand. "What the fuck is the big deal with the stupid SEAR knife? Lucan was freaked out about it, Inanna took it away, and now you."

She stares at me, her eyes briefly glowing. That's new. It reminds me a little too much of the Fallen Archer in the Fledge church. My breath is heavy as I stare at her.

"I understand your anger and hatred for Inanna. And I understand how you feel, but this body you have now…"

I look down at myself.

"This body is the picture of health. That scarred-up shell of a half-human you were before? That was not even close. And you were never, let me make this perfectly clear, never meant to be an avian. That was a mistake Tier made out of pure selfishness."

I stare blankly past her. Like Gideon. Who never went through the avian morph. "Then why? Did Tier know? That I wasn't supposed to be an avian? Is he in on all this?"

She shrugs. "Parts, yes. He knew he was supposed to kill you, but he doesn't know your Destiny."

"Which is what? Exactly?"

She waves a hand at me. "Later, Junco. We need to leave here right now. Ashur and Tier will be back in a moment and that will jeopardize our chances for success."

I snort at her. "How the hell are we gonna get off the ship?"

She smiles. "Teleport, Junco. How else?"

"You can do that?"

"No," she replies. "But you can."

Chapter Twenty-Seven

This teleporting business is news to me so I just sit back down and finish lacing up my boots.

"I've been told you can hold your breath for long stretches of time?"

She says it like it's a question, but we both know it's not a question. "Gideon told you that?"

She nods.

"Well." I shrug. "I suppose if I have to I can do a lot of things. But I'm not real excited about holding my breath in space, if that's what you're getting at. Besides, I have no suit, so the pressure will kill me anyway."

"You won't need a suit and I can tell you how to do it. It's not hard, I was with Lucan when he learned and he was several levels below you when he completed his first trip."

My mouth hangs open. "You can *tell* me how to do it? Are you fucking insane? Never mind, I'm gonna wait here for Tier and have him take me—"

"He won't take you back, Junco. Whether you believe it or not, you're currently a prisoner."

I roll that word around in my head for a few fractions.

She's right.

I am a prisoner.

But that doesn't mean I'm gonna let her take me out into space with no suit.

"I'll take my chances."

She storms up to me now, angry. Her normally green eyes blaze red, just like Lucan's do when he's in that demon form. "You will not take your chances. You'll teleport right now or I will throw you out into the dark emptiness and watch you writhe in pain until someone comes to save you, do you understand me?"

"That," I snarl at her, "will kill me. So go right ahead."

She relaxes and the corners of her mouth turn up slightly. "You will not die, Junco. But you will feel pain."

She points to the screen where the djed is beginning to self-assemble, growing like some mutated beanstalk from out of the ocean depths. "Tier is done now, he will be here soon, he commands the timespace pretty well these days. On three you will go into your mind and fling yourself to Earth, never mind where, just in that general direction. Don't fight my guidance, I'll get you to where you need to be. When we are on the ground we'll take the next step."

I just stare at her as I log the screaming coming from the screen in the background. The tsunami warnings are blaring and I can't help myself, I turn to watch. The split screen shows the growing Pillar on one side and the advancing wall of water on the other. The reporter is crying like a girl as he runs, trips, and then gets trampled by others even more panicked. His head bobs up, like he's gasping for air, then gets smashed down onto the concrete as feet connect with his skull. I watch, along with billions of others, as the blood seeps into his iriscam and blocks the view.

"One."

The feed switches—apparently reporters are expendable these days—and this one has a clear shot of Gideon and Tier fighting on the top of a building. They are a flurry of teeth and claws, blood is everywhere.

"Two."

Fling myself to Earth? That's her fucking idea? Tier becomes distracted, looking at the reporter, and Gideon takes advantage and pounds him in the head. Tier refocuses and the bloodshed continues.

Gideon is in my head urging me. *Go, Junco. Go!*

I'm gonna regret this. But he's in charge, so—

"Three."

My time slips and suddenly everything is in battle slow-mo. I do just what she said. I fling myself out of the ship, have a slight panic attack because I'm not facing Earth when I feel my body move, and then Sera's voice is in my head.

Do not draw breath. I will guide you.

We're not in space. We're somewhere else. Somewhere blurry, like a tunnel. I concentrate on not blowing out my last breath of air and close my eyes as the blur makes the acid in my stomach go into overdrive. It immediately makes me want to puke, but if hurling in your helmet is a bad idea, then this would definitely be worse.

My body is so cold I feel the crystals form and then spread across my skin, making a sound that pulls me back to the cracking of ice when I used to break the rules and walk across our mountain lake in the winters back in Council 3.

This memory hurts so bad I forget to hold my breath and it bursts out. I open my eyes in a panic and watch the air as it crystallizes in real time. The cold overtakes the warmth my body has been supplying the liquid that bathes the outer layer of my eyes and the ice-cracking noise is in my head now, blinding me. My lungs burn and every reflex screams to rid myself of the carbon dioxide that is building, second after second, as we advance through the tunnel.

Shut down the core, Junco.

I'm not sure if that command was from Gid or Sera, but it doesn't matter. I obey and slow my heart, making the blood coursing through my body slow as well. I pull every remaining molecule of glycogen from my leg muscles, ask for the calories the extra bit of fat on my body contains, and have a fraction to enjoy my exceptional self-control before I am slammed into the ground face first.

Chapter Twenty-Eight

The rapid wind and crackle of plasma fire erupts around me as I struggle to come to terms with what just happened. Sera is in my head, not next to me anymore, and her screams are so uncharacteristic I almost place them as foreign.

Port again, Junco! Port again!

"What the fuck does that mean? Port again?"

Teleport, you stupid child!

I don't think another teleportation is possible in this lifetime, let alone seconds after being slammed to the scrub that is scratching my face as I think.

But then the plasma fire grazes past my waist, taking out some skin and maybe even some muscle underneath for good measure as it burns a hole straight through my shirt and catches it on fire. I swat frantically, look around, and realize I need to do that port thing now or I'm gonna be gunned down by some nasty desert dwellers.

Go invisible, Junco!

"I can't," I croak out. "HOUSE has that power!"

Sera appears in front of me now, pulling me to my feet. "God, you are more trouble than you're worth. Do you really think—"

Another bolt of plasma flies past us, the arc reaching out to grab my arm, and I start shaking uncontrollably.

Sera drops me back to the scrub and turns.

I have just enough time to see the red fire she is emitting from her eyes before her rage turns into a crackle of electrons.

Electricity is pulled from a nearby power line and she wields it with the authority of Tesla himself. I duck my head, partly from the pain of the plasma burn and partly to avoid the dancing electricity.

Everyone else follows suit and the firing stops.

Teleport now, Junco!

I fling myself again and this time the tunnel is short and the landing quick. I crash into the side of a boulder next to a giant red rock, my shoulder flaming with pain as I look around to see how far I got.

Not far.

I laugh a little. Not far at all. About a hundred yards. Sera is gone now and the small troop of attackers are running around in a panic. I wait for them to see me but they are aiming at something else now. A cloud of dust and dirt is heading straight towards me from the east and I squint my eyes to see what it is.

A vintage HumVee. Like the Goat.

The armed men, who I am unable to identify by uniform but who might be Desert Republic soldiers, are following the racing vehicle on gravs.

Frantic screaming comes from the vehicle and I try and dial up the vision to see what's up.

A girl, it looks like. Flailing her arms out of the driver's side window.

She's screaming my name.

I try to get up and wince as the blood leaks out of the wound in my side, then crack a smile as I realize who the crazy girl is.

Selia!

I stumble over a few large boulders and half limp, half run towards her. She gets about fifty feet away, turns the wheel and skids sideways in the sandy dirt, then grabs a high-powered rifle and climbs to the back of the vehicle and starts spraying bullets. I reach the vehicle and take her place at the wheel.

"Drive!" she screams.

The engine is idling so I throw it into first and the tires spin for a fraction before finding traction, and we lurch forward. I shift again, and again as we pick up some speed.

I look back at my friend.

"What the fuck is going on?"

"Go north, Junco! We gotta get out of the Utopia!"

Oh shit. The Utopia soldiers do not fuck around if you're in their country illegally. I shift again, press on the gas, and we bounce along the uneven desert scrub. I come straight up out of my seat when I take the dozens of prairie dog holes at more than a hundred and ten miles per hour. I groan as I land hard on the seat and Selia curses at me in the back, but I'm preoccupied for a fraction by the pain in my side. My right hand reaches down and comes back sticky and red with blood.

I take my attention back to the road as the whine of grav bikes catches up with us and Selia starts shooting again.

"Get over the border, Junco! We gotta make the border!"

I can see the border. It's not that far away actually and I'm pretty fucking sure we're gonna make it. But the problem is that there's lots of soldiers over on that side of things as well.

"Those guys friendlies, Sel?" I scream at her.

"No!" she comes back with. "You gotta port us somewhere far, you got it, Junco? Somewhere far!"

"What the fuck? I just learned how to do that like five minutes ago, ya know! I'm not a fucking exp—"

"On three!"

"On three, what?"

She stops shooting, throws the rifle out the back window and then climbs up into the front passenger seat. "Port us!" She's flush with adrenaline, her face red and her eyes racing. "Right now!"

"This does not sound like a plan," I say back to her. But I have no time to wonder because they are shooting at us from the front now too.

"One!"

Oh shit. Tier is gonna kill me. *So bad.*

"Two."

We are only about fifty yards away now and I push down on the gas as we gain some speed. Bullets fly by my head as plasma fire reaches out to grab the metal chassis and the entire truck is electrified as Selia screams—

"Three!"

I tap her shoulder like Lucan and Tier do to me and pray to God she'll come along for the ride as I fling us forward.

Chapter Twenty-Nine

We fling forward in silence and I have a fraction to experience relief that Selia is indeed next to me. I can feel the tunnel more than see it this time, and I instinctively know that when the light becomes brighter the fling will end, so I concentrate on going faster, keeping the tunnel open, elongating it.

I only get a few second into practicing this new skill when we abruptly exit and roll in a jumbled heap until we crash into something relentlessly hard.

Another boulder?

No.

The hard thrum of music is interfering with my thought process as my hearing comes back.

I recover before Selia. She's shaking uncontrollably next to me even though the sand we're lying on is still rather warm from the sun that is still disappearing behind a relatively small mountain range.

"Sel? You OK?"

I push on her shoulder as her teeth chatter together and she manages a stiff, "Yeah, just great. Where did we end up?"

I look around. The hard thing we crashed into is a large truck and the music comes with party laughter.

"I think we're at a party or something."

She props herself up, her teeth chattering beginning to fade. "Who the fuck would have a party in the middle of the desert?"

I have no idea. It's all beyond my realm of worldly experience. We landed between two parked trucks actually, and when I crawl on my hands and knees to peer out behind the one closest to us, I realize it's a makeshift parking lot of sorts. There are people stumbling along and I have a small moment of panic that they will see me, but it dissipates when I realize they are all pretty fucked-up drunk.

I slink back to Selia who is sitting up now. "We're definitely at a party. They've got lights and listen…" I point my ear up towards the sky to show that I'm listening. "A generator to power it all."

Selia leans over and pukes.

"Gross, Selia."

She spits and drags her hand across her mouth with a snarl. "You're one to talk, you puke all the time."

"Yeah, but that's different. Anyway, what do we do now?"

Selia considers this for a fraction and then shrugs. "We get a ride to Vegas. We're meeting Irin there. And maybe Lili, but she's such a bitch, Junco. I cannot even explain it. Everyone makes fun of Ashur for being a piker, but shit. That girl has a stick so far up her ass she's ready to scare crows."

"Huh." I shrug back at Sel. "She saved my life back in Runout, so I gotta like her. Sorry."

Selia stands, wobbles a little, then shrugs off her backpack and starts to untie the sparkly gold halter top she's sporting. Her bottom half is a micro mini made of leather.

My eyes follow her tanned legs down to her high heels. "Selia?"

She's fussing with the spaghetti ties that wrap around her waist now. "Huh?"

"Did you just go into a firefight dressed like a whore?"

"Shut up and gimme your shirt."

I"m shaking my head when she flips my arms up and yanks my sniper tee off my body.

"Shit, Selia, you really gotta stop undressing me like this."

She stuffs her shirt in my hands. "Now put that on and take off your pants."

In the end I'm the one who looks like a whore and Selia has on my sniper tee, although she's cut the sleeves off and made it shorter so her belly button shows, her black mini, and my combat boots.

I'm wearing that ridiculous gold halter and it barely covers the bandage Sel slapped over my side to stop the bleeding. I figure that wound is no big deal since I'm an Archer now, but it doesn't hurt to be prudent.

I also have on her high heels and she's cut my perfectly good avian light armor pants into shorts that practically go up my butt crack.

Selia grabs a brush out of her pack and starts tugging on my hair, then separates it out and begins to braid it up like how Lili wears hers. The plaits run down the side of my head and the end in two long tails that drop in front of my chest.

"My hair is so blonde," I say, picking up the tails that trail down my chest.

Selia grunts as she twists the ends together in a hair tie. "Yeah, and your eyes are pure blue now too. What's up with that?"

I shrug. Like I would know. I'm always the last to know anything around here.

She finishes and steps back to look me over.

"Well," she huffs, "it will have to do."

"Thanks a lot, Sel. Way to make a girl feel special."

"Oh stop, Junco. You're amazing. I was talking about your disguise, you dumbass."

Oh.

I take a few hesitant steps towards the dirt alley between the parked cars. "I can't walk in these heels, Selia. Trade me."

"No, Junco. People will associate these field boots with the military and we need them to see you as anything but military. Besides, they're not heels, they're wedges."

I shake my head at her. "The fuck are you talking about?"

She squeezes my lips together and paints on some bright red lipstick. I just roll my eyes. "I'd really like to know what your plan is, Sel, because if you think I'm gonna fuck strangers to get something, I'd rather just kill them."

She lets out a little laugh before she can lock it down. "Junco, we just need a freaking ride to Vegas. Just be pleasant and follow my lead, we won't need to do anything, but we have to look like we might. We just need a ride."

"If you say so, but if they touch me I will not be responsible for—"

"You will not," she emphasizes, "kill anyone tonight, Junco. If you do we'll blow everything. If we didn't need to be careful and avoid detection I'd just steal this fucking truck and we'd be on our way. But we need a ride that cannot be traced, understand?"

I wave her on.

Whatever.

Like she's the grand pooh-bah of tactical war games or something. I'm the queen of war games. Hell, I'm the Goddess of War Games.

She grabs my arm and pulls me along with her towards the throngs of people, clustered around a raging bonfire.

The September night is a little cool, even for the desert, and my serious lack of proper clothing makes me long to stand next to it.

People start staring almost immediately and this makes me nervous. What if they recognize me like Cora did?

If Selia feels my apprehension she doesn't let on. If Gideon was here he'd be calming me right now because I'm not that great in crowds, and crowds of young people that require talking are *really* not my thing.

My breathing starts to speed up and Selia stops.

"Knock it off, Junco. It's a goddamn party for fuck's sake. No one cares about you, they're here to drink and screw. Got it?"

I nod. I guess she's a lot more like Gideon that I thought.

She leads us into the crowd and the throbbing music that was just a minor annoyance back where by the truck is now pounding in my head.

We weave in and out of various small social groups, then stop briefly to grab some plastic cups of beer near the keg, before continuing our circulation.

I taste the beer and spit it out all over some girl. Nasty. The girl gives me a death look and I growl at her.

"Sorry," Selia says as she pushes me to move away quickly. "Junco, come on, work with me here. I cannot find us a ride and babysit you all at the same time." She stops us and turns around. "OK, I found some possibles. Don't look now, but the two guys over my left shoulder… fuck, Junco! I said don't look!"

"Those guys standing over by the fire?"

"Yeah, are they looking at us?"

I shrug and look behind me to assess the possibilities, but no one else is even close to us. "How should I—Oh, no, wait. Yup. They are. He's motioning for me to come over to him."

Selia fluffs up her hair and says, "Ready?"

I wave her on. "Do your thing, Sel. I'm gonna head to the fire and get warm, I'm freezing my ass off here."

Regardless of what anyone tells you, the desert at night is almost always chilly and I'm practically naked, so I can't get to that fire fast enough.

We walk in that direction and just as the tall guy who was motioning to me starts to talk I circumvent him and continue walking. I hear Selia explain my behavior. "She's mute, don't mind Abi. So what's your name?"

I laugh internally because Selia must've finally run out of lies to explain why I'm not allowed to talk to people. I make my way over to a little log and cop a seat. It's a little close to the fire so I turn my back to the flames and look up at the stars.

And sigh. My stars.

I have no urge to count at the moment and I take that as a very good sign. This has been one of the better days since I was brought out of the morph. It's a lot like life in the old days—constant action and excitement. I've sorta missed it. Hanging out on a tropical beach is fun for a day or two, but it's boring.

Soft footsteps behind me make me jump up into a ready position but it's just the tall guy I was avoiding before.

"Ah," he says. "Then you're not deaf as well?"

"I'm not a mute, either. She tends to lie a bit." I sit back down and continue my survey of the sky.

"Mind if I sit?"

I shrug. "Mountain Republic is still a free country, right? Sit if you want."

"Not interested in the party?"

"I'm cold, that's all."

He walks out in front of me a few paces and then takes a seat on a small rock across from my log. "Your friend back there told me your name, but I'm not interested in her lie. So, you wanna tell it to me? Or should I guess?"

I look him in the face. He's got sandy blond hair from what I can tell and the firelight dances across his face in a way that creates shadows over his eyes, preventing me from seeing their true color. He's wearing a white tee shirt and a pair of jeans with those sneakers that are so popular in the Utopias. He sorta reminds me of Gideon with his looks.

"Go ahead and guess."

He drags his hand through the loose dirt for a few seconds and then looks up at me through the hair that partially covers his eyes. "Junco."

I'm not surprised, not really. "So what do you want?"

He straightens up at my questions. "Who says I want something?"

"So you're just here to what? Check up on me? See how I'm doing? Give me a break. Just tell me what you want, OK?"

He stares at me and I meet his gaze. It's pretty intense, enough to make me want to pull my eyes away, but I force myself to hold steady. "Maybe I should introduce myself first? Would that work?"

"Hey, it's your party. You can do it—"

He grabs my shoulder and we are… somewhere else. It's not space, because there are no stars. It's not a ship because there are no walls. It's… it's just nothing. Nothingness.

I take a breath and swallow down the fear. "Typically a name will do."

He lets go and turns me to face him. "I am Caleb. Do you know who Caleb is, Junco?"

There are probably millions of Calebs in the world but I know exactly which one he's talking about. "A spy."

He exhales a rush of air in an obvious sigh of relief. "Yes. Well done. I had my doubts about your father's early training methods but I guess those were unfounded. Continue."

I stare at him as these words sink in. "My father? What the hell does he have to do with anything?"

"Later." And then he prods me on with a slight wave of his hand.

"A spy who went above and beyond his call of duty to report back accurate intelligence to the Hebrews when they wanted to invade Canaan."

The description of Caleb slides off my tongue with ease, a result of my rather extensive recall training as a child. RR Sunday School was an endless barrage of memorizing passages and descriptions of every important person and act in the Bible. I went for fourteen years and never missed a day if you don't count my periodic bouts with insanity, and considering that I have a near perfect photographic memory of anything written, this recitation is not difficult.

"Nice," he says as his eyes sparkle with pleasure. "Those marks on your back, do you know what they mean?"

I shake my head.

"Try."

"Archer scars, I guess."

"They are the mark of the Fallen, Junco. You have been claimed and marked by Inanna for Lucan. And this will not work for us. It's unfortunate the way it turned out, and I'm sure we're not the only ones who are disappointed, but it cannot be undone, I'm sorry."

I blink at him.

"I'm Caleb and all I want is the truth so I can report back accurate intelligence. So tell me, Junco—who do you answer to?"

I know this answer as well, it was part of my Sunday school training along with the freaking Bible bullshit, but I suddenly have to urge to go off script. "Gideon," I say with satisfaction. "I answer to Gideon."

He sighs and turns his back to me for a moment as I take a small bit of pleasure in his disappointment. "But you made your promise back in the Runout valley, Junco. Surely you remember that?"

Wait. "What?"

"Was Gideon saved or not?" He turns back and his eyes dart back and forth, searching mine for answers.

"You know he was."

"So, I don't understand your confusion. You begged for his life, said you'd do anything, remember?"

I will do anything, God.

Anything.

Just save my friend.

"Gideon's powers come from us, Junco. So his survival is our gift to you."

I close my eyes and admit defeat. I prayed for his life to be spared. I should've known there'd be strings. I should've known. "I remember."

Caleb smiles and seems pleased with my admission. "You must not enter the Pillar with anyone else. Especially Gideon, Junco. Do you understand?"

I totally should've stayed with Tier. Maybe I can port back? I look around at the darkness, the nothingness of where we are and have a lot of doubts about that. "Why? I mean, maybe I will agree to go inside the Pillar alone, but just tell me why."

"Because Gideon does not belong to you, Junco."

I snort out some air at this. "The fuck he doesn't! Gideon *is* mine! And if that's your reason, well, that's definitely not good enough for me." Things start to take on more form and make more sense and then we are back in front of the fire, I'm sitting on a log and Caleb is across from me sitting on a rock. A trick? He tricked me somehow.

"This is your only warning, Junco. Do not cross me."

"I don't even know who you are."

"Look at me, Junco."

I lift my eyes and stare into him as he presses something cold into my hand. It takes a lot of willpower to look away from his face, but I finally manage to glance down at the object. "Tier's true north compass." I finger the smooth silver then pop open the clasp and wait for the needle to settle.

It's pointing to Caleb.

I drop it and stand abruptly, turning to find Polaris in the night sky. It's behind me, so the needle is pointing south when I turn back to Caleb. "It's pointing to you."

"It points to me because I am your true north, Junco. Fate can shift but Destiny is fixed."

Sera's words, back when I was in that virtual cabin after Deliverance.

"You can resist Fate if you want. You can refuse to play along and you can quit. But Destiny cannot be changed. And your Destiny is to meet the end, one way or another. You can go prepared or not. You can fight or surrender. You can control all those things, but what you cannot change is the fact that you will be there."

I swallow down the bile that is rising in my throat and scan the horizon, looking at anything but him.

He takes a step towards me and then leans into my ear to whisper, "Do not waste Selia, she is critical."

I just stare at him as he walks past and then I hear Selia's voice behind me. "Ready, uh—" She's still lying and forgot what name she gave me.

"Yeah, I'm ready."

Chapter Thirty

We're about two hours northeast of Vegas if what Caleb says is correct and really, after all the bullshit he just laid on me, is he gonna be lying about that? His buddy, Jacob, directs Selia to the backseat of a late-model Ripper that barely seats two, let alone four. I'm glad he's squished back there with her, I'd rather have control of the door anyway, you know? Just in case this guy goes apeshit on me and I need a quick escape route.

I shake my head after that thought. It's pretty dumb. I'm not interested in running. The next person who attacks me will find one pissed-off bitch to contend with.

They all chat endlessly as we rage down the desert highway towards the glow of light that spews out of the distant horizon. It's like a beacon. Or whatever the opposite of beacon is, because I'm pretty sure no one in Sin City wants me to drop by for a visit.

Someone pushes on my shoulder and I jolt myself out of my funk. "What?"

"Jacob wants to know what high school you went to, Abi."

I contort my body so I can look back at Selia. She's sitting in the seat behind me, so all I see is the friend Jacob. I narrow my eyes at him. "What the hell does that matter?"

Selia interrupts my bad mood. "We both went to Goshen High out on the Western Slope, five years apart."

I roll my eyes back at the Jacob guy. "How convenient." I'd forgotten that Selia was from the MR. That realization bothers me for some reason.

Caleb interjects before I can answer, "Which school, Abi?"

"My name is Junco, right? I'm pretty fucking sure everyone in this vehicle knows that, so why the fuck are all of you calling me Abi?"

"Answer my question, Junco."

"I'm a cadet rat, OK? I went to Council 1 Cadets. Happy?"

"Oh shit," Selia says. "We're getting out. Pull over."

Caleb just laughs. "I'm not dropping the two of you off in the middle of the desert dressed like prostitutes. Really, Selia."

Selia snarls at him as she pushes her head up through the slit that separates my seat from Caleb. "I said, pull the fucking car over or Junco will subvert the electronics and pull it over on her own."

I will? I probably could. If I can tap into phone lines, how hard would it be to take over this car? Easy, I bet.

My eyebrows shoot up when Caleb pulls off the road and settles into a small turnout, cuts the engine and the lights, and we all sit in the silent darkness.

"Now what?" Caleb asks.

Selia kicks my seat. "Open the door, Junco."

I sigh. "No, just go, Caleb. Selia, I'm not interested in getting out, walking to Vegas, or using an unorthodox method to get us there. Just let the man drive. What's he gonna do? Kill us?" I laugh. Shit, I'd actually love for him to try because it's been a while since I had a decent one-on-one fight.

Caleb starts the engine and pulls back out on the road before Selia can even answer me. I hear her slump back against her seat and huff out some air. The car is silent after that and I just sit and stare at my reflection in the passenger window, my face distorted with the curve of the glass and the orange glow that radiates out from the dashboard lights.

About an hour later, just as the sun is coming up in the east and bathing the desert in a wash of orange and pink, Caleb turns into a Chick-Chick-Chicken, parks the car, and opens his door to let Jacob out. "Selia," he commands, "go with Jacob so Junco and I can talk."

I expect a battle of words at the very least but she climbs over the hump that separates her seat from Jacob's and exits the car.

Caleb gets back in and I wait for it.

"Let me be very clear, Junco. You have rules and obligations, do you understand this?"

I shake my head. "I rule myself and I've been thinking about that whole prayer out on the battlefield." I wait for his anger and then smile and continue. "I'm just not convinced that I'm obligated to go forth with what you're asking, ya know? I mean, I figure Inanna taking me was a pretty severe trade for saving Gideon's life. So I think God and I are even, I don't owe you and I'm not interested in your plan for me. I'm taking Option B, Junco fate shift."

He reaches over and grabs my wrist and squeezes. It's painful, I'm not gonna lie, but it's not even close to the pain Inanna inflicted on me in the tank. "Break the bones. Go ahead. I'll heal."

He stares at me.

"Your rules, Junco—you will follow my orders and enter the Pillar alone. You will give us the results we're after and you will report back as instructed. Do you understand me?"

"I understand your words, yes. But I will not comply. Period. That discussion is now over. I follow Gideon's orders, and that's it, do *you* understand? I'm not your servant, I'm not your slave, I'm not your warrior. I'm nothing to you. I'm not interested in this job or mission or whatever the fuck you Bible people are calling it, and I certainly have no moral obligation to deliver results because I have no morals."

His eyes blaze at me, not in the way that Tier's eyes might, but just a normal I-hate-your-fucking-guts blaze of anger kind of way. "You will, Junco. You will do what I ask or I will revisit you and *make* you do it."

I laugh at this. "Oh, Caleb, that is a good one. And ya know, if I hadn't already been told by Tier that I have the Power of Decision I might've believed that." I stop just long enough to gauge his reaction. "But I'm pretty sure that I'm driving the float in this little parade we have going, so you can keep your threats and—"

His attack crashes me back against the passenger door and his hand is wrapped around my neck. I head-butt him in the forehead so fucking hard the blood that spews out of the wound splashes down on my face. He hesitates before grabbing both wrists as he leans back to stay out of the reach of my skull.

I laugh. "You fucking idiot. If you want to fight, get out of this car and let's do it right!"

He spits blood out on the floor of a vehicle that probably costs as much as a house in the RR. "Calm down, Junco."

"Oh, now you want to be reasonable? Before it's all violence and threats, but now you want to be reasonable? Fuck you."

My door opens and Selia has a gun pointed at Caleb's head before I can even register what's happening. "Get out, Junco, we're—"

"No, Selia, get in. He's done now. We're fine, right Caleb?"

He releases my wrists and opens his door to let Jacob in the other side. I get out so Selia can get in behind me. She keeps her TZi handy.

Everyone settles back down and after I clean the blood off my face with a wet-nap from the glove box, Jacob offers me food. My hand reaches out to take it before I can stop myself. Selia shoots me an incredulous look. "I don't even know how many days it's been since I've eaten, Selia. Sorry." I pull off the pickles and proceed to scarf down the sandwich.

"Which hotel?" Caleb asks Selia as we crawl into the early-morning traffic of the Strip.

"Asgarth's Dungeon," she answers.

You have *got* to be fucking with me. I laugh between bites of chicken. My life is one long bad omen after another. Nothing but one long motherfucking bad-ass omen after another.

Chapter Thirty-One

The car glides into the dropoff in front of a hotel that looks exactly like a castle from the Middle Ages. When the valet comes up Caleb waves him off, then pulls forward into a little alcove.

"Please stay a minute, Junco." He opens his door and lifts the seat so Jacob and Selia can exit, then settles himself back in and looks over at me.

"You will renege?"

"I made no promise to you."

"You made a promise to God, Junco. He held up His end. Now it's your turn."

I hold my temper, but inside it's raging. "God? You want me to believe you're the Messenger of God? After what I've seen, you still expect me to hold on to that shit? Caleb, the Devil swooped me up into the heavens so I could have a few moments of peace to stargaze. In the middle of an empty fucking vacuum, no air, no gravity, no nothing. And I'm still here to talk about it. He took me through time, he sees the future. And you want me to believe there's a God?"

I watch his expression for a few fractions but it is still.

"God is nothing but a trick of science. I've been resurrected by an AI, my mother reshaped my body in a tank of fucking gel, I've jumped out of a spaceship from a hundred and twenty-five thousand feet, met myself hundreds of times over in the face of Mountain Republic clones, and my twine died in front of my eyes."

It doesn't matter how many times I mention Isten out loud, his death is so raw and painful it takes my breath away.

"There is *no God*. Because if there is, and that God did this to me for his own Purpose, then I hate his motherfucking guts and I hope he loses. If Lucan's the Devil and he's the enemy of God, then I hope God loses. You got that?"

"He gave you a family."

"My mother left when I was six and my father left when I was sixteen."

"He gave you skills."

"Skills that are only good for killing people."

"He gave you strength."

"Strength to bear all the fucking pain!"

"He made you intelligent."

"Yeah, so I can figure out what a worthless piece of shit He is."

"He gave you Gideon."

I falter and turn my head. "And He'll take him away, too, right? It that what you're saying? He gave me Gideon and He'll take him away now?"

The tears stream down my face and I can't hold it in anymore.

"He wants very little from you, Junco."

"It's too much."

"What more do you want?"

"I want Isten."

His frustration comes out as a long breath of air. "You will disobey over one man? One man you were twined with for a few weeks? Who was not even a lover?"

"I want him back. I want to tell him I love him. I want to tell him I'm sorry, I want to tell him about my day and I want to hear his heartbeat under my cheek as we fall asleep together."

"You have Tier for that."

"Tier gave me Isten. He was a gift."

"Tier traded Isten for *you*."

"No."

"And God granted your prayer and saved Gideon, Junco. You never prayed for Isten."

"I never got the fucking *chance!*" I scream the last part and I feel myself losing control quickly so I take a moment to pull it together.

"You know what? Forget it, I want them all. I want them *all* back. You tell your God I want them all back and then I'll finish His job."

"No, that will not happen, nor is it even possible. Isten and your friends are gone, Junco. Gone."

"No, they're not. I know where they are." I look up and meet his eyes. He's unsure of this statement and it shows. "I've seen them, I know where they are and I want them back!"

"No!" His shout rocks me back against the window. "They cannot come back. They are somewhere else, that's true, but once you cross over there is no return, Junco. There is no proxy for that world. They are gone."

I drag my wet eyes away from his anger and play a card. "Then I want to go there too."

He laughs at this. "You cannot have it both ways, Junco. You cannot stay here with Gideon and go there with Isten. That's not how it works."

I smile. An actual honest-to-God smile. "Then I'll take them all with me."

"You'll kill your friends? Is that what you're saying? Because, Junco, that's what those words mean."

"We can go right now, can't we? I mean, I can just check out now and this whole load of bullshit is swept away, isn't it?"

The smile grows across my face as his arms sweep out and grab my shoulders. "Junco, stop. I cannot give you Isten, I cannot. It's not possible. But I can give you something else. Name it."

He's right about one thing. God did make me pretty fucking smart. I throw down more cards and I've got a full house. "You're versed in Bible trivia, right? You know what the name Gideon means, Caleb?"

He sighs. "Warrior of God."

"No. Wrong answer. Gideon means Man of Proof. When God asked for his compliance in ancient times, just like God is asking for mine right now, Gideon stood up and said, *Prove it.*"

Caleb turns away and shakes his head.

"You go back and tell your God I said prove it. And I'm gonna tell you right now, Caleb—I've seen some pretty spectacular things in my day. Lucan can do just about anything so you better tell that God of yours to come up with something better than any of the things Lucan's done. I want my miracle. I want my Isten and I will accept nothing less."

"It cannot be done."

"And if He takes Gideon, the whole deal is off. I'll kill everyone and we'll all go down together."

"You're insane."

A guffaw bursts out of my throat. "You're just figuring that out? Shit, Caleb, you're late to that party, it's pretty much over. I'm certifiable, absolutely. I will kill them all, Caleb. I will kill them all. I will destroy this whole fucking planet!"

"I cannot take this message back, Junco. I won't do it."

I shrug and open my door. "You do whatever the fuck you want, I've got some revenge to enact. Thanks for the ride."

I slam the door and head over to Selia who is waiting on the curb in front of the giant dungeon doors that lead into Asgarth's hotel. The absurdity of this setting makes me cackle with laughter.

Selia chews her fingernail as I walk up to her. "Everything OK, Juncs?"

I grab her hand and lead her through the doors. "Just great. We're all gonna be just fine, you'll see. We can't lose, Selia, we cannot fucking lose."

Chapter Thirty-Two

The elevator takes us all the way up to the penthouse and I'm just about to think this is excessive and unwarranted when the doors part and Irin is standing in front of me smiling.

The penthouse comes with a terrace.

A terrace that is easily accessible for avians.

I have a good team.

"Well, my psycho little sister, it's about fucking time!"

I let her hug me and breathe a sigh of relief. I think I love Irin, even though she's a total bitch.

Lili, on the other hand, is standing there with her hands on her hips, her mouth in a contorted scowl, and her eyes blazing. "Lucan is not happy with you. At all."

I flip her off. "You can tell Lucan I said that. OK?" I look around the suite and spy several doors on either side of the large sunken living room. The screen is on and the scene is familiar. People running, screaming, death, destruction.

Looks like Tier is in town, wherever that place is.

"Which room is mine? I'm fucking exhausted."

Irin points and I walk off, calling out, "Do not bother me," as I close the door and flop on the king-sized bed.

Oh shit. I really am tired. That Caleb guy might be an asshole, but he gave up some serious information. *Tier gave me Isten then took him away.* Sacrificed him for me.

It hurts.

So bad.

I want Tier to be my one, I really do, but every single time I get it in my head that he's a good guy, that we're meant for each other, I learn something ugly about him. I pull my comm out of my back pocket and fiddle with it until my dad's face appears on screen.

I push the tab associated with the picture and the connection starts. It buzzes a few times and then he's there.

"Hi, Snowbird."

I smile so big it makes my cheeks stretch. "Hi, Dad."

"You OK?"

I sigh. "Yeah, I'm OK. Just tired. How about you? Where are you?"

"Polar Friendlies."

"Is everyone there?"

"Yes, everyone is here now. Your mom's here, too."

"Oh," is all I have to say to that. I'm not interested in her. "Well, what's going on up there? Anything important?"

"Yes, you could say that. But you'll have to come see for yourself." He stops, and then adds, "When you have a chance, of course. You're busy now, so that's OK."

"Oh," I say again. I was just making conversation, but whatever.

"Tier called a few hours ago. Said you'd be calling."

"Did he now?" Must be nice to see the future. That's like the Powerball of superpowers. "Was he mad?"

"No, should he have been?"

"Ummmm… no. I guess not."

"You just call to say hi? Or do you need help?"

"Dad," I begin, "do you think Lucan is the Devil?"

"Yes."

Oh, shit. That was not the answer I was looking for. "Do you think he's evil?"

"Do you think I'm evil, Junco?"

Well, sorta, I want to say. I mean, he did nuke Peak City and Council 3.

"You don't have to answer that. It was rhetorical. I'm just saying that everyone has the potential."

"Do you think *I'm* evil?"

I hear the long draw of breath before he speaks and know he's gonna lie. "Junco, evil is not as black and white as you were taught. Evil isn't an action, Snowbird. It's an intention."

I'm not so sure of this, that road to hell is paved with stuff that sounds very similar. "Who's side are we on? Do you know? Is there a side? Is Lucan trying to destroy the world? Who will—"

"Junco." He cuts me off there. "Stop. I understand it's confusing. Evil is tricky in that way. You can never be sure you're on the right side. But love. Love is easy. Stay on that side of the road and it doesn't matter what it's paved with. You're on the right side."

"They keep hurting me, Dad."

I can hear the anger come out as long deep breaths on the other end of the comm so I elaborate before he loses his cool. "Not physically. Physical pain has no meaning, I don't even feel that anymore. They hurt my heart, Dad. And I don't understand how this can be love. Tier twined me to Isten and he knew Isten was gonna die in the Runout Valley. He knew, and still he let me get so close and depend on Isten. And then it was ripped away. And my heart, Dad. My heart after Isten died, it was so full of pain. Pain I can't even describe, pain that hurts me still. It hurts so bad I just want to crawl into a corner and die."

I pause to see if he'll contribute, but he stays silent.

"And Tier did that to me. But I still love him. I want him so much, but how? How can I trust him with my heart when he hurts me?"

"Junco, people are flawed. This is how we were made, we are not perfect. Everyone makes mistakes."

"But that wasn't a mistake, it was deliberate."

"The mistake, Snowbird, was hurting you in the process. He doesn't want to hurt you. He loves you."

"Oh." How can that be love? I admit I'm no expert on love, I barely know what it means. But it just seems wrong that it should hurt so much. "Gideon never does this shit to me. The only thing Gid ever did to hurt me was leave and it's not like he could've stopped that. He was just a teen when he had to go away. Tier and Lucan, they know exactly what they're doing and they do it anyway. Like I'm just collateral damage or something."

His sigh is long and loud. "Sometimes we have to kill to right our world. Sometimes we have to be killed so someone else can right their world. This is life, Junco. It's not good or evil, it's a delicate balance of both."

It's like the constellations. Like Laelaps and the Teumessian fox. A paradox that must be neutralized. It's like Lucan's lecture on perspective. Look at both sides, but neither side is right. It's like Inanna giving me this strong new body and these powers even though it turned me crazy with the pain.

I have a hard time with that last part. How can anything she did be good? But that's what Sera was trying to say as I ignored her words. Inanna made me whole again. But I never asked to be whole. I never begrudged what I was.

"You still there, Junco?"

"Yeah," I breathe. "I'm tired now, Dad. I'm gonna go to bed."

"I love you, Junco."

"Ditto, Dad. Bye."

I tap the screen to end the connection, then turn over on the bed and before I have time to think my eyes are closed and my world is dark.

247

Chapter Thirty-Three

I'm sweating like a motherfucker in the Dallas Underbelly humidity. The black covert ops outfit doesn't help things either. Fucking shit sticks to my skin and makes me feel like I'm wearing plastic. Who the hell needs heat shielding when it's ninety-seven degrees out? I mean, fuck! I highly doubt that single degree is gonna be the one thing that gives me away on this job.

This distraction makes me lose focus and my lens scope vibrates against my iris as it adjusts. I'd rather have a fucking pair of night-vision goggles strapped to my head than these stupid lens cams. Who the fuck planned this job, anyway?

The vibration stops and then I hear the internal beep that says it's found the target. He's got a marker on him that's been programmed into my vision equipment. It zooms in and out as it focuses—again.

I peer down the sight of my rifle and start breathing.

In. Out. Stop.

"Stand down, Semaj. Report back. Repeat, stand down, and report."

Now what the fuck? "H2, I'm on target, I've got him."

"Stand down, now. Report."

This whole night blows.

I slither back into the dead space and then crawl back the way I came. Over the railing, hop onto the next building, down the fire escape, jump to the ground, and book it down the alley. My stalk mocs are silent as my feet pound the pavement. I love those synthetic rubber soles. You could stalk anything in these shoes.

I slip into the shadows as some prostitutes walk by, then walk the wall and round the corner.

I slam into James and fall on my ass.

"What the hell, James? You're not—"

"Quiet, Junco. We've gotta get back now, your dad called for you."

"Oh."

I take his hand as he helps me up and we walk briskly to the waiting flier. He holds the door open as I get in and then we take seats opposite each other in the back.

"What's he want?" I'm suspicious because my dad hasn't called for me in almost a year.

James shrugs and pushes a bag into my lap as he takes my rifle. "Get into your uniform. I told him you were in training down here, but he's not aware of your extracurricular activities."

Obviously. I cannot even imagine a world where my dad sanctions civilian hits.

I struggle out of the wet plastic and sit there in my underclothes for a few minutes, letting the air conditioning blast me. James is uncomfortable with me undressed, but I don't care. It's so fucking hot down here and the last thing I want to do is put on a cadet uniform.

"Dress, Junco. Now."

"Why do I have to wear a service—"

"He thinks you're here as a commander, Junco. Not a student."

"Oh." I blow out some air and start tugging on the layers of clothes that make up the Senior Cadet Captain service uniform. Pressed shirt, tie, trousers, belt, socks, boots—in this fucking heat, boots!— and hat.

After I'm dressed I sit as still as possible. Every single time I move I sweat, even in the air condition.

"Fuck, why is it so damn hot?"

James shoots me an uncomfortable look and then adjusts the temperature lower. His flesh is pimpled with chill and I reach over and touch his arm. He's freezing.

"No. No, James, you better explain—"

"Junco, he's stable right now, but he's not doing well, I can't lie."

My body instantly breaks out into a sweat, living the fever that connects Gideon and I, and my breath is coming in short gasps as the panic rises. "He's dying! He's dying, isn't he?"

"Don't, Junco. Do not lose it, do you understand? Your dad is there, he's already suspicious of this trip, and if he sees this connection I guarantee you he will not let Gideon live. You listen to me now and hold it down."

I force the tears back because he's right. My dad is different. I don't know how to explain it or how it's even possible, but my dad has changed somehow. I haven't seen him since late spring last year and the last time I talked to him on the comms, he was acting strange. So many questions, things he already knows, like it's a test or something. Or like he forgot the answers.

And this heat thing started a while back with Gid and I. He broke his arm on a mission—shit, he got hurt a lot over the past few years. And each time the heat from his wounds was transferred to me. But it never felt like this. This is a fever that burns my whole body. Which means he's fucked up.

I swallow and look out the window. It's too dark to see anything but the occasional light or two until the perimeter security for the Stag comes into view.

I can see my dad's private flyer on the east pad and we land on the north pad.

When the door opens he's standing there, in full service uniform as well, and his hands crossed in front of his chest. He doesn't salute.

I raise my eyebrow at that. When I wear the service uniform I get a salute. It's always been that way.

"Weapon," he barks at me. His arms uncross and his hand extends as I untuck my shirt and pull out my SEAR knife, then hand it over.

He slips it into his front trouser pocket.

My eyebrow doesn't shoot up this time, but it wants to.

"What's going on, Dad?"

"Gideon is very sick, Junco. I wanted you to know right away that he will not make it."

My heart is crushed and my eyes close to protect myself against these words. "No."

He grabs my arm and pulls me towards one of the outer perimeter buildings. One that I've never been allowed into before. He flashes his biometrics and tugs on me as the double stainless-steel doors part to let us through.

My head is in a fog as I am pulled along several corridors, through more doors, past stations manned by nurses—or actually, when I take a second look, manned by scientists. I do a double take at one as we pass and my dad notices and jerks my attention back to him.

"Don't get nosy."

"Nosy?" Since when is being aware of my surroundings considered nosy? I'm about to call him out on this when we come around a corner and Gideon is in front of me.

I burst into tears.

He's nothing but machines and tubes, and wires. The large room is buzzing and underneath I can hear the tell-tale wheezing of the ventilator that is keeping my partner alive. "What the fuck *happened?" The words are out before I can stop them and I'm sprawled out on the ground, the pain radiating out from my mouth as the blood from my lip drips on the floor in front of my eyes.*

"Watch your mouth!"

Did my father just hit me for swearing? Since when?

James picks me up and smiles, but I see the panic in his eyes as I shake off his grip on my arm and walk over to Gid's bed. When I look back, Matthew is in the room as well. James retreats behind him, no more help for me. If Gid could talk he'd tell me to keep cool and stay alert. They're up to something.

I take a deep breath and look at my dad. "Please, tell me what happened."

He smiles at my manners. "He is not responding well to a treatment we gave him. He will not recover, Junco. We are taking him off the ventilators tonight. He will stop breathing, and you will deal with it rationally."

I swallow down my anger and growl, "Define rational."

"Normal, everyday grief is fine—"

My unexpected laugh cuts him off and then he continues.

"But we will not tolerate rebellion over this. He will die and you will go on. You will be agreeable and follow orders. Do I make myself clear?"

He sure does. One thing is very clear. This man is absolutely not my father. My father loved Gid like a son. He would never expect me to be rational upon his death. Never.

I nod up at him and look over to Matthew. He's smiling. But I almost miss that because the tiniest fraction of my sight is directed towards James. And he puts it all into perspective. We're playing a game, Junco. *I can almost hear the words come from his mouth. That's what he always told me as a kid when I had to behave but would prefer not to.* We're playing a game.

"Yes, sir," I whisper.

I can play. I know the rules.

"You may stay here with Gideon until we're ready to remove his life support, but do not wander the hallways. Clear?"

"Clear."

They leave me alone then. I pull a chair up to the bed and lean my head down on his chest. I can't even hear his heart, not through all the artificial breathing. But I don't need to hear his heart. I can hear his mind.

And I can feel his pain. His fever circulates in my blood, his life mixes with mine and for a moment I almost panic and think I'll take that from him. That I'll be responsible for his death.

But then the heat dissipates and I move on. Looking for the next problem, looking for the things that want to crush him. And I take them next. I take them all, one at a time, until my body is limp and his fever is my own.

If he dies, so will I.

I refuse to live without him.
I refuse.

254

Chapter Thirty-Four

The voices are what wake me. Not soft. Not talking to me. Not loud, more like hurried or insistent.

Not talking to me—talking about *me.*

I struggle to make sense of the words, but I can't catch it all. Only fragments that make no sense.

Life support… recovery… death.

Oh God. I start crying before I can stop myself and then someone is hovering over me, asking me questions.

But I'm not listening. Because their erratic conversation can only mean one thing. Gid has died. They took him off life support and—

"Junco?" This soft voice is talking to me. "Junco, he's still alive, so you can stop now."

James. *I say it but no words come out.*

The voice is no longer soft, it's my new dad talking now. He's screaming at me, question after question. I hear the words but I just can't make myself give a shit. Someone is pulling him out, I recognize the voice but it makes no sense. Matthew is calming my dad? Since when?

I feel the tube in my arm wiggle as someone pushes drugs into the line and then, almost instantly, the world ends.

When I come to I am fully awake and I am staring up at Gideon.

"Snowbird. Don't ever do that again."

He looks like total shit, his gown slipping down his shoulder, his arm still attached to an IV line that ends at a bag of something, and his hair—shit, what hair? Half his head is shaved bald and the remaining hair is sticking straight up.

I manage to croak out some words. "Don't you ever do that again."

He leans down and kisses me. He kissed me!

How many years have I waited for Gideon's kiss? It pecks my forehead, but so what. I cough out a small chuckle. "Is that what it takes to get a kiss from you?"

"Shit, Junco. You want a kiss, just say so. Don't ever do that healing shit again, you hear me? It's not safe, you're not ready."

I close my eyes because they are still so tired. "What is this place?"

"The outer labs."

I open my eyes again and find my attitude. "Yeah, I know that, Gideon. What is it, though?"

"It's not important. Just rest. I only wanted to come in and see how you were doing. They said you were gonna be fine, but I had a hard time believing them." He shrugs. "I need you, Junco. Don't leave me yet."

I smile up at him. "I won't if you won't."

He leans down and kisses me again. On the cheek this time. "Deal," he whispers. "That's a deal. Now go back to sleep. I gotta get to my room before they come back."

"Where is everyone?"

"Some sort of emergency in another building." He stands up and grabs his IV bag and squeezes my arm with his free hand. "I'll come see you tomorrow."

I manage a nod and then lose the battle with my heavy eyelids.

The next time I wake I feel spectacular. A nurse stands over me and smiles. "Thought that might bring you back."

"Who the fuck are you?"

She sucks in some air between her teeth and looks behind her shoulder. "Please, don't swear in here, Junco. Your father is not in a good mood. I saw that last smack, and right now you don't need any more smacks."

"I've never seen you before in my life. How long have you worked here?"

This time the smile is indulgent. Like she feels sorry for me. "A very long time. You just never got to see me when you were awake before. I've been taking care of your treatments since you were a baby."

I nod at her. "Well, then you know that man who hit me is not my father, right?"

She stands up this time and starts smoothing out her scrubs. "Don't say that, OK? Just don't."

Father status confirmed. Not. Mine.

"What treatments?" I pick up that admission to ease her back down. She's the one who mentioned them, so it must be safe for me to talk about it.

Her hands swiftly go to my IV line and she pushes more drugs in. Apparently not.

The bitch brought me up and then she sent me down again. All because I started asking questions.

The next time I wake it comes slowly, like the drugs are still working, but wearing off naturally. All I can hear is the incessant beeping of an alarm outside my open door.

I try to call out, but my voice doesn't work.

I have no idea how long I've been lying here when I decide I cannot take that alarm for one more second. I swing my legs over, stop and let the dizziness subside, then push myself up.

I feel surprisingly strong as I stand there, weaving a little, but steady. There is no IV in my arm anymore, so I pad my way over to the door and look out.

Stillness.

No one is there.

The alarm comes with a blinking light on a wall screen. A map of the outer perimeter buildings. Whatever's triggered it, this building is not where the emergency is located.

I look around a little, recognize the stations that looked like lab benches when that father guy was dragging me to see Gideon, and make my way over to them.

They are organized with neatly stacked datacubes inside clear plexiglass containers. Each column is labeled with numbers and letters.

While I don't recognize the number sequences, I do recognize the pattern they make.

They're genetic crossings.

This is a genetics lab.

The first stack says 1397P X 1447P.

It's the sevens that give me pause.

I'm Seven. Or Gid. We're the only Sevens left, at least that's what we've been told. And I know enough from school that P stands for parental generation.

I look around and take it in again, but this time I see it. I see it all.

This is a hub, not a room or a station. There are four wings that appear to branch off from here, all with double stainless steel doors. Each door has a biometric lock and each door is closed.

Except one. The one right in front of me.

It's almost closed, except for the bent piece of rubber flashing that sticks in the bottom corner where the doors should meet. Another breath and I'm standing in front of them, my fingernails gingerly prying them apart. The door slips, but I grab it again just before the weight of it and the air pressure difference on the other side can suck it closed.

If I get caught there is no telling what they will do to me.

But those labels have sevens on them.

I pull the door open, step through and let it swish closed behind me.

A high-pitched grunt in a room down the hallway stops me, my heart beating so fast it takes whole seconds for me to get it under control.

Another grunt, then a squeal.

I swallow.

Turn back, Junco. You don't want to know. You don't want to know.

I don't want to know. I really don't, but try telling that to my feet, because they're already at the open door when I finally snap back to my senses. I reach out and push the door so it can open fully. The hinges squeak a little as it swings.

The thing making the noises is small, not much bigger than a child of two or three. Her long blonde hair is wild and ratted up, her face an ugly distortion of features that make no sense, and her red coveralls remind me of the demented doll that starred in a horror screen Gideon made me watch when we were left in New York hotel alone on New Years when we were kids.

Her head swings like she can't control it well, and her eyes are crossing as she looks up at me from the bed, desperately trying to focus on me.

She's strapped down.

Finally, after several long seconds, her head is still and I can watch her gather me up in her mind.

"Who are you?" I ask.

She screams. It's not a human scream, not at all. It's the scream of a demon, of some ancient bird. The wailing pierces my ears and I fall to the ground clutching my head. "Stop!" And then I scream as well. My pain mixes with her pain and we scream.

Hands lift me to my feet and I am ushered towards the door, I look back one final time and read the chart on a table as I pass.

1397P X 1447P—Molly.

The nurse from before is frantic, she half drags, half pushes me back through the doors and into my room. She doesn't waste time with an IV, that ionspray is squirted up my nose before I even realize I'm still screaming.

Chapter Thirty-Five

Oh, God. Just make it stop. Please, I'll never ask for anything again, just make the memories go away.

No blue lights show up to deliver me from myself this time.

I pretty much burned that bridge.

"Junco?"

I bolt upright and see Lucan standing at the end of the bed.

What the fuck? "What're you doing here?"

His face is flushed and he's sweating, it reminds me of the heat in my memory. His wings are upright, in a position I'll call attack ready. I raise my eyebrows at him. "I said, what are you doing here, Lucan?"

When he speaks I understand his complexion. It's anger. He seethes at me. "I'm going to say this once, Junco. And only once. You will follow directions from this point on, you will forget this revenge scheme you're cooking up with Irin, and the two of you will do as you're told. Or else."

I jump up out of the bed and cut off his words. "Or else what? I am not your warrior, Lucan. I do not respond to threats."

His eyes change. The beautiful aquamarine is long gone and the red that appears now says I've crossed his line. His razors come out of his hands with a sickening crack and his teeth elongate into fangs.

I tuck down the fear and hold my position.

And smile.

"You think I'm afraid of you?" I run at him and spin. My kick misses and I am about to land hard on the ground when he snatches me up, only to throw me back down, making me scream out as my head slams hard and bounces back up.

He sits on top of me and forces my arms to the ground as he leans into my face. "You don't want to know what I might do, Junco. Do not challenge me. You have no idea."

The door bursts open and the girls stand there shocked.

"Out!" Lucan roars.

Lili and Irin slink away but Selia stays, waiting for me to give her an order. "I've got this, Sel. Just go."

She grunts out a laugh but still holds her position. "He's got ya pinned to the floor, Junco. I'm pretty sure you don't have this."

Lucan has me upright again before I can even process an answer. He steps away and fans out his arms. "Happy?" he asks Selia.

She takes a moment to think and then backs out, closing the door behind her.

"She's a keeper, that one," he mutters.

Selia seems awfully popular among the various higher beings involved in this whole affair. This is weird, but it's not really a great time to ponder shit like that.

I take my attention back to Lucan's face. His sweat is wafting off his body as steam now, he has literally boiled over. "Yesterday I was told Isten lives in another… place or universe or somewhere besides here. A place where I can go if I die, so do you really think I care if you kill me?"

He throws his head back and laughs. It's a giant outburst, actually.

I'm not sure what's funny.

"You had a visitor?" His eyes brighten as the laughter lingers on his face.

I just nod.

"Oh, and he told you about this place, did he? This *Heaven*?"

"No, not exactly. But I know it exists and I know I can't go there until I'm dead."

He watches me for a few moments, then runs his hands through his hair. "You can never go there, Junco. You're marked. The marked cannot move on. Ever."

I stand still and silent.

"Why do you think Tier refuses the Archer morph? Why would he refuse to be changed? He wants to die, Junco. He *wants to die*. And Archers have a very hard time doing that. You are one of us now. It cannot be undone."

I can't even speak, I just shake my head.

"I need your co-operation, Junco. We can all sit down and discuss the future once we know we have one. Understand?"

"That makes no sense, Lucan. Either we can die or we can't. If the High Order is coming to kill you, then how is it that you can't die?"

He turns a little but his eyes catch mine from the side. "There are far worse things than death, Junco." And then he laughs. "And don't even try blaming me for this situation you find yourself in, I would have preferred you die your natural death back in the Rural Republic, but Tier insisted you come back with *him*. I would've preferred that you died in Deliverance, but Sera insisted that you come back with *her*."

The words! Oh, holy motherfucking fuck. His words!

"And I would *never* have morphed you. Ever. Not the first time and most certainly not the second time. Tier would never have let me, but even without his disapproval, I would not want you to be an Archer, Junco." The last of his words are softer but somehow that makes it so much worse. Like he feels sorry for me.

I bite my lip and my brows furrows together so tightly I can feel the stress expand down to my neck. "No."

"Yes. This is what Inanna did when she made you an Archer. Immortality. You are a Goddess in every sense of the word. You will live forever, you will watch everything and everyone you ever loved die and disappear, you will find new mates, make new families, and then watch them die as well. And in the end you will be so jaded and bitter you'll look back on your life, your real human life and think all this hell you're going through right now *is* Heaven. You'll look back on that childhood you think was so awful and desperately wish to be that girl again. Being shot by your trainers, smacked in the mouth by your father, or losing that child who would never have survived in the first place."

"You fucking asshole! How dare you say that shit to me! You said you'd love me forever, but this! You are such a total piece of shit! You broke me! All of you! You *broke me!*"

He stops, maybe to let those words in, maybe to wonder what he'll eat for dinner tonight, who the fuck knows. "No, Junco. You are not broken. This," he waves his hand at me, at my insanity, "is but a crack. The actual breaking has yet to commence."

The chill travels up my stomach and bursts out through my mouth. "*What?*"

"I wish you'd left Amelia that day." He turns away. "Left with that commander, what was his name?"

"Slag," I whisper.

"Right. Slag. You should have left me standing there alone against the darkness of the universe outside. But you didn't. You chose to stay, and I even warned you what it would come to. And now that we're here, you want to feign innocence? Blame this on *me?*"

His words come back, through all the murky ramblings in my mind, through the insane voices of dead people, and AI's, and mind readers. They are still there, ready to haunt me again.

Just remember, when we are at the end, when I am standing over you as you break in half, and I am forced to leave you with nothing, Junco – don't say I never tried to help. Don't tell me I made your life a living hell, because you will have done that all on your own.

"You're going to use me, aren't you? Use me all up and then leave me there, sprawled out and spent."

My words cause a great exhale of breath from him, as if I'm boring him, or taking up too much of his time. "Junco, please. I'm trying my best. If you would push the insanity away and just listen we'd all be in a better place when the High Order arrive. And I'm sorry for being so callous with the facts of the morph. I understand, it's big. It's the biggest thing to ever happen to you and you missed it. You have no idea what it means, so I understand the craziness."

"No." I say it again, but it comes out even weaker than before.

He huffs and loses his patience. "Listen to me! We cannot die, Junco. But we can be dissipated."

Dissipated. Both Rikan and Sera used that word. Rikan to tell me he will not allow me to dissipate Lucan, and Sera to tell me that's the way I can kill Inanna.

"It means to shatter, Junco."

His fangs are longer now, still growing, along with his razors and his anger. "You will be shattered, into billions of individual atoms, and each one holds a tag that says 'I am Junco'. They will be scattered around the Universe and you will be left to wander the darkness for eternity. Your consciousness fractured yet at the same time intact, as you spend decade after decade, century after century, millennium after millennium—billions of millennia added together—drifting alone in a sea of insanity. Until finally, one day, after so much time passes you are incapable of understanding that you exist, let alone remembering the baby you lost, the love you felt for Charlie, or the lost opportunity with Tier—all those particles will finally bump into one another in such as way that you will be whole again." He sneers at me. "At least that's the theory. If you want to know who the Devil is, Junco. I'll tell you with one hundred percent certainty, it is not me. It is one of those shattered beings who drifted for so long the quantum laws brought it back together again."

I'm a spinning mess, my world is psychosis personified.

"I am not even close to being the Devil, but those Angels coming for us? Some of them have survived the very process I just described. And one in particular has survived it many times over. They will be here soon, Junco. And they will shatter you and Inanna and my Archer brothers in a way that makes it almost impossible to return on your own. Because all of you are High Order and all of you are Fallen."

I take a deep breath and just shake my head as I look past him, out the window into the dusky red of the MR desert. "What about you? Will they shatter you?"

He smiles. It's the most evil smile I've ever seen. "No, Junco. They cannot shatter me. Believe it or not, my curse is like a shield. I truly am the captain of my soul, that is why they need you."

God, I want to be anywhere but here. Maybe we can escape, just run away and forget all of it—some ship, surely the avians must have some long-term life support ship we can take and just float out or existence in the nothingness… I look up at Lucan and know he's reading me.

"But even if we lose, and as long as you don't shatter *me*, if you just do what I ask, Junco, I will be there for you. I will put you back together. You won't have to wait until your love for Tier is a long-forgotten memory and you won't have to wait for someone to search for you across eternity. I will not let them take you away and throw you into oblivion.

"I will be there, I promise I will put you back together. I *will* love you for thousands of years, Junco, because you'll have no one else to share it with. If you will be there for me for this, I will not let you drift. Just do what I ask."

"No." I whisper it this time.

"When I was holding you after your Archer morph I said I'd wait, Junco. And I will. If you do what I ask and I survive, then you can live your life with Tier, do whatever you want—have a family, the house, the dog for fuck's sake. Whatever." He waves a dismissive hand towards me, like the whole idea of Tier and me having this normal life is ridiculous. "Have it all. I will give it to you, Junco." He searches my eyes to see what my reaction might be, but these words are so repulsive they've yet to sink in. "And I will be there after your life with Tier is over."

I laugh and shake my head. "You're insane. This is so much bullshit I don't even know where—"

"Inanna sentenced you to Hell, Junco. This is Hell. You're there already and you can never leave. You cannot die, but you can be punished and I'll tell you right now, after billions of years, the High Order have come up with many very creative ways to punish those of us who defy them. Dissipation is but one."

"I haven't though! I haven't defied them! I don't even know who they are!"

"You defy them by existing. If Inanna would've left you a Seven, you might have come out of it OK if you agreed to scatter me. But she took the next step, took you to Hell with her. You *will* be punished."

I stare out the terrace window and think of Matthew's punishments. His violence was always something I could live with. I mean, it was scary, but he never disfigured me or anything. Some smacks mostly. He only punched me close-fisted once and I really fucked him up in retaliation.

I was eleven when that happened.

I feel Lucan's hands on my shoulders but I don't turn.

"You knew, didn't you? Just like Tier knew Isten would die, even after he gave him to me." I look up at him now and I count. My pain is so real and raw I need to count the scales on his armor to hold it back. "You knew I'd end up this way? As a High Order Archer sentenced to an eternity of Hell?"

"I'm sorry, Junco. I really am, and I know it's a lot to take in, but you need to forget about that for now and concentrate on the Pillars. We must have them, you must make sure Irin will comply, you must show up to your Pillar, and you must give it to me. Do I make myself clear?"

I hate that phrase. It reminds me of camp. They were forever asking me if things were clear, and ya know what? No, nothing about my life is fucking clear, thank you.

I am in Hell and I will stay in Hell for eternity.

For years I've clung to the fact that it will end, one day, once and for all, it will end. All the heartbeats will stop. And it felt powerful to know, even though I never would, that I could make it end any time I wanted. I have always, literally, had control over my heartbeats.

But now?

Caleb did not mention this but surely he would've known. "You used Isten, just like you used me. You wanted inside my mind, you wanted answers, and you used him to take that from me, didn't you?"

He sucks some air in through his teeth and sneers at me. "Isten used you."

"No. You knew he wanted another twine more than anything and you used that against him, made him love me, made me love him. And then you took him away."

"None of this has anything to do with Isten, Junco. He wanted you, yes. Tier and I decided to make his remaining days happy. You would've rather he never had that special bond with you?"

"Go."

"Junco, I need your promise."

"Get out." I turn and look at him now. "Get out! I promise you nothing, Lucan. You're on your own, just like me. Maybe I'll raise that Pillar and maybe I won't, I have no idea right now to be honest. I'm gonna get my revenge, that's all I care about. I'm gonna go kill those people who started this, who made me, and I'm gonna feel a whole lot better about things when it's over. Maybe then I'll show up and raise that Pillar." It's my turn to sneer. "Or maybe I won't."

"You will show."

"Yeah? I'm sure you've seen me show up, is that it? Just like you saw me kill Kush and then slice my fucking chest open in Deliverance?"

He shrinks back a fraction, but I catch it.

"I did not see that."

"You lie! You're such a fucking liar! You saw that and everything else, too! Tier saw Isten die, he traded Isten for me, right? You traded Isten for me?"

"Who told you that?"

I grunt and face the truth I've been pushing away since before we went back to Earth to get my Siblings. "It's true.

You guys gave him to me as a gift and then you took him. And not just killed him, you killed him in front of me, Lucan. You made me watch."

We stand there in silence for several seconds and then he puts a hand on my shoulder and I know it's all true. I shake him off and watch his expression when I say the words.

"I hate you." His eyes glow for a fraction and I repeat it without the malice. "I hate you. You used me. In the worst way, Lucan. You used me all up, broke me, then stepped on the pieces just to make sure I'd never be put back together again. You'll gather me up? Once I'm shattered? Well, I don't want you to come looking for me, and if you do come, I won't allow you to put me back together. Because you know what? I'd rather be floating in my own insanity for eternity than spend it with you."

He stares at me for a few seconds and then he disappears. Just like that, he's gone. Replaced by emptiness.

Like fucking hell he'll be there to gather me up. Like fucking hell. His promises are as empty as the air he left behind.

Chapter Thirty-Six

Someone, probably Selia, but maybe Irin, has left me some clothes in a bag in the closet. The bag is labeled Junco, so I know it's for me.

I take a shower, the anger from my confrontation with Lucan still replaying through my mind. I have to stop everything I'm doing, several times, and lean against the tiled shower wall to calm myself. I don't have the same control over my heart rate that I used to have before the morph. In fact, nothing about me is the same as it used to be.

And that was Sera's point in telling me that Inanna remade me into something better.

Maybe.

Maybe she did, but I'll skin that bitch alive if I see her. I will not hesitate. I consider myself a pretty forgiving person, I mean I put up with a lot from all my childhood handlers, my father, Lucan, Tier, Ash and the rest. But that anger I feel for them is nothing. Minuscule. Compared to the hate I feel for Inanna.

I finish up in the shower and dress in an outfit that once again looks suspiciously like my Fledge uniform, minus the wing holes. I don't have the sniper t-shirt to offset it this time. Selia cut it all up and who knows where it is now.

So I look like an avian, minus the wings. Which is just fucking fantastic. I love being reminded that I have no wings.

Whatever.

I leave my room and head into the common area and find Ashur and Selia sitting on the couch watching a horror screen.

I wave my arms at the screaming girl running from some horrible mutant thing. "What the hell, Selia?"

Her head is lying on Ashur's thigh and she's stretched out on the couch. Ash has one hand on her ass and the other rests on the back of the couch. Like he fucking lives here or something.

Selia doesn't even sit up to answer. "We're waiting for Esta's Pillar to come on the screen. They're about ready."

I blink at her—"OK, you're useless"—and take my attention to Ashur's smug gaze. "What the hell are you doing here?"

He smiles. "Babysitting, what do you think?"

"I don't—" My sentence is interrupted by the newscast on screen. The area shows nothing but open ocean with the exception of one small dot far off in the distance. The media team zooms in until I can make out avian shapes and I see Esta clinging to Ryse on the deck of a boat. Tier stands on the top level of the cabin, like he's watching the media team with interest. Like a predator protecting his kill, waiting to see if the hyenas will try and steal it, maybe.

The camera pans around them in a circle and the light from her Pillar comes into view. From his vantage point it's an endless column of photons shooting up towards the heavens. In a few more minutes, it's gonna be those nanotech things making the light turn solid.

What is up with these things, anyway? What could they possibly be doing with them?

My internal questions are forgotten as the camera zooms in on Tier. His face is calm but his wings say another thing altogether. They are definitely what I'd call attack ready—slightly uplifted behind him, not outstretched, but not folded either. His head is high, but maybe that's because he's looking up at the camera crew with intense interest now.

The light from this soon-to-be Pillar looks like it stretches on forever, that's how large the radius is. The video team pans the camera again, explaining the exact coordinates. They are off the southeastern tip of Africa somewhere. Hundreds of miles off-shore, but it doesn't matter. Tsunamis will travel until they lose energy or crash into something that will take that energy away. There are still plenty of places to demolish once this baby gets rolling.

The voice on screen is predicting the end of Madagascar.

They take the camera back to Ryse and Esta on the deck. She's still leaning into him, and he's still talking to her. Esta nods and then she's talking too.

I wish I could hear what's going on.

Tier's mouth moves and the reporter on screen tries to decipher what he's saying. Whatever it is, it's definitely for the benefit of the camera crew, who must be hovering in a copter or something. His mouth moves again, like he's repeating his words over and over. The reporter tries again, but Tier laughs and shakes his head and enunciates very slowly.

Everyone catches it this time. *Goodbye. They're saying goodbye.*

He's talking to me.

I feel Ashur's hand on my shoulder but I don't look at him. Tier grabs a small device that the reporters have thrown down to him.

I lean in to hear, I can't help it.

He smiles first. "You want to talk to her, Junco? To make sure this is right?"

I nod. *Yes*, my mind says, and Tier turns, jumps down to the deck, and leans into Esta's ear before handing the microphone over.

Esta's face is red and streaked with tears. "I'm OK, Junco. I'm just scared."

Oh shit.

"Stop." I look up at Ashur. "Make them stop."

"No, Junco. There's no stopping. If we don't complete the Pillars they'll *all* die. She's not scared of what *she* needs to do, she thinks you might leave her stuck in there. She's afraid she'll never see Ryse again."

My heart feels so small and shriveled up right now. *She thinks I'll abandon her.*

For a microsecond I figure I can teleport there and talk to her but Tier is talking into the microphone again, telling me that the timeshift required for such a jump would put me there hours or maybe even days later.

I feel deflated. "I'll show up, Ashur. Make him tell her I'll show up." I look up at him and catch the distant look that typically clouds an expression when the vision screens are being accessed.

The message gets through, whether it was Tier reading me or Ashur talking directly to him, it gets through. Tier leans down and whispers into Esta's ear and she smiles as she answers. "I never doubted you, Junco. Never."

Right.

Tier tosses the microphone into the ocean and both he and Ryse take Esta by the arms and fly her up and out towards Pillar Four. As they approach the light takes on a whole new energy, like it switched wavelengths or something. My vision screen pops to life and I can see the changes in the light as Esta approaches—it wiggles a little, then increases in intensity and the wiggle becomes a wave that originates somewhere deep below the ocean. The hovercopter pulls back as the movement takes on an almost violent intensity and I shrug off Ashur's grip on my shoulder to step closer to the screen. "I can't see them, I want to see them."

Ash's hand is back but this time he's gripping my upper arm. "You don't want to see them, Junco. You'll have your turn." The screen shuts off and he pulls me away.

"Wait! I want to fucking see her do it, Ashur! Let go of my arm!"

He tugs on me hard and I stumble and fall into him. "I said no." His eyes glow green down at me as I shake off his grip a second time and scramble to get away before he can catch me again.

"You think I won't do it, don't you? You think the only way you guys can get me to comply is if you lie to me, is that it?"

Ashur walks away and takes his place back next to Selia. She's siting up now, and I notice she's not really dressed appropriately for fighting. The pale pink nightie looks like she's definitely got other plans. It's the middle of the night here in Vegas when I check my vision screen. "You better get changed, Sel. We have work to do."

She shakes her head at me and rests her head on Ashur's thigh again. "I'm not going anywhere tonight, Junco. Sorry."

"Where's Lili then?"

"You're not going anywhere either, Junco." Ashur says it in a way that begs me to defy him.

And I ponder this for a split-second.

But then he's talking again. "We're waiting for Tier this time."

"Lili?" I call out as I walk towards the rooms on the other side of the common living area, but before I can reach the door Ashur slams me down on the ground and pins me to the floor.

Selia doesn't even get up off the couch.

"What the fuck, Selia? A little help here?"

She snorts. "Like I could stop Ashur, Junco. Please. That's not even funny. He'd kick my ass too, so just relax and wait for Tier, OK?"

I stare up at Ash this time. "You know what?"

He smiles, like I'm coming to my senses and I'm just trying to make conversation and be friendly like we were back on Amelia. "What, Junco?"

"You're a dirty fucking woman-beater. That's what. You've spent your whole life on Earth almost, and you still think fighting girls is OK. You're nothing but a dirty fucking woman-beater."

His eyes glow. Like fluorescent. "Really? When have you ever seen me fight a woman, Junco? I only fight soldiers. Besides, you barely qualify as a woman. You're the farthest thing from a woman I've ever seen. And that's the way you like it, remember? You're nothing but a soldier. Which makes you fair game in my eyes."

Ouch. He certainly knows how to play the game of Junco. I shake it off and continue. "You're so fucking full of yourself you think just because you're Lucan's pick you can man-handle me? You're a violent piece of shit, that's what you are. Kadian was right about you all along, wasn't he?"

He's not quite ready to take the bait so I add another worm to the hook as he begins to snarl. "And if Selia was smart, she'd fucking leave your ass and go for Aren or Gideon, because at least they're fucking gentlemen."

He leans down into my face and I can feel the heat inside of him. "Is that right? You think Gideon is better than *us*? Well, let me tell you a little bit about the guy you love so much, Junco. He's spent the last ten years feeding information about you to Inanna."

I shake my head but he reads my expression and smiles.

"Oh, yeah. That"—he pauses—"whatever he is to you—a brother, a father, a lover, a handler—*whatever the fuck* that guy is to you—it's not even close to being the perfect guy you envision."

"No. I know Gideon is not like that, if he's told things to Inanna it was to protect me. Or something."

He gets up and pulls me up and this makes my stomach do little somersaults because it means he feels he's got the upper hand and I need help. I need to be back on my feet to hear this news because hearing it on the ground just gives him an unfair advantage.

"He's plotting with her, Junco. He's got a plan and maybe you think you know the plan, but I'm telling you as your friend, he's got a plan you have no idea about."

"What fucking plan? If you're so well-informed, tell me his plan."

"Well, for one thing, Selia wouldn't be able to be with Gideon."

He stops to smile and I feel it again. The sickness that comes with punishment. Or in the case of my recent life, revelations.

"Because he's been fucking that bitch Iliana since they put you in the tank two years ago. And you wanna hear the really sick part, Junco? He turned that bitch into you. He made Inanna morph her into you, the way you look *right now*. Tell me that's not sick."

I shake my head and suddenly Selia is on her feet walking towards me. "That's enough, Ashur. Stop it."

I wait until she's right up next to him and reach out before that dumb fuck Ashur even realizes I just played him. My fingers tap her shoulder and I watch his open mouth start screaming at me even as the tunnel of time opens up and Selia and I are flung *somewhere else.*

278

Chapter Thirty-Seven

We crash face-first into the desert scrub. If you've never been in the Southwest Republics, then you might think deserts are made up of sand. But that's not the case. Deserts around here are made up of dirt like the Eastern Plains of the RR. And scrub is not even close to being soft like sand. Scrub means poky plants, and rocks, and small woody shrubs that scratch the shit out of you as you slam into them.

I sit up as Selia wails about her lack of lower body clothing, but shit, it's not my fault she was dressed for sex right when I needed her.

I look around. Dammit. I'm not very good at this teleporting stuff. I can see the lights of Vegas off in the distance, and when I look up at the stars and twirl, I can tell that I'm west of there, but other than that I have no idea where we are.

Selia walks up to me, still whining about her scratched legs, but I ignore her.

Or at least I try to, it's kinda hard to do that when she's slapping me across the face.

My hand goes to my cheek. "What the fuck, Selia?"

She bobs her head up and down, like this satisfies her or something. "That's what you get for slapping me back at Subjack's place, you spoiled rotten little bitch! How dare you take me away like that. I'm half-fucking-naked, you stupid piece of shit!"

Whoa. Selia is pissed. I've never seen her pissed.

"Shit, Sel. Sorry, we just need to get a move on, ya know. We only have—"

"*We* don't need to be doing anything, Junco. I'm tired of this shit. What the hell are you doing? You're going to ruin everything! Ashur and Tier are not the enemy."

I just stare at her raging face and then absently scratch my head.

She turns and walks off, stubs her toe on a rock, then kicks at something that scurries across her foot. "I'm probably gonna get bit by a black widow or something and it's going to be all your fault, Junco…"

Her voice trails off as she makes her way through the scattered shrubs and cactus.

I have definitely crossed Selia's line.

What choice do I have? I follow her. "Stop, Sel. Just stop. I'm sorry, OK?"

Selia spins around, walks towards me, and then slams her hand into my chest. I fall backwards on my ass and watch her lose control with slight amusement.

I tuck that smile down quick because Selia. Is. Pissed.

"I'm glad you think this is all funny." She stops her tirade for a few seconds to look around, finds the city lights, and I watch the wheels turn in her head as she calculates the distance from Vegas. Far. We're far and she knows it. "That's perfect," she seethes down at me as she turns back. "Just perfect. We're hours away, I bet. Now I have to sit out here in the fucking desert, freezing my ass off, and wait for Ashur to come find us. What the fuck?"

I shrug. "I can take us back, no biggie, Selia. I can—"

"Uh, yeah. No thanks. You suck at porting, you know that? Suck. I thought Ashur's first ports were rough, but you! You suck!"

I scramble to my feet and huff out some air. This is not going well. I'm just about to try and smooth things over when Selia spots a dust cloud approaching from the east.

"Oh, thank God. That was quick." She starts walking towards the vehicle racing towards us waving her arms, then calls back to me, "You can stay out here being all covert psycho badass Junco if you want, but I'm going back to the hotel and I'm gonna sleep with my boyfriend and have fun, and eat those bigass strawberries dipped in chocolate. Because if the world is gonna end next week, I'm going out with the one I love. So you just—"

"Next week?" That's a little soon for me, but Selia is not listening. She's still talking about her romantic night with Ashur and flapping her arms around wildly, as if the truck racing towards us doesn't already know we're here.

The vehicle emerges from the thick cloud of dust, but something seems off so I crank up my enhanced vision.

There's not just one truck, it's a whole shitload of them.

"Oh, shit! That's not Ashur, Selia! That's the fucking MR Defenses!"

She whirls around, her mouth half open and ready to speak, when the bullets start spraying us. I sprint hard, lose my footing in the sand, stumble and recover, and then reach out to tap her a fraction of a second too late. Her chest is riddled with holes as we move through timespace.

We crash into the desert again, but this time the blood squirts out of her and splatters my face as we fall into a heap in the scrub. Before I can even think about her condition the bullets are spraying again and I am forced to tap and port. We crash a third time, but this time I fall on top of her and her screams come out as gurgles as the blood bubbles up through her mouth. We're in a grocery store parking lot in Vegas and the high-noon lunch shoppers are screaming. A stream of plasma reaches out to slap my arm as I tap her once more and then I keep us in the tunnel of time for a little longer, try and point us somewhere and figure out a direction, and then finally, after several long seconds, I open us back up to the world.

It's night again.

Selia is shaking uncontrollably.

Oh, holy fuck. I just dragged her through time wounded and I don't even have wings to heal her.

"Selia?" I slap her like I slapped Gideon that night Inanna stole me. I panic and look around for Inanna now. Is this a trick? My breath is coming in fits as I slap Selia again. "Selia! Answer me!" Her eyes flutter and I swallow down the dread. *No, please, shit! I need help! I need help! Do not die on me, Sel. Please.*

The flash of light reminds me of Inanna one more time and I let out an involuntary whimper as it fades. I strain to see what horrible being will be there to take me away and torture me in return for saving this friend.

Caleb stands above me, the shine from the moon backlighting him and covering his face in shadows. He sighs, like Selia isn't bleeding all over me and in the process of dying.

I swallow and wait for his demand, but he picks her up with a gentleness I never imagined and disappears, leaving me alone out here in the desert.

I pace the desert in the dying light of dusk, racking my brain for what to do next. I'm not stuck, I mean I could teleport somewhere. I might not be able to get to somewhere specific, but I won't die out here.

This makes me let out an insane laugh.

As if.

As if I could die anyway. If what Lucan said is true, then who cares if I'm stuck out here. Who cares? No one, that's who. Because I'm pretty damn sure I was the last one to figure out that being what I am now means you can't die. No wonder everyone treats me different. I don't need help anymore.

I really truly am alone.

I check the ground for desert crawly things and take a seat, leaning up against a red rock. I tilt my head up to see the stars, but it's not dark enough to see anything.

Fuck, Junco. Selia might be dead.

I shake my head. No. That's not gonna happen. If Selia was meant to die, then that Caleb guy wouldn't have come to take her away.

That makes no sense.

Neither does arguing with myself.

My mind wanders as I wait for the darkness. I need the darkness tonight. I need these stars. I need something, anything that will connect me to what's going on down here on Earth, because if I want to be completely honest, I feel like one of those people in Ashur's horror screens.

Only I'm not the girl, I'm the monster.

And Ashur is gonna kill me.

Kill me.

I don't see any way out of a fight with him. He's violent to begin with and I just snatched his girlfriend away and got her sprayed with bullets.

He's gonna kick my ass.

I stare up at the sky, watching the light melt away one fraction at a time.

And remember.

Chapter Thirty-Eight

I wake up in my bed at school, the nightmare of the mutant baby girl still haunting me.

"Hey! There you are! I thought you'd sleep all day! How can you sleep in today, Juncs? It's graduation!"

The terror fades so fast I almost get dizzy. "What? It's not graduation. It's only May tenth." Yeah, I left to do that job for Hando on the ninth then I was flown back to the Stag that night, now it's the next morning. Gideon is—

Gid is what? I can't remember. Something about Gideon. Something…

"Shit, Junco, you need some coffee." Aren thrusts a cup into my hands and I take it, but do not drink. I don't drink coffee.

I look up at him and he smiles, but it's not a real smile. It says, Drink the fucking coffee and I'll tell you about it later.

I put it to my lips and force a long guzzle. He relaxes. "OK, let's get ready. You have your speech written?"

"What?"

"Oh, here it is." He pulls out a notebook and hands it over, flipping the cover open to show me the speech. The title is written out in longhand that looks a lot like Aren's and states Towards Destiny. *"Good thing you wrote it early, huh? A little too much partying last night, I'd say."*

I roll out of bed, notice I'm wearing bed shorts I've never seen before, and make my way to the bathroom.

The noise of the shower hides my gasp as I study myself in the mirror. I look like something ran me over out on the planet pad.

My head hurts all right, but this is no hangover. Who the hell would I have been partying with last night? I don't remember any partying. Aren doesn't even drink. And besides, if this really is graduation day, then we broke up last month. Why is he here anyway?

I peel off the clothes and look at the tags. They are from a high-end fashion store in Peak City. A store I have never, ever in my life, visited. But besides that little inconsistency, my clothes don't have tags. I refuse to wear clothes with tags on them, everyone knows this.

Except of course, the person who dressed me in these bed shorts.

My whole body shivers and I jump into the hot shower to push this shit down.

Graduation day?

Graduation day.

I accept it because I have no choice. I've lost time before, right? This is nothing unusual, just a little lapse in continuity, that's all. No big deal.

I finish, wrap the towel around me, and go back out to my room.

Aren is sitting on the bed waiting, his hands in his lap, not fidgeting. Wringing. He's literally wringing his hands.

He notices my gaze and pulls them apart, only to fiddle with the blankets on the bed.

I look at the door, then back to him. He shakes his head.

"Shit, that'll teach me to party like that again, right? I feel like I've been sleeping on the tarmac all night!"

Both his smile, and his relief, are real. "Yeah, I'll wait outside, OK? We'll walk over to the hall together.

"Yeah, sure. Oh, and Aren?"

He turns. "Huh?"

"Thank you."

He nods at me. "Yeah, sure, Junco. No problem. Everyone needs a babysitter every once in a while and graduation only comes once."

I nod back at him. "Yeah. Graduation is a big deal."

He leaves and I count the shuffling of extra boots on the other side of the door. Then strain to hear the whispers. I stand there, still dripping from my shower, and know with one hundred percent certainty that I barely escaped with my life.

Everyone is at graduation. Even my dad. He's dressed up in his service uniform, his hat straight and his dark glasses on.

I squint at him for a moment trying to place the weird feeling I'm getting.

And then Matthew grabs my arm and leads me to my seat. I squint up at him as well.

"What're you doing?"

"Your seat, Junco. This is your seat." He points to a chair and pushes me a little until I have to sit automatically.

Something is wrong.

I wince as a pain shoots through my head. "Where's James? Where's Michael? Where's…" Where's who?

"Everyone's here, Junco."

"Who the fuck are you?" I blurt.

He leans down, squeezing my shoulder a little too tightly. "Look at me, Junco."

I look.

"Who am I?" he asks.

I shake it off. "Matthew. You're Matthew."

He nods and takes a seat next to me. We are alone in the front row.

I'm the ranking cadet commander, so that makes sense. But Matthew is no one here. He doesn't even belong here. He belongs…

Where?

"Where's…" Where's who? "Someone is missing," I say. I turn abruptly in my chair but Matthew's firm grip has my shoulder.

He leans down into my face. "Behave."

I look up at him again as my father brushes past to take his seat on stage. "You belong at camp."

He laughs at this, but I'm not sure what's funny. "So do you, Junco. So do you. We're going back right after the ceremony, so just relax, read the speech, and we'll be just fine."

I look down at my hands and see the notebook Aren shoved in my hands before he left my room.

"How did I get here?" I don't remember walking over. Everything is so fucked up.

"Aren brought you here. Remember?" Matthew is talking softly now, and not just because he's trying to make sure no one hears him. It's soft in a way I've never heard him be before.

Like he's concerned or something.

"And as soon as this is over we can go home and it'll all be OK."

The name I was searching for suddenly comes to me. "Gideon. Where's Gideon? He was… sick. Or something. I was…"

My dad is introduced and people stand and clap. Matthew pulls me up and elbows me to play along, so I clap.

"I was at camp. In a hospital."

This time his words cut me. "Junco, I will kill you dead right here in this auditorium if you do not comply and behave. Just sit, read that speech word for word when you're called, and we'll both go home alive today. You got it?"

Am I afraid of him? I'm not sure. I don't feel afraid, but he's talking to me like I should be. Should I be?

My dad calls my name and then an usher appears to escort me on stage. Before I can even make a decision to stay or go I am standing at the podium.

Looking down at Matthew.

His mouth is drawn tight across his face, like he's wincing internally.

And I smile.

I know who you are, Matthew. And today just might be a very good day to show you exactly who I am.

That thought leaves as my father clears his throat and I snap back to reality. There are about five thousand people crammed into the auditorium, all there to see their precious children step into adulthood.

I look over at my dad and the feeling is back.

He's wrong. Just wrong.

But then Gideon's voice is in my head. Just play the game, Snowbird. There will be another day to get…

I smile and clear my throat.

"Today," I say into the microphone, "is a very good day." Small chuckles come from the various cadet groups. I look down at my main squadron and nod to them. "The day I've been waiting for my whole life. From the time I was a little girl I've thought of nothing but this day." I stop to add a dramatic pause.

And then the laughing starts. It comes from deep inside me, a place I keep for secrets. A deep, dark place where I hide all the bad things.

Someone has unlocked my dark place.

Matthew's eyes go wide and before I even know what's happening I'm flying through the air at him. I tuck and roll when I hit the perfectly polished hardwood floor, and pop back up, reaching for my weapon.

My hand comes back empty and I have a second to see Matthew laugh before he attacks. His arm chops me across the neck and I go flying backward. The crowd is screaming now, chairs are being pushed aside, my dad is yelling and hands are pulling me. At first they don't know which way they want me to go and for a few fractions I figure they're gonna rip my arms right from their sockets.

My words come out in a scream and no matter how many times that impostor who thinks he is my father hits me across the face, the words just keep coming.

"I'm gonna kill you motherfuckers! I'm gonna kill you all!"

I'm screaming it all the way out of the auditorium, their fingers dig into my upper arms with such force there is no way in hell I'm getting away. Someone is trying to slap some gag tape over my mouth but I shake my head with wild abandon until more hands are there to hold me still.

They force me down to the ground and step on the back of my neck, boots pushing me into the floor so hard I worry that they'll crack my front teeth before I can manage to turn my face to the side.

A sharp pain in my neck is the last thing I feel. But the words echo as they follow me into the darkness. "She's insane."

Chapter Thirty-Nine

I am completely immobilized and in the dark.

"Open your eyes, Junco."

They are open, *I think I say, but I can't hear my voice.*

"Open your eyes."

I try, I really do, but they are heavy so I just give up and go back to the dark place. I love the dark place. It's madness.

The slap brings me back. "I said open your Goddamn eyes!"

They open.

My father is standing over me and the rage in his expression briefly shocks me into full compliance mode. "Yes, sir," I say.

He backs off and smiles. Then lets out a long breath of air. "Welcome back. How do you feel?"

How do I feel?

I smile back at him. "Like a motherfucking truck just ran me over."

He smacks me again, but I just smile.

"Like a motherfucking truck just ran me over!" *I scream. The maniacal laugh bursts forth as my father walks away towards the door, but he's not getting away that easy. "You're not him,"* I *snarl. "You're not him! My father would never use that word!"*

He doesn't turn back, just thumbs his biometrics on the doorknob, waits for the lights to flash green, and walks out.

I don't struggle or even try to shift position. If there's a weakness in the bindings, you don't want to give it away. They're watching closely right now so there's no point in trying.

Just wait, Junco. *HOUSE's voice in my head brings me back from the edge.* You know what to do. You've been caught before and you made it out that time.

Right. Gideon came and got me, though.

Gideon might come get you this time, too.

No, he's not coming, HOUSE. He's gone.

He's here, Junco. He's here. Just stay calm and wait.

I draw in a breath through my teeth as my head throbs. What did they give me?

A MEDOXI cocktail, they're getting ready for erasure.

Oh, God, no. They can't! I'm too old! They can't!

They already did, Junco. You missed a whole month of school, James brought you back and—

Oh, shit! Where's James?

Silence in my mind from her.

HOUSE? Where is he?

They have him locked away. He's not doing well, not well at all.

Oh, fuck. Do they know what I've been doing?

Yes, they know of the Hando Corporation and the Texican jobs, but not the first one.

I breathe a small sigh of relief at that. I have one last secret.

They're going to deliver another drug, Junco. Not erasure yet, they think they'll kill you if they do that again, especially so soon after the last one.

Especially since erasing anyone older than twelve is totally off-label use, I don't add.

It's supposed to have similar effects, but with less psychological damage. They still need you and Gideon needs you too, so even though this cocktail will not work, you must be compliant when you wake up next, do you understand?

Will you still be here? When I wake up?

No, you'll be alone. Your father—

He's not my father!

Commander Coot is going back tonight and I have to piggy-back in the flier or someone will notice I'm not running things back home. If they call down to my engineers to see if I'm sick, they might figure out what we've been doing all these years.

What have we been doing? I'm not even sure.

It's OK, I'll remind you when we're ready. They're coming now, be good and be careful.

And then the door clicks and her presence in my head disappears as the doctors enter.

My eyes track them but I stay silent like HOUSE suggested. She's got a far better grip on what's going on than I do, might as well listen to her for once. If you can't trust your AI to take care of you— well, who else is there?

The doctor is not someone I recognize, but my memories cannot be trusted if they've erased me recently. It took me years to remember stuff after the last time. And that's the rub with this procedure, you never lose them forever. If they could make memories go away completely then things would turn out better. But that shit always wears off. The mind finds a way. The drugs might fry the connections, but the brain rebuilds them every single time.

Sometimes, if the patient is very young, you can direct the regrowth so that when the memories do come back, they are not as frightening. They did that to me when I was eight. Those memories came back. The ones with the lions and the test where I was supposed to kill them.

That hurts a little even now when I think of it. I can feel my fingernails lifting up from my skin as I frantically climbed, higher and higher, until the pursuing lion could not come after me.

It was heavy and I was small and light. I climbed so high I was swaying in the wind. It was a nice rhythm and it reminded me of riding.

When you're young, they can regrow the connections in a way that lessens the fear. And that worked too, that first time worked because I don't fear that memory as much as the next one. I feel rage instead. Rage against these heartless monsters who would do that to a little kid.

My dad was furious when they had to finally call him and get permission to end the test, drive a cherry-picker out into the wilderness, and pluck me from that branch.

I was a mess, all soaked with urine and shit, no water for days, no food, barely alive, really. I watched him beat the shit out of Matthew as I sat in his Jeep wrapped in a blanket and an IV sticking out of my arm.

I didn't cry or scream or do anything. I just sat. In silence. For months. I couldn't go back to weekday school that whole year. They locked me in my room and had doctors come talk to me.

But in the end it was determined that I was just broken. That experience was more than I could handle emotionally and I had simply shut down.

The erasure probably did save me that time. It was the only option.

But the next time was after Gideon left.

I told anyone who'd listen that I was an RR secret weapon, that I killed people for the government. My dad warned me after the first time that Matthew would kill me, but I did it anyway. I just couldn't stop myself, even when I tried, the words would just spill out, like I'd been hypnotized to say them or something.

Erasure definitely saved my life that time. No way around it. I was lucky.

And everything was pretty good after that. I went to cadets, did a few odd jobs, saw Gideon a few times when he was home from doing whatever he did for them, and life was pretty normal.

But things are anything but normal now. And what's normal, anyway? Sanity, maybe. Or insanity. It's hard to tell, really, because I always feel so much better when I'm insane. It's such a relief to be able to let go and not have to lie or pretend. Because normal is definitely not what I am.

The biometrics flash on the door.

I have to make a choice—either embrace sanity or the dark place that drives me to be crazy.

The handle on the door turns slowly and I wonder for a fraction which one of those monsters will be the one to come through.

Sanity is so much harder than crazy. It takes so much effort. And I'm just too tired.

The door opens and James is pushed through. He stumbles and falls on the floor. The sharp crack of his teeth against the hard tile makes me cringe internally.

But I show nothing.

They kick him, but he's so far beyond caring that not even a grunt of pain comes forth from his mouth that is now full of blood. I close my eyes as they undo the bindings and pull me into a sitting position.

And I make my decision.

The commander who looks like my father is barking orders at me but I can't even hear him. I look blankly at my friend on the floor and know this is his day to die.

And I'm his killer.

That's the plan, it's so obvious.

The SEAR knife is thrust into my hand and I look down at it. It's not my SEAR knife, not the knife that's coded for me and all my handlers.

They pull me off the bed and drag me over to James, not even waiting for my feet to find the floor.

I flick the knife on and they all back away, most leave through the door, but the man who is not my father stays, cautioning me that he is coded for this knife.

I know what he wants so I complete the task before he even gives the order. A single flick of the knife across the top layer of skin on James' neck, just below the right ear.

The little sizzle leads to a tiny tendril of smoke as my friend writhes in pain on the floor.

It's so much easier to just do what you're told and besides, this is my one true purpose and you can't be half a killer. You just gotta embrace your inner evil, that's what I think.

Just be who you were born to be.

Chapter Forty

My mind wanders back after the memory fades.

The pinpricks of light from the bright stars Deneb, Vega and Altair appear suddenly, like they just popped into existence, but I know this isn't true. I wasn't paying attention and now look, the brightest stars are not only out, they're already well on their way towards setting on the horizon.

These three stars make up the summer triangle asterism as it connects the constellations Cygnus, Lyra, and Aquila. Both Cygnus the swan and Aquila the eagle span the edges of either side of the Milky Way, their wings open, necks stretched as they reach out for each other. Lyra is on the Cygnus side of the galactic haze, playing music so the two lovers can find each other again.

If that were the end of it, it'd be a great story. Unfortunately the story is never complete unless there's some tragedy to fuck it all up. Because the lovers in this tale will never meet. In front of each bird is a wall.

This is one of the stories Gideon used to tell me. What purpose it served in the grand scheme of keeping Junco compliant and subdued, I have no idea, but he told it often. In Cygnus' case, the wall is the little fox Vulpecula who stands in front of her—ready to eat the swan if she tries to cross the river of stars.

As for Aquila, well, he doesn't fare much better because he's got Sagitta in front of him. The arrow of Jupiter, ready to stab him in the heart and break his love for Cygnus if he tries to save the swan princess.

So they float there out in the deep dark, helpless and miserable—separated by a mere river of stars—for eternity. With no hope of ever being together.

Great story, huh?

When I got older I started asking Gid questions like *Why doesn't Cygnus just kill that stupid fox and why doesn't Aquila just snap that arrow in two with his raptor beak?* And seriously—a fox is sorta small compared to a swan. If you've never been batted down with their massive wings you might think they're helpless. I mean, they're not fast or anything, but I have been mauled by a swan before, so I know what they're capable of. That year my dad took me to the British Museum for birthday week we were walking along the Thames and I got it in my head that I was gonna catch one of those suckers to see what kind of game they had.

It didn't end well for the swan, I can tell you that. It was almost an international affair because apparently all the swans on the river are the property of the Queen.

And I knew for a fact, even back when I was little, that a raptor beak could take that arrow out no problem because Gideon had a hawk all growing up and normally I was not allowed in the mew or to fuck with her in any way, but again, I just wanted to see if the arrow was strong enough to stop her.

That one did not end well for me. I couldn't just kill Gid's bird.

When I got a little older he got tired of the questions and changed the ending and put a happy spin on it. Some bullshit about magpies building a bridge one day a year so the lovers could reunite. Which is stupid because that's just a ripoff of the Chinese Qixi festival myth. He forgot I studied Chinese mythology in fourth year, I guess.

Tonight's sky is not that much different from the one Tier and I looked at years ago at my cabin. Not really. The months are different—that was November and this is still September. So everything is slightly shifted, but we're still up there.

He thought I should be Cygnus and I thought he should be Aquila.

It's a very bad omen.

Me, the swan, desperately flying towards Tier, the eagle. But we can't ever quite cross that river of stars that separates us.

And if what Lucan said was true, then we never will. Because Tier will die and I'll be left here all alone. Probably dissipated out into the nether for eternity with my luck.

I huff out a sad breath of air and direct my attention north to the Big Dipper and find Alcor. It's sitting pretty, right there in the second bend of the ladle's handle. I've always been able to see Alcor, which is actually a binary system that sits right next to its twin, another system called Mizar.

They call the two of them together the horse and rider, and if that little detail isn't enough to make you want to shut the book on mythology altogether, then how about this one?

Alcor is also known as the Lost Pleiad, of the infamous Pleiades Cluster, aka the Seven Siblings.

Gideon. He's the missing Sibling. He's Alcor.

He is the star I can see.

In ancient times it was a test of good vision to be able to distinguish between Alcor and Mizar and not blur them into one dot of light, so when Lucan and the guys said I can see Alcor but miss the full moon, it was a joke.

Junco, it means you miss the obvious so often it makes me cringe.

That's what he said to me that night I discovered he's the Devil.

Except I don't believe he's the Devil, even though my dad certainly does. And I don't believe Caleb works for God. Lucan's not the Devil, but there's no God here, either.

I don't know what other people see when they look up at the night sky, but I see a revolving story. My mind has been looking up at these patterns for so long, has been schooled in their history and mystery for so long, that I see it all with very little effort. When I look up I don't see points of light—I see every character, I see the story behind the stars, I see the cyclic movie made by the rotating Earth.

I see the swan, I see the eagle, I see the walls they built, I see the hunter facing down the charging bull, the Gemini twine, the scorpion chasing Orion, Pegasus and Cassiopeia, and Andromeda.

I see them all.

Whenever I had a good friend growing up, whether it was Gideon or Aren or John Hando, or even the various boys I dated on and off at school, they always asked me the same thing.

Why do you always look up?

When I was a very small child I had a compulsion to look up, but I was not supposed to talk about that. So I started telling Gid this excuse of seeing them as characters in a story. And then when I got older and other kids at cadets would start asking I used to just shrug, you know, not answer. But then Charlie said all that stuff about the starshine lighting up my night, and then it almost felt like that really *was* the reason.

It was the light, all right. At least part of it was. But I didn't need it to see or calm me down in the dark, although I admit, it's helpful, that reasoning.

I haven't really thought about the stars very much since that night with Ashur back on Amelia. But here they are again. They always come back because they are constant. They never leave me, they make their celestial orbit and move through the night, but they are one hundred percent predictable. If I want to know where Vega will rise a thousand years from now I could find out. And barring some major galaxy-wide disaster, she'd show up, just as predicted.

And while Charlie's reason got me through some minor insanity issues, that was never the reason why I always look up. I like to find my friends in the stars because that's the only thing that connects us.

Starlight.

It's the only thing that touches every thing in the universe.

Well, that and because light breaks all the rules. No matter how hard we try, we cannot justify the unjustifiable nature of light. Light just *gets* to break the rules. The little photons travel outward in waves, and then, when we start paying too much attention to light, those photons change. They switch and start acting like particles.

Light is a mystery. Light has duality. That's the word they always used in physics class. Duality.

I always look up at the night sky because the entire galaxy is blanketed with stars, and if you go out further, to the billions of other galaxies out there, they're all blanketed with stars, too. And each one of those trillions upon trillions of stars emits a gazillion bazillion photons that spew out as light.

Light comes from the stars and I am forever looking up and drawing those imaginary lines that make up the constellations because light is the only thing that proves we *can* be two things at once.

I need to hold on to that because light is my proof that I am Junco as well as not-Junco and if Caleb really was God's Messenger, he could've just said that to me. He could've just said—*Look at the light, Junco. The proof is right there. It's everywhere around you. Light can be two things at once and that breaks all the laws of the Universe. That's your miracle. Light.*

And I would've been like—*Yup! That's right! I'm good now, glad you guys finally decided to show up.*

It's such a simple answer but he didn't even have it. The proof is right there, but he missed it.

God's Messenger should not miss the proof, and that's how I know Caleb is not part of God. He might talk a good talk, but he's not what he says he is because God's Messenger would know that light was special. He'd know about the duality and he'd know the significance behind that and my proof would've come right off his tongue, would've been the answer for thousands of years, each time someone or something had questions and wanted proof, light would be the answer and would come out with practiced clarity.

And most of all, if Caleb really was God's Messenger, he would've known that the stars always gave me comfort and he'd know *both* reasons why. He'd know that I look to the light because that means I won't have to be this monster forever. I can have duality too. If light can be two things at once, well, then so can I. I can be something more than Junco when I'm done doing what I need to do. Tier can be more than just Tier and Gideon can be what he wants to be, too. We don't have to be these monsters forever.

And not only that, if Caleb was God's messenger and he'd paid any attention to me at all, he'd know that the stars calm me for another very special reason. One I'm not quite ready to talk about, but if he was God's Messenger, then he'd already know that.

If God was real, God would know because I went to church every week. I prayed the same prayer every time. How could he *not* know?

It's disappointing, really.

I sigh to myself in the desert night.

Because if Caleb doesn't have my proof and he *is* part of God, then they were never paying attention to me in the first place. I am nobody to them. Just another chrome-steel sphere sliding down the Embryon playfield in this giant game of multi-ball.

Chapter Forty-One

Tier is standing in front of me before I even have a chance to accept the reality that he is there.

"I can't do this anymore, Junco. Yer fucking up the whole mission!"

I stare forward, past his legs, and don't even bother to look up. "You're wrong, Tier. My mission is still very much on track."

"What mission?" He rages at me, pulls me up so I'm standing and shakes me by the shoulders. "What mission? I want to know what the hell yer doing!"

I shake my head. "I'm getting ready to finish what they started, Tier." My voice is so calm it's scary. He lets go of my shoulders and turns his back, walks a few paces away, and then spins on his heel.

The green of his eyes is filled with glow. I'm not sure what it means, but I'm guessing hate. Or disgust. Or something to that effect.

I can feel him inside my head, picking through my thoughts. I'd be pissed at this, normally. But I've suspected for a while now, so whatever. He's been reading my mind. I guess he figures addressing that thought is a losing battle. He can deny it and admit he's reading my mind or he can shut up and let me keep thinking about it, accepting it as truth. I might not know a whole lot about him and vice versa, but I do know one thing. Tier and I are having a moment right now, one that might decide our future.

He draws in a long breath between his teeth. "Am I wasting my time, killing humans with tsunamis and building Pillars? Just let me know now, Junco. Because if you're gonna kill off every single living creature next week when the Order gets here, then I'd like to spend my remaining days doing something other than flying around the world trying to save us."

"Us?" I ask as I let out a small snort of disgust. "I have no idea who *us* is, Tier, but your inclusion in that little club is dubious, at best." I turn my back and walk out into the desert.

"Darlin'," he laughs at me, "you have no idea who us and them is, I get it. But when those things get here, you'll know. There is no us and them. We're all us. Even Inanna."

I bristle at her name. How dare he say that name in front of me. How dare he?

He catches my tension and continues, "Inanna is nothing. Lucan is nothing. I am nothing. You are nothing. We are all nothing compared to the things coming to judge us."

"Us?" I ask again. "I think not." I turn so I can see his face as I deliver the words. "You're definitely not one of us because you're not even an Archer. So don't you stand there and talk me up with some we're-all-in-this-together bullshit. I'm not interested."

He swallows so I know this is a sore spot with him. What was it he said on our trip back to Earth? *People don't know us, they don't really like our power and status, and they have a difficult time trusting us. Especially me.*

Now I know why. And shit, can I blame them? I'm having a very hard time trusting him myself right now, and he's the only one besides Gideon I ever handed that out to in the first place. "Those High Order things are gonna come here to Earth, they'll take one look at you and slice you in half or something, right? You're not immortal, so you get to die. That's a fucking blessing as far as I'm concerned. But not me. I get the pleasure of having them dissipate my body into individual particles or *whatever*, then I get to float into oblivion for millions or even billions of years until quantum physics pulls me back together. And from what I've been told, Junco will be long gone before that even comes close to happening. So really, all I have to look forward to is spending the rest of eternity in some insane state of non-existence."

I laugh as I look up at him. "But it's almost funny, ya know? I mean, shit—all this time I've been fighting the insanity and for what? Why? It's the most futile act of resistance ever, because insanity is easy, Tier. It's way too easy. I was born into insanity. The crazy isn't my problem, it's pretending to be sane that fucks it all up. I can do madness, but normal? Now that's something I've never been. Sane? No, I can remember being a very small child and the only thing that kept me going was plotting the deaths of the people around me, at some far distant point in the future."

His expression is unreadable, just blank.

"Do you hear the words that are coming out of my mouth? The only thing that's kept me going since I was a very small child were plans for revenge."

I stop again, but still, he's got nothing for me. Just nothing.

"And that's what I'm doing right now. That's why I left Sargassum, why I got my HOUSE back, why I left with Sera from your quarters, and why I'm still running right now. Because I'm not interested in saving you or anyone else. I'm interested in dying for my revenge." I laugh and shake my head. "And you assholes have even taken *that* away from me because I can't even go out fighting!"

I hate him right now. I hate all of them. The tears well up with the heat in my face and I turn away, forcing them back inside. Pushing them into the dark place.

"I'm done crying. I have no sadness left, only rage. Rage that has been built up over decades of horror. It's the only thing I have, really. And I'm not giving it up for anyone."

He clears his throat and exhales a long breath. "OK. Well, you can do all that if ya want, Junco, but just so you know, Sera was never in my quarters when ya ported out of there. She's got nothing to do with your plan."

"Save it, OK? I'm not interested in any more of your lies."

"Junco, I saw her the instant ya ported. I was looking at her, she was with me at Soli's Pillar. She was helping me calm her down."

"No, that's not what happened. You saw something else, a projected version or something. I have Sera inside me still. She was there, she helped me port, she—"

"No!" His sharp command stops me mid-sentence and I just stare at him. "You're hallucinating. Your Archer morph was unsanctioned and sub-standard. You have to be prepped from birth to become an Archer, Junco. You don't just wake up one day and say, *I think I'll become immortal.* You had no pre-treatment which means you cannot have any post-treatment because you can't do one without the other. Inanna messed with your head, Junco. She made ya crazy, but if you just listen to me, I'll———"

"You'll what? Make it all better? You and your lies about Isten and your judgment about Kush? Fuck you, Tier. I don't need you, you need me! All you've done is lie! And before you open your mouth to say it was for my own good, you look me in the eye and tell me you didn't know that Isten was gonna die back there in Runout."

He looks away and I laugh. "I hate you. I hate all of you, hell, I hate everyone, how about that? It's me and Gid against everyone, how about that? Hurt much?"

"Gideon, of course," he sneers. "That guy who's been selling yer secrets for years, the one who's fucking that clone of a twin you have. He turned her into *you*, Junco! He had Inanna morph her up into some copy of you! Tell me that's normal!"

"I don't know if that's true, you and Ashur say it, but we all know that the words coming out of your mouths are more likely to be lies than anything else!"

"Junco," he continues, "I've got to tell ya, yer off-yer-meds crazy if you think Gideon is on yer side right now. He's selling you out and you don't even have the good sense to see it."

I hold down a chuckle. "Right, You keep telling yourself that, Tier. Whatever it takes to get you through the night. And by the way—how stupid do you think I am?"

He cocks his head to the side slightly.

"You think I don't know you were fucking that first Iliana, too? I mean, come on! You tell her your deepest secrets, secrets that could ruin all of Lucan's plans for—whatever the hell he's doing. Of *course* you were fucking her. Of course you were!"

I see a slight shift in his expression and I hold back the hurt, because if I let it out I will say things I regret.

"Yer careening off the cliff, Junco. And yer gonna take the rest of us with ya."

"You bet I am, Tier. You fucking bet I am. Just consider it my gift to humanity, OK? Because at least all of you will be dead. But me? I'll still be around wondering why the fuck I'm always the one who gets shafted in the end. I wish I could kill you myself, right now!"

"You want to go down this road, Junco?" He knocks me to the ground with one forceful shove and then stands over me, raging. Everything about him is rage. "You want ta fight me?"

I pick myself up and brush the dust off my pants while Tier backs off a few paces.

"I asked you a question."

My silence pisses him off even more, but what can he do? He asked me a question so he either has to wait for my response or make a move. If he makes a move, he's lost ground. If he waits, he hands me the advantage.

I've played this game before.

"I'm not playing, Junco."

"Oh, yes you are. You're playing all right. Because you don't get to tell me off for sleeping with Kush and choosing Gideon and then leave me to find out from Lucan that you *knew Isten was gonna die!*"

His back straightens with my accusation. Which means it's true.

I turn away so he can't see the glaze of tears covering my eyes. "I hate you."

He exhales.

"I hate you. And the whole Isten thing is only the beginning, Tier." The threat of tears is over now, so I turn back. "I mean, that's bad enough, but you're the one who sent me down this path in the first place. You gave me wings and you let her take them away. All of this. Everything that's happening to me is your fault!"

I've stunned him. I can see it. He was not expecting this.

"Why didn't you just kill me? Why? Why did you turn me into this *thing?*"

The muscles twitch in his face as he narrows his eyes at me. His words come out slow and calm. "Why didn't you just kill me? I could say the same thing to you, Junco. Why did you save me?"

I choose to ignore that. "You knew Isten would die, you knew and still, you let me twine with him." I wait for him to give me something but he remains silent so I just keep going. "Everyone in my life has left me. Every single person took off. My mother, my Gideon, my father, my Aren, my Charlie. Each one disappeared just as I got comfortable. Wiped away."

Everything about me aches as the words come out.

"And then you give me this gift. This perfect gift of a man who wants to live in my mind and be with me forever and all he wants in return is for me to do the same. And against my better judgment, I said yes. Because I wanted what he had to give, *so bad*."

He cringes at the words that I pulled straight from his mouth that day on Gideon's terrace.

"And you told me that we had to be together, that this bond we were forming was the secret of a successful mission on Earth."

"Junco—"

"No." I cut him off. "Just don't. OK? Because that mission, in my eyes, was a complete fucking failure! But you guys all got what you wanted, right? You got all my Siblings, you got your perfect gene pool back, you got your *promotion*." The word is dripping with disgust. "You have a lot of nice new powers now, Tier. You get to have them all, right? But you don't have to pay the price, right? That's what everyone was pissed off about back on Amelia. Why the fuck should you get all those motherfucking powers and not have to pay the same price as the rest of us?"

"That's not how it is, Junco."

"That is the most pathetic attempt at a lie I've ever heard. Pathetic!" My scream echoes off the walls of a nearby rock formation. "That's exactly how it is, Tier." I take a deep breath and watch his face. I'm not sure what it's saying, but it's not saying anything I want to know. "And now I'm so far away from being human, so far away from the girl I was born to be, I'll never get back. And I'm gonna stew in this anger and insanity for eternity because I get to be cast out into infinity, blowing in a galactic wind for billions of years until all my pieces miraculously float back together under the goddamn laws of physics!"

"I'm trying my best to stop that, Junco. That's the whole reason we're—"

"Liar!" I let out a small choke of a sob as the tears build again. "You're a liar. You're doing this for Lucan. He's your master, you are the closest thing to a God's piece of property that ever existed. Right, Aquila? That's who you are, right? You're nothing but Jupiter's stupid property."

He waits for me to continue but I'm done for now. I walk back over to my rock and sit down. I'm tired. I'm just so fucking tired.

"Junco, I understand that's how it looks but yer missing the obvious, darlin'."

"Fuck you. If you say that stupid line about Alcor I'll port away and never come back. I'll dissipate myself if I have to hear that stupid analogy one more time. I'm not blind! I see the goddamn full moon!"

His look says I'm insane. I am insane, I've totally lost it. Shit, he might not even know what I'm talking about, I never heard him say that Alcor stuff before. That was Isten and Lucan.

"Isten knew he was gonna die, Juncs. He knew that either way he was not coming back from Earth. And he wanted ya. He begged me for weeks on Earth before I even met you. It was my fault his twine was killed. I let Iliana in, I trusted her so I couldn't say no."

I keep silent and let him talk.

"He said he'd be with you after, that you'd keep him in your head as memories. He told me what it was like to have Tanner, that it was comforting."

I snort at this. "Comforting? No. Painful, it was very fucking painful." I stop and rub my eyes as the hurt comes back. "It hurt. There isn't even a word to describe how bad it hurt, Tier."

He kneels down in front of me, his hands on my shoulders. "But it's better now? You have him and it's better now?"

He's pleading with me to tell him yes, it's better.

"No, I don't have him. So the pain is gone but so are the memories. I have nothing. He's gone! I have nothing!"

"What do ya mean? He can't be gone, where—"

"HOUSE has him, I left Sargassum to go get HOUSE, and well, to see John Hando too, but he's fucking married now and has kids and everything!"

I do cry now, an ugly cry complete with sobs and chokes and gasps for breath. I'm crying for my mistake with Hand in front of Tier. That is so wrong but I can't stop. I've fucked up every single good thing in my life. "I should've never left Dallas that weekend. He took me up to the Sagitta Arrow building to look at the stars. He took me to the stars and even though everything was coming apart, I *didn't* come apart. I was pulled back together that night. He pulled me back together inside that giant building that points to the stars."

I look up but he has no idea what I'm talking about, so I just wipe my eyes and keep going. "He said he'd get me out of the RR and we'd go to the Desert Republic for a while, lie low until his dad smoothed things over with my dad, who was not even my dad by that time, and he said he'd take care of me. And you know what, Tier?"

The sobs come again as Tier waits patiently.

"He would've too. He would never have asked me to save his race or sacrifice my humanity for anyone. He would've hidden me away in some little hole-in-the-wall reservation house and let me get fat and happy with kids." I breathe out. "I made a mistake. I said I'd be back before he could even miss me."

I stop to swallow down the pain and his green eyes search me.

"Did ya go back, Juncs?"

"No, I never even got a chance to leave properly. I was on the roof, ready to take my shot, and then Hando called and said we had to abort and—"

"Wait, what?"

"I was doing a job, ready to take my shot and go home with him forever—"

Tier looks so confused it makes me stop. I take a giant sniff and then continue. "I was a hit-girl for the Texican mafia my entire senior year of cadets," I say, as if that explains everything. "Hand is the company heir."

He bellows out laughter.

"What?"

"You're pining over a gangster? You're talking shit to me for being Lucan's Angel of Death, yet you were gonna settle down and get fat and happy with a fucking common criminal?"

"Don't. Just don't."

"Just don't? Fuck that! I'm tired of tiptoeing around yer temper tantrums, ya got it? That's over. I'm gonna speak my mind from now on. Yer so tough, right? You can take it, right? So fuck you and your *don't*."

Well, fuck him right back because I fling myself right out of this conversation.

Chapter Forty-Two

Something goes wrong and I feel a jerk, like someone is pulling me back through the tunnel. I gasp and try to break free, seeking a way out of the time shift, and then I crash into the ground once again.

Only this time I am not alone.

"You think I'd what, Junco? Just let you fuck up everything I've build over the past two years because you have some goddess complex?"

Ashur grabs my arm with some kind of super-strength and pulls me to my feet. The blood vessels under my skin are immediately crushed and I know there's a massive bruise on my upper arm from his fingers.

"Where the fuck is Selia?" His growl comes out so low the adrenaline bursts into my bloodstream with the threat. He shakes me and his grip takes on a whole new level of pain.

"Let go!" I squirm but he's not letting go—he's very much not letting go.

"I'm going to ask you one more time, Junco, and then I'm gonna beat the shit out of you if ya don't answer. You're immortal, but you're not immune to pain."

I want, seriously want, to talk back to him right now. But he scares me.

"Where is Selia?"

I swallow and give him his answer. "That Caleb guy took her."

I'm crashing into the ground before I can even register he's moved. Something tells me that all those fights we had before were nothing but play to him. He stands over me, his legs straddling my body, and his words come out as a hiss. "Took her where? For what purpose?"

Oh. Fuck.

"I'm not gonna ask you again, Junco. Took her where and for what purpose?"

"Ashur, I just need—" I try to get up, but he kicks me back to the ground. "I just need you to be reasonable and listen to me, OK?"

I swallow hard again as he waits, silent.

"We left the hotel and ported—"

"You mean you stole her from the hotel and ported, right?"

"Right." I nod. I'm not gonna argue with him. "We ported to the desert and she was all pissed off telling me how she wanted to spend the night with you, and—"

"That won't work on me, Junco. Either you get to the point right now," he pulls me up in a rush of pain, "or I'll show you how far over my line you've crossed."

"And then the MR troops came, or someone came, I'm not clear on that. They had—"

He shakes me to stop my babbling.

"And she only saw the cloud of dust and she thought it was you." I stop and take a deep breath. "But it wasn't you."

His face drops the anger and picks up panic. "What. The. Fuck. Happened?"

"Ashur, I tried, I just want you to know I tried—"

He smacks me and I go flying.

"I asked you a question, now answer me. What happened to her?"

"They shot her, Ash. They sprayed her with rapid-fire! I tried to get her away but I tripped and by the time we ported she was—"

"What! She was what?"

I gulp some air. "Filled with holes. And so we ported again, twice, until we got to the desert again, and then I was sitting there praying for help and that Caleb guy appeared. He didn't say anything, he just took her and left me there."

His fist is flying at me and I frantically port to get away, but his fingers find my arm just before we go into the timeshift, and again, I am slammed into the ground with the force of his anger.

Ashur is breathing hard. "You suck at porting, Junco. I can find you no matter where you go. And if you think for a minute I'm not gonna square up this debt you have with me, you're mistaken."

I scramble to my feet as his razors come out and slash through the back of my Aves shirt, but I slip past and run.

It only takes a few fractions before he's got me by the ankles and I go down again. I squirm and wriggle to loosen his grip, I try out every single move I know on him, but he knows me too well. Better than I know myself, probably. I end up pinned to the desert floor, my head being painfully smashed against a small rock that I had the bad luck to land on.

He leans down into me, the sweat dripping off his face in the desert heat, his chest expanding and contracting with anger and effort, and I lie still.

"Ashur, please. I know it's my—" I stop when I see his fist coming at my face and brace for the impact.

It never connects. Instead Ashur is flying up in the air and Lucan is pulling me to my feet.

"Are you all right?" he asks, leaning down to look me over.

I nod, but my whole body is trembling. "Ashur was gonna kill me."

Lucan only nods. "Yes, and if you could die, you'd deserve that to be quite honest. But since you can't die," he stops to scowl at Ashur who is now next to him, still angry and breathing hard, "and we need you for the Seventh Pillar, it is an extremely stupid plan to dismember you today."

"Lucan," Ash starts.

But he's cut off with a wave of Lucan's hand. "Not now, Ashur. Selia has been delivered back to the ship. I suggest you concern yourself with that and leave this to Tier and me."

Ashur disappears as I look to my right and Tier is standing next to me. Lucan demands my attention with a shake of my arm. "A private moment, Tier. Please."

Tier doesn't even look at me, just throws his hands up and walks off. I watch him from behind, his shoulders slightly slumped, his head shaking, like he's talking himself out of something.

"Junco, look at me."

I force myself to look him in the eyes. They are red again, glowing, or maybe churning is a better word to describe what's happening to the color in his eyes. Churning like lava. Like Hell.

"What will it take to make you understand?"

I snort out a laugh. "What kind of question is that? I mean, a little bit of truth, obviously. Why don't you just admit that you've been using me, Lucan. Just fucking say it already. Because it's so painful—" I stop and choke on the word for a few seconds before I can pull myself back under control. When I'm ready to talk again I only have a weak little whisper. "It's so painful to know that that you're lying to me. That you all hate me, see me as this insane girl that you have to keep around so you can save yourselves."

I turn back to Tier. He's stopped walking and is facing us again. He waits with me. To see what Lucan will say to that.

What comes out is unexpected. "Did you know that I love sunsets, Junco?"

"What?"

"Sunsets, Earth sunsets specifically," he clarifies. "I love sunsets but I had to spend thousands of years without ever seeing a single one. Coming back to Earth and seeing my first sunset again after all that time… well, it was something fantastical. I felt alive again. Not the dead thing I turned into. The stoic leader of the avians. Not the Archer of Fledge or Aves."

My eyes are still fixed on Tier as I think about this.

"Look at me, Junco. Not just glance at me, but look at me. See me for what I am right now."

I turn back to him, studying his ancient armor. The black interlocking scales remind me of a reptile's skin. I've touched it before, of course, and the smoothness is like a bucket of paint or a vat full of melted chocolate. Something that begs to be touched. I reach out. They are so soft. I'm not sure how something that's supposed to protect you can be so soft.

Lucan stretches out his bat wing and it curls around his arm a little. I touch that now too and it makes him shiver.

"Sorry," I say, looking up at his eyes again. "I see you, Lucan."

"I'm sorry as well. I know we've been dishonest."

"Pffft. Dishonest? Please."

"We've lied, kept things from you on purpose, misled you. We're guilty. And I'm sorry, I have no excuse except to say that I don't understand you at all. I misjudged you at every turn. It's all my fault. If I could go back, I'd do it all differently. Which should prove to you that I never saw these things you accuse me of. I didn't, Junco. We all knew Isten would die, but that it would affect you like this? No. We never saw that, we do not understand you. Not what you really are, not where you come from, not why you were made. The only thing I understand about you, Junco, is that you're capable of a great number of things. You are very powerful, you are a force. So it just never occurred to me that it would be so easy to break you. I did not see your end in Deliverance. Or how Kush would die. I knew Kush wouldn't make it out of the fight, but I never saw that end." He stops to search my face for some sort of comprehension, but I just swallow and look away. "You must believe me. Do you believe me?"

Do I believe him? No, not really.

"I'm not the Devil, Junco."

"I know that, Lucan. I really don't think you're the Devil but I'm not sure why you care what I think of you."

"I care because I see myself in you. I see your potential, your possibilities, and I'm worried that I'm sending you down the wrong path."

"What's this got to do with sunsets?"

He laughs softly and I look back over to Tier. He waits with me, still and quiet.

"When we had our first honest conversation, the one outside Fledge after you killed those boys, you lamented over the stars. Do you remember?"

I nod. "Yeah. I remember."

"And I thought about how I missed the sunsets on Earth. That's why I took you to see the stars that night. I wanted you to know that I understand. I really do. I have been you, Junco. I was forced to make choices when I was young and I stand by those choices to this day. I regret the price I've paid. I regret that Tier has to complete a job he wants nothing to do with. I regret that you are my saving grace and you'd rather be anything but that. I have a lot of regrets, but I am not unhappy. I am, in fact, very happy, all things considered. I never thought the Seven would be like you. I've imagined it millions of ways, but none of them even came close to what I got. I'm so glad you're my Seven, Junco. And I want you to know, above all else, that you're doing a pretty good job."

I laugh again. "Oh, crap. I hope that's not true, Lucan. I suck." It was meant to come out like a joke but the tears steal away any hope of pulling that off and suddenly they are streaming down my face.

"I know it hurts, Junco. I know you're tired. I know you have doubts and you think you're doing it all wrong. But you're doing just fine. Not perfect, but I can't expect you to comply with everything. That's not who you are. You can do it your way. I'm OK with that. I believe in you, Junco, so I will step back and stop interfering with your goals. I trust you. I know in my heart you will do the right thing in the end."

I sniff as I wipe the tears away. "I wouldn't count on that, Lucan. Seriously." When I look up at his face he is smiling. "What?"

He just shakes his head and motions for Tier to join us, which he does, and then he continues as Tier and I both wait it out together. "I understand your need for revenge, Junco. But you might be surprised to hear that I've taken care of all of that for you. We got the Vegas lab this morning. The lab where they held you."

"You have? You did?"

"Your killing is over now, Junco. I got them all, except for a few technicians in the lab that we kept for questioning. And Inanna, of course. I have no power to kill her." He stops and stares hard at me after this revelation.

"What?" I ask again. I hate it when they stop short in their explanations.

He looks like there are words on the tip of his tongue but he can't manage to get them out. He stares into my eyes for a few fractions that to me seem to stretch out like years. "It takes a certain skill level to kill a member of the High Order. I could not, for instance, kill you now that Inanna has changed you. But you could kill me. With your SEAR knife. If you had it."

My gulp is audible, I'm sure of it. He doesn't know I have one? I look over at Tier for some kind of confirmation.

"It's true, Juncs. The SEAR knife, the knife coded for you specifically, is the only thing that can dissipate Lucan."

"I am protected, you see. By..." Lucan stops here, maybe wanting to take it back, or maybe to think up a lie, or maybe just to find the right words to say it. "By another party to this whole mess. The High Order did not agree with the actions I took against the semi-sentient beings that used to populate this planet. But this other party, my counter-part, He did, so I was protected. I flooded the Earth using many, many Pillars and wiped out the pre-humans and then made a new race. I created the code that messed up the High Order genetics and corrupted the avian genome along with them. I was given that power and I used it."

"Oh," is all I can manage to say.

"But everything has a weakness, Junco. And you and your knife are mine. You could kill me right now if you had it. Just slice me in half and I'd never get back up. I'd be flung out into the Universe for a very long time. Eternity, for lack of a better word. Of course, I would fight you and I'd win. I'm much stronger. That's why Inanna won when she took you. She never gave you a chance to use the knife, did she?"

That day creeps back into my brain, the shock of her being in front of me, so close. The revelation that I was High Order too and she wanted me to go with her and wait for them to come back. But Lucan was there as well. And I chose Lucan instead of her. "No, I tried, I was gonna cut her head off. But she just raised her palm at me and I went flying backwards."

"She is strong, but she is also weak, Junco. She is not protected, she is just lucky. You are her weakness. Her daughter. Do you understand?"

I nod.

He stares at me. Hard. Like he's not quite sure if I understand or not. I'm not quite sure either, to be honest. In fact, I've probably got it all fucked up in my head, but I nod again. With more conviction this time. This makes him smile and turn to Tier.

"Take her to the Vegas lab, show her everything."

"Lucan, I'm not sure that's a good idea. She doesn't need that—"

"Raubtier, this is not a request. Take her now and show her everything."

And then he is gone.

Tier stares down at me and frowns. A deep frown that stretches across his whole face.

"What?" I ask. "What are you guys hiding now?"

"Things better left hidden, Junco. That's all." He reaches out for me, not a shoulder tap as per Lucan's usual method of transporting with me, but actually draws me into his chest. He holds me that way for several uncomfortable seconds, and then we're in the timeshift.

And this is not like any kind of timeshift I've ever experienced. Tier presses himself up against me and we are one as we travel. It's not like taking a step, it's not quick and clean. It's long and filled with heat and heartbeats. His heartbeat thumps against my body. The rhythm of it fills my head, it relaxes me and I press my cheek against his chest and wrap my arms under his wings and back around to his shoulders. We stay that way, entwined in each other's arms, until we are out of the tunnel and back to reality.

"What was that?" I ask, looking up at the soft green of his eyes.

"That, Junco, is how I feel about you."

Chapter Forty-Three

We are definitely in a lab all right. It's filled with avians, bustling about and doing things that look suspiciously like logging a crime scene to me. Cataloging things, analyzing things. It has an atmosphere that says they're trying to put all the pieces of this little puzzle back together.

Annun is over on the far end of the expansive room, past the many genetics stations that are neatly lined up down the center of the lab. He spots me watching him and raises a hand in a half wave, then turns and walks into a room that through the small crack in the door I see has a crowd of white-coated scientists in it.

The leftover technicians.

"This is where Inanna made her mutants and clones, Junco. This is where Irin lived."

"Oh crap." I look around with renewed interest.

"Follow me. Lucan wants you to see everything, so that's what we'll do."

I hesitate, wondering if I really need to see everything. "Maybe—"

Tier takes my hand, squeezes until I look up at him, and the rest of my objection is lost. "You'll be OK, I promise."

A long breath of air escapes before I can stop it. I'm nervous.

"And by the way, Snowbird?"

My eyes are searching the room, scanning, and looking for horrifying things. When Tier doesn't continue his thought, I snap back to him. "What?"

"Thank you for not saying shit."

I laugh before I can stop myself. "You know, it's hardly fair that you get to cuss all you want and I'm held to some girl standard."

"Since when has life ever been fair? If life were fair I'd have you back on that little habitat and we'd be lazing around in bed, wondering if we'd make it all day with no food or if we have to put clothes on and actually go into town to find some."

"I'd make it all day with no food, I promise."

His mouth twists into a sly grin as he leads me over towards a shadowed hallway.

And that's when I see what's been going on here. The glass rooms are filled with a hazy kind of smoke and I have to press myself up against the window to make out the small shapes lying on the ground inside.

"They gassed them," Tier says in a low whisper. "We did not do this, Junco."

The air scrubbers create a small wind and the thick gas moves in an almost clump-like mist, exposing a pile of children on the floor. The cloud moves up one body and I can make out the pants. A pattern of flowers and suns. I wait, holding my breath, until the gas drifts up over to expose the face.

Mutants.

Dressed up like children.

"They did this in the Stag too," I reply. I stare at the horror a little longer before turning away. "Only I was the one who killed them all back there."

Tier stays where he is as I pass down the line of windows. There are dozens of these little room and all of them are filled with the mutant children.

I keep my back to him as the words come out. "Does that change things for you, Tier?"

I hear him clear his throat and walk towards me as I continue slowly down the hall. "What would change things, Junco?"

"Well, now you know. I'm not just a killer of mutants on the range," I say, turning back to him. "I'm a mass murderer. I murdered hundreds of them."

"Why did ya kill them, Juncs?"

"Do you know the genetics of these monsters, Tier? Did you guys find the records?"

He swallows and nods.

"Well, the ones they were making in the Stag were children of Gideon and me. So I can only assume these little bundles of horror were made along the same lines."

He nods. "They were."

"And obviously they all come out the same way when I'm involved. Monsters. I'm not the Teumessian fox at all. I'm the Mother of all Monsters." He stays silent for this and I start moving again. I turn a corner and stop short when I see a glass-front door. It has pink curtains drawn back from the glass so you can see inside the room.

I'm twisting the handle to open the door when Tier rounds the corner. "Junco, wait. It's not what you think."

What do I think? I ask myself as I step inside. It's a nursery. A very proper, first-class, Farm Family-looking nursery made specifically for a little girl. There's a crib piled high with extravagant blankets and matching bumpers and pillows. Soft teddy bears and stuffed puppies line a few shelves on the wall, and there are those flash frames hung up everywhere cycling through dozens of images of Inanna holding a baby.

A very normal-looking baby with bright green eyes.

I read the painted wooden letters decorated with pink polka-dots that line one of the walls. The baby's name is Savannah.

"It's not what you think, Junco."

"I don't know if I believe you, Tier. It all pretty much looks like what I think."

He walks up behind me and wraps his arms around my chest as he leans down to whisper his words across my cheek. "She's not real, Junco. She's not ours. I'm sorry, darlin'. When you said you were never pregnant back at the Subjack camp, you were right. Layla found your records here, too. This was Inanna's sick idea of a trick. A trick to make you behave and do what she asks."

"But—she's got your eyes. And her name is Savannah."

"A nasty trick, that's all it was. If there ever was a baby living in this room, then it was human, Junco. One hundred percent human. We've tested the whole place, looked very carefully for any sign of avian genetics. I'm not sure who she belongs to, and she wasn't even here when we came in this morning, so she might not even exist. But one thing is for sure, she's not ours."

"Who would do that to someone? Why does she want to hurt me like this? I don't understand. Why does she hate me?"

"It's an old fight, Junco. It's got nothing to do with you, darlin'. This fight is all about Inanna and Lucan."

I look up to Tier. "Does she love him?"

"I guess, if you can call that love. Obsession maybe."

"Did he ever love her?"

"No, Junco. He never did. She has always wanted things she couldn't have and she wanted Lucan to give them to her."

"What does she want, besides his love?"

"To cross that Bridge, Junco. The Bridge that no Archer, let alone member of the High Order, can cross."

"Oh." I'm sorry I asked. Because I can relate. "Does she have a loved one over there? On that side of things?"

He simply nods.

"Oh." I can relate to that too.

"Inanna is losing, Junco. She's desperate. She took you, and what she did to ya, morphing you into an Archer, was just about the most heinous crime there is in the avian world. You cannot even understand the horror of what's she's done to ya. But we all understand, and that's why we've been patient. It's not your fault this is happening to ya. But going forward, Junco, you need to be very careful. The Archer morph has consequences. Violence and anger sets off these consequences and you do not want to know what you might become if you give in to the urges."

My chest is rising and falling in a weird pattern and tears start to form in my eyes.

"Do you hear me, Junco?"

"I do want to know, Tier. What will happen? Just tell me now so I can get used to the idea."

"You'll become like that thing ya saw in The Book."

"A vampire bird thing? With knives as claws?" I look down at my hands and wonder if they're in there right now.

Tier takes my hand and lifts it up. "You're not human, Junco. You're not avian. You're not Archer. You are High Order."

"I don't understand what that means," I say, confused. "Aren't all of the Archers High Order?"

He shakes his head at me. "No. Lucan, Gib, Rache, Inanna, and now you. You five are the only High Order in the Sol System at this moment. And when they get here, next week," he says, lifting my chin so I look him in the eye. "When they get here next week they will want things from ya. All five of ya."

"What will they want?" I ask, still watching his eyes.

"Full compliance." He drops his fingers from my chin but I don't look away. "And Inanna, Lucan, Gib, and Rache have been planning for this moment for thousands of years. Inanna has a plan to appease them. She took you as an offering so they wouldn't kill her and she's hoping she can trade ya, darlin'. For that trip she wants so desperately."

Holy fuck. What kind of mother does that shit? Even Carolinia Coot looks like Mom of the Year compared to Inanna.

"But Junco, we have a plan. So if ya just do what we ask, we might have a chance. We cannot fight them outright, Snowbird. As much as I admire your willingness to do so, you cannot fight any more. Or you will turn and they'll take you away. They'll take you and kill us. And that's the best-case scenario, really. They'll probably shatter ya after they get you to dissipate Lucan, Rache, and Gib anyway. We are walking a very thin line, Junco. It's microscopic. And all this running yer doing is making everyone nervous. So just tell me what you want, tell me what you need and I will provide it. Because Irin is waiting to enter her Pillar, and we need the Halo. It has potential and possibilities and we must have both in order to have any hope of living beyond next week."

I really wish I knew what he's talking about. This thought causes me to laugh and that makes me look a little crazy. Tier's expression goes from soft to confused in a span of fractions. "Sorry," I say, still stifling down a chuckle. "It's just, I have no clue here. What you just said has practically no meaning to me, I—" I shake my head, that's what I do. "I want to talk to those lab workers."

He huffs out some air. "Why?" is all he comes back with.

"Because I want to look them in the eye when I ask them if they know anything about this room." I swallow hard. "And that green-eyed baby."

"She's not ours, Junco. Layla found yer records, yer Archer tank is on the other side of the compound. You were not pregnant."

I nod, but don't look at him this time. "I understand that. But I need to ask for proof."

He frowns and this makes his brow crinkle with annoyance. "Proof? That sounds a lot like Gideon if you ask me."

I smile at the name. "I wish I could see him right now. And it is his word. Man of Proof, that's Gid. I just need to double check everything."

"Man of Proof," Tier snorts. "I'll fucking give him his proof. He's got a lot of nerve, ya know that? Leaving ya to fend for yerself, even when he knows the consequences of what that bitch did ta ya."

"Wait, isn't Gideon High Order, too? She made him an Archer. He's got the marks."

"He's got marks, all right. But they're not High Order marks, they're not even Archer marks, from our point of view."

"I don't get it, then what are they? He's got a triangle, like me, on his back."

"No, Junco. Your mark is not a triangle."

"What?"

"It's a series of stacked horizontal lines that form a triangle, but Gideon's shape is closed. An outline. Your marks are open."

"What's the difference?"

"He's not on our side, that's the difference."

"He's not on Inanna's—"

"No." Tier cuts me off. "She has no side. He's marked by the other party Lucan was referring to earlier. The one who protected him."

"So, why then? Why don't you trust him?"

"Because, Junco—they only helped Lucan to defeat the High Order to further their own interests. They have no loyalty to us."

"Well, I can't just dismiss decades of help and support by Gideon, Tier. That's absurd. I owe him, He saved me—"

"Sure." He cuts me off again. "He saved ya. I get it. We'll talk about this more later, OK?" He grabs my hand and leads me back out to the main lab area, then over to the closed door where I saw Annun disappear. He knocks and it opens a crack to reveal Arel. I lean in to see him better and he catches my eye as Tier and him whisper.

"Hey, Juncs!" Arel pushes past Tier and closes the door behind him, then makes a grab for me that almost sets me off in a panic. But his embrace is warm and friendly so I relax and let him squeeze me. "Did you get your HOUSE, Junco? I think about her every day, I swear. I'm like obsessed with knowing how she is."

"I got her," I say, leaning into him a little. "She's back in New Peaks causing trouble, I think. She took it over and—" I shrug. What can I say? She's commandeered an entire city. My little sister AI is so much like me as a child it's scary.

Arel laughs. "What a little shit, huh? OK, what can I do for ya?"

"She wants to talk to them, Arel." Tier waves a hand at the door.

"Oh, all right. But be good, Junco," he warns me.

"I already told her. She promised."

I shrug as I walk through the door. I never said any such thing.

Chapter Forty-Four

The technicians are lying face down on the dirty tile floor and Annun is pacing back and forth barking out threats as we enter.

Interrogations. Looks like I'm just in time for the fun. I slip in the room and lean on the far wall, trying to stay quiet so that I don't disturb the atmosphere Annun has going. Which is the atmosphere of shit-your-pants fear. One tech turns her head towards me and cries out despite her gag when she realizes who I am.

This breaks the atmosphere, so what the hell? I might as well join in the fun.

I bend down and smile at her as she panics and wriggles in her bonds, trying to scoot away from me on the floor. Except she's got nowhere to go. The body next to her, which might be unconscious, or possibly dead, blocks her escape.

Bitch. Now who's helpless and scared?

I grab her hair and pull her head back and watch, with a lot of satisfaction, as she starts the ugly cry. My razors come out. Just regular old razors, not metal knives like the vampire dude, and I slit her binding, taking care not to cut her mouth in the process.

The wailing starts immediately and I slap her.

She shuts up.

Sort of. There are noises still coming out of her mouth, but they are not screams and they are not words. She's trembling, almost convulsing, really, and the tears are streaming down her face.

I lean into her face and whisper, "Listen very carefully, OK?"

She nods emphatically, her eyes darting behind me for a moment. I turn my head slightly and see Tier's boots standing next to me, then take my attention back to my victim.

"Was there a baby in that pink nursery?"

She nods.

"Whose baby was it?"

She looks around frantically. "I don't kn—"

I stand up and kick her hard in the stomach before Tier grabs my arm and tugs me back. "That's enough, Junco." He reaches down and pulls the woman to her feet, standing her up between the two of us. "Tell her where the baby came from. I won't save you again. And next time, it'll be my warrior's boot in your face, so think hard before you answer."

She gulps so much air I'm afraid she's gonna start hyperventilating and we'll have to move on. But she nods at Tier and gets herself under some semblance of control.

"It came out of the Stag labs."

"You fucking lying bitch!" I punch her close-fisted in the face and the anger overtakes me as I knock her ass to the ground. Both Tier and Annun are pulling me off now, and Arel is dragging the woman back to the other side of the room. "That baby was human!" I scream. "Whose baby is it?"

She's hysterical now and can't or won't answer.

My hands are vibrating with the rage that is pouring through my blood. My fingers begin to itch and I scratch at them while my mouth is running off about torture and mutilation. Tier picks me up, throws me over his shoulder and physically removes me from the room as I scream my threats back at her.

He dumps me on the hard floor and every eyeball is suddenly watching us.

They are staring at my hands with a look of revulsion. Utter disgust.

I look down and there they are. The knives are assembling real-time, just like the Pillars do when they climb up into the sky, and I watch with horror as the nanotech inside me creates my new body parts.

"Out!" Tier barks. Avians everywhere are on the move and within a few seconds the room has been cleared. "Junco, don't panic. I'll explain."

My chest is heaving in and out so hard I might have a heart attack. "Oh God. I'm like *him*! Oh, fu—" I stop the curse mid-word and Tier laughs at me.

"Yer fine, OK? So you have knives as claws. It's kinda cool, right?"

I shake my head. "I'm gonna grow fangs and rip things apart with my mouth? Because that's what it looked like he was doing in that picture!"

"I told ya, Juncs. The anger sets it off. It's like Lucan that night when he took ya to the clutch cages. You have to control yourself, or yes. You'll become like him."

I look down at my hands and the tech has stopped growing. They are thin and they look like they can cut paper, that's how tight the edge of the blades look. "Well, there goes my piano career."

Tier's uncharacteristically upbeat mood continues as he takes my hands. "Here, let me show ya. You can make them go away if you just massage the palms of yer hands." His fingertips rub across my left palm and then he moves up each individual finger, being careful not to cut himself, but not entirely succeeding. The blade on my new pinky finger grazes his skin and blood spurts out. He wipes it on his pants and continues until the razors start to un-assemble.

"It feels good."

"Does it now?" he asks as he drops that hand and starts on the other one. "I'll remember that."

I turn back to the interrogation room door. "What about them? She never really explained anything, Tier. She—"

"Junco, the baby in that room was human. Yer records say you were never pregnant. Do you have memories of yer morph that contradict this?"

A sigh escapes as I give in. "No. And I was awake almost the whole time, I think. I don't know for sure, but it felt like a long time before they put me to sleep. And I don't remember my belly getting big, but maybe they took it out and grew it in a tank or something?"

"Maybe," he admits. "Maybe she went to all this trouble of planting human DNA into that room to confuse us. Make us think there was no baby and give up searching. It could've happened that way, I suppose. But it's more likely that she was setting you up the way I said, Juncs. To make you think there *was* a baby when there wasn't. To get you to comply."

"Yeah," I concede. "And there's no way that baby came from Stag Camp, right? I mean, you blew it up, I killed them all once, we got Dale's lab…"

I wait for his answer but it takes a little too long to draw any comfort out of it. "We got them all, Junco."

He stops the massage and when I look back at my hands they are normal again. No blades. "What makes the fangs grow, Tier?"

"Anger. You have to let us take care of this stuff now. No more killing, no torturing," he says with a slight nod towards the closed interrogation room door, "and no more swearing."

I scowl up at him. "Swearing? That's not a trigger, you're lying."

He shrugs out a grin. "Better not chance it though, huh? And one more thing, just so ya know. I'm not saying this to scare you into compliance or anything, I promise. But once you turn it's very hard to *not* turn. Does that makes sense?"

It does. "It has programmed memory or something? Like those little self-assembling toys I had as a kid?"

He looks at me funny. "I never had toys, so—"

Oh, that's kinda sad. I wonder if it's because his human family were such assholes or if avians don't play with toys? I don't ask, I just explain. "You have this little dot of metal and you stick it out in the sun and it grows into a toy. It takes hours to make it assemble the very first time, but if you take away the heat, it collapses back into the dot of metal and the next time you put it in the sun, it grows in seconds."

Tier just stares at me. "That sounds like a pretty cool toy. Yeah, I guess that describes it. The first time ya start to turn, it comes in stages. A claw here, a fang there. Then there's the primary trigger event, that's what they call it. Where all of the different parts emerge at once, making you into the final being."

"Is that the vampire guy?"

"No, Junco. That's a pretty tame version of him, actually. There's more than wings and fangs and claws. They get horns…" He shrugs. "Lots of stuff."

I stop hearing him at horns but my mind continues and it adds hooves against my will. *Oh my fucking God! I'm the Devil! I'm totally gonna turn into the Devil!*

"Junco." Tier is shaking me. "Just don't let it happen and you'll never have to worry about those later stages. OK?"

The door to the interrogation room opens and Annun and Arel emerge. I lean a little to get a look inside before they close the door but I only see one thing.

Blood pooling up on the floor.

"All done?" Tier asks.

Both warriors grunt out a yes and continue onto another part of the lab.

"OK, ya satisfied now, Junco? They're all dead. Can we go see Irin? And get the sixth Pillar up today?"

I look around, not quite ready to let all this go. "I've been waiting for my chance to confront people. Any people, ya know? Just someone to ask, what the fuck? Why? And all that now seems out of reach once again. I'm right back where I started, Tier."

He groans. "How the hell do ya figure that, Junco? Yer nothing like the girl I found out on the hill. What more do you possibly need?"

The Enki nargala comes back to me as I process his words. When Inanna was bitching to her uncle that he never gave her what she wanted, he replied with a laundry list of things, and yet she was still not satisfied. She wanted more. "Does it seem unreasonable to you," I ask him, "that I require some sort of closure? Do you think I'm selfish and wild? That I'm… what was it that you said on my birthday? I'm preoccupied with death or something?" I look up and he cringes and turns away as his words come back to haunt him. "And I am, I guess. It consumes me, this drive I have for *something*. Something to make it all OK. To make me feel like everything happened for a reason that will be good for *me* somehow, and not just good for everyone else."

I pause to see if he has anything to add, but he doesn't.

"I'm not really looking for death, Tier. I'm looking for answers. Why? Why did they do this to me? Why did that clone kill that baby? And Charlie? Why me? Why is this my life? How did they make me? For what purpose? Just—why me? How was it that Glory Sheffield down the street from us in the RR was born to a normal family, purely human, went to school—regular school—like all the other kids. Never had to kill anyone, or learn to shoot and throw knives so she could pass tests every summer. Why did she get that life and I got this one?"

He grabs my shoulder and pulls my head into his chest. "Because, Junco, your soul has a destiny. And besides, I'm pretty sure Gloria Stepfield from down the street is dead right now. Blown up in a nuclear explosion."

I sigh a little because he's right as usual. "Sheffield, Glory Sheffield."

"Whoever. My point is, you can't waste time on that kind of stuff. You can't change who you are and I don't know what they did to ya, all growing up. So I can't help ya there. You never tell me anything, you keep me guessing. I know the little bit Isten decided to share with us, and I'll be honest and tell ya that he pissed Lucan off with how tight-lipped he became after the twine. He clammed up fast, so I can only imagine that what he saw inside you scared him pretty bad."

A long drawn-out breath escapes my lips as I pull away and slump down into a station chair. I let me face fall into my hands and drag them across my cheeks.

"Why don't you just ask your father, Junco? I don't get it. He's the one with the answers, just call him up and ask him."

"I don't want to ask him," I mumble between my fingers. "I love him. I want him to be my dad forever. If I ask him," I say, looking up at Tier now, "then I might not love him anymore. I need him, Tier. I need these people from my past. Gideon, and HOUSE, and my dad. Because everyone else is gone. They made me kill James, did you know that? He was the one person at camp that I could trust and—"

I shake my head and get up to walk away, but Tier reaches out and taps me on the shoulder.

Chapter Forty-Five

When we come out of the timeshift we're on a large red rock that overlooks the entire Front Range. The sun is rising behind us, just like that day we sat out here and I learned that I was the one who killed my dad's clone. Back before I knew he was a clone, of course, so I really thought I'd killed my father.

Tier drags me over to the edge of the rock and sits down, then scoots back and pulls me into his lap and almost crushes me with his embrace. Our feet swing over the edge and I relax and lean back into him. "What's all this for?"

"We've got time, Junco. I don't know anything about a guy named James, not a thing. I barely know anything about you at all, so tell me something, Junco. Tell me anything, just make it about you, OK?"

I pause for a while. Tier just sits there, letting me think until I finally know where to start the trainwreck of a story that is me. "Do you know what OCD is?"

I feel him shake his head behind me, but he stays silent.

"It's a disorder that makes you do things compulsively. Things like count, or rock, or tap." I look over my shoulder and find his green eyes glowing. "I count and rock and tap. That's what I do." The last few words come out between my trembling lips and I feel the tears because I have never said those words out loud before. "Lucan once asked me why my dad gave me a sport and taught me piano. Well, that's why. I count and rock and tap because I have OCD. So when I was very small they gave me a piano to stop the tapping. And it worked, too, because one day I figured out that if I tap the keys in just the right way, it makes a song. So I stopped tapping and started playing songs."

"I've never heard ya play the piano, Junco. Not for real anyway. I heard the music coming from the house before, but never got to watch you."

I am stunned. "How is that possible?"

"Because, Junco, you've been running from me since the moment I met ya. You haven't shared much of anything with me."

The sadness washes over me as I realize what he's been going through for all this time. I've treated him like total shit—he knows less about me than just about everyone, how is he even still hanging around?

"Keep going, Junco. Please."

My fingers slide across my face to wipe away my tears as I try to explain myself. "The rocking was taken care of with the horses. I learned to ride and they figured out that the rhythm calmed me. That I was a lot more manageable if I was riding and downright normal when they started teaching me to do that acrobatic crap. So the horses took care of the rocking."

I can't quite get myself to address the last one, but Tier can only wait so long before he gets impatient and asks. "And the counting, how did ya stop that one, Junco?"

I shake my head. "I never stopped counting." Before I even know what's happening I'm sobbing. "I never stopped counting, Tier."

He hugs me close. "Is it bad? To count, Junco?"

I nod as I try to control my runny nose. "It's very bad. Because once I start it's very hard to stop. And that's why I first started looking up at the stars. The light and the stories about heroes and swans and hunting bulls, those all came later. It's the sheer number of them that draws me up."

He squeezes me as I calm myself. "What happens when ya count?"

I sniffle and wipe my face once again. "When I start the count it all goes away. My insanity, my life—everything is all wiped clean. And it draws me, ya know? Like that count is calling my name. But it's dangerous because once I start on the stars, I won't be able to stop. I'll be lost. And deep down, I want to be lost, Tier."

I stare out at the new city between the blur of tears. It has migrated north of the old city, where the mountaintop still dominates the horizon. But New Peak City is in the shadow of Mount Evans, near the old Red Rocks Amphitheatre, not Pikes Peak. It takes a little getting used to, trying to think of this new place as Peaks. The Old Peak City down south by the Springs is still nothing but concrete. They're not even working on it yet.

"Continue, Junco. Please don't stop talking."

I nod into his chest. He's been so patient with me these past few years. Why didn't I see it before now? He's practically been an angel with all the shit I've pulled.

"At first I would count steps, like the number of steps it takes to get to the shooting range, or the number of steps from my bed to Gid's after a nightmare. He was across the hall from me. Or when I was at home I counted the stalls in the barn or the tiles on the floor or the light fixtures in church. But I had been learning about the constellations for a while already when I looked up to find Perseus and noticed I could count the stars. The only problem is that the stars go on for infinity. And I had a very hard time stopping. I went insane actually. That was the first time I remember them talking about my mental issues. They didn't erase me, I was only like five, I think. But they had to lock me in a sensory deprivation tank for a while. It felt like a really long time to me, but I have no idea how long it took to pull me back from that little episode."

"I'm sorry, darlin'. I'm sorry they did all those things to you."

I shrug. "It hurts a little when I have to talk about it because I was so scared, so that's why I'm crying. I was scared a lot as a little kid, but now that I look back I realize something that scares me even more than what they did back then."

"What's that?"

"That my life was not so bad, Tier. I mean, in the early days. It was not so bad when my dad was there. Even Matthew—he was my handler when I was little, when I was at camp and before Gideon took over. But even Matthew wasn't that bad back then. Not like the stuff Gid says they did to Irin. But those years with the clone father, they might as well have been Hell. They were the stuff of nightmares. And when they found out I was going down to Texas to see John Hando, and traced it all back to my weapons trainer James, they made me kill him. With my SEAR. The same way I killed Kush. The slightest snap of the plasma grazed lightly across his top layer of skin."

I stop and remember the screams. From both of them.

"If you're going to die of a SEAR knife wound, the best way to go is fast because the pain involved in the slow version of SEAR death is almost unimaginable. And that's why I did it slow for that clone who killed Charlie and the baby. But that spring when I had to kill James was probably the worst time of my life. There are still things I push down from that time."

"What year was that, Junco?"

"That year before sniper school. Right before you guys showed up to start watching me. James came to Texas to pull me from that job I mentioned—we were doing all sorts of secret jobs that year. John Hando and I were becoming close, we started thinking about getting closer. He wanted me to stay with him and never go back, and he took me up to the top of the Sagitta building in Dallas because the Hando Family owns the whole top floors of that place. Did you know it's not just a building, but a transmitter too?"

Tier shakes his head at me.

"And it's got a duality AI. The only male AI on Earth. I met them that night that John took me to the top to look at the stars. But James showed up in the middle of that job and said my dad was asking for me. He was the clone of course and it turns out that the reason they wanted me back in the Stag was because Gideon was dying. They did some procedure on him, something I now think has to do with all that Archer stuff. And he *was* dying."

I let out a deep breath of air. "I knew my dad wasn't right, that he couldn't possibly be the same guy who loved me so fiercely as a child and then all of a sudden couldn't even spare the time to acknowledge me on my birthdays anymore. So when everyone left me there to say goodbye to Gideon, I healed him using the connection we had, don't ask me to explain, because I can't. But giving him whatever it was I gave him nearly killed me in the process. To make a long story short, while I was recovering in that place I found a lab full of mutant offspring of Gid and I, and killed them all. I was erased twice in the span of a few weeks because I just refused to forget. And that was the end of Junco. Whoever that child was, that piano-playing, horseback-riding child who lived in a sentient house and was loved by Johann Coot through her fifteenth year of life? She left with those memories."

"No, Junco. She's right here."

I dismiss his claim with a shrug because he is just plain wrong. "When I was small, they used stories and rules to make me compliant with orders and of course, my illness. So Gid told me I was only allowed to have one weakness at a time and I happen to be a crier, if ya haven't noticed." I feel him let out a little laugh behind me.

"So that was my one weakness. Gideon always said I wasn't allowed to count and cry. That was the deal that kept me sane, kept me from counting. I made the decision to stop counting because crying just felt better. Crying exhausts me. It feels good to sleep afterward. And then when I wake up, I'm OK again. I have new courage, and new faith, new everything. It's like a big reset button or something.

"But," I add softly. "I have a confession to make. I have been crying and counting now for a very long time. I counted your heartbeats when I fell apart back at Subjack's mountain. I counted Isten like every chance I could. I counted Lucan a few times, too. I even count myself." I look up at him and wait to see what he says. His eyes are soft and have just a slight hint of glow to them.

"But yer doing pretty well, Junco. You're still OK as far as I can tell. You're still OK." He sounds like he's trying to convince himself.

I know the feeling.

"I'm some other girl now. Maybe when I was avian I could accept that was still me. Just a better version. But this girl?" I point to my chest. "I have no idea who she is. But I do know one thing, she is definitely not in control, she's not reasonable, and all she can think about is revenge. I only count heartbeats, not stars. At least not yet. I might decide to count the stars again, I'm not ruling it out, but right now I count heartbeats because heartbeats have gotten me through everything for a pretty long time. And

I've been telling myself since I was little that there will come a day where there are no heartbeats left to count and I'll never have to think about or struggle with it again. Because there will be nothing left to get through, and then I'll know that's the time when I can let it all go. It will all be over when the heartbeats stop and I can let it all go."

I turn to look up at him again, just to make sure he's getting all this. "I only have two ways out, the way I see it. Counting stars or no heartbeats. And I was holding out for the final heartbeat, Tier. Because I'm never gonna stop counting the stars once I start. And now Inanna took that away from me. There will never be a final heartbeat now. Ever. I just want them all to end, Tier."

He sits quietly for a long time, still embracing me and burying his face in my neck. His breath dances across my cheek and I think of the night we first met and he charmed me with that little trick. How easy it was to be consoled back then. Even with all the bad stuff going on, even with my slip in sanity, it was easy to have hope that things would get better. It was easy to believe that I was powerful and had control over my life. But everything I've done since then has proved otherwise.

I have no hope.

I have no faith.

And the way I see it, I have only one power left. I've used up all my powerful gifts to get to this place right here, right now, and I have only one more left.

When he finally speaks I can hear the fear. "I hope that's not true about the heartbeats, Junco. I sincerely hope that's not true."

I can only sigh at that because it absolutely is true. One hundred percent true. But I don't want to talk about heartbeats anymore, I have something else to say now. "I have a regret I'd like to tell you about, if that's OK." I look back at him and he nods. "I wish I had let you kiss me back in the hot springs. I wish I could go back to the beginning and do it all differently. I wish—" His lips kiss the back of my neck and I stop for a second. "I wish I had turned around in that hot spring, climbed in your lap, and just given myself to you right then."

"But then we'd never make it to our end, Junco."

"Yeah, I know. But when I add up all the good and compare it to the bad I'm not sure it's worth it anyway. So screw it. I'd go back. I'd make changes."

He moves to get up, pulling me up with him, and then takes my face in his hands and leans down to press his lips against my forehead. "Don't leave me, Junco," he whispers. "I know I haven't really told ya how I feel about you, but please…"

My eyes find his. They are begging me.

"Please. Do not leave me here alone. I have regrets too. I regret not getting Lucan's permission to bring you home. I could've saved us so many bad memories if I had been honest with him from the start. And I would never have given you to Isten. I'm so sorry for that." His expression is so painful to watch, it makes me want to hug him close but he's still holding my face in his hands. "Just give me another chance. Please, don't leave me. There are more good things coming, I promise. Please don't leave."

I swallow and force the words out. "But you're the one who will leave me, Tier."

He swipes a finger down my cheek, taking a tear away with his touch. I look away but he gently turns me back. "Yer the only thing I want, Junco. I'm worthless without you. I promise ya, it'll get easier. I will take care of you. I will carry you, Junco."

"But you won't stay with me forever. You'll die and I'll still be here. I've always been alone and it's not enough anymore. It's just not enough. I'd rather float in the nothingness and drift away for eternity than get a stay of execution on my unhappy ending, Tier. I'm tired and I just want it to be over."

"Junco, just give me a chance to work through things. I never said I'd leave ya here alone. I never said that."

"I know." I swallow hard and look at him. "But you never said you wouldn't either. And now it's too late." I wait and watch him. Hoping for a fraction that he will somehow find a way to change our fate. And then shrug it off and accept what's true as I pull back. "We should get going, huh? Irin is waiting."

Chapter Forty-Six

We port back to a ship, but this time I'm in what appears to be the mess. There are food machines and tables. And it's empty. Tier is getting Irin, who has been kept here since I ported off and went on my little adventure through the desert.

Ashur is here somewhere, so Tier is trying to hide me from him, I think.

I'm pretty afraid of Ashur when I think about it too much. He's never been one to let me get away with having my way all the time, and he definitely has no issue with beating the shit out of me if I deserve it.

Right now I'm just another soldier who disobeyed orders.

I jump a little as the doors swoosh open and Tier enters, tugging Irin along behind him.

Her hands are bound and she's crying.

"What's going on?" I get up and walk over to her, but she won't meet my gaze. "What did you do to her, Tier?"

He ignores me and pushes her over to the table, then forces her to sit down before he speaks to me. "Do not cut her free, Junco." He lifts up her sleeves and her arms are wrapped with membranes.

"What happened?"

"You'll have to ask her," he says, and then turns and walks out.

"Irin?"

Silence as she stares at her bare feet.

"Irin? You OK?"

"Do I look OK?" she growls.

"No, you look like hell, actually. You wanna tell me what's going on?"

Her head flips up and her demon-yellow eyes are in full glow. "What's going on? You know what's going on. You're gonna let them kill us in those Pillars, you're gonna make me go and I'll end up like all the rest, stuck in that thing. With those things!"

"In that thing with those things. OK, that makes a lot of sense." Her unreasonable attitude is eroding all the softness Tier has built up in me over the course of the day and I have to restrain myself from slapping the shit out of her. "Do you know something I don't? Because no one has said anything about killing us in the Pillars."

"Oh no? Well, you wouldn't know would you? I mean, you've been off porting your way around the MR, getting Selia all shot up, making everyone crazy. So I guess I can see how you'd be so fucking ignorant of the whole what's-inside-the-Pillar thing."

I wait to see if she's got anything else to add. But she doesn't. "Well? You wanna fucking enlighten me?"

She sneers her lip at me.

I change the subject. "What happened to your arms?"

"What does it look like happened to them?"

"It looks like you tried to kill yourself, actually. That what happened here?"

She stays quiet.

"So you don't want to talk to me? You just want me to have Tier and Ashur take you to your Pillar now, or what? I hear we're on a timeline."

I let the silence hang and say nothing. Just lean back in my chair, put my hands behind my head, and close my eyes. Like we've got all the time in the world. I stay like this for several minutes. So long that I'm actually starting to drift off when she finally speaks.

"It's a trap, you know."

"What's a trap?" I ask without opening my eyes. It feels good to rest, actually.

"The Pillars."

"You're gonna have to elaborate, Irin."

"Getting us in there. We can't come back. It's a trap. We'll all be stuck on the other side. That's what Lili told me, even though she wasn't supposed to. She told me because she was pissed off and wanted to make me crazy."

"Well," I say, laughing. "You showed her, huh?"

"Bitch."

I force myself to open my eyes and take control. I'm anxious to get this whole thing over with now. "Look Irin, even if that was true, I have a feeling the other side is not that bad. I mean, Isten is over there. And Mish, and Braun, and my Aren. Even little Isec. So if we get stuck over there, I'm OK with that. For real. In fact, I *wish* I could get stuck over there. Because then I could just pretend that none of this is happening. Just hide and pretend it's all OK." I stop and let my words rattle around in her brain for a few seconds before picking it up again. "But that's just a fantasy on my part, we're not gonna get stuck there, Irin. You understand?"

I look over to her face and wait.

She keeps her silence so I try another tactic. "Lucan and them got the people in your lab, Irin. They tell you that? Annun and Arel killed the last of the technicians this morning. I was there. That place is nothing but a puff of smoke right now."

She breaks down and starts to cry. Leaning forward into her own lap, her bound hands trying desperately to cup her face so I can't look at her.

I walk over to the kitchen, find a knife, and return to her. "Give me your hands, sister."

She looks up at me and I recognize the crazy in her. It certainly didn't pass her over, Archer morph or not. I'd hate to see what she turns into if Inanna ever tried to put her through the same shit she did me. "Your hands," I said. "This is an order."

She lifts her hands and I slit the bindings. Her fingers immediately begin to massage the dark red peeking through her bandages. I listen to the quiet methodical humming of cleaning servos and environmental conditioning units in the large hall and wait for her to be ready.

Finally, after several minutes of counting my own heartbeats, she speaks. "Who said we're not going to get stuck?"

"Sera," I answer as I turn towards her. "Sera said. She's rigged something up so we can all return. Don't ask me what because I have no idea. But regardless, these Pillars need to be built, whether we come back or not."

"Will you come with me?"

The fear in her voice takes me back a second. She's really screwed up. More than me, even, and that's some new record. Whatever they did to her, it must've been pretty bad. "Of course I'm coming, Irin. Why do you think I'm here?"

"You didn't help any of the others out, why help me?"

"They didn't need me. But you do."

She takes a deep breath. "You don't think we'll get stuck in there? That other place?"

I shrug. "Maybe we will, who knows. But like I said, I think it's not all that bad in that place. So who cares? If we do we do. If we don't we don't. We have no control over it, so let it go, Irin. Just let that fear go, it's such a useless emotion. Fear gives you nothing. It only takes."

"But…" She stops, squinting at me in confusion. "You're not ever scared, Junco? I mean, that's not even possible."

"Of course I'm scared. All the time. You just can't let it control you like this. Just push it away and think about the job. The job always pulls you through the hard times. When you have a mission, Irin? Life is easy. It's when the missions end that should worry you."

"I never had any missions, Junco. I'm not a soldier, I was just a—" She stops and looks away, almost as if she's embarrassed. "I was nothing but a test subject, that's all. I never did anything brave or special. I just complied because I was so scared of everything. So, what can I do? How do I stop being afraid?" She sniffs and wipes her bloody hands across her face, leaving a long streak of residue.

I get up and take her hand, pulling her with me over to the kitchen sink. "Just stand here quietly, OK?"

She nods out a yes.

I grab some paper towels and get them soaked with water and lathered up with soap. Then I wipe her face like she's a little kid. "Close your eyes," I command, "so the soap won't get in." I scrub her, then rinse, and hand her a dry towel.

I wait for her to finish patting down her face and she looks a bazillion times better. "Fear, Irin, can be beaten with one simple exercise. Gideon taught me this. Are you ready to learn it?"

She bobs her head up and down.

"OK, the secret to conquering fear is to embrace the worst-case scenario. So, tell me… what's the worst-case scenario if you go in the Pillar?"

She thinks about it for a moment. "Death."

I shrug. "All right. Death. What happens if you die?"

"How should I know?" she snaps.

"Exactly. How should you know. It's the great unknown, right? You die and then you're gone, just blipped out of existence. Now what?"

"What? Nothing, that's what. You're gone."

"Right. So you'd never even know you died. Who gives a fuck if ya die, Irin? You're never gonna even know about it!"

"What if I do know about it?"

"Well, then that means there's an afterlife, in which case, it can't be worse than here, right? Just think about it, you've had a pretty fucked-up life so far. How can an afterlife be any worse?"

She stays silent.

"Irin, the secret to fear is to accept the worst-case scenario. Embrace it as truth. That way when it doesn't happen, you're better off than you were. And if it does come true, you're prepared. Of course, if death is the real end, then who gives a shit? You're done. That's the worse thing that could happen to you. You're done and sometimes being done can sound pretty fucking awesome."

Silence again.

"Don't just accept your fate, Irin. Change it to suit you. And don't just accept your Destiny either. Meet it on your own terms. Go forward with courage, because fear gives you nothing in the end. It only takes away your dignity."

She looks up at me now. Her yellow eyes are normal. A golden hazel, just like my own, before the morph, of course. It occurs to me that I've never seen her eyes without the glow. Who knew they'd be hazel?

"You were so lucky to have Gideon growing up, Junco."

"I'm still lucky to have him, Irin. He told me these same words the last time I saw him, right before we found ya screaming for us in my dad's old marketplace." I wait for another response but none comes forward. "Well, actually, him and Lucan."

"Oh, for fuck's sake. Just what I need, second-hand advice from the Devil."

"Smart-ass remarks mean you're back to your old bitchy self, I think."

She curls her lip at me and growls as the door swooshes open and Tier enters again. He looks her up and down real good and when her eyes finally meet his, he speaks. "You're ready then, Irin?"

She nods and Annun comes forward to take her out.

"We're right behind you," Tier calls after them. And then he turns. "I thought I told ya no swearing?"

"Sorry, but it's Irin, ya know? She needs a heavy hand, sorta like me."

He laughs and pulls me close as we follow them out. "Like you? That's cute. The last thing you need is a heavy hand, darlin'. If ever there was a person who required a light touch, it's you." He leans down to kiss me, his lips brushing past mine for the briefest of fractions. "What's the term they use for horses that require gentle guidance? A soft mouth, right? You've got a soft mouth, Juncs."

My whole body goes warm with his words. "Where did you learn that?"

He shrugs. "I looked up all kinds of shit about horses and pianos when you were missing. Spent entire days sitting in your room back at the 039 looking at your stuff. I stared at that piano for hours sometimes, wishing I could hear you play it."

"I think that's the most romantic thing I've ever heard." He leans in and kisses me long and good this time. "Don't ever stop," I whisper.

"You'll be begging me ta stop when this is all over, Snowbird. And I'll have ta tell ya no every time."

Chapter Forty-Seven

I feel all the breath leave me when we land on the side of a mountain ledge in South Central Columbia. This part of South America has been controlled by terrorists for more than a hundred years. Or I guess I should say *was* controlled. Because right now there is nothing left to control. It is hundreds, maybe thousands, of burned and charred acres of what once used to be thriving rainforest vegetation.

Forest fires are not all that uncommon in the jungle, but the kind powerful enough to burn the entire canopy into dust is truly End of Days stuff. The only other time I can think of where this occurred is when the planet pad explosion took out a large portion of Brazil. But that was due to tens of thousands of gallons of liquid hydrogen from the refuel station being sprayed into the air upon impact from the suborbital.

But this?

This comes with a smell that goes far beyond chemicals and green trees. The odor curling up my nostrils and invading my olfactory receptors is nothing short of thousands of charred and disfigured bodies. They are strewn about the landscape, what's left of them, anyway, curled up and still smoking.

"What happened?" I ask in a whisper as Tier comes up behind me.

"War happened, Junco."

Ashur walks up next to me, his posture still angry and stiff. "Is that righteousness I detect in your voice, Junco?"

I want to smack him so bad. Or at the very least tell him to fuck off. But Tier grabs my hand and addresses Irin. "Ready?"

She backs away quickly and Ashur has his hands wrapped around her chest, restraining her, before I even notice he's moved. "Not so fast, Psycho Number Two."

"Ashur!" Tier barks. "Shut the fuck up. I don't need this today."

Ash does shut the fuck up and I feel a little satisfaction that he still has to take orders like everyone else.

"Irin, we've talked about this," Tier says, trying to be reasonable. "You know what's gonna happen, you know you're not leaving here any other way, so do not make this difficult. Comply or I will knock you out like I did with Soli and drag your ass to that Pillar. You are out of options."

I look over at Irin and she begins to whimper. She's scared and I don't blame her. I've asked to go along and watch because I have this overpowering need to know what happens before I go to my own Pillar. Tier agreed because I insisted, but that means that Irin will have to fly herself over there and the guys will have to fly me with them because I have no fucking wings and if I can fly or float or anything like that, no one's told me about it and this new body did not come with a manual.

Tier prods me with his shoulder, a signal I figure. *Go shut her up and let's get a move on* is the message it sends.

But I just look out past the blackened remains of countless humans, and probably an equal number of avian warriors as well, to the column of light bursting forth from the forest about a dozen miles away. This is the first Pillar that will erupt on land, all the others have been in the ocean. A small relief to coastal populations everywhere I bet, but unfortunately for South America, this Pillar lies close to a major fault line that will be severely disrupted once the mechanism deep inside the earth is triggered.

It will cause yet another horrific natural disaster.

I swallow. How many will die because of Irin today?

And when they take me back to the Runout valley where my Pillar is located, how many people will die because of me?

I look up at Tier as a horrible thought strikes. "What about HOUSE?"

His brows flatten down over his eyes. "What are you talking about?"

"HOUSE? She's in Peak City." I start shaking my head and I hear Irin getting more hysterical behind me. Ashur is talking low to her, maybe to issue threats without me and Tier knowing. "There's gonna be terrible earthquakes, New Peaks is not that far from Runout, only a couple hundred miles, that's not nearly far enough away to be safe. Who will save my HOUSE?"

"Junco, this is not the—"

"The fuck it's not the time!" I scream—a bit hysterically, I admit. "I need her, I told you that. I need her!"

"She's an AI, she has a backup, right?"

"No." My head is shaking out the word and I'm trying to move away now. "No. She's not an AI, she's a little girl! And… and… even if she was still just an AI, there is no backup! I took the—"

He wraps his arms around me like Ash has his around Irin. "Darlin', listen. I'll get your HOUSE. OK? I promise, when you come back, your HOUSE will be there. OK?"

"But she might not be able to leave… what if she can't leave? I have to go see her, we can go there, it's on the way. I—"

"Junco." He interrupts me with a hand over my mouth. "We're not stopping there. The teams at your Pillar have a very tenuous hold on the area right now. We have no more time. We need to get Irin in that Pillar and then port directly to number seven. You understand? I will take care of her, I promise ya."

I stare up at him, my eyes glowing like fuck I'm sure.

"OK?" he asks again.

I nod and wriggle out of his hold so I can turn back to see Irin. Ashur has removed her to a place farther away from Tier and me and she is sobbing uncontrollably.

I'm not helping her at all, I'm making it worse.

"Go talk to her, Junco. Quickly, or you'll have to wait here and Ashur and I will have to drag her over there."

I take a deep breath and walk over to Ashur as I put on my soldier face. "I've got it, thanks," I say with the voice of a former cadet captain. It's pretty weak, but Ash just nods and lets her go. Irin turns to me, wiping her eyes.

"Please, help me be brave."

Oh my God.

I hug her. So tight.

"Irin," I whisper in her ear. "I'm scared too, OK? I'm scared too. But remember what I said, embrace the worst. This is it, OK? The end. We've got no choice."

This does not console her. Her whole body shakes against mine as we embrace our terrible futures together.

I try another tactic.

"When Gid and I were little and had a hard time dealing with something scary, we played a game. Do you want to hear about it?"

"Junco?" Tier barks.

"Wait!" I command him. "Just wait!"

Irin pulls back and nods at me. "Tell me, quick!"

"We'd take turns telling each other about a time when we were scared, and then we'd say how we overcame our fear with rational thinking."

She watches my face as I talk, her sobs slowing down a bit, and since we're pretty much out of time, I start with the most heinous thing I've ever had to do. "When I was back on Amelia fighting my way through Fledge I had to kill a friend because it was my duty."

Irin looks at me with horror.

"I struggled with it, but to be honest, there was never a doubt in my mind. I am a rule follower, and most of all, I always obey an order when it comes from the top. Lucan said I had to do it, and he was my top. So I did it. I am always afraid, Irin. But I get past it by following orders. For me, there's a lot of satisfaction in doing my duty." I shrug. "It's not very brave, I admit, but that's just how I work, I guess."

Her mouth hangs open as she processes my words.

"I've had a hard time living with myself ever since I killed Isec to be honest, but now I know that my friend went to a better place. I really believe that, Irin."

I pause and look back at Tier. He nods for me to keep going because Irin has stopped crying and is paying close attention, just like I did when Lucan came to me in the Fallen Archer church and told me about the state of their gene pool after I killed Isec.

"So we just have to put aside the fear and go forward. I'll go with you, the whole way, but only if you agree to fly alone. They'll leave me here if you fight them."

She stands up a little straighter and wipes her eyes. "I was never brave, Junco. I never overcame anything, I've never risen to any occasion. I have nothing to tell you back."

I smile at her. "Irin, brave only counts in the present. Past deeds of courage are just memories, it's the present that counts. Just be brave today and I swear, we'll leave that place together."

"We can leave together?"

"I swear I will not leave without you, OK? But will you make me a promise too?"

She nods. "Yes."

"Don't leave there without me, either."

Her whole face crumples and the tears stream down her cheeks again as her words come out as a whisper. "I promise, Junco. I won't leave you there either."

I mumble out a thank you as Tier and Ashur come up and grab my arms, then Tier nods to Irin. "Ya ready?"

Irin swallows down her fear and nods out a yes back to him.

And then we are airborne, flying out towards a massive column of light. The very same photons that I insisted were proof that God exists just yesterday.

Holy shit, I am so fucking dumb.

Irin flies as close to us as she can get and not be caught up in Ash and Tier's wings. I can't hear her heavy breathing over the wind we create, but I can feel it. I can feel it like my own heartbeat because it *is* my own heartbeat.

When the distance from the Pillar is reduced by about half I start to feel the heat and my heart turns into a jackhammer—pounding in my chest so hard I feel like it will explode, like I am about to die and the last moments of my life will be staring into hell, because that's how fucking hot it is.

We stop suddenly and Irin bumps into us from behind and starts flapping wildly to compensate. Ashur leans down into my ear and yells for me to climb on his back. It's only then that I notice the noise, coming out of the waves of light, bouncing around inside my ear canals, almost able to smother out all other sounds. I look at Tier to confirm this is what I should do and he nods and lets go of me as I frantically grasp onto to Ashur's uniform, clawing my way onto his back and wrapping my arms around his chest as my knees squeeze his waist.

His wings flap against me, and we bobble in the air a little which forces a rush of adrenaline into my system. I shut that down as best I can. What a waste. I'll need that adrenaline later, I can't afford to use it up. Ash reaches his hand back and pats me on the head then grabs me under my knees and holds on tight. "I've got you, Junco."

I lean into his ear. "I'm sorry, you know?"

"I know."

Tier has his hands on Irin's shoulders, giving her encouragement or maybe instructions. Ashur takes us a little off to the side so I can't hear what he's saying, and Tier has his back to me, so I can't read his lips.

But I can see Irin watch him with an intense concentration. Then her eyes dart to me and she nods as she turns away and begins to pump her great wings. I've never seen her fly before today and it hits me just how spectacular she is. Her wings thrust hard for a few beats, then she soars, banking left a little, drooping downward then pumping again and rising back up, moving more slowly now. I feel Ashur take a deep breath and hold it, then look over to Tier and he does the same. I turn my attention back to Irin and she's got her hand in front of her face, and then she's shaking her head wildly as she pumps her wings hard one more time and bursts into flames.

I'm thrashing against Ashur, screaming out her name, but I'm no longer on his back, he's got my hands and Tier has my legs.

And then everything goes black.

Chapter Forty-Eight

I come to lying on the ground as boots shake the earth around me with their shuffle. Slowly voices begin to make sense and I log the chatter of a stressful military mission. Tier, Ashur, Ryse, Arel, Lucan, and Annun. Their voices flood my head as they yell and argue, some boots come very close to stepping on me and then someone is thrown down to the ground. I open my eyes and I'm staring at Annun's stunned face for just a fraction before he is pulled up by Tier and thrust out of my sight.

Annun announces my return to the world and then heavy hands are pulling me up. "Junco?" Tier's voice is low in my ear. "You're OK, Junco."

"No," I croak. "She burst into fucking flames! I am very much not—"

His hand clamps down over my mouth and then he's talking to someone else. "How fast?" he asks.

"Twenty-five meters per second," replies Arel. "And increasing steadily."

An audible sigh of relief escapes everyone in the circle and my eyes dart around wildly as I consider biting Tier's hand to make him let me go. He leans down and tells me sternly, "Do not even think about it, Junco. That will really piss me off."

Then everyone is moving, Tier is barking orders, Arel is collecting some sort of tech from the ground, and Lucan and Ashur disappear without a word.

Annun approaches Tier just as he finishes ordering Ryse to go back up to the ship and then the blue lights are there, picking up Ryse and Arel. "You want me to help with her?" Annun says, as he motions to me with his head.

"No, I got it, back on ship, and secure that area. Twenty minutes is what we've got, understand?"

He nods and then steps into his blue light and is swept up into the sky.

It's only then, when we are alone, that Tier removes his hand from my mouth and turns me around. His hands are firmly clasped onto my shoulders and he's leaning down in my face. "Look!" he says, pointing to the Pillar. The nanotech is not a column of light anymore, but a solid Pillar that is self-assembling as I watch. "She's alive, Junco. If she wasn't, that thing would not be growing. Do you understand me?"

I don't. Not really. "She burst into flames, Tier! How the hell can she still be alive? She exploded!"

"She's in there, I promise."

I pull away and take a few steps, waiting to see if he'll stop me.

He doesn't.

"Junco, you just have to trust me, OK? I know what it looks like, but I swear, she's OK."

I spin around, furious. "How could you possibly know that? Are you inside with her or something? Because I'm pretty sure none of you assholes know what's going on in there. And I'm so fucking tired of this shit! You guys have no idea what you're doing! You're guessing, like everyone else!"

He stares at me, his eyes glowing a bright green.

"And you just blew up my sister!"

He looks away and I take my chance, flinging myself into the timeshift. But I feel his grip on me as I enter. He overpowers it and brings me back out and we land hard in the spongy rainforest floor. "Stop it!" he screams down at me. "Just stop it, Junco. You're going to that Pillar, you will complete the Halo and you will survive, do you understand me?"

I take a moment to gather my anger and then I spit the words at him. "I do not take orders from you. I do not take orders from *you!*"

He laughs. "Ya do, Junco. You absolutely do take orders from me."

I shake my head and spill the secret I've been holding close since Gideon and I left the Subjack marketplace. "No, Tier. I take my orders from the top, and my top is Gideon. So you can take me to that Pillar and I *will* go inside, but it's happening on *our* terms. So take that, you arrogant piece of shit! I'm done being lied to, do you understand me? I'm done!"

He stands and pulls me to my feet with him. "Lies? You wanna hear about lies, Junco? That fuck Gideon has been lying to all of us since the day we met him at Subjack's! He sold you out to Inanna, he told her to take you for the Archer morph, he let her cut open his neck in just the right way so not too much blood was spurting out, and when Layla went to clamp it off, it was already sealed. Already sealed! They fucking played you!"

"No," I say, shaking my head. "I will never doubt him. I will never doubt him." The words just keep repeating, over and over like my own personal mantra, until Tier is shaking me so hard I bite my tongue and just stop.

"You better fucking start doubting him, Junco! Because whatever he's got planned for ya at that Pillar, it's a trap!"

I'm just shaking my head.

"What's the plan, Junco? What's the fucking plan?"

My head continues to shake out a no. "It's not true, this is our day. This is our day!"

"He's a clone, Junco! He's a motherfucking clone! You said yourself, he came back broken, he wasn't the same, he's not Gideon! He's a clone!"

"No, he's my Gideon."

"No, Junco." His words are soft now. "I'm sorry, I'm so sorry, but he's not your Gideon. Your Gideon is gone, darlin'. He's probably been gone for a long time. I think they killed him, back when you were dragged from the safety of John Hando's influence that last time, that day you thought you saved his life, Junco? He died." He shakes his head at me. "It's a trap."

I squeeze my brows together. "No."

"Yes," he says with a soft conviction that makes me hesitate. "Please, listen. I'm not asking you ta do anything other than enter that Pillar alone, ya hear me? I'm not asking ya to give it to Lucan, even though he wants it. Or Sera, even though she wants it. I'm just asking that ya go in alone. Please do not take Gideon in there with ya."

My gaze drifts out and tracks Irin's Pillar as it makes its climb into the sky. She might be dead. They might all be dead. The thought of losing Esta and Moju just makes all the fight go right out of me. But I know one thing for sure. When I enter my Pillar I will absolutely not be dead. I will live and there's something so wrong and so right about that at the same time.

"Junco?"

I just shake my head and take a deep breath as I count a few heartbeats to bring me back down to a manageable level of insanity. "Do you know the story of the Magpie Bridge, Tier?"

He stares at me with a very strange look on his face.

"It's a story Gideon used to tell me about the swan and the eagle." I stop and point up to the canopy of rainforest trees. There are no stars on the forest floor so there is no way to see them now.

I have Tier's undivided attention all of a sudden. "How's it go, darlin'? Tell me, quick!"

I take a long breath and try to make my point as efficiently as possible. "Well, you know. It's the same old story. Forbidden love and all that. Cygnus and Aquila want to be together, but they've got to overcome impossible obstacles. Cygnus can't cross the Milky Way to be with Aquila because the little fox Vulpecula will eat her. And Aquila can't cross the Milky Way to be with Cygnus because Jupiter will shoot him in the heart with his arrow and break his love."

I sigh.

"Is that it?" he asks.

"No, it's got the proper unhappily ever after. They find a way, the magpies make a bridge that allows them to cross the Milky Way. But the doomed lovers only get one night a year." I stop again and picture it up in the sky one more time. Cygnus diving down, Aquila soaring up. And the freaking Milky Way that separates them for eternity. "Every time Gid told me that ending I always thought about that one night and it isn't enough, ya know? It's just not enough. I need more than one night of happiness a year. I'm just greedy I guess, because that won't satisfy me. It's not worth it." I look up at him and stare in his eyes.

"What's not worth it, Junco?"

"All the hurt that comes with that little bit of love." I shrug out an apology. "That's just how I feel. It's not worth it. And really, that ending is the total happy version, because in the one Gid told me for years, they never got to be together at all. Ever." I look over at Tier and feel so freaking tired, I want to lie down and sleep for eternity. "But when I saw Gideon that last time, back in the Stag before I really went insane, I was so upset at our goodbye he told me a new version of the story's ending."

"What'd he say?" Tier is gripping my arms so tight I think he might squeeze the life out of me.

"He said that the swan was God's princess and the eagle was Jupiter's favorite and they were blessed and got to live together for eternity. And how would he know to soothe me with that new ending if that wasn't my Gideon, Tier?"

He shakes his head and loosens his grip.

"He's still my Gid. I know it. He told me that new ending for no other reason than to make me happy."

"Maybe," he concedes. "Maybe he is, but you cannot take him in the Pillar with you, understand? He's a Seven, he will fuck everything up if he enters, Junco."

He waits for me to say something, but I stay silent.

"We have to go now, Junco. We *have* to go. Will ya do what I ask?"

I take a deep breath and nod my head. "Yeah, OK. I won't take Gideon into the Pillar."

He watches me, reads my mind probably, looking for any inkling that I am lying. But I'm not, so he straightens up and lets out a long breath of air. "Thank you. When this is all over, Junco, I swear, I'll make it up. I will make it up, OK?"

"Don't forget about my HOUSE," I say. "She's just a little girl. Don't leave her there to die alone. I couldn't stand it if she had to die alone."

"I won't, Junco. I promise. She's not gonna die. I won't let her die."

I try and hide my surety of her approaching demise, but I fail miserably and Tier picks up on it. "I will not let her die, Junco. OK?"

"Just do your best. That's all you can do. Take me, I'm ready." He holds me close in the timeshift and my prayer from the Fallen Archer church back in Fledge comes rushing back. *Please let me accept my fate with courage. Let me be brave in the end.*

It might've worked this time as well, except for one small detail. The time for fate is over.

Because this is destiny.

Epilogue

Where am I?

Who am I?

What will happen to me now?

These questions have no answers.

I'm pretty sure Gideon and Sera planned for me to win this fight, but that would require pushing away the possibility that I might lose. And losing a fight with Inanna had such big consequences that it just wasn't possible.

So I embraced the worst-case scenario instead. But I left out one little detail about how this conquers fear when I gave Irin my secret.

You must *want* the worst-case scenario as much as you want the best.

They are equal partners and fear must be canceled out with acceptance.

And I want this. *No matter what you think*, I want this.

I want to float in the shower of starlight, empty and alone. Because at least I know that bitch Inanna went with me, I went down fighting, and there is nothing left to be afraid of. Ever. Again.

I won

I lost.

I am.

I am not.

The heartbeat is still there. I am immortal and that will never change—it will never stop so I have no other way out. I can't change much. I have very little power, and I have no hope, or faith, or future.

Or tears.

But I can still count.

My pieces travel up and out like a comet dragging ice across the galaxy. I watch it from every angle, from the inside and the outside. From Earth and from space. I am my own scattered pieces. I am like starlight, I am all of me and none of me at once.

I am like light.

I am not Junco.

I am just light.

I am nothing but my own shattered pieces.

"The path to paradise begins in hell."
— Dante Alighieri

MAGPIE BRIDGE
PREVIEW
BOOK FIVE CHAPTER ONE
THIS NOVELLA IS ALL <u>TIER'S</u> PERSPECTIVE

This story is far from over - so if you skip The Magpie Bridge, you're missing a whole bunch.

The high-altitude wind whips past my face, leaving it raw and dry as I watch the scene play out down below. I cross my arms in front of my chest and ask my pupils to dilate and then contract, trying to keep Junco in focus as she makes the walk to the waiting pillar of light.

"What's she doing?"

I look over and see Arel and Annun, looking at me and down at the valley, respectively. I sigh in the general direction of my brother, although my eyes never find his face, and shrug. "I'm not sure, Arel."

"Was this part of the plan?"

"Not our plan."

"Gideon?"

Sometimes Arel can really piss me off with his questions. It's like he's got no internal filter. Just spews out words without thinking. "Do I look like I know Gideon's plan?" I hiss at him.

He ignores my mood, as per usual, and just lets out a long whistle. "This is about to get interesting."

It's hard to upset Arel. Even with the existence of our entire race on the line, he can shrug it off. "Interesting?" I scoff. "That's one way to put it."

Annun spits on the ground and comes around to the other side of me. "You think she knows what she's doing?"

I want to rip his fucking head off and my hands are even reaching for his throat when I stop. Annun just spits again and pretends it never happened. I think he's been spending too much time with Arel.

"I mean," he continues, "she's typically got a handle on stuff, right? Even when you think she's fucked and lost her mind, she pulls through, right?"

He's right. On most days Junco pulls through. She's tough. She's powerful. She's a force.

"She's Junco, for fuck's sake," Annun continues, more to himself than any of us.

But today is not most days. Today was *her* day. The day she's been waiting for.

Lucan appears by my side and we let out a collective sigh as her body begins to glow, then Inanna's follows suit. Seconds later they are gone.

"Well, that's pretty much it, then." Arel flips open his tablet and begins punching in data.

I wait, not looking at, nor acknowledging, Lucan. Because if I want to be truthful, Lucan's the one I want to rip apart, not Annun. I want to blame him. Just fucking once, I want to make it all his fault, tell him off, push back and walk away. Just once I want to lose control instead of standing by his side.

"Ten meters per second and slowing." Arel slaps the tablet shut, like that's the end of it. "This one is not on track for completion, initiation is delayed by one point five minutes for every minute completion fails." He looks up to me and shrugs. "We're stuck until she finishes whatever she's doing in there. I'm assuming she's slicing her mother to bits? But maybe not. They could be having a fucking picnic for all I know."

He disappears, leaving Annun behind.

Annun barely notices, just spits one more time and picks up where he left off. "Take the Deliverance fight for instance. She went into that with no clue. None. So, I think this time, they maybe have a plan." He looks over to Lucan. "What do ya think, Luc?"

Lucan growls at the nickname and I don't blame him. Annun pushes buttons on purpose, not like Arel who's just being good-natured. Annun is a mean motherfucker and to be honest, he's very lucky I'm tired of constantly kicking his ass, or I really would throttle his throat right now. "Get to fucking work or I'll send ya back to Amelia to babysit."

"He can come with me," Lucan states matter-of-factly. "I'm going back soon to wait it out with her, anyway. She's unhappy. And afraid."

Annun shrugs. "I'll go, sure. Why not."

"Annun," I growl, "your ass is supposed to be scouring the Stag for that child."

"Tier, I like to delegate, right? I have a team down there—"

"What fucking team?"

"Merkar, Pike and Tessen. And I gave each of them a legion of their own. If the kid's down there, we'll find her."

The heat from my eyes tells me they are red. I direct the glow towards Annun.

He disappears.

Lucan turns to me then, but I don't look at him. I've had enough and he knows it. "What's that look?" he asks. "Sadness?"

"Don't, Lucan. I'm at the end here. I asked you for one thing and that was to keep her safe and you go and tell her to *do it her way*." I stop to look him in the eye. "This is her way, Lucan. Congratulations, she did exactly what you told her to do."

"You have very little faith in her, Raubtier. I find it quite disturbing. She always has so much faith in herself, it's a shame you can't see what she's capable of. Besides, Sera is with her, correct? You said she mentioned that."

"Have you talked to Sera?" His expression is unreadable.

"No, not in several weeks, actually. But Junco said—"

"Junco is fucking *sick*, Lucan. Sick." I wait to see if he's got anything to say to that, but if he does, he holds it in.

The cold air is heavy with the silence, and once again I notice that the wind is making my face chapped and raw.

"She's sick. She told me she's got a condition. Some mental disorder that makes her want to count things, or tap things. Some condition that makes her want to count stars and never stop. A compulsion to embrace insanity. Does this make any sense to you?"

A loud boom shakes the mountains and an explosion of light erupts from the top of the Pillar. The ground shakes and snow begins to slide down a nearby mountain where it's gotten too deep from the early fall snow.

"Fuck!" I look over at Lucan. "What the fuck was that?" I call Arel to come back via vision screen and watch Lucan's surprised face as he studies the sky. It looks like a fireworks display—particles shooting out of the top of the Pillar and up into space.

Arel appears and his fingers are in mid-slide across his tablet. I wait as they fly across the screen and then he looks up at me and shakes his head. "Dissipation particles. That crazy little sparrow fucking dissipated her ass!" He barks out a laugh and looks up at the light show in the sky. "She fucking dissipated Inanna!"

I look up as well, a slight wave of relief washing through my heart when Arel's voice interrupts my almost

celebration. "Wait. There's two sets of particles, not one—
"

He doesn't finish his sentence. He doesn't have to because this can only mean one thing.

They scattered each other.

I enter the timeshift before my anger can manifest as knives and fangs.

CHAPTER TWO

I've never been to New Peak City and I only went to the old one a few times when I was here watching Juncs. But my body finds the Circus like I've been there every day of my life. I even exit sitting on the side of the fountain, my face in my hands. Lost.

The people around me begin to panic and the screaming starts. I'm not the most popular guy on the planet right now. Something to do with millions dying in the floods I've unleashed with the Pillars. Why they're still here, I have no idea. Technically, if all went well, the Pillar eruption should've been well on its way to demolishing New Peak City in a massive earthquake, just like Subjack blew up the old one with a nuclear bomb.

I raise my head for a moment to take in the bedlam, then let it sink back into my hands.

I knew this moment with Junco was coming. I mean, she was one hundred percent honest about the way she saw her future when we were out on the red rock. She told me exactly how she'd meet her destiny, I just never suspected it would be in the Pillar. I never suspected she'd even consider taking Inanna in there because I counted on her finishing the job. It's not like her really, to leave her job unfinished. And after all those words to Irin about the mission keeping her sane, I figured I had time to change her mind. To tell her I'll be there—that I will *find a way* to be there.

I scrub my face with my hands and allow the grief to wash over me. My whole chest hurts. Like hands are crushing me to death. Twisting up my heart and making every breath a struggle. I have no frame of reference for this feeling. It is dread. Overpowering dread, and hopelessness and sadness. I feel like a part of me is gone. And this is nothing like the moment when we all realized Inanna had taken Junco for the morph or even those years she was in the tank. Because I knew where she was and I knew she'd be back. No matter what, I knew that one day *she'd be back.*

But this time I can't count on that.

I've failed her.

Again.

It's not Lucan's fault for handing her his trust. It's my fault for not hearing her last cry for help.

I'd rather float in the nothingness and drift away for eternity than get a stay of execution on my unhappy ending, Tier. I'm tired and I just want it to be over.

How much clearer could she have made it?

I heard what I wanted to hear. A hypothetical. Not the promise she was making.

When the shooting starts I begin to get annoyed, but it takes rapid fire and plasmas to make me give a shit. I put up a shield and don't even bother to watch the feeble attempts of the New Peak City security to kill me, I just continue to hold my head in my hands.

As if it were that fucking easy to kill me now, anyway.

"Why are you here, Beast?"

I force myself to look up and find a small child standing inside my shield perimeter with a pretty severe scowl on her face. She's got shoulder-length brown hair, hazel eyes, a pink shirt, pink flipflops, and some scraggly denim shorts.

"I said—"

"I heard, ya, girl. I'm looking for HOUSE. Junco sent me."

Her whole demeanor changes in an instant. "She did? Where is she? Is she OK? Is she in there?" Her little finger points up to the sky where the light Pillar is still shining up towards the heavens.

I nod. "She's in there. But she wanted me to take ya out of here, so go get your stuff and I'll wait for ya." I look back at the Pillar of light and drop my face in my hands one more time, suddenly exhausted.

And then I feel her little fingertips pry one hand off my cheek. "She's dead, isn't she?"

I study her face. The face of Junco at about age eight. I know this because I've seen all her photo albums. I looked at them endlessly over the last two years. At first I'd just sit in her room and look. But eventually I moved all her personal things into my own room to keep them close. I almost moved into her room instead, but she was never there long enough to put any sort of mark on it and besides, Kadian was always spying. "She's not capable of dying, HOUSE. So, no. She's not dead. Now go get your stuff."

She stands there pouting. "I have no stuff."

"No? Well, OK then. Can you leave here? Junco didn't seem to be too sure about that."

"I can leave, I just wanted to take New Peak City for myself. My house was so small in comparison and besides, they made a place for an AI here but she hadn't moved in yet. How could I resist?"

It fucking figures.

It's entirely appropriate that Junco's HOUSE turns out to be a conniving, sneaky little look-a-like who's dead set on getting her way about things. I scoop her up in my arms and we go back into the timeshift together and exit on Gideon's Sargassum terrace.

She squirms in my embrace and I loosen my grip and allow her to slide down. "Wow! Where are we?" She runs to the edge of the terrace, climbs the bottom railing, and leans over. Far over.

My heart thumps a little as I watch her begin to step up on the second railing. "Hey, get the hell off that thing! Put yer feet on the ground, right now!"

She makes no move to obey and I'm crossing the terrace to yank her down when she turns, smiling. "It's far, isn't it? Wow, is this where you live?"

"Very far," I say, grabbing her arm and pulling her off the railing. "And no, this isn't my house, it's Gideon's. I'm looking for him."

She's already run off, squealing her way into the living room yelling something about automated shopping and bathing suits.

It's my turn to lean over the railing. I look down at the black rocks Junco was sitting on when I came here the night of her birthday. I turn my gaze down the beach looking for people, but it's empty. Totally evacuated. They weren't sure what I had planned and since Sargassum is nothing but a floating man-made archipelago, they took the conservative approach and got everyone off the resort before I had a chance to wipe it out with tsunami waves.

I walk back towards the terrace doors and when I reach them, I turn and pace back the other way. I continue this for a while. Just pacing. Thinking. Part of me wants Annun to come back and tell me how Junco's always got a plan. How together she is on the inside. How sneaky she is. That she can pull it off just because she's Junco and she finds a way to pull everything off.

But the rational part sees nothing but the dissipation particles shooting up into the sky like those fountains they have in Vegas.

She's not coming back from this one, Tier. Face it. She's not coming back.

But I've had that thought so often it's becoming cliché. How many times have we sat around and discussed rumors of Junco's demise?

Pretty much once a week since we located her more than four years ago.

She's been dead and gone and then revived and reborn in my mind so many times, I'm not sure what her actual life status is any more.

I look up.

But there's no Halo circling the earth. There's no defense system to protect us. I have no Junco, I have no future that I can see. I have no hope.

There's no hope.

We are fucked.

End of Book Shit

This is my favorite Junco book. I know I said that about Fledge, but really, it's Range. It's funny, because of all the books, this is the one people generally don't like. It's too dark. It's too introspective. It's too depressing and sad and it has a nasty cliffhanger. But I like all that stuff, and believe it or not, I wrote this series for me, not readers.

This book especially.

I had this world and these characters on my mind for five years before I decided to write it all down. This book was really the beginning of the story when I first started imagining it. Gideon was the star, Junco was still crazy as all hell, and Sera was Gideon's partner in crime.

But when I started to write this series I was worried that I'd fuck up the story if I made this my first book. It was all very complicated, as a good epic SF series should be, and I had only written non-fiction before this.

So I decided to write a "paranormal romance" with some SF elements to get some practice. That was CLUTCH. It was supposed to be more romantic, but Tier ended up being less than reliable, and I liked him that way, so I messed with the plot until I got it set up right. And I only ever planned on giving Junco three books, but when I got to the end of FLIGHT and she lost her wings, I knew she had to carry the rest of the story and Gideon would only be a side character.

The original RANGE, which never had a title, started out pretty much the same. A broken girl, a partner who could read her mind, and a nefarious AI called Sera. None of that really changed. The cities, Peaks and Low Dallas, were always the cities.

There were always Pillars, the original version had them as sentient AI's, but I cut all that out.

The mythology was always there. And even though you have no idea who Lucan is at this point, I've always known.

Every sentence of this series was planned.

Every theme.

Every character.

Every city.

Every scene.

Every kill. Every kiss, every betrayal, and every revelation was planned.

In fact, the very last chapter of the very last book was known, down to the exact words, back when I finished CLUTCH. People might think I had no clue where I was going in this series, but I've always known. It's just not everyone was meant to take this journey with me.

So be it. That's me giving zero fucks.

I'm glad I gave Junco the starring role. I have no regrets.

I have very particular tastes in science fiction. I think it comes from loving the dark side and having two science degrees. I try to keep things as logical as possible, but insanity isn't logical. And let's face it—you might not have believed it before, but after this book you should have no doubt. This girl is insane. She was completely insane in CLUTCH too, but she was hiding it. Yeah, not so much anymore.

So Junco is a character you either love or hate. I love her and that's all that matters. You can think what you want of this book. I do not care. Everything Junco has been hiding comes out in this book right here and I would not change a single word.

It's perfect.

Magpie Bridge is not optional. It's got a lot of answers and it's all from Tier's perspective. If you skip it, skip RETURN too, it won't make any sense.

ABOUT THE AUTHOR

JA Huss is the New York Times Bestselling author of 321 and has been on the USA Today Bestseller's list 21 times in the past four years. She writes characters with heart, plots with twists, and perfect endings.

Her books have sold millions of copies all over the world, the audio version of her semi-autobiographical book, Eighteen, was nominated for a Voice Arts Award and an Audie Award in 2016 and 2017 respectively, her audiobook, Mr. Perfect, was nominated for a Voice Arts Award in 2017, and her audiobook, Taking Turns, was nominated for an Audie Award in 2018. Five of her book were optioned for a TV series by MGM television in 2018.

She lives on a ranch in Central Colorado with her family.